Georgianna

Georgianna

– A Virginia Family Saga –

Fay L. Logan

Brunswick

Cover art by Talia Logan.
Text illustrations by Cathie Logan Sharpe and Claire Logan English.

Library of Congress Cataloging-in-Publication Data
Logan, Fay L., 1918–
  Georgianna : a Virginia family saga / by Fay L. Logan.--1st ed.
    p. cm.
    ISBN 1-55618-191-4 (hardcover : alk. paper)
      1. Shenandoah River Valley (Va. and W. Va.)--Fiction.
  2. Southwest Virginia--Fiction. 3. 20th Century family
  saga. 4. Girls--Fiction. I. Title.
PS3562.O4457 G4 2000
813'.54--dc21

                                     00-046814

All names in this book are fictitious. Any resemblance to actual persons and events is purely coincidental.

First Edition
Published in the United States of America
by

(👹)

Brunswick Publishing Corporation
1386 Lawrenceville Plank Road
Lawrenceville, Virginia 23868
Tel.: 434-848-3865
www.brunswickbooks.com

Dedicated to my precious family.

Acknowledgments

Heartfelt thanks to my niece, Mary Davis;
my son, Paul; my daughter, Claire Logan English;
and my friend, June Nolley.
Additional appreciation to my daughter,
Cathie Logan Sharpe, for her wonderful artwork and
support, and to my granddaughter,
Talia Logan, for the book jacket illustration.

Table of Contents

CHAPTER 1

Georgianna's Birth

Anna had slept lightly throughout the night as a gentle rain cooled the September night. She was awakened by the brushing of the hemlock against the house. Anna knew by the way her abdomen had dropped that the time was near for the birth of her ninth child. She hoped this child would be a girl. She would name her by combining her name and that of the child's father. Since she had borne six boys, a preference for a girl was natural. She hoped this child would be extra special, and her hopes were high that this little one would have a deep desire to achieve and would be able to escape this hard mountain life. Here the women were expected to serve the men, have babies, and raise them without much assistance from the father. She truly wanted more for this child she had carried within her for nine months. The wee one stirred within her as she pulled the thin coverlet closer to her hoping for a couple more hours of rest before arising for the many chores of the day.

Just as Anna was becoming drowsy, she felt the first twinge of pain. It was then that she realized that she did not have much time. Fubby, the two-year-old, stirred by her side, cuddling closer to her as she stroked his soft white hair while trying not to wake Bidgy, who lay on her other side.

George, her common law husband, had not come home the night before. This gave her no concern. She was accustomed to being independent. He was probably spending the night with his legal wife and children, which he did occasionally. Even so, he was aware that her time was getting short.

As Anna lay there expecting the next pain, she began musing over her life and wondering why or how she had gotten herself into this situation, with all these children, including two sets of twins born two years apart. Most of her children were two years apart. Nursing her children on the breast seemed to be the way children were spaced. Nursing mothers usually did not get pregnant.

The fact that she had no husband did not bother her a great deal. That seemed to be the lot of some mountain women. George did provide shoes for the children along with some other items from the store, which he owned. He often slept there overnight with his bottle for company. Moonshine was plentiful in the area, and you could obtain it even when you had no money. George liked his liquor and his women. Anna wondered why he paid so little attention to his children, both legal and illegal. Oh! Another pain, sharper than the first. Since they were not too close together she felt safe in delaying, getting two of the older children up to go for Mrs. Emore.

Anna had been born in the late eighteen hundreds in a nice house a few miles from where she now lived. She was one of five daughters and one son of a very stern father, who was tall and gaunt and seldom smiled. Her meek, humble, tiny mother had very little to smile about.

As the third pain came closer, she decided she had better not wait. Carefully getting out of bed so she didn't awaken the two little ones in bed with her, she lit the lamp and trimmed the wick, leaving a soft glow in the sparsely furnished room. She quietly opened the folding cot that she had previously placed under her bed to have on hand for this occasion. Near it was the box of clothing she had made for this new baby. She gently moved the two small boys to this cot, placing one at each end, and was thankful that neither had awakened.

Another pain prompted her to go upstairs to wake Billy, her oldest son.

Billy," shaking his shoulder, "Billy, Billy! My, you sleep soundly. I need you and Cory to go fetch Mrs. Emore."

"Aw, Ma, it's too early."

"Wake Cory and get dressed so you two can get goin'. Please hurry. You know it is a good three miles even if you take the short cut."

Anna's pains were getting closer and harder. She hurried the boys out the door, cautioning them to be careful with the lantern. No one had mentioned anything about a baby, but Billy knew every time Mrs. Emore was summoned there was another baby at their house.

Anna knew how long it would take for the boys to run this errand. They were strong and healthy and could step lively. The rain had ceased falling, and they had a good path. She felt they would have the midwife there in plenty of time.

She filled the large teakettle and laid the kindling in the cookstove. The children kept the woodbox full. Thankfully, she didn't have to fret over that. A hard pain took her breath just as she was reaching for the delivery pads she had made many times before and had placed on the high shelf. She got a pair of embroidered pillowcases and clean sheets for later use. A fresh gown was ready, also an outfit for the newborn.

Her pains were getting closer and harder. She would have liked for the birth to have been when the children were asleep or at play. The way things were shaping up, they would all be up and clamoring for their breakfast. The children were accustomed to working, though, and could manage without her help.

Just as she was thinking that all was in readiness, she remembered the safety pins for the band, a strip of cloth wrapped firmly around the baby's middle to prevent rupture. As she looked at the long gown, she wondered why baby's clothing had to be so long. It certainly made them more expensive, and she had so little money. She felt fortunate she could get material from George's store, sometimes for free. Then other times butter and eggs and, when in season, garden vegetables were traded.

After another sharp pain, Anna decided she had better not chance going to the springhouse for things for the children's breakfast. She removed a large box of oatmeal from the high shelf. The children knew how to cook that and could manage nicely. She was raising them to be independent.

Bruno, the hound that had recently taken up residence there, began to bark. She knew the boys were returning with Mrs. Emore, and none too soon, as another hard pain was easing. She heard feet hit the floor upstairs as the children began awaking and calling, "Mommy, Mommy, why is Bruno barking?" By then Fubby and Bidgy—who had acquired the nickname after he began reaching for the biscuits saying "bidgy, bidgy" (this name stuck with him for his lifetime) — were both awake and the chorus of "I'm hungry" had begun. Noona, the only girl, would have to help with the little ones, even though she was only seven years old. She had been a twin. Her brother, Otis, had fallen into the fireplace after the cradle turned over and had died at eight months from the burns. Noona always felt like she was not a whole person.

As Noona and Corbin, Cory's twin, raced down the stairs, Billy and Cory were at the door with Mrs. Emore and the little black bag of necessities she always carried.

"Mommy, why is Mrs. Emore here? Are we getting a baby? Are we?"

"We'll talk about that later," Anna answered. "You children all get in the kitchen. Billy and Noona will make breakfast, with everyone's help," she said as she ushered them into the kitchen. Bidgy and Fubby carried their clothes and obeyed, reluctantly followed by Corbin.

"How have you been, Mrs. Emore?" Anna greeted her. "You were sick a while back."

"I'm right spent now after that little sick spell. I think you had better be getting into bed. Doesn't look like we have a lot of time to waste. Ah, good, I see you have everything ready. I suppose you want a girl this time, what with all those rowdy boys."

Anna was comforted to have Mrs. Emore there, with her kind face and long sturdy arms and that crisp white apron she always wore when midwifing. She could be trusted to perform in an extraordinary manner, since she had delivered many a baby in these hills. She had lost very few, and those through no fault of her own. Seldom did anyone use a doctor with her in the locality. She had hoofed many a mile in all kinds of weather day or night to birth a baby. Many times her only pay was thanks.

Mrs. Emore removed the sterile scissors from her bag, laying them on a clean towel spread out on the dresser in the sparsely furnished bedroom and sitting room combined. She got the string to be used to tie the umbilical cord and placed it there also. She dashed into the kitchen, where the kettle was boiling and the big wash pan that she needed was ready. Anna called out, "Mrs. Emore, you'd better hurry."

Fubby was right behind Mrs. Emore as she entered the room, oatmeal still on his mouth. "Mommy, Mommy, I want Mommy."

Anna said, "Just let him stay. He can sit in the rocker. It's all right. It will not be long."

With him settled in the rocker with his doll made from a sock, Anna got down to business. Mrs. Emore knew it was time to do some coaching. Even though Anna was experienced at having babies, she still needed some coaching. She always came through in good shape, though, and after a couple days' bed rest, would be up and tending to the usual duties.

The delivery pads were in place as the coaching began, first with wiping the sweat from Anna's forehead. Mrs. Emore said, "Now with the next pain, push, now relax. Spread your knees a little more. We've been through this enough times, you should know how it's done. There, that's it."

Anna began moving with pain. Fubby wanted to know, "What's the matter with Mommy?" Mrs. Emore was much too busy to pay him any mind, much less give him an answer.

"Now, push hard as you pull on the rope, tied to the head of your bed. We will soon have this job done. The cap is in view."

Another hard pain and a lot of pushing, and the head emerged. "Now push, push with the next pain."

"Ah! Ah!" Anna cried as she pulled on the rope and pushed with all her might.

There emerged a healthy baby, as pink as a rosebud. "It's a girl," Mrs. Emore said as she cleaned mucus from its mouth and the baby let out a lusty cry as the first breath of air rushed into its lungs.

From the kitchen came sounds of excitement and laughter as one after the other exclaimed, "We've got a baby! We've got a baby!" just like there was not a new baby every two years!

"Yes, Anna, it's a healthy little girl and you should make this your last one, seein' as you can't have a proper father for them. You have to work so hard to feed them, keep clothes on their backs and shoes on their feet in the cold mountain winters," the midwife remarked as she busied herself getting the baby cleaned up and taking care of the afterbirth which she placed in a bag. She called to Billy in the kitchen to go out back and dig a deep hole where she would later bury the bag.

After gently washing the infant and being sure she had the bands on firmly, she fastened on the feedsack diapers that had been bleached white with lye soap. The long outing gown almost swallowed the baby. Then she cleaned Anna and helped her into a fresh bed so she could hold her tiny daughter who was wrapped in the soft pink blanket with the blanket stitch around the edge.

"Anna, are you comfortable in your fresh bed?"

"I'm still having some pain as usual, but that will pass like the morning dew. Let me have my baby, my little Georgianna. Did I tell you I had this name all picked out in case it was a girl?"

"Are you honoring that worthless man by naming your child after him?" the midwife asked.

"Now Mrs. Emore, he does give me some help from the store, even though he seldom notices the children. It's his loss, 'cause they are all bright children and good looking too," talking while she pulled the baby's gown up to see if she had the right number of toes. "Look at those short legs. They're George's all right. He can't deny her as his, and look at her short arms. She is going to be a shorty for sure."

Anna stroked Georgianna's corn silk hair. The baby opened her blue eyes and the corner of her mouth turned up as if she was smiling.

Fubby had been prancing around the bed, wondering what was going on. He had been very quiet during this time, clutching his sock dolly and sucking his thumb. "Wanta see Mommy. Wanta see Mommy!" The midwife lifted him, so he could give Mommy sugar and marvel at the new baby beside her. It hadn't dawned on him that he was no longer the baby, and that Georgianna would claim a lot of attention that had been given to him.

The remainder of Anna's brood were eager to see the new family member. As Mrs. Emore unlatched the door leading to the kitchen, all five tried to get through the door at once, almost trampling Bidgy in the process. He began to cry. The baby awoke and joined him. Soon they quieted down and everyone had his first peek at the wee one in the pink blanket.

To the older ones it was no big deal, and they soon wandered off to take care of the morning chores. The nine-year-old twins, Cory and Corbin, went for Old Bessie, the cow, so Billy could do the milking. Usually this was done while breakfast was being made, but this was a different kind of morning and everything was a mite late.

Soon things got back to normal, except that Mommy was in bed, and it was unusual for this strong woman to be anywhere but hard at work. Mrs. Emore began collecting all of her equipment to put in her black bag.

"Well, Anna, I don't suppose you will be needing me again for a couple years, but like I said, you oughta make this your last one. You already have more than you can handle, seein' as you have to handle everything by yourself, not gettin' much help from that man, and workin' the younguns so hard, too. They ought to have a better life. I'd best be getting over to home. I think my son Frank is gonna' bring me some dropped apples so we can get a kettle of apple butter made. You may not be strong enough to make any this year, so I'll share mine with you. Taste mighty good on your hot biscuits. Maybe you can do some sewing for me, seein' as my sewing machine is on the blink. I'll send over some apple butter as soon as it's ready."

"Thanks Mrs. Emore. I don't know how I would get along without you, helping me with these babies and in times of sickness. I'm thankful we don't have much of that. You're always helping somebody and I know you are not as young as you used to be. I'll be glad to sew for you and do anything else I can. And come butchering time, I can send one of the younguns over with some fresh meat, seein as how you don't have hogs and ours are in fine shape for butchering. That apple butter will be mighty good with ham and hot biscuits."

The early morning excitement died down in Anna Marlow's happy dwelling. The older ones took care of the chores. The sun was out and the grass was soon dry. Fubby and Bidgy trotted out to play leaving Anna alone with Georgianna sleeping peacefully by her side. Anna began her musing over her past life and how she had gotten in this situation with all these children and no legal father for them. She felt trapped with no way out. Deep in her heart she did want a better life for the children she had brought into the world, but she could see no way to improve things.

Anna had grown up without many material things and also without much affection from her parents. She had closeness with her sisters Marty and Marilyn, who were older, and Kate and Lizzie who were younger. Kate and Lizzie had both died while young married women. Anna missed their letters and occasional visits. Elmer, her only brother had also died when a young man. She visited Marty and Marilyn once in a while taking some of the children to visit their cousins. She could get the train at George's store that served as a depot, Post Office and general meeting place. Anna could leave some of the children in the living quarters adjoining the store while she took some with her. In the spring she would take the new baby to see them for she was eager to show her off. Her sisters' husbands didn't like for their wives to leave home because they were afraid Anna's lifestyle might affect their wives and make them long for independence such as Anna had. Secretly, Anna wished she had a husband who really cared about her and helped care for the children. Since this was the way things were, she had to be the one to keep in touch and do the visiting. As soon as she sold some hams, she would put that money into the special blue jar in its secret place, in the far corner of the pie safe. She would have enough for her ticket and the three little ones could ride free. She would even have some left over.

This would be her little secret that would get her through the icy mountain winter. From October until May, there was a bit of snow in the shady spots. She would not mention this to the family until after the seeds were in the ground in the spring.

Hearing the children at play jolted her back to the present. It was nearing lunchtime. Noona and Billy were trying their hand at making potato soup. They had raised plenty of potatoes and had milk from ole Bessie. Noona was only seven years old and was not yet skilled at cooking. She had a lot of responsibility to help with the younger children.

She heard cries from outside and Bidgy yelling "Fubby bleeding, Fubby bleeding on his toe." This was not an unusual occurrence because someone was always getting an injury of some kind. Fubby appeared at the door and trotted to the bed, leaving bloody footprints. Hearing the commotion Billy appeared with a rag, pan of water, and the bottle of turpentine. Placing his little brother on the cot in the corner, he began to cleanse the wound after Anna told him how much turpentine to add to the water. Soon the tears were dried and off they went to call the twins in for a lunch of potato soup, milk and some fried pies Mommy had made the night before.

The two little ones napped after lunch while the others washed the dishes and did the chores. Anna nursed Georgianna, smoothing her corn silk hair and looking into her bright blue eyes. She needed a change again of course. Anna always kept everything close at hand so she would not have to call any of the children. With a full tummy and a dry bottom, Georgianna slept.

Things were quiet and Anna felt tired from the early morning labor. She also fell asleep. A few hours later she awoke to a disturbance among the chickens. The guineas were squawking. "Billy, Billy," she called, waking the two little ones. "Bidgy, find Billy and tell him to see what's the matter with the chickens.

Billy had gotten up so early to fetch Mrs. Emore that he was taking a nap. Being the oldest he had to assume a lot of responsibility when Anna was unable to take care of things. The twins both appeared at the door, excitedly yelling, "There's a snake, there's a snake, a big un." By this time Billy did not have to be told to get the hoe from the side of the house and take care of that snake. He took great care not to get bitten.

Georgianna stirred and nuzzled her mother, looking for her next meal. Anna noticed that the little one did not cry. She assumed that the baby would be easy to care for. When the baby was fully awake, Anna offered her the nipple and she attacked it with gusto. Billy came to the doorway bearing his trophy, a huge snake hanging from the hoe. "Look, Maw." Since he was twelve he was accorded the privilege of addressing Anna as Maw. He felt very grown up.

"Oh, my," Anna exclaimed."
"Another copperhead. Throw it away and you younguns be careful, I can't doctor a snake bite right now."

The sun began to set behind the stately pines that abounded in the area and the children had to be reminded to take care of the evening chores. Fubby climbed onto the bed to watch the baby nurse. The twins were assigned the task of rounding up ole Bessie for milking time. Bidgy would be feeding the chickens as Billy took care of feeding the pigs. Noona checked the cupboard and springhouse to see what they could have for supper. Leftovers were kept in the springhouse. They still had fresh vegetables from a late garden, so there would be some variety.

Anna reminded Noona of her daily chore to see that the lamps had oil and that the chimneys were clean. As she looked at her new baby daughter she thought, that will be your job in a few years. All the children learned to work while they were still very young, and they accepted that in stride without too much grumbling.

After all the necessities had been take care of and the lamps were lit, night was their favorite time. Following the evening meal, the children one by one drifted out into the twilight for a few games before darkness enveloped their home. Then they would enter the house and wash their feet before going to bed. Normally, this brought a protest, but they were ready to comply since they had all gotten up earlier than usual.

Billy helped Fubby (whose real name was Earl but Bidgy had tried calling him brother and it came out Fubby, so Fubby stuck.) Billy saw the two boys comfortably on the cot in the corner before turning the lamp wick down. It still gave Anna plenty of light to care for the new baby, which she had placed at the foot of the bed so she would not roll over on her.

Soon everything was quiet until the whippoorwills began their familiar evening serenade. The children would often mimic this lonesome sound. Anna was tired and ready for sleep, but she continued her musing about what Mrs. Emore had said about the children having no legal father.

CHAPTER 2

Anna's Marriage

"**O**h! the man of my dreams," Anna thought as she spied the handsome gentleman across the room of the dance floor. She was sure she had seen him somewhere. Was he that fellow that she had glimpsed at Mountain Lake Hotel where she had been cooking? Yes, she believed he worked there.

Anna and her two sisters, Kate and Marilyn, had arrived by horse and buggy, and she was looking forward to a good time. Not much social life occurred in these parts and she, being a beautiful dancer, wanted to make the most of this evening. Dancing around in her head were thoughts that this looked like the sort of man she would like to marry and set up housekeeping with. She just could not keep her eyes off this handsome fellow. She wondered if he had brought anyone or if he came stag as she and her sister had. She also noticed that he kept glancing her way and she thought he had started across the room in her direction just as a casual friend, Bob Jones, asked her to dance.

Bob complimented her on how pretty she looked in her long blue dress that matched her eyes and her black hair in a bun with a jeweled comb to hold it in place. She knew she looked pretty good, but she felt good knowing someone noticed. She felt this would be an evening long remembered. Bob was a good slow dancer and they cut a fine figure as a lively number was played by the local musicians. Everyone else stopped and just watched the couple.

As the music ended, the stranger who had caught Anna's eye immediately approached her, introducing himself as Tom Marlow. He asked if he could have the next dance. Her shy reply was, "If you would like. My name is Anna Goodman and I live in the big house not far from the railroad trestle at Kire."

The evening was pleasant. Kate and Marilyn had partners, and Anna was in ecstasy that Tom had asked her to dance more than once. He danced as well as Bob Jones and he was much more handsome. He asked if he could see her again. They made plans for the following Sunday for a buggy ride. There was not much in the way of entertainment in the mountains other then quilting bees, church socials, and apple butter stirring.

Much later the three girls hopped in the buggy for the ride home. Their giggles lasted all the way home, each one vowing they had a better time than the other.

Maw and Paw were listening for them while pretending to be asleep, Maw whispered to Paw, "I hope they behaved as ladies and did not drink too much hard cider."

Anna was in a tizzy and could hardly wait until next week when she would see Tom again. In her mind she could see his handsome face and she spent most of the night reliving the evening and how comfortable she had felt with his arms around her. After deciding which dress to wear for the date the following week, she fell asleep. Kate and Marilyn were already fast asleep.

Everyone was up bright and early next morning. Since there was only one boy in the family, all had to help with the farm chores. It didn't matter that you were late getting to sleep. Paw was a demanding man who bossed Maw continually and ruled with an iron hand. This morning Anna didn't even notice his gruff manner and sang merrily as she performed her tasks, only thinking of Tom and the upcoming date.

Maw had noticed, "What makes you so happy?"

"Oh! Maw, I met the most wonderful man, Tom Marlow, and he asked me to go for a buggy ride." Maw replied, "I hope he's a nice young man and will let no harm come to you."

"Oh!, Maw, you know I can take care of myself. He is so handsome and I believe he is a gentleman and can be trusted."

The week passed swiftly. Anna tried several hairstyles and finally decided on the same one as the night she met Tom, with the jeweled comb that seemed to suit her best.

Finally, the big day was at hand, a bright sunny Sunday afternoon.

She knew better than to plan an evening meeting, as Maw would surely have had her bring a chaperone. She wanted this time alone with Tom after church service at Jesus Christ of Latter Day Saints, commonly known as "Mormons." Paw was a dedicated Mormon elder. They only missed church if deep snow or family illness prevented them from being there.

Most of the cooking was done on Saturday, so dinner was soon on the table. Anna was so excited that she ate very little. Paw noticed and says, "You sick, girl?" Everyone laughed and someone spoke up, "Yeh, lovesick." At this, Anna excused herself to add a few last minute touches to her appearance. She had traded dishwashing duties with Kate on Saturday night, giving her more time to primp.

Kate and Marilyn discussed the afternoon while doing the dishes. Anna preened before the mirror and practiced a few bewitching words and some special smiles which she hoped would spark a real interest from Tom. She could tell Tom liked her but she wanted more than that.

Tom arrived on time and she introduced him to Maw and Paw. He was very mannerly and promised to have their daughter home well before dark. They were impressed by his appearance and good manners.

The afternoon was very enjoyable. They rode several miles and stopped at Big Stony Creek. Tom tied the horse to a tree and they sat on a flat stone near the water, tossing pebbles into the water, watching the dragonflies, while they talked. Anna learned that he had very recently gotten a job at Mountain Lake Hotel. "Oh, I thought I had seen you somewhere. I cook at the hotel several days a week."

"Well, I work mostly at the stable caring for the horses."

The sun began to disappear over the mountain as Tom remembered his promise to have Anna home before dark. He took her by the hand and helped her to her feet and into the buggy. She thought he held her hand longer than necessary, which she liked.

There were many Sunday afternoon buggy rides and a few dances. Anna knew she was falling in love with Tom and she wondered what his intentions were. She did not have too long to wait. Getting ready for the Sunday afternoon ride, Anna heard the buggy drive up early. She thought, "He must be eager to see me."

As Tom approached the porch where Paw was nodding in the rocking chair, he said, "Mr. Goodman, I need to talk to you."

"What about?"

"Uh, uh," Tom stammered. "I would like to ask Anna to marry me. I'll try to make her happy. I know where I can find a place to live." Without any visible emotion, Paw says, "Go ahead."

Anna came out to the porch to find two somber men, and she was puzzled as she greeted Tom in her shy manner, "You're early."

"Yes, I know. I had some business to take care of with your Paw."

"Thanks Mr. Goodman," he said as he helped Anna into the buggy. "Where would you like to go?"

"Let's go down by Big Stony Creek, where we went the first time you took me out." This sounded like an ideal spot for him to let her know what was on his mind. It was evident that the horse had been brushed, the harness polished, and the buggy was clean and shiny.

They drove under the railroad trestle, and neither had much to say. They could hear the water rushing over the large stones from which the creek got its name. Tom removed a horse blanket from the buggy and spread it on the rock where they had sat on their first outing together, when the laurel were in full bloom. Now the leaves were floating down stream. As the leaves fell from the trees, you could hear the squirrels rustling the leaves, gathering nuts to store for the winter. It was just a perfect afternoon for what Tom had in mind, but he was unsure just how to start. He had kissed her a few times at the door when he took her home. Sitting on the rock, listening to the flowing of the water and rustling of the leaves, he tried to get the courage to ask the question. Tom took her hand and raised it to his lips, saying, "Anna, I love you, will you marry me?"

She was somewhat surprised and said softly, "If you really want me to, I would be happy to be your wife. Was that what you wanted to see Paw about?"

"Yes, and he said, 'Go ahead'." It was then he kissed her passionately.

They were married by a Mormon elder in Pearisburg, Virginia. With whatever pieces of furniture they could afford, their small house was a cozy place. Tom was a good husband and was kind to Anna and her family. Anna was happy and in a few months she realized that she was expecting a child. She liked children and eagerly anticipated the birth of their first child. It seemed like a long wait before a beautiful, blue-eyed dark-haired baby girl was placed in her arms. Anna thought she had never seen such a beautiful baby. She was ecstatic with happiness and enjoyed cuddling her to her breast while she nursed her. She named her Elva.

Kate had become pregnant out of wedlock, and her Paw had asked her to move out. Anna and Tom asked Kate to come live with them. Six months later Kate's son was born. Anna gave her all the help and sympathy she could and things went well. Elva was a year old, and Anna weaned her from the breast. After Anna stopped nursing Elva, she soon found herself with child again. She was happy over this because she would have Kate to help her, and Kate's son would be a playmate for Elva.

As Anna's belly was gettin' rounder by the day, she noticed Tom paying a lot of attention to Kate. She thought he was just being sympathetic because Kate was unhappy over her plight. However, she kept her eyes open when the two were together. As Anna became increasingly larger, she noticed that Kate was also gaining weight, and she became more suspicious every day.

While Tom was at work one day, she pinned Kate down. "You are not pregnant again, are you?"

Kate turned ghostly white and dropped her head mumbling, "Yes."

Anna was aghast, "I wasn't aware that you were seeing anyone to get in a fix like that. Who is responsible?"

At this, Kate began to weep and then it dawned on Anna. "It's Tom, isn't it?"

Kate confessed that it was, that it just happened. Anna decided she must leave Tom. She was heartbroken, and they separated before her son Billy was born. She filed for divorce shortly after he was born. Tom said, "You will never get Elva from me. I'll see to that." Could this be the same Tom she had fallen so madly in love with? Her heartbreak was almost more than she could bear. Tom concocted some falsehoods about her that were so convincing that during the divorce proceedings the court awarded Tom custody of Elva and allowed her to keep Billy. Anna suffered greatly over the loss of her beautiful little girl, and knew she would never fully recover from this great loss.

CHAPTER 3

Georgianna's First Year

Georgianna thrived on mother's milk, oatmeal, applesauce, mashed potatoes and coffee soup, which was coffee with lots of milk and biscuits soaked in it, as well as lots of attention from her siblings. And a sugar tit was usually handy when she became fretful or sleepy. A sugar tit was a lump of sugar tied in a cloth. This item was in later years replaced by a pacifier that served the same purpose of quieting a fretful baby.

Spring arrived and Georgianna shed her long dress for a shorter one. Anna would tie her in the big porch rocker with pillows around her so she could watch the children at play, the chickens, and ole Bruno as he roamed the yard. When naptime came, Noona watched the house and the two young children, while Anna, Billy, and the twins planted the garden that Anna had plowed earlier. Bidgy was given the job of covering the seeds after being shown just how to do it. He soon grew tired and was allowed to go to the house with a message for Noona to bring a pail of water and the dipper since everyone was growing thirsty. The twins were tired and were allowed to go back to the house with Noona. Anna and Billy would work a couple more hours, raking fresh soil around the cabbage plants and the peas which were looking good.

Anna thought how good it would be to have fresh vegetables from the garden after months of dried beans, potatoes and onions from the root cellar. The root cellar was a large hole dug in the earth and lined with a bed of leaves. It was sectioned off to hold potatoes, cabbage, onions, apples and other fruits and vegetables, then covered with

16

more leaves and a board or piece of tin, then more leaves piled on top to prevent freezing. This was a very effective way to store your vegetables for the winter. When snow was expected, the items that would be needed were taken out with a minimum of trouble. The root cellar had to be covered well so the bears that sometime came close to the house couldn't get a whiff of the foodstuffs and raid the root cellar.

Georgianna had been fretful for a few days and had finally cut her first tooth, to the delight of her siblings. A first tooth was a major event in the mountains where there was not very much excitement. A new calf, a litter of puppies, or baby chicks hatching usually happened in the springtime, along with the gardening. It was indeed a busy time for anyone big enough to do any work. You did not have to be very big to begin working at Anna's house.

Georgianna's first summer was uneventful, a lot of her care fell to Noona, while Anna stayed busy caring for the brood of seven, the gardening, harvesting, canning, pickling, preserving and sometimes caring for a sick farm animal. The children got a hands-on education as Anna sometimes had to sew a wound using turpentine and muzzling the animal and tying its feet.

The summer ended and Billy, Noona, Cory, and Corbin started to school four miles away. Georgianna's first birthday had come and gone before Anna realized her baby was a year old. Birthdays were just another day. Sometimes mountain folk were not exactly sure of their correct age. The young ones just knew they were two years younger than the one next to them.

Fubby was Georgianna's constant companion when he was not occupied with his three-year-old chores. She was now pulling up and walking around the furniture, falling many times, crawling over the rough floor, and getting splinters on her little knees. She quit crying when rocked by Fubby who cuddled her as he rocked. They were very close.

George, their father, stopped by occasionally after the children were asleep. He was usually gone by the time they were awake. He had to open the store very early in the morning when the train brought the mail in. They thought this was the way things were supposed to be and never questioned Anna about this. None called him Dad, it was

George. Occasionally he brought them a treat of candy or gum and always gave them a treat when they visited the store.

Indian summer was beautiful in these hills, time for gathering chestnuts, walnuts, hickory nuts and chinquapins. There were a lot of outings in the woods, gathering food for the winter. Anna's family lived off the land as much as possible. It was hard work but satisfying and no one had trouble sleeping at night.

The harvest was almost completed. Apple butter was made, apples canned, beans canned, and pickled and dried vegetables readied for the root cellar. Only the hog killing would come later when the weather was colder. There was a little break from all the hard work outside, and a few weeks could be used to get sewing done and take care of other things.

CHAPTER 4

Shoe Shopping

Anna announced at supper one Friday evening that the following day they would go to the store for shoes. Excitement reigned as they hurried through the dishes. The big wash tub was put on the kitchen floor and filled with warm water for their Saturday Night bath a day early. Anna always checked their necks and behind the knees that they usually missed. Sleep was slow in coming they were so excited.

The rooster only had to crow once before feet were on the floor to begin their exciting day. Anna had placed stockings in a poke. None of the children wore shoes until it snowed and they would go barefoot to the store. They did wear shoes to church on Sunday if their shoes were not outgrown.

It dawned on Anna that George had not even held Georgianna, and here she was a year old. Georgianna was always asleep when he was at the house, so this would be his chance to see her awake and maybe hold her, if he were not too busy.

Everyone helped with breakfast. Noona stuffed oatmeal into Georgianna while the others ate a hearty breakfast of canned sausage, fried eggs, apples, and hot biscuits to keep them from getting hungry before they got back home. They would be treated to a candy stick at the store.

When all eight of them were ready, ole Bruno was tied so he wouldn't follow them. Seven children were enough to keep up with. They did not need a dog to chase after. No one minded the four-mile walk. On they marched past the area they called the paint bank, where the rocks were of a soft clay of varied colors. They loved picking the soft clay rocks from the bank and marking on other stones. None of them became artists, but they had fun. The next fun spot was called Sandy Bend because of the accumulation of loose sand in the curve of the road. They spent many hours playing there. This morning they were too eager to get to the store, so all they did was wade through the sand.

The walk was by no means boring for them. They spotted a bunny rabbit or a squirrel scampering up a tree with a nut in his mouth. The older ones took turns carrying Georgianna. Even Bidgy and Fubby helped. One carried the poke of socks and another the poke of diapers, one extra bib, and Georgianna's sugar tit. She was still nursing and needed no bottle. As they passed Mrs. Emore's house, Bidgy asked if they could get her to bring them another baby. The older ones laughed at this question.

The store was soon in sight, and they all chattered like magpies and ran to see who would get there first. Billy handed Georgianna to Anna so he could get in the race. Even though he was getting quite grown-up, he liked to compete. His legs were the longest, and he was the winner, much to the dismay of the younger ones.

George came to greet Anna and to quickly hold the baby for a moment, remarking on her "white hair" and blue eyes. He rarely thought of the children as his and called them Anna's children. He remarked, "You've got a pretty girl," as he handed her back to Anna, and waited on another customer. Fubby marched behind him, expecting a little attention, which he did not get just yet. Saturday was a busy day at the store, especially in the morning.

After the morning rush, George finally had the time to pull out the children's shoes so Anna would choose. Of course there was not much to choose from, just black and brown high top shoes, but they were bright and shiny and smelled good. Georgianna would wear a pair that Fubby had outgrown, and Fubby would get Bidgy's outgrown ones that still had lots of wear. The rest got new shoes, all a little larger so they would not outgrow them before the winter was over.

Anna handed Georgianna to Noona so she could get her list of supplies she needed. George let each child select a favorite candy stick, much to their delight.

Anna took Georgianna to the back room to nurse before the long walk home. She almost forgot about the mail. They heard the train whistle in the distance and they all begged to stay and watch. This was exciting. They loved to watch the wheels turning, the big puffs of smoke, and the people at the windows. They knew the conductor, Otis Adkins, and thought of him as a special friend. All this excitement made this a very special day, and they happily returned to their humble mountain home, all starving. It was a good thing Anna had baked bread on Friday and there was plenty of milk in the springhouse and jams and preserves on the shelf.

Anna placed the sleeping baby on the bed and joined the children who were helping themselves and fixing Fubby's bread and jam. After eating they had to admire the new shoes, poking their noses inside to smell the new leather. Fubby moped in the corner. Bidgy's old shoes didn't smell good. Then he remembered that George stuck something in his pocket when the others got their shoes. He checked his pockets and found a licorice whip all rolled up, that made him feel better.

Bedtime found them all happy and content with the expectation of wearing new shoes for church the next day. Bidgy's were polished so Fubby would look good too.

CHAPTER 5

Georgianna from Two to Five

Georgianna was two when it was time for Mrs. Emore to arrive with her black bag, and Lancy, a chubby golden-haired boy, was born. This delighted all the children.

By this time Georgianna was talking a lot and could recite little jingles mimicking the older children. She soon learned 'Rock a Bye Baby' and sang as she rocked Lancy in the cradle. When he became fretful she would stick the old stand-by sugar tit in his mouth. This saved Anna many a step while she was recovering from Lancy's difficult birth. He was the largest baby she had given birth to and it took her awhile to grow strong again.

Georgianna was beginning to feel like a big girl—helping Mommy take care of the baby. However, it was not unusual to hear her say, "Take me Mommy, I'm your baby," while she had Lancy on her lap.

Springtime arrived and gardening time came. Planting time found everyone in the field. Lancy was placed on a quilt under a shade tree with Georgianna by his side to shoo the sweat bees away and see that no harm came to him. Those dreadful sweat bees would sting Georgianna and she cried softly while trying to protect her baby brother. A jug of water and a baby bottle with sweetened water was on hand. Sometimes when they were working a distance from the house, they carried a lunch so more could be done without stopping to go to the house. Anna was a hard working woman, and she expected the same of her children.

Even though Anna was a hard worker and a strict mother with more problems than she needed, there was a happiness about her

22

and she sang hymns she had learned in church as well as folk songs. Georgianna picked up on these songs and often sang even if she did not always get the words right. After hearing Anna sing "Take the Name of Jesus with You," she took that up as her favorite. When she came to the part "Hope of earth and Joy of Heaven" and it came out "Opal Verth and Joy of Heaven," the older ones laughed at her.

The summer was over, the crops were harvested, the root cellar was stocked, and the family were settled in for the long cold winter. Georgianna and Fubby were great companions and spent many happy hours playing with paper dolls cut from the Sears Roebuck catalogue when there was no work to be done.

The days came and went, Lancy was a year old, had a mouth full of teeth, and was walking, climbing, bouncing, on the move constantly. This kept Georgianna pretty busy trying to protect him from the hot stove, the stairway, and the other things that could happen to harm him.

Billy had gone to work over the mountain at a sawmill. Noona, Bidgy, and the twins had started school, so they could get some time in before the weather got too bad for the four-mile walk.

By late October Anna began getting up every morning feeling sick, and she realized that by late April or early May, Mrs. Emore would be bringing that little black bag again, and there would be another baby. She was not exactly happy about this, as George had not been giving her as much help lately, and the responsibility of raising the children was a tremendous job. Billy had gotten a job at a logging camp and saw mill and brought some money home. Georgianna looked forward to his homecoming, always with something for her. She was already four years old and alert to all that was going on.

Fubby and Georgianna were a good team setting the table at mealtime. Georgianna would stand on a chair and wash the dishes, and Fubby would dry and climb on a chair to put them in the cabinet. They had very few material possessions. There was always plenty of nourishing food, wood for cooking and warmth, oil for their lamps, and they were a pretty happy bunch. Anna discouraged quarreling among them. By mid-November the snow had begun to fall making a winter wonderland of the surrounding forest.

The family settled in for evenings and popping the corn that was a bumper crop this year. The children all learned to play a card game called 'Set back'. Also time was spent with the scope and views, a contraption you held to your eyes and inserted a double picture that was magnified as one. This was a never-ending enjoyment that had to be shared. An old phonograph stood in the corner with a few records that were badly scratched and sounded terrible.

Georgianna asked every day, "When is Billy coming? He's been gone too long," not knowing when he would be dropping in for a few days when it was too cold to work. And she was right. The next day he appeared with a small brown package under his arm, teasing Georgianna with it, then asking for 'sugar', a kiss on the cheek. She excitedly pulled the string from the package, unwrapping it to find not one, but two cupie dolls. It pleased Billy to see how happy this made her, and he felt like a real grown man to be working away and bringing something home. Anna was no longer 'Mommy' but 'Maw, all the time.

The snow continued to fall, and Georgianna was happy to have something new to play with. Heat was only in the two downstairs rooms, and it was quite crowded. Bidgy was sort of rascally and picked at Georgianna. She accidentally dropped one of her dolls from the table and its head broke off. She knew it was dead, so she took it out and buried it in the snow, shedding a few tears. When the snow melted, there lay the doll that had to wait for the ground to thaw before a proper burial could take place.

The older children went for a few weeks of school, before the weather became too difficult.

CHAPTER 6

Springtime in the Mountains

Spring arrived in the mountains with all of its splendor. The birds were singing and busy building nests. The hens were singing and laying an abundance of eggs, some of them laying their eggs in a secret place. You could tell by their appearance, all fluffy and excitable, that they were getting ready to set, and there would be lots of baby chicks scurrying around in a few weeks. An assortment of Rhode Island Reds, Dominicans, White Leghorns, and several Bantams all roamed the yard.

The red sow had thirteen piglets and a new calf would be arriving any day. There was a lot of activity going on and Anna wondered if she was going to be able to handle everything. She was getting heavier by the day and knew that in another month she would be having another child. The early garden was planted with everyone working until dark every day after school was out.

In late April, just as Anna thought she may have some spare time, Mrs. Emore was summoned once again to deliver Anna of a handsome dark haired baby boy, which she named Russ. The children were excited as usual at the arrival of a new baby even if it did mean more work for everyone. Georgianna just knew it would be her job to help take care of him, and she lost no time in taking over to see that he did not want for anything. She had learned how to fold a three-cornered diaper but couldn't yet put it on him. Anna was soon at her usual work. There was still some planting to be done, and hoeing of the things that were coming through the ground. Georgianna was left

by Cathie Logan Sharpe

with Russ for short periods while he slept. The others went to the garden to finish planting and hoeing.

This Saturday was to be a greens gathering outing, and Noona would stay with Russ and Lancy. Georgianna loved to go into the woods, and she was looking forward to seeing all the spring flowers, as well as learning what greens were good to eat.

The woodland was lush with many wild flowers. Violets, columbine, honeysuckle, and the most beautiful lady slippers kept getting the little girl's attention. Anna let her know this was a working outing and she planned on a good supply of greens to can for the winter. They would need to make several trips in the woods. Anna knew all the edible plants that grew there. This would be a weekly chore while the plants were young and tender and at peak flavor. One plant resembling a bear's paw, was called bear foot. There were Star of Bethlehem, poke, lamb's quarter, dandelion, sheep sorrel, and others. Each child learned to gather the proper plants. With many hands, a large quantity was soon in the burlap sacks. This would be greens for dinner seasoned just right and served with spring onions and vinegar. Then there would be enough for canning a few jars for the wintertime, thereby keeping the children in good health.

The spring and summer were just as busy as could be. Corbin and Corey had gotten some work at the sawmill and were gone part-time. This left more work for the others, but there were two less hungry mouths to feed. Springtime quite often found spicewood or sassafras roots simmering on the cookstove for hot tea they all enjoyed. The warm sunny days and cool evenings of late summer found everyone scurrying around to get all the harvest in before the first frost that came early in these mountains, often before mid September.

CHAPTER 7

Georgianna Learns to Read

The older children were in school. Bidgy and Fubby were going this year, and Georgianna missed Fubby and looked forward to the end of the day when they would be coming home bringing their books. How Georgianna loved looking at those books! She was learning to read, and Lancy was an avid listener. One of her favorite stories was "The Fox That Went to Squitims and Back." She had practically memorized that story.

When Anna's friends would drop by, Georgianna was encouraged to read for them, and so often she selected her favorite. She had not been to school and they were surprised that she could read so well. Many grown ups in the mountains could not read or write. She was soon helping the other children with their reading, and pounced on any new book they brought home. She read them all. Her pleasure was evident when she picked up a letter from Aunt Marty and proceeded to read it. Now she could read writing as well as print. There were times that she was asked to read the Bible for the Ladies' Bible Class at Sunday school, which was held in the small schoolhouse near the store. There were times that no one there could read well.

Learning to read at five years of age did not make Georgianna feel like she was doing anything special and she wondered why so much attention was given to this. She just enjoyed reading to Lancy and the older children and watching them study. This stuff called arithmetic was something she could not understand, and she didn't think she would ever go to school if you had to do arithmetic. She would just stay home and take care of the baby. She just knew there would always be one, and she liked taking care of them. She could already pin a diaper on Russ without sticking him or have the diaper fall off when you picked him up. She felt proud of that.

The winter passed quickly and once again there was the busy hustle and bustle of another beautiful springtime. The rhododendrons that usually bloom in mid-June were especially lovely. They grew almost like trees and hung gracefully over the clear sparkling stream that flowed by the house. The warm sunny days of summer soon turned to cool evenings as the harvest was once again gathered and stored.

Georgianna knew she would soon be six years old. The exact day of her birth was somewhat fuzzy, since birthdays were just another day.

Billy was away most of the time, and the twins were away some, and when they were there, they would pick a fuss with Bidgy who was growing up fast and wanted to be sassy to Anna who would not tolerate any of that kind of behavior from any of her brood. Age made no difference when it came to parental respect and she let this be known in no uncertain terms. No one was exempt from the consequence of misbehavior. Georgianna kept this in mind, not wanting to do anything that displeased her Mommy, who had to work so hard to care for her children.

CHAPTER 8

The Trip

Anna could plainly see the twins and Bidgy were getting restless and hard to manage, and she desperately wanted to make a change and get them into a different environment. While sitting with Russ in her lap one day, she picked up the booklet she had gotten with her mail. She leafed through it and an ad caught her eye. "Small farm near Scottsville, Virginia, low rent, needs attention." Maybe she should look into this.

This had been a good year, and she had taken produce over the old stagecoach road into neighboring West Virginia. She had been able to save a little money. She gave this a few days' thought before she made up her mind to look into it. She checked with George to see if some of the children could stay at his living quarters back of the store for a few days. She took Georgianna with her.

Anna wrote the agent in charge of the property, telling him when she would like to see the farm. A letter arrived from the agent that he would be happy to show her the place and answer any questions she might have.

Anna made the mistake of telling Georgianna that Mommy was taking her on a trip. Every day was the question "Is it today?"

"No, not today, it will be Thursday." It seemed like Thursday was never coming.

"Tomorrow is Thursday, Georgianna. Tonight we get ready." Her hair was washed, and she got a good scrubbing before going to bed. Anna had put their clothes in the big black suitcase that was seldom used and laid out Georgianna's good new navy dress with matching bloomers beside her navy blue coat suit that she still looked good in after many years wear.

Georgianna was looking forward to the long ride on the train. She had not been on a long trip, only a few short ones to "Goodwin's Ferry" or to "Paint Bank" to visit her aunts. She was so excited it took a long time to go to sleep. She would get to wear her new black shoes instead of Fubby's old ones. Anna put items in a box for Noona and the other children to use while they were at George's store, before she went to bed.

Early morning found Anna in the kitchen, and Georgianna right behind her to help get breakfast. "Go wake the others, so we can get things done and not miss the train." She was quick to respond, not wanting to miss out on this trip. As soon as breakfast was over, Bidgy was instructed to get their sturdy homemade wagon to haul the luggage and the box of belongings for the ones left behind. The nearest neighbor would take care of the farm animals while they were gone, using the milk and eggs for pay.

They arrived at the store in the early afternoon so as to get the children settled in before the train arrived. Russ continued to cling to Mommy like he knew she was leaving him. George would see that there was food for the children while she was away and that Noona would take good care of Russ. She had much experience.

All rushed out at the clanging of the train bell and the loud whistle, as the train rounded the curve belching black smoke and making a hissing sound as it slowed and came to a stop. Otis Adkins, the conductor, was first off the train, being warmly greeted by all the children. Following him were two passengers. Fubby piped up, "Mommy and Georgianna are going with you." Otis smiled, "That so?"

"Yes, it's so."

Anna took the children into the back room and bade them good-bye, telling Noona and Bidgy to keep them there until the train had pulled out.

George helped her on with the suitcase, and the train pulled out after the conductor found them a comfortable seat. The train went fast that the trees and poles seemed to be moving. The days were getting shorter and before too long it was dark. They ate the sausage biscuits they had carried with them and the bottle of pop George had given them.

The porter would come through the train and announce the next stop they were approaching. They stopped a lot, so did not get up much speed until it was time to stop again. Coming into a large town called Roanoke, they had to get off the train and wait for another train. So many people were coming and going. A small girl with braces on her legs was being walked back and forth, back and forth by her mother. Georgianna asked "What is the matter with her?"

"She probably had "Infantile Paralysis.""

"What's that?"

"A bad disease that cripples you."

Their train was announced. Anna picked up their baggage and they boarded the train. They missed their old friend the conductor. Just as they found a seat that suited them, the "all aboard" was sounded, and you could hear the hissing of the steam as the train began to move.

The black porter came into the car and said, "Ma'am, your berth is ready," and showed Anna to a bed pulled out of the wall. Georgianna hadn't thought about going to bed on the train. It was like a dream, a nice dream, but a little strange—she had never been away from the other children and already missed them.

In the morning Anna and Georgianna got up, went to the toilet, washed their face and hands, and on their way back to their seat, they met the porter calling out, "Next stop, Scottsville."

"That's where we get off," Anna remarked, as Georgianna peered out the window, just when the little town was coming to life. A milkman with his horse drawn wagon was putting bottles with milk in them on people's porches.

Anna took her child by the hand as the conductor helped them off the train with their baggage. There were several houses quite close to the depot. Anna approached the ticket agent who tipped his cap politely as she inquired if he knew where she might find a few nights' lodging. "Ah yes ma'am. Mrs. Moore, a widow lady in the big white house, puts up folks who are in town for a few days. It's the house next to the depot."

Anna knocked on the door of the big white house. It was early in the morning and Mrs. Moore pulled back the curtains. After seeing a woman and child, she opened the door. Georgianna, being shy, tucked her head and stepped behind her Mommy. "I am looking for a room for my daughter and me for a few nights."

"Lands yes and what a sweet little girl. Come right in and I'll show you to the room. My two girls are still in bed."

They went upstairs and were taken into a neat clean room with pretty white curtains and a big rocking chair. Mrs. Moore quoted the price and said she served three meals a day. She would also care for the child if needed. A twelve-year-old boy lived there. His name was Jimmy Bugg. The Moore girls, hearing voices, were soon up. Mary, who was in her teens, was a big hit with Georgianna. Daisy, the other girl, was older and not too friendly. Jimmy Bugg reminded them of Bidgy, sort of a rascal.

Mrs. Moore hustled around fixing a big country breakfast while Mary set the table. Anna told Mrs. Moore why she had come and asked where she could find the agent, Mr. Elam. "Oh my yes, he's the man across the road with the afflicted son. They say the boy don't have any bones in his fingers. He goes around shaking' them all the time. You can telephone him or just go over to see him."

"Thank you, Mrs. Moore. I didn't think I would be this lucky."

Anna contacted Mr. Elam as soon as breakfast was over, and they arraigned to go look at the farm early Saturday morning.

Georgianna was already following Mary around and helping her with the dishes and making the beds, always keeping an eye on Mommy to see she did not go off without her. Anna enjoyed this little bit of free time from all the work and activity. She had not been away from the children much and she had been taking care of her mother during illness. It was nice talking to Mrs. Moore whose husband's death a few years back had compelled her to take in roomers to have an income.

Anna explained her reason for being in Scottsville. "Oh, I remember that farm. I've heard some things about it. You may not want to move your family there."

"We'll see," remarked Anna as her daughter climbed up on her lap saying, "What are we going to do now? Can we take a walk?"

This was a good idea. The village was not heavily populated, but it gave the appearance of a big city to a little girl who had spent most of her time miles from the nearest neighbor. Mrs. Moore let them know what time dinner, the midday meal, would be on the table.

They walked slowly up the road admiring the many neat homes painted white and the fall flowers that were blooming. Georgianna spotted a sign that said 'Country Store', and Anna reluctantly took her in knowing she could not spare much money for a treat of any kind. They could just look. It was fancier than George's store but had about the same items—jars of stick candy of different colors and peanuts in a jar that were measured with a small scoop and put in a small brown poke. "Can we get some, Mommy? They smell so good." After pausing for thought, Anna gave in and purchased two small scoops for six cents. This gave them something to munch on as they continued their walk. Noticing the clock in the store, Anna found they had plenty of time before dinner. Anna was going to enjoy someone else's cooking for a change.

After dinner, a leisurely afternoon was spent walking in a different direction. They arrived back in plenty of time for the generous supper that filled the house with its aroma. Anna approached the kitchen to tell Mrs. Moore, "I do believe you could out-cook me with all them pots on the stove."

Saturday Morning was bright and sunny, an exhilarating crisp autumn day. Some of the leaves were beginning to fall. Anna took her child by the hand and walked across the road for the ride to the farm. Another gentleman had joined Mr. Elam. They were both dressed in a suit and tie and appeared to be gentlemen you could trust; but not used to seeing many strangers, Anna was skeptical.

It seemed like a long ride in the buggy where Anna and her child sat in the back seat. The men were busy chatting as they traveled over the dusty country road. They soon spotted a small white house that was overgrown with weeds and brush. Anna thought, "Plenty of work here for lots of people."

Parting the tall weeds that surrounded the house, they went inside. Anna began having second thoughts about considering a move. This would not be any better than the beautiful mountain area where they now lived. However, she looked at all the possibilities as the agent pointed them out to her. There certainly was plenty of work to keep the boys busy for a long time. She would have to give this a lot of thought.

The house tour was completed and they moved to the big front porch to talk over the deal they wanted to make. This held no interest for Georgianna, who began to explore some on her own. Seeing a row of barrels, she stretched up on her tiptoes to see what they contained. After looking into several of them and seeing that bones were in all of them, she was puzzled and scurried through the weeds yelling "Mommy, Mommy," in her loudest voice. Mommy was engrossed in conversation with the two men.

Georgianna tugged at her skirt, "Come look. Come look!" Seeing Georgianna more excited than she had ever seen her, Anna decided she had better have a look. Anna viewed the barrel of bones with astonishment. They looked very much like human bones. She took Georgianna by the hand because she had a very strange feeling about this place. As she walked around the house, one of the agents flashed a large shiny knife. This was too much for Anna, added to the strange feeling she was having.

Tightly holding onto her child, she walked around the other side of the house. She was just going to walk back to the village. Apparently she was fearful for herself and her child's safety. In the twenties children did not question their parents and usually just accepted their judgment, so Georgianna skipped happily along the road picking some fall daisies for Mrs. Moore. She never thought this would be a weekend that she would still be puzzled over sixty-five years later.

The clatter of horses' hooves and rumble of the buggy soon reached their ears. There was no place to hide. Mr. Elam urged them to get in the buggy, since it was quite a distance. They did and the ride into the village was quiet and uneventful. Georgianna thought that everything was all right.

Arriving at Mrs. Moore's after dinner was over, Anna saw food was still on the table waiting for them. Stew pots were on the cook stove keeping some foods hot. Serving two plates, Mrs. Moore sat down to talk while they ate. She asked, "Well, Mrs.Marlow, what did you think of the farm?"

Anna answered briefly, "I have some doubts about it that are hard to explain. I'll just have to think about it."

Anna sat on the porch rocking while Georgianna romped in the yard and picked at June Bugs as she had dubbed Jimmy Bugg. The day's events had faded from her mind as she raced around playing tag and hide and seek.

Anna wished she had brought some handwork along, feeling so useless just sitting. She asked Mrs. Moore if there was anything she could help her with. "My lord, you are supposed to be a guest, but I'd be much obliged if you would peel some potatoes for salad. I always cook food on Saturday so I do not have to do much on Sunday. That's my day of rest." Anna was glad to have something to do with her hands and keep her mind off the day's events.

Sunday morning was a bright, beautiful day. Yesterday's events were forgotten. Georgianna looked forward to the train ride home in the evening because she had missed the family, especially Fubby and Russ.

Mrs. Moore invited them to go to church with her after she had everything in readiness for dinner. The church was much prettier than the little schoolhouse back at Kire and the people were friendly.

Mrs. Elam was on the phone before they were finished with dinner. "Mrs. Marlow, my husband wants to talk business with you. What time can you come?"

"As soon as we are through dinner," Anna said.

Mrs. Elam, a soft-spoken woman continued, "Afterward, we can take a walk and look at the new bridge recently built over the James River." A small town like Scottsville did not get a new concrete bridge often, so it was quite an attraction.

Georgianna tried to keep everything in her head so she could tell Noona and the boys all about it. As they entered the Elam home, she looked around at all the pretty things, even nicer than the Medley's home back at Kire.

Georgianna stood by Anna who was seated at Mr. Elam's desk, with papers he wanted her to sign. Anna, with a disturbed look on her face, was hesitant about signing anything. Mrs. Elam walked in and picked Georgianna up—she was quite small for almost six years of age—saying, "I'll wait for you in the yard."

Georgianna thought they had been waiting for a long time when Mrs. Elam began to cry. Never having seen an adult cry, Georgianna was puzzled and wanted to be put down so she could go to Mommy. Mrs. Elam was unwilling to let her down, as if she was afraid. Being very shy, Georgianna didn't protest.

Anna came around from the back door to the front yard where they were waiting. She, too, looked like she had been crying. All this was a big puzzle to the small girl, and she didn't know how to fit the pieces together. She felt better, though, having Mommy by her side and holding her by the hand.

The walk across the bridge was exciting. The only bridge Georgianna had ever been on was the wooden bridge over the creek. To her, the James River was a lot of water, and from the bridge she could see Mrs. Moore's house and the nearby depot. She was eager to get on that train and be on her way back home, not knowing that fate would create a delay for several days by events she had never dreamed of.

Arriving back at Mrs. Moore's, Mrs. Elam said goodbye. She gave Georgianna a big bear hug, and looking unhappy, she walked across the road to her home.

Anna went upstairs to see that all their things were ready for the trip back home. They were both still in the navy blue outfits they had worn to church and for the train ride home. Mrs. Moore was getting the leftovers from the warming closet (an extension over the stove to keep food warm) as Anna and Georgianna came down the stairs bringing their baggage. "My, you are in a hurry. Train ain't due for two hours."

"Just saving a few steps," said Anna as she set the baggage down and asked for a paper poke for their dirty clothes.

Mrs. Moore handed her one, saying, "Hope you don't mind left overs. That's what we always have Sunday evening. I baked a lemon pie to go with them, and we are just going to leave the dishes. The girls will wash them when they get back from visiting. You need to rest a spell before getting back to all that work. You look a mite tired."

The Moore girls came home, ate their supper and washed the dishes. Georgianna would like for Mary to come home with her because she had liked her and June Bugg, who was nice to her like Billy. Anna sat her luggage on the back porch so when they heard the train there would be time to pick it up and walk to the depot and flag the train down with a lantern. If no one was getting off the train, it did not stop when the depot was closed. Mrs. Moore lit the lantern and would walk to the depot with them.

The whippoorwills had begun their evening serenade now that darkness had fallen. "That train must be late. I am going to see if I can hear it in the distance." Anna walked out the door. Georgianna waited at the door. Mommy did not come back. Then she heard the train. She was very much afraid they were going to miss the train. She had to hold back the tears. Still her Mommy did not come back. Sadly, she watched the train as it rolled on down the track.

Now she was really scared. Where had Mommy gone? She was more puzzled than ever. She knew something must be wrong, when Mrs. Moore and her daughters talked in hushed tones, and Mrs. Moore made a telephone call from another room.

Not much time had passed until two men came to the door. One looked like he might be a sheriff. Georgianna did not know what to think. Mary picked her up and sat with her in the rocking chair, while Mrs. Moore and the two men went into another room. You could hear them making phone calls. The little girl was soon fast asleep and Mary carried her to bed.

Georgianna awakened to find everyone up, but Mommy was nowhere to be found. It was then she asked, "Where's Mommy?" No one seemed to want to answer her. Now she really felt abandoned and thought she would never see Mommy or her family again. It was all she could do to keep from crying. Meanwhile, there was lots of coming and going and people talking in private and low tones like they didn't want her to hear what was being said. Still the child did not question. She was quiet and timid and usually just accepted things good or bad. It was a strange and long day for this child who was not quite six. Jimmy and Mary tried to keep her amused and busy.

Darkness came and still no Mommy. Even then she did not cry but stayed close to her friend Mary, afraid she, too, might go away. She clung to Mary with one hand and a doll with the other. There was much coming and going of strangers and Georgianna heard someone mention bloodhounds. She knew what they were. She had never been separated from her family and felt like she would cry any minute. Her loneliness was almost more than she could bear. She was trying to behave like a big girl, but she didn't feel much like one.

The day was almost over and Mrs. Moore was busy as usual amid all the interruptions getting her supper cooking. Mary continually tried to keep the child busy hoping she would not be too unhappy. For once in her life Georgianna didn't have much appetite when she sat down next to Mary. The thought passed through her mind this must be what you call being homesick. She surely was.

Mary took her upstairs to bed and lay down beside her until Georgianna was fast asleep. Yet the child tossed and turned throughout the night. The rumble of a buggy and clap of the horse hoofs woke Georgianna the next morning and she just knew that Mommy would come for her today. It was a dreary morning with light rain falling and heavy dark clouds hanging in the air. She knew she was supposed to be a sunshine girl, but this was not her kind of day. Pangs of homesickness engulfed her, and she was miserable.

Softly, in her bare feet, Georgianna descended the stairs to hear one of the strange men say, "We have found a shoe, and the blood hounds have picked up a scent. We'll find her."

This was such a mystery. "Mommy must be lost. She would not just go away and leave me." These thoughts whirled through her head.

By mid morning the rain had stopped, and later the grass was dry. She and Mary could play in the yard and romp in the grass that was turning brown from the cool nights. For a few minutes she almost forgot that she was alone among strangers.

In late afternoon she heard, "Whoa, whoa," as two gentlemen and a lady stopped in front of the house. Georgianna hoped this was Mommy. She was about the right size only skinny. She didn't have Mommy clothes, and she had scratches on her face and hands, and her skin was very dark. The child slipped inside as they made their way up the steps and into the house. Georgianna stayed out of the way. She had seen enough strangers.

The lady was led to a chair. Georgianna stood awkwardly near the doorway. Mrs. Moore spoke, "Don't you know who this is?" Anna held out her hand and smiled briefly. Now Georgianna knew her Mommy had returned, but she was different and so quiet, not at all like the Mommy that went out to listen for the train.

Georgianna tried to learn everything that was being said. Apparently

Anna had been frightened by something or someone as she stood near the railroad track and had swum the river to escape and had become lost. Her clothing had been torn to shreds by brambles. From fatigue and fright she had begun to hallucinate and had followed a blue light that led her on and on along the river. She saw no signs of a settlement where she could get help. When she was found by the bloodhounds, most of her clothing was gone, and numerous cuts and bruises covered her body. Georgianna was a little hesitant about going to her mother, but finally she shyly climbed up on her lap. It was then that she burst into tears. She could restrain herself no longer.

A kindly Dr. Harris was summoned to the house to examine Anna. Finding nothing seriously wrong, he decided that after a couple days' rest and some nourishing food, she would be able to go home. It was then he asked, "Why did you go away and leave your child?"

"I knew Mrs. Moore would care for my child. I was concerned that she would be upset, but there was nothing I could do about it."

CHAPTER 9

The Trip Home

An Episcopalian preacher, Rev. Meredith, with his pretty wife and eleven-year-old daughter, Nancy, came to visit. Georginna really liked Nancy. This kindly couple offered to travel part of the way home with them to be sure the change of trains went smoothly.

The morning of departure, the Merediths were at Mrs. Moore's early to be of any help they could. Nancy carried a beautiful big doll in her arms. Georgianna asked, "Can I hold your doll?"

"Here, take it. I brought it for you." It was the most beautiful doll she had ever seen.

Georgianna threw her arms around Nancy and said, "I am naming this doll Nancy and I will always remember you." Georgianna now had three things to be happy over: Mommy was back, she had a new friend, and best of all she was going home. It had been a long and strange week.

The train arrived at the small depot. Two people got off the train. Preacher Meredith took care of their tickets, helped them all up the steps, and found vacant seats across from each other. Nancy and Georgianna shared a seat. Georgianna liked the way you could fix the seats facing each other because she was afraid to let Mommy out of her sight.

As the train sped along the tracks, one had the feeling of standing still and the trees doing the moving. The Merediths talked with Anna, while the two girls kept up a lively chatter. Nancy was told all about Fubby, Lancy, and baby Russ.

Anna appeared more like her old self but not in total command of

41

the situation. The Merediths would be leaving them at the next stop to take the train back to Scottsville, while Anna and her child would be on another train on their way to Kire.

The porter came through the train announcing, "Next stop, Roanoke." Anna retrieved their baggage from overhead as the train slowed down.

They would have a wait before the train arrived for Kire, shortly before the next train for Scottsville would be in. Georgianna was so eager to get home that she often asked, "Is it time yet?"

Checking the big clock in the depot, Anna answered, "About fifteen minutes."

Reluctant good-byes were said as Anna thanked the Minister and his wife for their kindness. Georgianna wanted Nancy to go home with her, and she thanked her for the beautiful doll. The train arrived and many people came off the train. Mr. Meredith helped Anna and Georgianna on board with their baggage and saw them comfortably seated on the side facing the station, so they could wave to each other as the train began to move.

The last they saw of the Merediths were their hands waving from the platform. "I wish Nancy could have just gone home with us. I want to keep this pretty doll forever." Mommy didn't notice. She was deep in thought. Georgianna watched the trees and telephone poles fly by, much too excited to take a nap. She looked forward to seeing the family again. Being gone a week seemed like a month. She had never seen her Mommy so quiet. She wished they could sing a hymn together or talk, but she, too, kept quiet. There would be plenty of noise when they got home. The family had expected them home several days before and would be watching for them on every train that came through the town.

Georgianna asked from time to time, "It sure is taking a long time. How much longer?"

Anna would reply, "Ah, we will be there before dark."

Georgianna was relieved to hear her Mommy say a few words and she continue the conversation. "I'll bet Fubby missed me and Russ too, since I hold his bottle sometime. I am glad he is off the titty, so I can help feed him. I sure don't like to change his dirty diaper, though, he smells as bad as the pig pen."

Anna would tell her, "Sh, sh, that's enough talk."

Anna had no timepiece, but she could tell it was about four-thirty in the afternoon. Another forty-five minutes would find the train at Kire. She was tired and weary from the week's events and riding most of the day.

As the territory became familiar, Georgianna once again asked, "How long is it? Can the train go faster?"

Anna told her, "If it is necessary. Now quit fidgeting; you'll wear your bloomers out. They have to last you all winter."

Excitement reigned when friendly Otis Adkins came striding through the train announcing, "Next stop, Kire."

Home at last. The other children greeted them on the store porch. George had gotten a phone call so they were expected. There was quite a bit of hugging and back patting. Russ had already forgotten them and clung to Noona. Lancy was a bit shy. Anna did not appear like her old self because of her recent ordeal. She was glad to see the children who had fared well except for Lancy's swollen foot.

The children wanted to know, "What took you so long?"

Anna just said, "Well, we had some problems that caused the delay." Anna was eager to get the children home. They had gathered their things together since the phone call came. While the boys loaded the wagon, Anna gathered a few items from the store, including thread she needed to make over some warm coats for the cold winter ahead.

The four-mile trek home began with lots of chatter, and all were glad to be back home.

CHAPTER 10

Granny's Death

No sooner had things settled down to the usual routine than a letter arrived from Grandpa telling that Granny was very sick and he could not wait on her. He asked Anna if she could come and help care for her. There was nothing for Anna to do but put her sewing aside and pack a few clothes in the saddlebags, taking only what she would need.

She made arrangements once again to have the animals fed. She saddled ole Maude, loaded the little wagon, left the children at the store, and went on up the mountain. She took Georgianna with her, for she would be lots of help in caring for Granny.

As they rode by Mountain Lake, Anna knew it would be nearly frozen in another six weeks. She was reminded of the good times she had skating on the ice and the bad fall that had left an ugly scar across her chin.

Anna and Georgianna arrived at Granny's to find her in worse condition than they had expected—she didn't recognize them. She later rallied enough to ask for a drink of water. As Georgianna went to the kitchen for a cup of water, Grandpa said, "Don't give her any water." Giving Grandpa a mean look, Georgianna decided he was a mean man to not want Granny to have water.

Grandpa showed Anna the pile of dirty clothes that had accumulated since Maw had been sick. He didn't offer to help, just left the job of scrubbing the clothes on a washboard to Anna and her daughter.

Anna didn't get much rest at night and "Maw" was getting more feeble every day. Grandpa was very little help around the house. She wrote to Marty to come and help. Marty's oldest daughter could take care of the home while Marty was away. Marty managed to arrive in time to be recognized, before Maw went into a deep coma.

The two women stayed busy trying to care for their mother. They knew that she was not going to get well, and they kept her warm and as comfortable as possible. Anna had very little time to pay any attention to Georgianna. Once when she checked to see if Georgianna was covered, the bed was empty. Searching the house for her, Anna found her in a warm spot behind the cook stove, curled up fast asleep in the wood box. Anna gently lifted her up and placed her in the feather bed, removed her shoes and covered her up. Georgianna never awakened.

Georgianna awoke early the next morning and was surprised she still had on her clothes. She pulled her shoes on and tied them tight. She noticed the house was very quiet. No one seemed to be up. She peeked into Granny's room and saw that Granny was asleep in her best dress. Georgianna though that was odd, until it dawned on her that Granny must have died while Georgianna slept.

Aunt Marty and Anna had been up most of the night and were now sleeping. Georgianna found Grandpa sitting quietly in the rocker by the fire. She wondered if he was thinking how mean he had been to Granny when she was alive.

Granny's funeral was small, attended by only a few friends and relations.

After the funeral, Anna hurriedly gathered their few belongings, saddled ole Maude, led the horse up to the porch so she could put their clothes in the saddlebags. She lifted her child onto the mare, and then climbed on herself, hoping to cover the twelve miles home before dark. She did not relish the idea of being out after night.

As they passed beautiful Mountain Lake again, Anna said, "Whoa!" They paused to admire the beautiful fall colors: reds, yellows, golds, and some purple. With all the evergreens and the shimmering lake, it was a beautiful spot. There were lots of shady spots, and Georgianna was glad she had on her overalls, as well as her long black stockings. You could feel Ole Man Winter on the way.

They arrived back at the store. Anna let Georgianna walk the rest of the way home and put Lancy behind her on the horse and Russ in front. They hurriedly made their way over the mountain, getting home just as the sun's last rays were fading.

Noona was the first to ask about Granny, and Anna told them about Granny's death. Many people died fairly young in the early nineteen twenties, and unless you had a telephone or lived near someone who had one, death messages were not always sent. This was an accepted way of life and seemed normal to people in the backcountry.

Georgianna noticed that the lamp chimneys were black with soot. There had not been time to clean them before they left for Granny's. This was her daily job, and she seldom had to be reminded. Noona was different; she had work to do but liked to stand around and daydream and let someone else do it. Noona often had to be reminded. No one in this household got out of working!

Anna spied a bushel of apples just inside the kitchen door with a scrap of paper on top. It had Will Perkins' name on it. She said, "That ole horse trader has been by and left us some apples. It's a good thing, too; we didn't have too many this year. I'll get busy and work some into preserves tomorrow." She busied herself getting supper ready. She was surprised to find Billy had found work for the twins and had come for them while she was at Granny's. Her family had suddenly diminished to six and there was less food to prepare because they were her biggest eaters!

CHAPTER 11

Home Remedies and Other Stories

Anna Marlow was a skilled woman with many ways of keeping her family in good health. She knew the herbs and plants that were beneficial for many ailments, and the trusty bottle of turpentine was good for sterilizing and keeping down infection. Someone was forever stepping on a nail and, because the animals roamed the yard, a good disinfectant was important. The large jar of Vicks Vaporub took care of the colds and runny noses during the cold season. A good night's rest was aided by a pan of water containing Vicks salve setting on the wood heater, acting as a vaporizer. Croup attacks were treated with a steaming pan of water and a sheet draped over it and the patient. The moist air was an aid in clearing air passages. Croup attacks were few and far between. An asthma attack was treated by burning leaves of the Jimsan weed and using a sheet over the pan so the patient could inhale the fumes.

Home remedies were extremely important when you lived in the mountains and the nearest doctor might be many miles away. The nearest doctor to the Marlows was many miles away in Pearisburg, and by horseback you could either be dead or well by the time you reached the doctor, and he could make a visit. If you were poor, doctors did not always respond.

Twice yearly Anna wormed the children by making vermifuge candy and feeding it to them. This was done by boiling the vermifuge plant in water, taking the water, adding brown sugar, butter, and vanilla, and cooking it just right. It resembled caramel fudge. To most of the children this was a treat, but not to Georgianna. She fed hers to Bruno. Guess that dog did not have worms.

A fretful, feverish child usually got a good dose of castor oil to clean them out. These remedies must have worked for no one ever had to spend much time in bed because of sickness.

Stubbed toes and lost toenails often occurred in the summer time. Usually this was a minor occurrence and one just sprinkled some sand on to stop the bleeding and kept on playing.

Mullin leaves soaked in warm vinegar were used to treat swelling from any sprain or sore muscles.

Farm work could be hazardous. One incident during rail splitting time almost cost Fubby a finger. When he was brought to the house with his little finger hanging by a piece of skin.
Anna skillfully put it back in place, soaked a clean white cloth in turpentine, bound the finger firmly, and placed his hand on a board for a splint. The finger grew back without any trouble, and only a slight crook and an almost invisible scar remained.

An anti-itch lotion was made from boiling witch hazel bark, straining the liquid and adding camphor gum. This was effective for stings, insect bites, poison ivy, and other itches.

Lancy had a problem with what was called spasms in old days. He often began screaming and thrashing about wildly while in a deep sleep. Anna kept the camphor bottles handy. After several attempts at holding it under his nose, at which times he clutched the bottle with tremendous strength, he would eventually waken and settle down. Needless to say, this ordeal awakened everyone in the house. They all got things under control.

An excellent cough syrup was made by simmering vinegar, brown sugar, honey, and a small amount of butter. This was kept warm, so the butter remained melted. This was very effective, more so than many products currently on the market. A container sat in the warming oven throughout the winter and was used as needed. It had a pleasant taste and there was no objection to taking it.

Bee stings were frequent and treated with a paste made from baking soda and vinegar. This worked well and was applied immediately. It was very inexpensive and the ingredients were always on hand.

Occasionally, a stubborn cold was treated with a mustard plaster on the chest. This was made of a paste of flour and dry mustard spread on a piece of flannel and kept warm. With Anna's expertise at doctoring her children, no doctor was ever needed.

The soil in the area was very fertile which was a good thing, enabling one to grow many things and live comfortably off the land. Much wisdom was a real necessity if you expected to survive, stay in good health, keep your animals cared for, and manage through the harsh winters, when the winds howled and the snow covered the ground from early fall until mid spring.

This "Sun Flower story" reminds some folks of "Jack and the Bean Stalk" and is almost unbelievable. However it is very true. One especially good season produced a giant sunflower stalk that survived much climbing from the youngest members of the family. By the end of the summer the stalk had been stripped of every leaf and had a well worn shine. It took both Fubby and Georgianna to carry the giant head to the house where the seeds were beaten from the head and filled a very large pan of feed for the chickens and the pigs. Sometimes a squirrel or a bunny rabbit would bravely join the chickens for a few nibbles before being frightened away by the confusion they caused.

Fubby was the choice when it was time to ride to West Virginia on the small gray donkey to bring back flour and occasionally a loaf of light bread, which he proceeded to call heavy bread. He always wanted to add a little comedy to every thing. Some days this was quite a journey, not because it was so far, but because the donkey was not always cooperative and often wanted to go backward when one wanted him to go forward.

On one occasion Fubby was lucky to have a string in his pocket, along with the nails, marbles and other things that boys his age were in the habit of sticking in their pockets. "Don," short for donkey, decided to lie down against a barbed wire fence, tearing a hole in the sack of flour. After taking the bull by the horns, so to speak, and tying the hole, with lots of persuasion, Fubby managed to get the donkey on his feet and arrive back at the mountain home to devour a well-earned supper.

Teaberry picking was many a Sunday afternoon venture. For folks who do not know what a teaberry is, it grows close to the ground on a plant with a glossy leaf. The berries are quite small, pink in color, and remind you of a tiny apple. Georgianna liked to put hers in a poke and pretend they were apples. Sunday was always a special day and no work was done that did not need to be done. Of course, animals had to be fed, cows milked, and eggs gathered. Most of the cooking was taken care of on Saturday, so everyone could get some much-needed rest, along with church services that were held in the small schoolhouse.

Georgianna occasionally made the four-mile walk to the store and post office to get the mail and bring back some needed items. One particular cool autumn day as she was returning home feeling a little scared, her overalls were brushing together and she kept looking behind her to see if anyone was following her and making that brushing sound. As she strolled along she heard someone whistling. It was then she felt really scared. Mommy had always warned them about tramps. She thought, "I'll speak nicely and they will not hurt me." As she rounded the Sandy Bend, she came face to face with a stranger. When she spoke softly, he dashed into the woods. Georgianna ran the rest of the way home. Totally out of breath, she cried, "Mommy, I saw a man and he looked mean. I spoke to him, and he ran into the woods."

Anna covered her mouth after speaking, "That might have been that convict that escaped from jail."

CHAPTER 12

The Hog Killing

Hog killing was an extremely busy time, one that farm folks were glad to get out of the way. The weather needed to be just right, cold enough to chill the meat but not too cold to hamper the process. First, you had to have stones heated in a brisk fire and placed in a barrel of water to heat it to a high degree. The slain hog was then dipped into the barrel to loosen the hair so that it was more easily scraped from the hide.

After the hog was shot and the throat was slashed in order for it to bleed, the hog was scalded, scraped, and hung from a high pole, supported by braces at each end or, if you had them, two trees close enough to support the pole. A strong stick was inserted through the lower hind legs and over the pole to secure it in place.

The hog was then gutted and its head removed. Buckets of water were thrown over the hog. Then it was ready for sectioning into hams, shoulders, tenderloin, spareribs, fat back, and side meat for bacon. The liver was separated from intestines, and some of the liver was made into liver pudding or liverwurst, as it is now called. Scraps of lean and some fat were ground and seasoned for sausage. The head was cooked and made into souse. The fat was stripped from intestines and other parts and was cooked and rendered into lard. This had an unpleasant odor while cooking. The pig feet were pickled and were enjoyed. Very little of the hog went to loss. Fried ham and eggs with hot biscuits and lots of freshly churned butter was often a generous breakfast for the hungry brood. If Anna could have devised a way to make use of the hog hair, she certainly would have used it!

November arrived and all were just awaiting the perfect time for this busy activity that nearly everyone except the baby was involved in. They were anticipating the enjoyment of the fresh pork that would be on the table.

Anna decided the weather was ready and so was she. Arranging for Deck Emore to help her on Monday, she sent Bidgy to the lumber camp for Billy, Cory, and Corbin to come home for a few days. Lots of help was needed to get the meat taken care of fast, in case warmer weather should arrive.

Anna and the children had just finished a hearty breakfast when Bruno began barking loudly and a knock at the door let then know that Deck was there. "Howdy Deck, you are here good and early. I see you brought your shotgun. I am glad you didn't forget it."

"A day like this I'm not apt to forget my gun. I'll see the boys have a good fire going and the water in the barrel. Your bunch got up early too."

Noona and Georgianna were kept busy washing the dishes and keeping Lancy and Russ out of the way. Fubby was given the job of gathering the knives and scrapers together. There would be lots of scraping for two good-sized hogs, and small children could help with this. The twins retrieved the hanging pole from its storage spot overhead in the granary.

Anna, in her bib overalls, bustled around giving everyone instructions on what to do next. A large table was readied for cutting up the hogs. Everything was falling into place.

Georgianna kept an eye on everything, knowing that her pet pig "Ole Rooter," given this name because he was continually rooting in the ground, would be getting the bullet this time, and she neither wanted to see or hear, when it happened. She had selected her place of refuge. As the pigs were driven into the pen, lots of squealing was heard, as if they knew their time had come.

Georgianna said to Noona, "I am going to the spring for a bucket of water," and she hastily grabbed the bucket and dashed out the door. She went behind the huge hemlock tree and stuck her fingers in both ears and waited until the shots and squealing had ceased. She then filled her water bucket and went back to the house, being careful not to look in the direction of the hog killing. Noona scolded her for taking so long. "You know I need you to help me get food ready to cook for dinner. Everybody is gonna be starving by twelve o'clock." Georgianna didn't let this bother her because she knew she did her share of the work, usually without being told.

Noona responded to Anna's call from the butchering area, and asked Georgianna to take them a bucket of water with the dipper. "I've got to fix Russ a bottle. You take it," Georgianna said. She wasn't about to go out there and see "Ole Rooter" dead, even if she would be eating him all winter. She still felt sad. She would be helping to grind the meat up for sausage to be cooked and canned, but it would not be so bad. It would not look like Ole Rooter.

The butchering area was a hubbub of activity. The crew scraped furiously using a variety of tools, some a piece of sharp tin or metal nailed to a small block of wood, others a knife.

By dinner time the scraping was over with, the hogs hung, gutted, and rinsed with buckets of water, and their insides placed in a wash tub and covered to keep the dog out. At last, the group came in to satisfy their ravishing appetites.

by Claire Logan English

Cory, Corbin, and Fubby debated about who would get the bladders, as they noisily slid into their familiar place on the bench beside the table, doing a little pushing and shoving. Anna quieted them down in a hurry and remarked, "The bladders will belong to everybody, and that settles that." The bladders made a great ball after tying one end, inserting a hollow end into the other, inflating it like a balloon, then leaving it to dry for a few days.

The day was long and tiresome. Deck did most of the cutting while Anna did the trimming, sorting, and inserting of a wire hook through the lower end of each leg to hang them to cool overnight, before curing them with her special mixture of brown sugar, salt, and pepper. The boys were kept busy finding containers to hold the small pieces. The side meat was also wired and hung to cool, and the liver was placed in a large crock with a flat stone as a lid. Fresh liver was on the menu for the evening meal.

Anna checked the spices and decided that she would need more sage, as well as a few other things, and someone needed to go to the Post Office. Calling to Georgianna, who responded quickly, she said, "I need you to go to the store first thing in the morning, so wash good before you go to bed, and you can go as soon as breakfast is over." No one had to be told to go to bed after the long hard day!

Georgianna awoke to the noise of the rattle on the stove lid. She knew Mommy was up, and she needed to get up and help her. She was excited about going to the store on Old Maude; she liked being by herself once in a while and doing a little dreaming.

Breakfast was over and Billy bridled Maude and put a burlap sack over her back. No need for a saddle—they often rode bareback. Items gotten at the store would be divided and placed in the sack for the ride back home. And with the list in her overalls pocket, Georgianna was off. Her overalls felt good this cold morning and so did Fubby's outgrown coat that she was wearing, even if it didn't match the toboggan on her head. It had been Fubby's too.

The brisk air did not make Maude increase her pace, and she just wanted to plod along, probably because she was getting old. Georgianna decided she would fix that and she pulled up beside a tree to break a switch. This usually was enough to make the old mare increase her pace and almost leave one hanging on the tree. Georgianna used the switch whenever the pace slowed. She did not want to be accused of dawdling; she had been instructed to come back as quickly as possible.

At the store, George told her that he had been sick with asthma. He looked at her list and mumbled, "Musta butchered hogs."

"Yep, yesterday; gotta make sausage and all that stuff." He filled the order, placed items in the burlap sack, divided them up, and threw the sack over Ole Maude with the items balanced so it would not fall off. He stuck some candy in her overall pocket, picked her up, sat her on the horse, and told her to be careful.

The yard was a beehive of activity as the horse and rider pulled up along the porch to join the sausage grinders, taking turns. Georgianna slid off the horse onto the porch. Bidgy came to get the sack of items, take the bridle off, and shoo Maude off to pasture.

The aroma of fresh meat filled the air. Liver was simmering on the stove, spareribs were cooking, and potatoes would be added for dinner.

Georgianna took her turn at the sausage grinders, all the while trying not to think about Ole Rooter being ground up for her to eat.

Anna mixed her curing ingredients together, and in a large wooden box in the spring- house, she packed the hams, shoulders, and sidemeat for bacon, covering each piece as she placed it in the box before having Billy hang the box to the rafters, leaving the meat to cure. She was trying to get the heaviest work over, so Billy and the twins could go on back and work at the lumber camp. She and the younger ones could take care of the rest.

Pan after pan of sausage meat was mixed with the fragrant spices as soon as possible to preserve it until it could be cooked and canned. Tenderloins and spare ribs would be cooked and canned. Anna reminded the children, "No wash will get done this week, except Russ's diapers, so try to keep clean."

The week was perfect for working with fresh meat, cold, but not too cold for working on the porch where the grinding was done. The hog heads had been boiled in a big pot and the proper parts of it were ground, and mixed with other ingredients for souse. The livers were ground and made into liver pudding. This was molded and then cut into blocks for slicing and browning. The skins were cut into strips and baked in the oven until crisp and were then crumbled and used in cornbread, making delicious crackling bread.

By Saturday Anna felt satisfied as she stood back and surveyed the jars of sausage, spare ribs, and tenderloin that lined the shelves and the four hams and shoulders hanging high to be out of the way of any animal seeking to satisfy its hunger. She knew meat would be on the table of the Marlow household for many months.

CHAPTER 13

Games They Played

Something that was never heard in this large family was, "I don't have anything to do." There was never a lack of some kind of work to do, and when work was completed at the end of the day, there was a little playtime outside, especially when the days were longer. The hog bladder was then used as a kick ball, a dodge ball, and sometimes just for tossing and catching and for their favorite game "Annie Over," with groups on opposite sides of the building. When the words, "Annie Over" were heard, the ball was thrown over the building, and the person catching it threw it back while yelling "Annie Over." Sometimes one side waited, trying not to be caught off guard.

The older boys built wagons and raced them down the hill, while the others cheered. They occasionally lost a wheel and wrecked.

Hide-and-seek was a great favorite. There were many places to hide: buildings, trees, bushes. Small ones could even hide under a washtub.

Blind Man's Buff was where "it" was blindfolded and attempted to catch the others. Meanwhile everyone continued to try to throw "it" off the track, by calling his name quickly to another spot, or maybe giving "it" a pat on the back and moving quickly away. Whenever "it' caught someone, he had to guess who it was. Meanwhile, caps or jackets were exchanged for a disguise. The one caught and identified became "it."

by Claire Logan English

Baseball was played often. When no ball was available, one was made by stuffing rags into the top of an old sock putting a small stone in the middle to give it some weight.

A race was in progress just anytime, trying to match the racers according to size as close as possible. Another little bit of entertainment was played only during the month when the new moon was visible. You recited this rhyme, "New Moon, bright and fair, please give me the color of my true love's hair." You then stooped and picked up a handful of whatever, while looking at the moon, then searched to see if you found a hair in what you picked up. One occasion for hilarious laughter was near where the butchering had been done. Fubby picked up a handful of Ole Rooter's red hair. Members of the family could laugh about this sixty-five years later.

Tag was another favorite, as was crack the whip, statue, and a number of guessing games. Even the work was turned into games. Who could make the biggest rock pile gathering rocks from the garden? Who could shell the most ears of corn? On one occasion, Fubby said to Georgianna, "You can't shell enough corn for one chicken," to which she replied, "I do, but I don't," meaning I can but I won't.

A game at bedtime was placing your shoes with toes pointing together reciting, "I set my shoes in shape of V. Tonight my true love I shall see." You were supposed to dream of the person that you expected to marry. You could name the corners of the room and on awakening in the corner you were facing was your true love's face.

CHAPTER 14

The Move to West Virginia

Mid-winter, Anna began to have that queasy feeling every morning, and she knew exactly what that meant. She was not going to let it interfere with her move to West Virginia. She had spotted a neat little house with a yard when she had taken produce over the mountains in the fall. She really felt like she needed a change. George had not been giving her much help.

She had inquired inside after seeing a sign in the yard that it would be for rent in the late springtime. The rent was low. There was a good garden spot and a field for Maude and the cows. Anna decided that she was going to move her family near the end of school, hoping that she could manage on her meager income from what she could grow and sell. The boys could find odd jobs to help buy their clothes.

Two trips with the wagon full of their belongings rumbled over Peters Mountain, the last load with the cows being led by Bidgy.

Many hands helped unload and carry items into the one story house, in time to get the beds set up before bedtime. A cold supper staved off the hunger. The stove would be put up the first thing next morning. The family were excited about this house. It was nicer than their other house, painted white with a nice fence around the yard. You could actually see some other houses not too far away.

Everyone was ready for bed early and soon fast asleep. Anna had settled down with Lancy on one side of her and Russ on the other, and had just drifted off to sleep when she heard noises from the boys' room. Getting out of bed and stumbling over a toy Russ had left on the floor, she picked up the lamp, turned the wick up, and went to investigate. They complained of something biting. Looking closely she saw several bedbugs. Noticing that Noona and Georgianna were restless, she checked on them and found the same condition. The house was literally infested with them. No one had a very good night's rest.

Anna had few material possessions but she kept things clean and could not tolerate bugs. On top of getting settled after the move, now she had this problem. Kerosene applied to every crack and crevice should get rid of them, and if that did not, maybe the store in the village had something that would solve the problem. She was not going to move out so quick.

As soon as the cook stove was installed, the bug problem was attacked. They were everywhere, around the baseboards, around the door and window frames. It took several treatments with kerosene to complete the job, and you needed to be aware not to strike a match for fear of burning the house down.

The next big job was getting the garden out to be able to feed all the hungry mouths. The garden had been plowed in the fall. Anna was thankful for this. She was over the morning sickness, but not feeling quite up to so much hard work. Harnessing Maude with Bidgy's help, she hooked up the harrow to loosen up the ground and by the end of the week, all the seeds were in the ground. It was too late for potatoes or early peas, but they could probably trade butter or eggs to a neighbor for potatoes.

Everyone had been much too busy and too tired when evening came to even think about whether they liked living here. Georgianna missed the brook that ran by their other house, and she also missed the beautiful forest of trees and the fragrance of the many blooming trees. The family were together, though, and that was the most important thing.

The new home was not far from a small white church. It was here that Georgianna experienced her first vacation bible school. She loved the bible stories and the singing, and learning bible verses. After this came the handiwork, and this was where her first piece of embroidery was done.

Billy came home and brought a doll for Georgianna and abruptly said, "Maw, I have joined the Army, and I leave for camp next week. What do you think of that?"

Somewhat surprised, she replied, "It'll be good for you, teach you things you'd never learn in these parts." The new doll was beautiful, and the family liked having Billy home for a few days. Georgianna liked the extra attention that he always gave her, holding her over his head, pulling her braided hair, or just holding her tightly. She never thought it would be over twenty years before she would see him again! Bidding all goodbye, he walked out the door. Everyone watched until he was out of sight.

Things did not work out like Anna expected. She was having a hard time, and she was homesick for the old home in the mountains. She decided that as soon as the garden was harvested, they would move back. While she was pondering this move, she heard that George had died. Now she realized she was doing the right thing. The land was more fertile, the woodland provided wood for heat and their greens in the springtime. She would no longer get help from George's store. No family member knew of this expected child in October. Some of the older ones may have suspected it, though, since Russ was past two years old.

By the time most of the garden was ready to pick, things were being packed up for the move.

One evening as Georgianna was putting her things in a box, Lancy pleaded to hold her new doll. Georgianna knew he was destructive and held tightly to her doll. He began to cry. Anna did not want the children to be selfish, and after Lancy promised to just hold it, she coaxed Georgianna into relinquishing her doll. Very reluctantly she handed him the doll. He looked at it for a few minutes and then threw it against the wall, smashing its beautiful head. Needless to say he was spanked soundly, and the two sat down and cried together. This was just one more child heartbreak, still remembered many years later.

The next few days were a beehive of activity. The vegetables were picked and what was not going to be eaten or dried was canned and packed in boxes. The canned foods had not been unpacked since they moved. Every one was excited about the move back home. They had missed all the familiar things that had created such fond memories.

Mostly they had missed the clear sparkling stream, with the water wheel, their home made boats, and just splashing in the water. Two more days and they would be on their way. They were ready and would leave today, if they had their way.

A neighbor loaned them a horse and wagon that would not be available until the evening, and many things were loaded onto their wagon, just leaving the beds, the straw ticks and some of the food so they could have something to eat before loading the second wagon.

They were a gleeful bunch as they started back to their mountain home with a cow tied to the end of each wagon.

Arriving at their old home to find it looking very desolate, each one tried to be first to get off the chicken crate where they had been riding. The usual race was on to see which would be first onto the porch that hadn't been swept since they left and was covered with lots of debris.

Bidgy untied the cows and put them in the cow lot. Anna handed Georgianna a broom. "Take care of the porch and steps." Noona swept the kitchen, so the cook stove could be put up first thing and they could have hot water for cleaning the place. It would take several days to scour the floors, wash the windows, and get everything in place.

It was indeed a busy household with everyone doing their share. All were happy to be back home and did not mind the hard work. Georgianna unpacked the lamps and chimneys that had been packed in a good supply of crumpled Sears & Roebuck catalogue pages. Anna filled the lamps with oil, while the older boys set up the beds. By bedtime a lot had been done, and all were ready to go to bed, listening to the whippoorwill serenade.

CHAPTER 15

The Secret Is Out

U sually Anna did her sewing in the fall and winter, when the weather was cool, but now the sewing began while the weather was still warm. Georgianna loved to watch. Taking note that everything that was being sewed was white, she piped up, "What you making, Mommy?"

"Just some pillow slips." It did not look like pillowslips to her. She had never seen pillow slips with sleeves. She continued to watch without saying anything.

Anna spent several days at the sewing machine, then she closed it up, and spread a scarf over it. Apparently she was finished with sewing for now.

Several pounds of butter and lots of eggs had accumulated. Anna knew she probably had less than a month before the birth of her twelfth child. She would make one more trip to West Virginia and sell her farm products to get her a little money for necessities.

Bidgy was wandering around somewhere. She would take Fubby with her. She would sell some of her canned goods, as well as some buttermilk. Fubby could save her a few steps. She was tiring more easily. The horse and wagon were readied and loaded up and off they went.

Noona and Georgianna, with the two little boys, had the house to themselves for the biggest part of the day. Noona was somewhat of a snooper, and this time she involved her younger sister. Noona was old enough to know that there was going to be another baby. She got busy looking to see where baby clothes were stored. Leaving the boys downstairs in care of Georgianna, she searched high and low, and noticed Mommy's large trunk. She knew this was off limits, but she opened it anyway. There they lay, all neatly folded in the top section of the trunk. She would show them to Georgianna when the boys were taking a nap.

The two boys ate their lunch, and Lancy climbed onto the bed, while Russ was rocked until he fell asleep. With both boys asleep, the house was very quiet. Noona stuck her head in the door. "Wanna see what I found?"

"Yup, don't wake the boys." The two went quietly up the stairs, and as Noona began to open the trunk, Georgianna said, "You better not do it, Mommy will get you."

"She will not know it if you don't tell her. Promise not to tell." Noona knew Mommy was trying to keep a secret. "All right, I will not tell anybody." The heavy lid was lifted, and Noona held the tiny garments up for Georgianna to admire. There were long white gowns, some with touches of embroidery, a long white dress for Sunday best, bands for around the baby's middle to prevent rupture, feed sack diapers, bleached white with lye soap, and three new undershirts from Sears & Roebuck. So that's what came in that package from the post office.

"What are they for?" asked Georgianna.

"A baby of course, Silly. Mommy is gonna have a baby." Now the secret was out. Mrs. Emore would be coming again carrying that black bag. Georgianna didn't know how she was going to keep quiet about this secret, but she had promised to keep quiet, so she must. She enjoyed caring for babies. She was very excited and hoped that it would be a girl. She was tired of all these boys. They were so rough and always picking on her. A little sister would be good to have around.

Anna and Fubby arrived back home shortly before dark. She ordered Fubby to get the milk pail and take care of the milking, while she unharnessed the mare and with a slap on the rump, shoved her out to pasture.

Anna was feeling sad now that George had died and she would not see him again. He would not be there to give her any help with the children. He would not even see this child of his, which would certainly be her last one. She wondered how she would handle one more all by herself, but handle it she would.

It had not been easy to deal with George's death. She had not been able to go to the store which was now operated by someone else. One of the children was sent, more things were ordered from Sears & Roebuck, and they did without what she couldn't afford. None of them would go hungry or cold and they would be adequately clothed with hand me downs made over and an occasional donation.

October arrived with the beauty of Indian Summer after several cold days with heavy frost. Much of the foliage was showing off beautiful colors. Anna felt a little sluggish and noted the lowering of the baby within her. She knew the day was near when Mrs. Emore would be summoned. She was hoping for another girl because boys were rough and harder to handle.

There were bags of dried beans to be shelled and corn to be shelled to feed the cows, Maude, the two hogs, and the chickens. Early October found all hands busy while they could work outside. The bean hulls were crushed and placed in a round container with a coarse screen bottom which rubbed the beans, loosening the hulls with a lot of shaking of the container. With a lot of lungpower, they blew the chaff away before pouring the beans into a burlap sack.

Lots of activity was prevalent during these bright sunny days, and surprisingly, a lot was accomplished with all hands busy. Even Russ could do many things.

On the morning of October fifth, nineteen hundred and twenty-five, Anna awoke with a backache, and the grain storing came to a halt. Before dinnertime Anna began to have pains. She was glad she had put the pot of pinto beans on to cook early that morning. As the pains progressed, she knew she had better send for Mrs. Emore. Preferring to send two children, she looked them over to see who was the most presentable. She decided on Bidgy and Fubby after checking Georgianna's neck and the back of her knees, troublesome spots, and finding she had not washed good. Bidgy and Fubby were sent with the orders not to dawdle and to tell Mrs.Emore that she was needed. No mention was made of what she was needed for. Most everyone knew already.

Anna gathered all the necessities together while leaving the finishing of dinner to Noona who was the oldest at home, and Georgianna, who could just about keep up with her. There was no concern that anyone would go hungry.

There was a sigh of relief as the boys and Mrs. Emore came in the door, none too soon. The pains were getting harder and closer. Anna had been staying close to the bed.

Mrs. Emore greeted her with,"Well, I reckon this'll be my last trip for this sorta thing, seein' that man is dead."

"Yes, it will, I have all I can take care of," Anna said.

Mrs. Emore went to the kitchen to get the water and whatever she needed, while the children washed their hands for dinner. Georgianna helped Russ, so he didn't upset the wash pan.

Everything was ready and there nothing else to do but wait until the time was right. Anna had been through this enough that she needed no coaching. The door had been closed between the bedroom and kitchen. As soon as Russ finished eating, he banged on the door. "I want Mommy, I want Mommy."

This was a familiar happening for the youngest of the family, and as before, he was allowed in the room. Not really knowing what was going on, he settled himself in the rocking chair and was content.

The two women got down to the business of birthing this baby, and with a few hard pains it was soon over with. Anna gave a sigh of relief. Mrs. Emore remarked, "Well you got what you wanted." The baby let out a lusty cry when mucus had been cleared from her throat. Then the cord was expertly tied and cut. Gently Mrs. Emore bathed and dressed the baby, wrapped it in the soft outing blanket Anna had made, then placed the baby by its mother to be admired, while she took care of other things. "What you gonna name that pretty little thing?"

"Not exactly sure," said Anna, as she looked the baby over to be sure it was all there. Finding her to be perfectly formed as all her children had been, she said, "I have decided on Dela, looks like it will suit her." So Dela it was.

The brood in the kitchen knew they would be allowed to see the new baby after hearing its first cry, and there was a mad scramble to see who would be the first one in the room. After everything was cleaned up, Mrs. Emore opened the door. Georgianna and Lancy were against the door and literally fell into the room. The others stepped over them and raced ahead. The older ones pretended unhappiness at another baby to take care of. They were only faking. Georgianna plainly

displayed her delight and wanted to hold her. "She is asleep, but I'll
let you carry her and put her on the far side at the foot of the bed."
This seven-year-old was excited to hold the baby for this little bit and
knew she would love helping take care of her.

CHAPTER 16

Caring for Dela and Other Things

Helping care for Dela was a genuine pleasure for Georgianna, never a troublesome chore. She soon learned to change the baby's diaper. By springtime Dela was sitting up and she was carried around on Georgianna's hip when she wasn't asleep.

Churning was a twice-weekly chore and was shared by members of the family. When Georgianna's time came, she made sure to scoot the churn near the cradle, and as she churned, she used one foot to keep the cradle rocking. In no way did all this attention spoil Dela, who was a good baby from the very beginning.

Anna did not have a lot of time to give her babies very much personal attention other than keeping them clean and fed. At times, cradle cap would form on Dela's head. Then vaseline was applied and Georgianna would take it from there. Gently using a fine toothcomb, she worked until the scalp was clear and ready to be washed.

When garden vegetables were ready to pick and all hands were busy, Georgianna spent her time at the house taking care of the baby. Once a week, Anna and Noona took the produce, eggs, and butter over the mountain to West Virginia to sell or barter for items that were needed, usually leaving very early and not getting back very long before dark. A special jar of milk was left in a special spot in the springhouse for Dela. Fubby and Georgianna were left in charge of the three little ones, seeing that they were kept fed and free from harm.

No one was afraid of the many wild animals that could be heard and sometimes seen in the distance, such as black bear and wild cats. They were very afraid of tramps that sometimes passed by the house back and forth from West Virginia. On one occasion, when he spotted

69

by Cathie Logan Sharpe

an unfamiliar figure in the distance, Fubby helped the others to climb up on the roof from a ladder at the back of the house. He then pulled the ladder up after them until the man passed by the house and they felt it was safe to come down. They never had any serious emergencies while in charge of the little ones.

As independent as Georgianna was, Anna still had to comb her hair which was long and fine and was worn in three braids brought together in the back with a ribbon tied in a bow. It was not combed every day. Vaseline was applied to it occasionally to help eliminate the tangles and make the combing easier. The boys dubbed Georgianna, "Ole salve head."

One morning when the combing was extra bothersome, and there were ouches and whining, Anna decided she would put an end to the problems, and got her scissors from the machine drawer. As the golden locks fell to the floor, so did the tears as Georgianna wept over the loss of her hair. As she looked in the mirror she wept some more. She was ordered to "Dry up, and from now on you can comb your own hair, and I will not have to listen to your whining."

Georgianna carried Dela around on one hip and looked forward to the time that the baby would walk and could learn to play the games she was eager to teach her. She was getting heavy.

CHAPTER 17

Chestnut Harvest and Preparing for Winter

The bright sunny days of summer soon changed to the crisp days of autumn. Frost usually came early in the mountains. Anna would have to order the children's shoes from Sears & Roebuck. She would not overlook any opportunity to add to her cash. She would need every cent she could get together. The move to West Virginia a year and a half before had set her back, and not a thing was accomplished by the move.

This had been a good year for nuts, and the chestnut trees were bearing especially heavy. Bidgy was home. He could shimmy up a tree like a bolt of lightning and could be a big help, if he was in a cooperative mood. Fubby was good at this job also.

During supper Anna informed the two boys, saying, "It looks like tomorrow will be an ideal day for gathering chestnuts." Everyone wanted to go, but it was not a good job for little folks. "You two boys need to be up early and hunt up some gloves. You know how prickly those chestnut burrs are." The boys were excited to be going somewhere, even if it was hard work. The boys were up as soon as they heard Anna building the fire in the cookstove. When the milking was done and breakfast was over, Fubby was sent to the garden for the burlap sacks to carry the chestnuts in while Bidgy found some gloves. He found six of different colors, but three were left hands and three for right hands. Meanwhile Anna fixed some biscuits with leftover sausage and a jug of water to carry, knowing they would be hungry and thirsty before the day was over.

Noona was given the instructions for the day, and off the three went, Bidgy's heavy shoes making a clumping sound as they trudged along. Chestnut picking was certainly no place for bare feet; the burrs were very prickly.

What a great day they had filling two sacks full and making plans to go back the following day. Winter evenings were spent roasting chestnuts and eating them while the nuts were still warm. No one even thought about the food value or that nuts were a good source of protein. They only knew how good they were.

The next day was nice and the three were off early with their gloves and sacks, expecting another successful day, only to be disappointed by an accident. About the middle of the day, Bruno began to bark and the children at the house just knew someone was coming. It was not time for Mommy. They surely hoped it was not a tramp that would hurt them.

Noona peered up the road and could recognize her mother. She was carrying something on her back, and it didn't look like a sack of chestnuts. Fubby was dragging a sack and trying to keep up. Of course everyone ran to meet them to learn why they were coming in early. Fubby piped up before anyone could ask. "Bidgy fell out of the tree into the rock pile."

Everyone was upset, afraid he was dead. He was not moving and had blood on his face and one side of his head. Noona was sent to the nearest telephone to call Doctor Brown to come as quickly as possible. She hurried to the Medleys and asked Rosa to phone the doctor. She had run most of the way and was out of breath. She plopped into the nearest chair. Rosa asked, "What do you need a doctor for?"

"Bidgy fell out of the chestnut tree, and he won't wake up."

Rosa made the call and explained the accident to the doctor. Rosa said, "He said to tell your mother he would be there."

"I've gotta get back. Mommy had to carry him home."

Anna had gently placed this big gangly twelve-year-old on her bed. With a wash pan of water and a clean cloth, she wiped his face and hands and cleaned his wounds as best she could, hoping he would wake up and not be seriously hurt.

Noona arrived home out of breath, having run most of the way home. "He's coming, he's coming as quick as he can."

The doctor arrived on his beautiful sleek bay horse that was frothing at the mouth from the several miles gallop. Throwing the reins over the limb of the nearest tree, he hurried up the steps and walked in. "Howdy, Ms. Marlow, what we got here?"

"Howdy, Doc, I hope he ain't hurt bad. He had a long fall into a rock pile." The doctor began checking to see if there were any broken bones and found none. As he examined the head injury, Bidgy began to awaken.

Dr. Brown decided that he must have a bad concussion, but no fracture. "You are going to have to be quiet for the next few days, and let this head wound heal. This medicine should help heal it up, and you will be as good as new."

Anna gave the doctor a bag of chestnuts for pay. He stuffed it in his saddle, mounted his horse, and was gone. This was the doctor's one and only trip to the Marlow home.

Bidgy tried to stand up but was still groggy and lay back down. All the children wanted to wait on him, they were so glad he did not die. The next day he spent sitting around the house, while giving orders to the younger ones.

The mornings were cool and frosty. Fubby and Georgianna had the job of going for the cows who spent every night in a different spot. Sometimes there was lots of looking before the cows were found. By then, the children's poor feet were plenty frosty, but they knew how to warm them up in a hurry. The cows were driven from the warm spot in the grass and the two danced around in their own warm spot, making a game of who could dance the fastest. Fubby always won, chanting, "I'm the fastest, I'm the fastest."

"Well you are older and have longer legs." She dearly loved him, even if he did tease her sometimes.

All of the older boys would often tease her just to see her pout. Whenever she was injured or punished and began to cry, the boys would chant, "Poor little thing," and this only brought more tears. Fubby would pet her. Then she was all smiles again. Fubby would make doll furniture for her and help cut out the figures from Sears & Roebuck catalogues. He also played paper dolls with her.

Bidgy recovered from his fall and was very anxious. He was getting
very hard for Anna to handle, and with no man to help, she was afraid
he would end up in some kind of trouble. He had a fiery streak that she
had not noticed in her other boys. This gave her a lot of concern.

Anna stayed busy trying to get everything taken care of before
the hard winter began. There was a large crop of late green beans,
part of these were broken and threaded on a long thread and hung
around the porch to dry. Later, they were soaked over night and
cooked with side meat. Some folks called them 'leather britches'
because they were quite tough.

These Indian summer days were perfect for the drying of beans,
apples, and sweet potatoes, that were all threaded onto a string and
hung to dry. Sometimes the cows would hang around the yard instead
of going to pasture. Georgianna was assigned the job of keeping the
cows away from the drying beans. She really tried to keep a sharp eye
on the cows, but Dela's crying claimed her attention, and she just
had to see what the matter was.

After being gone only a few seconds, she returned to find ole Bessie
chomping on her second string of beans. Georgianna's tears began to
fall, even before she got the switching that she knew was in store for
her. Mostly she felt that she had betrayed the trust that had been placed
in her, and she vowed not to leave the porch until the cows had gone
away.

The day was a good one for traveling, and when Bruno began his
company bark, they knew someone was approaching the house. When
Mommy was home, there was no fear of tramps. Everyone was eager
to see who was coming and watched from the porch until their friend
the horse trader, Will Perkins, pulled his horse and wagon to a stop.
He always stopped on his travels to and from West Virginia, having a
meal, a snack, or maybe just a cold dipper of water. He was a short
stubby fellow with a mustache and a round belly and was a sloppy
eater, spilling his food down his front. He always wore a tie that was
covered with remains of his last meal. The children liked him. He
usually had some candy sticks or licorice whips in his pocket for
Anna's youngest. Georgianna forgot about her recent whipping.

The cows were gone for the day, and the eight-year-old girl could
devote her time to her little sister. She liked combing her blond curly

hair that formed many ringlets when rain was imminent. One could usually tell that rain was on the way when the curls clung close to the baby's head. Anna depended on Georgianna for a lot of things, and she did not need to constantly remind her of her responsibilities.

Before time for the cows to come in, all the dried foods were safely taken down for the night, to be hung out again the following day, weather permitting.

Noona made the remark, "Miss Jenny has not been by for awhile; it's about time for her." By mid-afternoon, who should appear but Miss Jenny with her sack on her back, as usual, when she traveled the stagecoach road back and forth to West Virginia. "Howdy, Miss Jenny, come in and have a chair. We have just been saying it was about time for you. Can you spend the night?"

"No, I best be gettin on soon. Days are gettin shorter and much colder when the sun sets." Anna busied herself to fix an early supper with some of last year's ham. The daily potatoes were fried with onions, and a pot of green beans was all ready to eat with some of Anna's good hot biscuits. Supper would be over in time for Miss Jenny to get home before total darkness.

The younguns climbed onto the bench behind the table, filling it full to make room for Miss Jenny, who looked as if she was about starved.Miss Jenny filled her plate and began eating. "I declare, Anna, you are just about the best cook in Giles County. I reckon you learned some of this when you were cooking at Mountain Lake Hotel."

"Well, maybe, I learned a lot from Maw while I was growing up."

Miss Jenny spied the dish of Anna's famous apple preserves. She pulled the dish over to her, picked up the cream pitcher, and poured cream over the preserves. "Miss Jenny, them's apple preserves."

Miss Jenny remarked, "And they shore are good." Some of the kids snickered at this, while Miss Jenny finished off the dish of preserves. After Miss Jenny left, the whole family laughed about it.

All too soon winter arrived with the first deep snow and howling winds that whistled through the big hemlock tree out back. The butchering was over with, hams hung high in the springhouse. Wood was stacked high with a good supply on the porch covered with a burlap sack.

No one ever became bored. There was always someone to play with. Evenings were spent playing "set back," a card game everyone knew how to play, and taking turns with the Scope and Views. Looking through the Sears & Roebuck was entertaining, dreaming of all the things you would like to own.

There were walnuts to crack and eat and chestnuts to roast. Chinquapins were bountiful, and when fresh snow was on the ground, many a large bowl of snow cream was enjoyed. This was made with snow mixed with cream, sugar, and vanilla or lemon extract. Everyone hovered around the heater to keep warm while enjoying this winter treat, that was so cold it would give one a bad headache if eaten too fast.

Old catalogues were made into chains, airplanes, lanterns, and other things, using paste made from flour and water. Someone was always coming up with a new idea for entertainment. They discovered that by throwing their wash water in the same spot, they eventually had a great place to skate.

Anna fussed about them wearing their shoes out. Nevertheless, they took every chance they could for a few slides. Anna remembered the time she fell on the ice that left the scar on her chin.

Anna kept busy scrubbing clothes on the wash board, having to hang them on a line in the kitchen and on backs of chairs near the stove. On sunny days when they could be hung outside, the clothes froze before you could get them pinned on the line. She also used this time for mending and making shirts for the boys and dresses and bloomers for the girls. She was making over a black and white striped coat that had been hers, into one for Georgianna. The pretty half round red buttons would spark this coat up. "Georgianna," she called, "go upstairs and get those red buttons from the button box." The button box had held candy from Tom before they were married, and she wished they could have stayed together and things would have been different. Georgianna brought the buttons, and after selecting the number she needed for the coat, Anna gave her the others to take back upstairs, warning her not to put one in her mouth. Georgianna, she remembered the time before Billy joined the Army, when she disobeyed and put one in her mouth. As she started up the stairs, it slipped, and she was choking but was not about to go back downstairs and face Mommy. Just as she thought she was going to die, Billy came down the stairs. "What's the matter?" he asked, and she managed to say, "I'm choked," while the tears rolled down her face. He had picked her up, carried her downstairs, turned her upside down, and slapped her soundly on the back. Out rolled the pretty red button. Mommy did not punish her, hoping she had learned a good lesson.

Anna spent many days at the sewing machine making outfits for the children. She had sold a calf and ordered material. She never used a pattern but did a remarkable job without one. Georgianna loved to watch and was eager for the time to come when she could make her own clothes. The boys were only interested in running the treadle and watching the wheels turn when the machine was not in use. They got scolded in return. Anna didn't need a broken sewing machine.

The winter had been a rough one. The children were getting restless from staying in so much and were longing for the days when they could shed those long black stockings and high top shoes. They wanted to feel the soft green grass on their feet, play in the dirt, and gather the lady slippers, Johnny jump ups, and other spring flowers that grew abundantly. They wanted to make sassafras tea and smell its fragrant aroma. Spicewood tea was good, too.

Early spring found hens singing around the yard, and you knew they were storing their eggs in a secret nest and getting ready to set. Georgianna loved peeping into the nest, if you could find one, to see if the eggs had pipped. This was where the baby chick pecked its first little opening in the shell, starting the hatching process.

Spring was an interesting time as well as busy. The first few nice days were used to clean the yard, it being too early to put garden out. Noona, Fubby, and Georgianna were given the job of cleaning rocks out of the yard while Anna was away. Georgianna decided she wanted a break and climbed up on the picket fence, where she would crow, flap her arms, and jump down.

Noona and Fubby continued to work. Noona wasn't too careful where the rocks went, and one got Georgianna just over the right eye. She began to cry as blood flowed down over her eye, and she had to be helped down from the fence to get patched up. Noona tried combing the bangs as far down as possible, hoping to hide the wound so Mommy would not know how careless she had been. She remembered the time she was splitting rails and cut Fubby's finger so that it hung by a small piece of skin. His hand was tied to a board for several days. Georgianna teased him a little now, telling him if the cows did not move fast enough, he could swat them with the board.

CHAPTER 18

The Unforgotten Punishment

The summer had been hot and dry and the pasture was short. Anna knew that she would have to get pasture for Maude. She only had enough shelter for the two cows and shelter was a must for the cold snowy winters.

Georgianna responded to her Mommy's call, knowing that Mommy had a job for her. "I need you to go to the Switzers' and see if they can keep the horse for the winter."

"Can I ride ole Maude?"

"Yes, but you will have to come right back it gets dark early and I do not want you on the road after dark."

Georgianna washed her face, donned a clean pair of overalls and a sweater, and called Maude to the porch so she could slip the bridle over her head, feeling proud that she was able to do this. There was no need for a saddle. She often rode bareback. She fully intended to do as Mommy said and come straight back.

When she arrived at the Switzers, she found the children into a game of "Dodge Ball." It didn't take much encouragement for her to join them, after she looped the horse's reins over the nearest limb she could reach. They played game after game, the time flew by, and Georgianna noticed the sun had disappeared behind the treetops. It dawned on her what she was there for. "I gotta go, I gotta go," she said as she hurried into the house to ask Mrs. Switzer about pasture and housing for the horse.

"I reckon we can handle it. We have one extra shed. You better be getting on home. It's nearly dark." Swiftly Georgianna headed for the door.

"'Bye, Mrs. Switzer. Thank you."

Leading ole Maude to the nearest stump, she climbed on and headed for home. She was not really anxious to get home, she knew she had been disobedient and what she was in for. You did not disobey Mommy and get away with it, no matter what your excuse. Mostly she felt remorseful for having disobeyed.

By the time she reached the barn, it was very dark. Sliding off the horse and pulling her head down to slip the bridle off, she turned to face her mother with the switch in her hand. She was switched every step of the way to the house, while the tears streamed down her cheeks. Fubby being the big brother, tried to comfort her. Her tears were not as much from the sting of the switch as the thought of disappointing her Mommy. Anna depended on her, and she always tried to be helpful, knowing that her mother had to work hard to take care of them.

She knew she had good fellowship with Mommy and remembered the times she would fix a wash pan of warm water to bathe her Mommy's feet after a long day in the field and she sat on the porch to rest with a child or two on her lap. She knew Mommy would not stay angry with her for very long, and before the evening was over, she was climbing on her lap. She was eight years old. She still sought the comfort of her mother's lap and would often say, "Take me Mommy, I'm your baby." The boys would mimic her.

By one year of age, Dela had a mouth full of pearly white teeth, and she liked to use them on anything or anybody that was convenient. When Lancy tried to take a toy from her hand, she held on tight and bit him on the arm. That drew blood. Discipline started early with Anna's children, and she was switched in spite of the older children's protests. They were so mad, they decided they would run away, only getting as far as the barn and climbing into the hayloft, where they expected to spend the night. They had not been gone long until Georgianna heard her mother calling her name. Over Noona's protest, she went back to the house and told where the others were. Anna knew they would be back as soon as they began to get cold. Anna thought maybe she had been too harsh, and since all the children were so protective of Dela, her being a baby, she would think twice before punishing her again soon.

CHAPTER 19

Fubby's First Long Pants and Another Springtime

This early April Sunday morning dawned clear and bright. All the children had new clothes and were eager to wear them to Sunday school, having been home during the winter while the weather was so cold and snowy.

Fubby was especially excited. Mommy had ordered him a navy blue suit with long pants from Sears & Roebuck and she made him a new shirt. He was really going to strut today, and maybe that pretty girl would be there again. He had caught a glimpse of her before the bad weather kept them home. He would not have to wear those stupid brown knickers which he hated.

Noona marched down the stairs in the beautiful white Hamburg lace dress with the wide red ribbon sash tied in a big bow. Oh, how Georgianna was looking forward to the time when she would be big enough to wear this beautiful dress. Knowing that eventually it would be passed on to her, she wanted to grow fast.

Georgianna put on her new pink dress with lots of lace and combed her short straight hair that was getting darker as she grew older. She smoothed her long black stockings as best she could, using a safety pin to fasten her garter that had come loose. Looking in the mirror, she felt satisfied except for the black stockings. Maybe some day she would have white ones.

Bidgy and Fubby in their suits and ties, Lancy in short navy pants buttoned onto a white shirt with tiny navy dots, and the girls in their finery, Anna beamed over her fine looking family and was sorry she could not accompany them. Russ had a slight fever, and Dela has spent a restless night, so she thought it best that she keep them at home.

The children ran, they hopped, they skipped, and they jumped, as they happily made the four-mile trek to the little schoolhouse that was also the church. As soon as they arrived Fubby cast his eyes around the room to see if that pretty girl was there. He surely wanted her to notice him. She was nowhere in sight. He continued to look around as they began to sing one of Georgianna's favorite hymns, "Take the Name of Jesus With You." When they came to the chorus, she was belting out loud and clear "Opal Verth and Joy of Heaven," and enjoying every minute of it. It made no difference to her that the words were not exactly right!

It was good to be back after such a long time and to see other folks in the neighborhood. The service was over much too quickly. Rosa Medley asked them to stop by her house for milk and cookies before the long walk back home.

The Medleys appeared to be rich. They lived in a nice big white house and had lots of pretty furniture. Georgianna loved the pretty dishes in the cabinet with a glass front. They were the only family in the area that had bought a car. Their girls had pretty clothes, some with strips that hung loose down each side. Georgianna dreamed of the day that she could own a dress like that and go out with Levi, the youngest of six Medley boys. She claimed him as her boyfriend.

After the little treat, the children knew Anna would be expecting them home. As they came out of the house, the sky was gray with heavy clouds. No one had thought of umbrellas, early morning had been so clear and bright, but typical of April, sudden showers could appear seemingly from nowhere. A few drops fell, and then the sun came out, but not for long. As they hurried on home, clouds covered the sun, and a steady rain began. Fubby always tried to look after Georgianna and, being gentlemanly, he took off his navy blue coat and put it on her to protect her from the rain. The rain continued, and Georgianna looked down and saw blue streaks streaming down her pretty new pink dress. She lost no time in taking the coat off and handing it back to Fubby. He immediately put it on over his new white shirt.

They arrived home and were met by Mommy. "What in the world happened to your new dress?"

"Fubby's coat did it." Fubby removed his coat to display a blue and white streaked shirt. Anna immediately put them in a soapy solution of lye soap, hoping to get all the stains out. The stains came out beautifully and were Sunday clothes for a long time. This little incident was laughed about many years later. They would remember to carry an umbrella next Sunday and anytime there was a threat of rain, making sure this didn't happen again.

The spring planting was underway whenever weather permitted. A litter of piglets had arrived, and Ole Bessy was dry. Each day they looked for the new calf. Fuzzy baby chicks were in evidence, a new flock making its appearance every few days, following the clucking mother hen as she scratched for bits of corn, bread crumbs or any other treat. There were many interesting things going on and each new day brought excitement to the Marlow family. They were happy with what they had and were not aware that they had so little material possessions. They had each other and that was great satisfaction. They did do some dreaming over the "Sears & Roebuck" catalogue each time the new ones came out. The children did notice that the Medleys had so many pretty things and the girls had pretty clothes. Mrs. Medley was Anna's cousin, and they visited occasionally after church. The Marlow children shared a lot of love and were not bothered by having few of the world's earthly goods. Many folks they knew were in the same boat.

The beautiful days of May were producing lettuce, fresh onions, radishes, and green peas, which were a welcome treat after the winter of dried and canned foods. The longer days were indeed welcomed. Sometimes play was still in progress in the moonlight, with stars twinkling overhead. Many a shooting star was visible. Anna's children called the big dipper the big bear and the little dipper, the little bear, liking to use their imaginations, thereby making life more interesting.

As summer progressed, gardening, pickling, preserving, and canning were in full swing as in many summers before. Dela was on the move and kept Georgianna busy. She was learning new words every day with coaching from her big sister, who knew that she would be nine years old in September and that Dela would be two in October, not exactly sure which day.

CHAPTER 20

Anna's Death

Georgianna's eighth year was spent like many before, always busy at work and watching out for Dela when she was not occupied with other chores. She joined in the boisterous play times that were not real frequent but always a lot of fun.

The hot summer was near an end with some things from the late garden still to be harvested, when tragedy struck the Marlow family. Just after dinner on a bright sunny day, Anna asked Georgianna to help her and the boys round up the hogs for the boys to drive down along the creek, where vegetation grew in abundance. The hogs would graze and the hog feed could be saved for later when all vegetation had died. This was done quite often.

The boys had their switches to drive the hogs on to pasture as they trotted happily down the road. As Anna and the girls started back to the house, Anna clutched at her side and grimaced with pain. Georgianna did not know what to think as she helped her Mommy to the house. She had never known her to have a pain. At least she had never mentioned it.

After she was helped into bed with a quilt pulled up over her, Anna began to have chills and said, "Get some kindling and build a fire in the heater."

The child was puzzled. Why in the world did they need a fire on this bright sunny day that was not the least bit cold. However, she looked around and, not finding any, she said, "I can't find any kindling."

Anna was getting angry. "You'll find some when I get out of this bed and get a switch."

Georgianna knew she would have to make more effort to get a fire started. She gathered every little twig she could find and lots of crumpled pages from an old Sears & Roebuck catalogue, along with a couple chunks of pine, and she soon had a fire going. She knew just how to set the damper, so the fire would not get too hot. She surely did not want Mommy mad at her and was hoping that she would soon be feeling better. It was a little frightening to see Mommy in bed in the daytime. The only time she was in bed in the daytime was when she had a new baby.

Another quilt was placed over Anna before Georgianna looked for Noona, who had gone to the springhouse to put leftovers away. Noona was upset also, never knowing her mother to be sick.

Anna thought it might be the buttermilk that she had for dinner. This had never made her sick before. She stayed in bed with quilts piled high and a good fire in the heater. Still she could not get warm. Her teeth were chattering. She knew she must be very sick. Georgianna brought her a cup of hot coffee, and she felt a little better. Russ and Dela were kept as quiet as possible.

Fubby and Lancy were back from driving the hogs to the creek and were whooping and hollering like wild Indians. Noona told them to play outside as quietly as possible, that Mommy was sick. They stared in disbelief. She was all right when they left. They knew she would be all right tomorrow. They tried to keep quiet and to take care of all the chores that needed to be done. They had to do Anna's share, too, and keeping quiet was pretty hard for them to do. It was very strange for Mommy to be in bed while the children ate their supper, quietly tidied up the kitchen, lit the lamps, washed their feet, and tried not to make any noise.

Fubby and Lancy took Russ upstairs to bed with them, and Dela was put into Noona and Georgianna's bed. She and Russ usually slept with Mommy.

The lamp that was turned low and placed on a table near Anna cast a soft glow on her flushed face. A glass of spring water was nearby. They settled down expecting everything to be back to normal by morning.

Anna was awake most of the night. She had ceased to have chills, but the terrible pain in her sided persisted. By dawn she knew that she had a high fever and would need some help. As soon as Fubby was up, before he had a chance to milk the cow, he was sent for Mrs. Emore. She usually knew what to do when anyone got sick. Sticking a cap on his head, Fubby set out for the four-mile walk for Mrs. Emore. One thing he knew, there would not be a new baby this time, since George was dead. He had learned how babies were made and was puzzled why he needed to get Mrs. Emore. He did not think anything bad could happen to Mommy.

Mrs. Emore was feeding the chickens when Fubby approached her. "Hi, young man. You are out awful early this morning."

"Mommy sent me to get you."

"Who's sick?"

"Mommy is in bed."

"What's she complaining of?"

"A pain in her side since yesterday."

"Tell her I'll be there just as soon as I take care of a few things here." With hands in his pockets, he whistled as he walked away.

One by one the children were up, and Russ pleaded, "Get up, Mommy," not believing she couldn't get up and cook for them. Her food was better than what Noona cooked.

Shortly after Fubby arrived home, Mrs. Emore was at the door with her little black bag. She was shocked to find Anna so ill, and she knew by feeling her forehead that she had a very high fever. Asking for a towel, she slipped it in a pan of tepid water and wiped Anna's face and hands and then placed it across her forehead, trying to reduce her fever and make her more comfortable. Mrs. Emore mixed a glass of Pain King, a liniment with sugar and water. With great effort Anna raised her head long enough to drink the liniment and then lay back down.

She related how the pain had struck her the day before and that she thought it may have been the buttermilk. Now she knew it was not that. Mrs. Emore was baffled and at a loss as to what to do next, other than wait and see what developed. She knew that appendicitis caused a lot of pain, and if it ruptured, there would be a lot of fever. She had never nursed anyone with appendicitis and wondered if should she get a doctor. The family were too poor to pay one, and the nearest one was in Pearisburg, about twenty miles away. He probably would not come if you got in touch with him. The only time they had needed a doctor was when Bidgy had fallen from the chestnut tree, and the doctor's pay was a bag of chestnuts.

Noona, being the oldest at home, was instructed to keep the children outside or in the kitchen and as quiet as possible. They handled things pretty well, feeding the animals and taking care of the usual chores.

By late afternoon Mrs. Emore knew she would have to stay overnight. She called Fubby from the woodpile, where he was splitting kindling. "You and Georgianna go tell my son Deck to do my milking and feed the chickens tonight and in the morning." The two children delivered the message, then, for a while forgetting that their mother was so sick, they began to race back home.

Georgianna had been having some serious thoughts of her own, afraid Mommy may not get well, and she knew there had been times that she wished Mommy was not there and she could do as she pleased. But she surely did not want her to get sick and die. Mrs. Emore would not let her in the room to help take care of her Mommy. She had opened the door a little and peaked in to see if her Mommy was out of bed, only to see her lying very still. This created a very sad feeling for the eight-year-old girl.

While getting the children ready for bed, she heard moans from Anna's room, as Mrs. Emore's soft voice tried to comfort her. This kind lady did not get much rest during the night, and as soon as Fubby's morning chores were finished, she asked him to go see if Mrs. Switzer could come for the day and she could rest awhile. "See if she can phone Dr. Brown to come as soon as possible."

Fubby whistled as he hurriedly made the trip. Mrs. Switzer was surprised to see him this early in the day and inquired as to the purpose of his early morning call. "Mrs. Emore wants you to phone Dr. Brown and see if he can come. Mommy is sick in bed. And can you come for awhile so she can sleep. She has been up all night taking care of Mommy."

"What's the matter with your Mommy?"

"We don't know."

"Tell her I'll be there as soon as I finish churning, and that will not take long."

As Fubby left to go home, his thoughts turned to his mother's sickness. What if she didn't get well and had to stay in bed, and even worse, what if she died? What would happen to them? He hurried home to find Mrs. Emore nodding in the rocking chair near Anna's bed. She looked really sick, not at all like herself. Fubby touched Mrs. Emore's arm and startled her awake, relating the message. He left the room to look for Georgianna. They were a comfort to each other.

Mrs. Switzer arrived shortly in her crisp white apron and her usual sunbonnet, ready to give Mrs. Emore a much-needed break. She was shocked to find Anna so sick. They stepped out onto the porch so Anna would not overhear their conservation. "Did you get hold of Dr. Brown?"

"I tried, but couldn't get through."

"Well, I've given her a good dose of Black Draught. Her bowels haven't moved since she got sick, and she has vomited a lot of green fluid."

"We'll send Fubby a little later to try and get the doctor."

"It don't look good to me. She is out of her head part of the time."

Noona and Georgianna were managing the three younger ones well, keeping them fed, quiet, and out of the sick room, and getting whatever was needed for the sick room.

Fubby was sent to the nearest phone with a note to summon the doctor. When he arrived home, he reported the doctor was not in, but a message was left for him to come as soon as possible. Fubby busied himself getting in wood for the cook stove and taking care of the outside chores, while trying not to think about his mother's illness. Alas, no doctor arrived at the humble Marlow home. Anna was in and out of delirium most of the afternoon, as the two women took turns sitting by her bed, often talking in hushed tones.

Mrs. Emore tried to get as much rest as possible, knowing that Mrs. Switzer would have to go home to see to the needs of her family of boys, who had never learned to cook. She might have to keep a lone vigil again tonight.

Before the day ended, Anna had vomited often. At one point the vomit contained large roundworms. The two women had never seen anything like this. The Black Draught had no effect. The two women knew that she would probably die and leave all these children orphans. Mrs. Emore had nursed a lot of sick folks and some through grave illness. She had done all she could, and she was concerned about what would happen to these children. Most of these mountain folks had big families and couldn't take six more. Mrs. Switzer interrupted her thoughts by saying, "I need to go home and cook some vittles. I should have taught some of these boys how to cook. They'd starve for sure if I ever get sick. They only got in my way. It was easier to do it myself."

"I'm glad Deck can take care of himself. Since I am away a lot caring for the sick or birthing a baby, my men had to learn to cook or go hungry."

Mrs. Switzer left with these words, "It may be dark when I return, I'll carry the lantern. I'll fix something, so the men can have some breakfast and have something for dinner."

These mountain folks were generous with their time, when anyone was in need. They knew Anna would do the same for them, if the need arose.

Shortly after dark Mrs. Switzer arrived swinging her lantern and walking at a brisk pace. This was a welcome sight for Mrs. Emore, who did not relish a night alone, if Anna didn't make it through the night. Tomorrow would be the third day, which was often crucial for someone this sick, without medical attention. As expected, Dr. Brown never showed up.

Noona saw that all the children were in bed, using the back stairs. No one was allowed in Anna's room where the main stairway was. The little ones were getting crabby, wanting Mommy throughout the day. The days were long for Georgianna, and before she went to sleep, she made plans to go in to see Mommy the next day. She certainly should be better by then, and with this on her mind, she cuddled up to Dela and fell asleep.

All the children slept soundly, unaware of the commotion that was going on downstairs. Neither woman had a chance to rest. Anna was burning up with fever and in and out of delirium. They knew that she was not going to get any better.

The day dawned sunny and bright. All the children were up early, the older ones shushing the young ones to keep the noise down. Georgianna dressed Dela, combed her silky blond hair, and thought what a good little girl she was. She reminded Noona, "Don't forget to fix enough food for Mrs. Emore and Mrs. Switzer."

"Oh! I almost forgot," as Noona added two extra pieces of meat to the skillet.

Georgianna took a pitcher to get milk and butter from the springhouse. Hearing the sound of the running water, she was tempted to jump in the water and play awhile. This was such a favorite play spot. While dreaming about this, she heard Noona call her name and she took her pitcher of milk and dish of butter and went to the house. She knew what she was going to do after Fubby milked. She would bring the milk to the springhouse, carrying Dela along, and they would wade in the brook, hoping this would make her feel better. She had really missed Mommy.

After a good breakfast, shared with the two women taking turns at eating so Anna was not left alone, Georgianna washed the dishes, while Noona strained the milk. She was looking forward to a little playtime in the water with Dela. Maybe they would catch a minnow or a crayfish. She wanted to think of something beside her mother's illness. Mommy was better to work with in the kitchen, not fussy like Noona. She was hoping Mommy was not mad about her not finding the kindling right away the day she got sick. She wished she were allowed in the room. Maybe she could do something to make her Mommy feel better.

After the dishes were finished, Georgianna handed Dela the empty water bucket while she picked up the jar of fresh warm milk, and the two girls left for the springhouse and a few moments of play in the crystal clear stream. The best play spot was near the big beautiful hemlock tree. Georgianna held on to Dela so she would not slip on the smooth stones. They waded from the springhouse to the hemlock having great fun. Dela was gleeful as she splashed and kicked the water. Both girls had wet bloomer legs, which didn't bother them one bit for they knew they would soon dry.

Hearing Noona call, they climbed out of the water, walked a few yards to the spring, filled their water bucket, and walked back to the house. Noona was building a fire under the wash kettle to wash sheets, and they knew it would be a busy day. First many buckets of water had to be carried from the stream. Russ could carry a gallon bucket. This was a lot of help.

Georgianna fixed a glass of the fresh water she had just brought from the spring, hoping the women would let her in the sick room. She knocked softly on the door, and as Mrs. Emore opened the door a crack, she could see her mother lying very still. They did not let her in the room. Some way she was going to get in the room today.

The washing was in full swing, with Noona scrubbing on the washboard, while Fubby and Georgianna squeezed with all four hands, trying to wring the water out. Using a bench to reach the line, they hung the clothing out and propped the line up with a pole so the clothes would not drag on the ground.

The morning passed quickly, the clothes on the line. A pot of beans were cooking while Noona mixed up some corn bread. Georgianna peeled onions with teary eyes and wished she could have a good cry. She was feeling very sad.

Things had been quiet in Anna's room, with only an occasional moan as if she were in pain. Mid-afternoon she rallied enough to ask for Noona and Fubby, the two oldest ones at home. Georgianna was in charge of the three younger children and was kept busy keeping them occupied and quiet. This meant that Mommy was better, and she would find out when Fubby came out of the room. She waited anxiously for them to come out of the room. The two came through the door with very solemn faces, and neither one wanted to answer her questions. Georgianna repeatedly asked, "What did Mommy want?"

Fubby told her, "Mommy said she had tried to teach us right from wrong, and she wanted us to always do the right thing and to look after the younger children." There was no mention that she loved them. They knew that she did. She had taken care of them and had given them all she could and had always wanted them to be nice to each other.

There seemed to be sudden movements from the next room, things being moved around and the two women talking in hushed tones for some time, and then all was quiet. The two women came into the kitchen, washed their hands and poured two cups of coffee from the coffee pot that sat on the cookstove. They sat down at the table.

Georgianna knew this was her chance to get into the sick room, and, going onto the porch and through the other door, she quietly entered the eerie stillness, walking up to see her Mommy lying still with her eyes wide open. She stood there a moment and then said softly, "Mommy?" and waited for an answer. She went to the foot of the bed and lifted the sheet and looked at her mother's feet. It was then that she realized that Mommy was dead. She slipped quietly out of the room and took refuge behind the big hemlock tree and wept. The lump in her throat was choking her, and she wondered if she would ever be able to swallow.

Fubby was sent to the store to spread the word. He carried a note from Mrs. Emore. Word was spread quickly around the neighborhood. People came for their mail, and by evening practically everyone in the neighborhood knew of Anna's death. By nightfall several people had arrived at the house. The children were all aware of their mother's death, but didn't talk about it.

by Cathie Logan Sharpe

Mrs. Emore and Mrs. Switzer left for home to get a night's rest, while other neighbors stayed all night just sitting and talking softly. The children went to bed and slept, never realizing exactly what had happened and that their lives would never be the same again.

A coffin had been ordered from Pearisburg along with a light blue shroud. It would come by train to the station and by horse and wagon to the house. The neighbors had made all the funeral arrangements.

Lancy and Russ couldn't understand why all these people were here just sitting around. Georgianna had been to Granny's when she died and people came to the house. Some stayed overnight. She supposed it was to keep the family from feeling so lonesome.

Billy was in the Army, Cory and Corbin were working away, and so was Bidgy. No one knew how to get in touch with them. Georgianna stayed close to Fubby for comfort, while Russ and Dela kept asking for Mommy, and no one knew just what to tell them. Picking Dela up into her lap, Georgianna rocked her to sleep and carried her upstairs to bed. Lancy was keeping on the move, not knowing what else to do with all these people around. It was all so unusual and puzzling to the six year old.

CHAPTER 21

Anna's Funeral

Early the next morning the coffin arrived from the depot on a neighbor's wagon. The children watched from the end of the porch, while the coffin was being unloaded, all looking very somber, not fully aware of the impact this event would have on their lives or that they would be separated and end up in different parts of the country with lengthy separations. The neighbors were in the kitchen, on the porch, and milling about the yard.

The coffin was placed on one of the beds and the pale blue shroud was removed from the box so the ladies could dress Anna and place her in the coffin. By this time, a terrible odor was coming from the corpse. The ladies tried to remove the gown and replace it with the shroud and had to go outside for air. After several attempts without success, they folded the pretty shroud and placed it back in the box to return it. Then they placed the body in the coffin, leaving the nightgown on, and the coffin was closed.

Some of the neighbors drifted away, while a few just sat on the porch waiting to go to the cemetery with the family.

Noona, Fubby, and Georgianna found something for the younger children to eat and washed them, and everyone dressed in their Sunday clothes they usually wore for church.

Shortly after the coffin was loaded onto the wagon that had brought it to the house, the ladies went home to put fresh clothes on for the burial. Only two gentlemen were with the children when they left for the funeral, following the wagon carrying the coffin for the four mile walk to the cemetery. It was a somber group trudging along behind

by Cathie Logan Sharpe

the wagon bearing the coffin and stirring up some dust. The older ones took turns carrying Dela. She was not quite two years old and couldn't walk fast.

Arriving at the cemetery, the gentlemen placed the coffin beside the freshly dug grave. The Mormon elder stood by with his black Bible. On the other side of the coffin stood a beautiful dark-haired lady the children had not seen before. They wondered where she had come from. Georgianna whispered to Fubby, "Is that Elva?"

"It might be."

Someone was with her. They walked over to where Anna's children stood and she said, "I am your sister, Elva." The children just stared in amazement. This was their first meeting with her. Anna had often talked about little Elva that was taken away from her when she was just a baby, and how she longed to see her. Elva and her companion had come on the train.

The summer flowers were almost gone. One lady had brought a small bouquet. There was a small crowd. Most had walked from nearby. The Elder waited a few minutes to see if there were late comers. He then began to read from his black Bible. Georgianna looked up at Noona. She had begun to cry. As her tears began to fall, she noticed Noona had a handkerchief in each hand and asked her to let her have one. Noona would not let her have it. Georgianna just wiped her tears on the back of her hand, feeling this must be the saddest day of her life. Now her nose had begun to run, and she needed a hanky bad. Still Noona wouldn't part with one, and she just had to wipe her nose on the back of her hand, something Mommy had taught her not to do. Feeling pretty bad toward Noona, she knew she would never forget this. A hymn was sung. The Elder prayed. Then the men placed the coffin in the grave and shoveled the dirt on top of it. Mrs. Range placed the glass jar holding her bouquet on the grave, and the service was over.

Mrs. Switzer walked with the children as far as her home, and, telling her goodbye, they proceeded on to an empty house that suddenly seemed very lonely. The neighbor ladies had straightened the room, putting fresh sheets on the bed and things looked about as usual. They had taken the soiled bedding home with them to wash, trying to make things a little easier for the children.

By now the children realized that Mommy was never coming home again. No one knew exactly what to do next. They did know that hogs had to be fed, eggs gathered, ole Bessie to rounded up and be fed and milked, food to be cook for supper. They removed their Sunday clothes, Dela getting help from Georgianna, who had already changed. Georgianna breathed a sigh of relief to get those horrid black stockings off that she disliked so much. Before long she would have to wear shoes every day to protect her feet from the cold. She put her little sister to bed for a nap, patting her on the head and telling her to be good.

Russ was four and a half and was assigned the job of getting the kindling from the woodpile, while Lancy fed the chickens and gathered the eggs that had been laid that day.

Fubby filled the wood box, while the two girls got the fire started to cook supper. The lamp chimneys had to be cleaned. After helping get supper on the way, Georgianna joined Fubby to round up the cow, so he could milk as soon as supper was done. The children thought maybe they could still live here and that everything would be all right. They knew how to do most things for themselves.

A few days passed with things going very smooth, not as good as when Mommy was there, but they had food, and the animals were getting fed. Someone they did not know came to the house and told them they could not live there any longer. They would be going to stay with Aunt Marty for awhile. They would get the train the next day.

Georgianna thought this would be temporary, as she excitedly gathered up her few belongings. Noona decided they had time to wash the dirty clothes and get them dry if they worked fast. Evening found everything clean and dry and in whatever container they could find. Georgianna was excited about the train ride and visit with Aunt Marty and, of course, coming back home when the visit was over. She thought how she wished Corbin, Cory, and Bidgy were there. What if they came home to an empty house and didn't know where to find them? She didn't think this would be her last night in their mountain home.

Just as they were putting the dishes away, Deck Emore brought his horse and wagon to take them to the depot. He loaded their clothing on the wagon and closed the door, wondering who was going to feed Bruno and the other animals. The six children climbed into the wagon for the last ride down the road, going around the sandy bend and past the paint bank and on to the depot.

The train arrived soon after they reached the depot, and they were ushered onto the train and told where to sit. "Your Aunt Marty will meet you at the train. You are going to live with her for awhile." The three little ones were excited about the train ride, and all wanted to sit by the window. Georgianna stuck close to Fubby, while clutching Dela by the hand and wondering what would be happening next. Everything was a big puzzle.

CHAPTER 22

Living at Aunt Marty's

Aunt Marty met the train which ran not far from her home. She didn't look too happy to see six children aged fifteen years down to two years coming to her small house all at once. Georgianna's first thought was, "She is not much like Mommy, even if they were sisters." She began to feel the first pangs of homesickness and hoped the visit would not be too long.

The cousins were nice. All three were older than she and wanted to boss her like Noona did. She had Dela to care for and the other siblings were there, so it would be bearable for awhile. Madge and Elsa were in their teens, and Marshall was about Fubby's age. He was already eleven years old.

Several of the Marlow children developed the whooping cough one after the other. This did complicate things. Aunt Marty was very grumpy. Not only did she have six extra children, they were all sick, the house was small, the weather was getting colder, and because of the whooping cough, all were having to stay inside.

Uncle Ell worked in the coal mine, and the first day that he came home from work, the children were sure that he was a black man. He was covered with coal dust, and the whites of his eyes were about all you could see. They had seen very few black people and were somewhat afraid of them. It soon became Fubby and Georgianna's job to carry several pails of water and fill the tub to heat for his bath every evening. These children had been accustomed to some singing around the house, along with some laughter. Mommy was stern and made them behave, but she acted happy part of the time.

Within a few days, a man and his wife came and took Lancy along with his clothes to their house. Georgianna was sad to see him go, but could do nothing to stop it. At this time, she was afraid they would all be separated eventually.

Noona was crabby a lot of the time. The small house was crowded with eight children and two grownups. If Georgianna had her way, they would just pack up their clothes, get the train, and go home. She missed the mountains and the pretty clear stream where they would play for hours. She missed her Mommy and everything else and was just not very happy living here.

Christmas came and left, and no one at Aunt Marty's paid any more attention to it than the Marlow children had when they lived back in the mountains, so this didn't bother them.

Noona had been gaining weight. Aunt Marty thought that she looked like she was going to have a baby and had asked the doctor to come to the house and examine her. The doctor confirmed her suspicion that there was indeed going to be a baby, and it would be in a couple of months. At this news Aunt Marty was ready to throw up her hands. Her small house was overrun with children. What in the world would they do with a baby? No one knew who the father was, possibly one of the older brothers.

Aunt Marty hadn't had any experience birthing babies, and her youngest was eleven years old. She surely did not want this added responsibility. Talking to Noona and learning that Mrs. Emore was a well known midwife, she made her decision. She wrote to Mrs. Emore inquiring if she could keep Noona and Georgianna until after the baby was born. She received a reply that she did not have room for two extra people, but they could stay at her son Frank and his wife's until the baby was born, and that she would take care of the delivery.

This was a big relief for Aunt Marty, and she instructed Noona and Georgianna to get their clothes together. Georgianna was pleased to be going back to the mountains, but reluctant to leave Dela. After Fubby promised to look after her, she happily put her few clothes in the box she had brought with her. She was looking forward to getting back near her old home place. Noona had already been back there when everything was sold. Kent Medley had been in charge. Shortly afterward the house had burned down, probably from a tramp seeking shelter and building a makeshift fire to keep warm.

CHAPTER 23

Noona's Baby and Russ's New Home

Noona and Georgianna arrived at the Emore home in time for sup-per, after walking from the depot feeling pretty happy to be back among friends and familiar surroundings. The young Mrs. Emore was pretty upset that Noona was having this baby, while not being married, but they treated her kindly. Both girls were given some specific chores, so they could earn their room and board.

The young Mrs. Emore helped Noona sew some baby clothes. She used her own money to buy material. Noona had no money and no way to earn any. There would only be the meager necessities: a few changes and enough diapers to manage. These were made from feed sacks bleached white.

Noona never mentioned anything about having a baby to Georgianna, but she knew about it. Fubby had told her. She now knew how a girl got this way, but she didn't know much about how it was born or how you knew it was time for the birth. She guessed Noona or the young Mrs. Emore would know. She might need to go for the midwife like when Russ and Dela were born. Then she could help take care of it.

Georgianna missed Dela, Russ, and Fubby, and she also wondered about Lancy, whether he was happy and if the new family were good to him.

Evidently they could never go home again since their things had been sold and the house was burned down. She did not want to see the ashes, knowing how sad it would make her. The chores kept her fairly busy. She still felt lonesome. Mrs. Emore had two big sons that did not give her any attention.

No matter how hard she tried, she could not push the thoughts out of her mind about them all being together again. As she climbed into bed with Noona, she remembered how she would snuggle up to Mommy, and Mommy made a lap to warm her feet. Then she thought of the day her Mommy was buried, and Noona did not let her have a handkerchief, and she softly cried herself to sleep.

Noona awoke and, not feeling well, didn't want to get out of bed, saying her back hurt. The young Mrs. Emore told her to "Just stay in bed, until you feel like getting up. Georgianna can take care of your work." The extra work kept Georgianna busy and, as she worked, she thought that it must be time for the baby to be born. Noona spent the day in bed only getting up to use the chamber pot, which Georgianna had to take to the toilet to empty. By the next morning her labor pains had begun, and after the men had gone to work in the field, Georgianna did indeed have to go for Mrs. Emore, who came immediately, thinking Noona, being only sixteen years' old could have some problems.

Georgianna knew she would not be allowed in the room, so she stayed busy doing whatever she was told, in addition to Noona's chores and the ones that had been assigned to her. No noise was coming from the room where Noona was. Everything must be all right. Having no one to talk to was so boring and the work was taken care of. She tried to have some fun all by herself and began running around the house. She found a big Rhode Island Red rooster and proceeded to chase him around the house. He began squawking, and other chickens were cackling. She heard moans coming from Noona's room. Trying to blot out the noise, she began singing and chasing the rooster.

The midwife came to the door with a frown on her face and called to the young girl, "How can you be so happy with your sister in her suffering?" Georgianna hung her head. She was shy, and her feelings were easily hurt.

She sat in the rocking chair on the porch and kept very quiet while listening to the moaning and groaning coming from the room. She wished she had Dela to keep her occupied and keep her from thinking about the way things used to be, when they were all together and never ran out of things to do. She didn't know why she could not be happy. Noona was just having a baby, and Mommy had birthed twelve babies.

It seemed like she sat there for a long time when she heard a very loud moan and then a baby's cry. Now she could go back to being happy again, and she could help care for the baby. Feeling like she could get out of the rocking chair, she quietly opened the kitchen door and walked into the kitchen, where the young Mrs. Emore was filling a wash pan with warm water.

"Your sister had a baby girl. What you think of that?"

"I'm glad she is a girl. We already have a lot of boys."

"As soon as we get her washed and dressed you can hold her."

When the baby was a few days old, Georgianna was informed that she was to go back to Aunt Marty's, but that Noona would stay with the Emores for awhile longer. She never dreamed that fifteen years would pass before they were together again.

Georgianna was happy to see Fubby, Dela and Russ. Aunt Marty and Uncle El were as grumpy as usual and acted like they wished these extra children would go some place else to live. Fubby and Georgianna kept the wood box full and a good supply on the porch. Aunt Marty's three children were in school every day. These two carried the water and had it hot for Uncle El's bath every evening. They were not really happy, but it was a place to stay, and they had food to eat.

Georgianna never knew what to expect, always having the fear that they would all be separated for good. She missed Lancy. She loved him and missed him, even if he did break her dolls and tear her paper dolls.

It was no surprise when, a few days after the arrival back at Aunt Marty's, it was announced that Russ and Georgianna were going to visit another family. She became suspicious when all of Russ' things were placed together, while she was only taking a change of clothes and a nightgown. She knew this was going to be another separation.

The kindly gentleman, Walter Hutchinson, arrived early next morning with his horse and buggy to take them to his home, where his wife, Anna, and their three daughters lived. Mabel, Pauline, and Sue were waiting for them. The three girls made a big fuss over Russ, while mostly ignoring Georgianna. Mrs. Hutchinson picked Russ up in her arms and called him her little boy. He squirmed to get down, and when he did, he ran to Georgianna and threw his arms around her.

The Hutchinsons seemed really happy to have them in their home. It was a welcome change from Aunt Marty's home.

Georgianna missed Dela and Fubby, and thought of all the changes they had been through in a few months time, and wondered what would happen next. It occurred to her that if Fubby and Dela could come here, this would be a good home for them.

Mrs. Hutchinson made hot biscuits nearly every meal, had fresh butter on the table, and always a pitcher of molasses. Mixing the butter and molasses together to spread on your biscuits was really good.

Russ had been the last one to get the whooping cough and still was having periods of coughing, especially at night. The kindly couple had him sleep in bed with them so they could look after him. When Russ would have a bad coughing spell, Mr. Hutchinson would get out of bed, pick Russ up, place him under his arm, and dash outside in his long underwear, so the boy would not vomit in the bed.

Everything was pleasant, and after school, the girls would give the two children some attention. In spite of everything, Georgianna sensed that this would be one more separation and tried to not think about it.

The time came when it was decided that Georgianna would go back to Aunt Marty's. Russ's clothes were purposely washed and hung on the line to dry. That was used as an excuse that he couldn't leave until the next day because his clothes were still wet. She knew better. They were not going to bring him back at all. She did not say anything, only felt the lump in her throat.

Mrs. Hutchinson had noticed how much she had enjoyed the molasses and gave her a quart jar to take with her. They knew how she dreaded leaving Russ. The girls took him to the back of the house, so he would not cry when she left. She was crying on the inside.

It seemed like a very long ride, as the buggy rattled over the rough road and Georgianna sat by the old man. At least he looked old to her. People aged faster in the twenties. Farm folks had to work hard.

Before getting to Aunt Marty's, Mr. Hutchinson stopped at he general store in Newport and bought a bag of candy, trying to make Georgianna smile a little. They traveled on another road to Spruce Run and onto Goodwin's Ferry, where Aunt Marty lived up on the hill overlooking the New River and railroad tracks. There had not been much talk between the two from the Hutchinson's Clover Hollow home to Aunt Marty's. Georgianna could not get rid of the lump in her throat and did not feel much like talking.

The house was in sight. Pulling up to the back gate and stopping the buggy, the old man gently lifted Georgianna down from the seat and fetched her belongings. Dela came running out the door and gleefully grabbed her sister by the legs, chattering like a magpie. The older girl was just as gleeful, and for a few moments, forgot how sad she felt. Fubby left his woodcutting for a few moments to greet her. He did not ask about Russ, having been told that his home was going to be with the Hutchinsons. They had the three girls and really wanted a son.

They stood on the porch and talked a few minutes. The old man remarked, "I reckon I better be getting on back. The days are so short, and I have a lot to get done before dark. Now that I got me a boy, he will be a lot of help, when he gets older. He is a sturdy lad, and I think we will get along just fine." Hearing this, Georgianna was sure he was not coming back and that the excuse of the wet clothes was a lie in disguise.

It appeared to this girl that nothing had gone right, since her Mommy had died. She did have Fubby and Dela, and that was more than her siblings had. She wondered if Corbin, Cory, or Bidgy had been back to their home and found no one, not even a house, and what turn of events would come next. She did not have long to wait.

It was evident that Georgianna and Dela were glad to see each other, and they stuck close together for the time they had left, not knowing that it would be such a short time, until they would be separated for over seven long unhappy years.

Chapter 24

Dela's Departure and Other Things

No more than a week had passed when Georgianna spotted Dela's belongings all placed in a box. Panic gripped her heart, and that big lump was again in her throat. She knew without being told that Dela must be leaving. Her first thought was to take Dela after everyone was asleep and run away where no one could find them. Then she thought of Fubby being left all alone, and where could she run to? And how would she get food for Dela? Her heart was indeed heavy, and she didn't feel like talking to anyone, with the big lump in her throat.

Aunt Marty gruffly spoke, "I want you to wash Dela's hair and give her a good bath before she goes to bed."

"It's not Saturday."

"Just do as I say," was the harsh reply. When the supper dishes were put away, Georgianna got the big washtub while Dela removed her clothes, filled it with warm water, helped her little sister into the tub, and spent a long time soaping and rinsing, pouring pitcher after pitching of water over her head, just trying to stretch the time they had left together.

Georgianna tried to go to sleep, hoping she would not even wake up when morning came, knowing it would be a very bad day for her as well as for Dela and Fubby.

The whippoorwills were not heard here like back home. The train sounded its whistle as it rounded the curve along the New River, and it only made her feel more lonesome.

Thoughts of former times filled her mind. She thought back to the time Dela was born, and how Mommy had let her carry her to the foot of the bed, where she always put her new babies, so she would not roll over on them. She had loved and cared for her sister since that time, and now it was all coming to an end, and there was no way that she could stop it. Crying softly until she could cry no more, she fell asleep.

Morning found Fubby shaking her by the shoulders, "Get up, get up, sleepyhead." All the dread surfaced, and she did not want to wake up. She knew she could not dawdle, or she would be scolded, and she sure couldn't handle that, not today.

The cousins left for school. Fubby and Georgianna washed the breakfast dishes, and Fubby brought in a bucket of fresh water. Dela was still in her gown sitting near the heater in the bedroom sitting room. Aunt Marty brought the box containing Dela's clothes and set it by the door. She then spoke, "Get your sister dressed. I left out her best white dress. She is going for a visit with her Aunt Marilyn." This made the older girl feel a little better. Dela would be with family, and maybe she would come back after the visit. She dressed Dela and combed her golden curls for the last time, trying to think pleasant thoughts and instructing Dela to stay clean.

The dog barked as a lady whom the children didn't know came to the door. The children were sent to the kitchen and told to shut the door behind them. Shortly, they were called into the room. Dela was given a sweater. The lady picked up the box and reached for Dela's hand, while Dela clung to her older sister and was very reluctant to go. After being promised a treat after getting on the train, she let go of Georgianna and went along, not looking very happy. Fubby didn't look very happy either, and Georgianna certainly was not happy.

Standing on the porch, she watched until they were no longer visible. Then she went inside, not knowing that it would be many years before she would see the little sister with the golden curls again.

The wood box in the kitchen had been filled, wood nearby for the bedroom, living room heater; and Uncle El's bath water was heating. For once in her life Georgianna didn't know what to do with herself. She had never felt so alone. Unable to find any books to read, she noticed Aunt Marty's black Bible. She could read that, but so much of it she could not understand. Uncle El came in, black and dirty and as unsmiling as ever. He took his bath in the pantry, while the two cousins helped Aunt Marty put dinner on the table, and called everyone to dinner. For once in her lifetime Georgianna did not feel like eating and said, "I am not going to eat."

Uncle Ell spoke up, "What's that you are not going to do? We don't talk like that around here. Get to the table." Trying to eat with the lump in her throat made her very uncomfortable.

The following day Aunt Marty noticed how very unhappy she was and tried to cheer her up. "Would you like to help me make you a pretty new dress?"

"Yes, could I have a yellow one with pockets?" The nearest store was at Newport, about eight miles away. They had to wait until a neighbor was going and would give them a ride in the wagon. They found a bright yellow broadcloth, and together they decided on how to make it. It was to have box pleats from the shoulder to the hem, with pockets in the proper place over the box pleats, and with matching bloomers. She really would like to have one with the strips down each side like the Medley girls wore for church. It was good to be helping to make her own dress and keeping busy so she would not be thinking of Dela continually.

The dress and bloomers were finished, and Georgianna wanted to wear them to the little white church at the foot of the hill. Aunt Marty said, "You can't wear it yet. It's for something special." Now this something special made her curious and a little suspicious.

It had been a year since Anna had died and Fubby and Georgianna were the only ones left together. Many thoughts were in the back of Georgianna's head. What if she were leaving him? No one had mentioned anything. She knew something was up.

A few days later, Georgianna came upon Aunt Marty and Midge putting all of her and Fubby's clothes in a box. Now she knew that "something special" that her dress was made for. She just wished she could die and go on to heaven and be with Mommy, but she didn't want to leave Fubby all by himself with none of his family.

CHAPTER 25

Leaving Aunt Marty's

The next morning at breakfast, Aunt Marty told them to put on the clothes that she had laid out for them. A nice lady was coming and was taking them on a train ride. She didn't tell them why or where they were going.

By the time they had dressed and combed their hair—Fubby liked to wet his hair and comb it straight back—they heard the dog bark, and a buggy drove up. A man was driving, and a pretty lady in a coat suit stepped down from the buggy. The man did not get out of the buggy. Aunt Marty walked onto the porch to greet her, and they came inside. The lady smiled and spoke to the children. "Hello, I am Mrs. Hopfield, and I am taking you to a new home." Georgianna had never taken up with strangers, but this lady seemed nice and talked kindly. She supposed it would be all right to go with her. Fubby would be along. Of course, she didn't have a choice.

With both carrying a box, they said goodbye and climbed into the buggy for the short ride to catch the train. Neither had any idea where they were going. The past four months had been a time of many changes, and neither child was very happy. None of these changes had been good changes, that made anyone happy.

They boarded the train. Shortly they heard the "All aboard!" before the train began to move, and they were on their way. They had not been made aware of where they were going, and both felt lost and very lonely. Mrs. Hopfield sat across the isle from them looking very calm and composed.

The train picked up speed, the wheels making their familiar clickety clack sound. The trees and telephone poles seemed to be flying by, while they felt as if the train was standing still.

In a short while, nothing familiar was in sight, and Georgianna could contain herself no longer. She began to cry, softly hiding her face with both arms. Fubby tried to comfort her every way he could, all to no avail. Mrs. Hopfield joined him and tried to console her, telling her about the nice place she would be living. The harder they tried, the louder she cried. Eventually her face was so red and puffy, her eyes were nearly swollen shut. She was a pitiful sight. Mrs. Hopfield spoke softly, "You really do not want to leave here, do you? Georgianna just shook her head and continued her sobbing, until she was totally exhausted.

Neither child had asked where they were going. In the twenties, children did not speak out much or ask questions. They just accepted whatever happened. Adults made the decisions, and children abided by them.

by Cathie Logan Sharpe

The train sped along what seemed a long time. Scenery kept changing along the way, as they went by small villages, making a stop now and then. At every stop, the two children wondered if they were getting off.

The train lessened its speed as buildings came into view, then lots of buildings. This must be a big city. As they were pondering about whether they would be getting off the train, Mrs. Hopfield reached overhead where she had placed their boxes of clothing and their warm coats, handing them the coats to put on before getting off the train. Georgianna was glad she still had her warm black and white coat her Mommy had made. It felt like fur. She handed them each a box to carry.

The conductor helped them down the steps, followed by Mrs. Hopfield. They were met by a man who was driving a black car. These two children had only been in a car one time, and that was the Medley car back home. They perked up some thinking about the car ride.

After they had climbed into the car, Mrs. Hopfield informed them that they were going to stay with a widow lady for a short time and were then going to the children's home, where they would have lots of children to play with.

Georgianna had pangs of homesickness even with Fubby nearby. She had never felt so alone in all her life. Her hands itched, and she felt like her world had completely fallen apart. Fubby was behaving like a real man and did everything that he could to comfort his sister.

The car pulled up to the curb of a pretty white house. Carrying their boxes, they followed Mrs. Hopfield up the steps. She rang the door bell, and a nice looking lady appeared at the door. "Mrs. Hopfield, I've been expecting you."

"Well, Mrs. Howell, I have brought you some company for a few days." They entered the living room that had pretty furniture, nicer than Georgianna had ever seen. That did not help at all. She just wanted to go back home, where they had all been together and she could sit under the hemlock tree with her feet in the brook and watch Dela play.

After a good night's sleep, Georgianna awoke feeling better, and curious about all the different things. The light switch held her fascination. She had never been where anyone had electricity. It was sort of like magic. No need to clean the lamp chimney or put oil in the lamps and then strike a match to light the wick.

They each had their own bed but were in the same room. Mrs. Howell came into the room saying, "Wake up time, wake up time." They were both already awake and dressed.

While they were having breakfast, Mrs. Howell kept trying to get them to talk without getting much response. "Mrs. Hopfield is coming to take you to the doctor."

"Why are we going to the doctor? We are not sick," Fubby responded, and Georgianna agreed.

"They always take children to the doctor before taking them to the children's home. You do have some breaking out on your hands."

"If Mommy was here, she would put salve on it and make it go away," Georgianna spoke up. "One time the doctor came to our house and fixed Bidgy when he fell out of the chestnut tree." Now that Georgianna had started talking she felt more at ease.

Mrs. Hopfield soon arrived with the man driving the black car. Georgianna tucked her head and mumbled a weak "Hello" as Mrs. Hopfield greeted them. Fubby was a little more outgoing. He had his hair slicked back and his tie on and felt confident he could handle anything that came his way. Being a couple years older probably helped.

Mrs. Hopfield said briskly, "Well, we are going to pay a call on Dr. Phillips, and its almost time for our appointment."

This was another experience that was foreign to both of them. At the doctor's office they were taken into a room separated by a curtain. Georgianna was afraid of another separation, and she began to cry. She had certainly done more crying in the last few months than she had done in her entire lifetime.

The nice nurse placed her arm around her and explained that the doctor was just going to examine them and that everything would be all right. "You need to take all your clothes off and put this sheet around you."

"I can't."

"Why?"

"Mommy told me never to take my clothes off in front of boys. The doctor is a boy."

She knew she had to do as the nurse said, and she began removing her clothes. She could hear the doctor talking as he examined Fubby and heard him say, "You will need to be circumcised."

She wondered what that was. The nurse stuck something called a thermometer in her mouth and said, "Keep it under your tongue, so we can tell if you have a fever." Mommy just felt your forehead and your hands to find out if you had a fever. After the nurse took the thermometer out of her mouth, "Goodness, you are running a temperature." Georgianna was not surprised at this. There had been so many things to upset her, it was surprising she was still alive.

Dr. Phillips finished with Fubby and came to check the girl. He first looked at her hands. "Ho hum, well, they both have the itch, and both of them are running a temperature." He turned to Mrs. Hopfield, "I think these two should stay in bed for a few days. This ointment should clear up their hands, and within a week, they can be put with the other children."

They climbed into the back seat of the black car and went back to Mrs. Howell's. Mrs. Hopfield handed her the jar of ointment. "This is to be put on their hands every three hours, and they are to stay in bed, until their temperature has been normal for twenty four hours. Give me a call when they are ready to leave."

"I'll take care of them. You two get ready to get in the bed."

Georgianna put on a nightgown. Fubby just wore his underwear. This was strange, to be going to bed in the middle of the day. They didn't even stay in bed when they had the whooping cough. The days really dragged, Mrs. Howell sticking the thermometer in their mouth every so often and looking at the little red line in the thermometer. Georgianna really did not feel good. Mostly she was homesick for her family. Mrs. Howell concluded they had a mild case of flu. Their temperature was slowly dropping.

Georgianna awoke feeling very thirsty. Hearing Mrs. Howell stirring in the kitchen, she called, "Mrs. Howell, I am thirsty."

"Just a minute," and she appeared still in her nightgown, bringing the glass of water. Reaching for the glass of water, Georgianna could see something in it beside water. She looked into the glass and looked up at Mrs. Howell. "It has teeth in it."

"Ah! My goodness," Mrs. Howell said as she quickly retrieved the glass. Evidently Mrs. Howell did not have her glasses on or her teeth in. Georgianna hoped she would bring a clean glass. Her family always drank from the same dipper. She surely didn't want to drink after Mrs. Howell's teeth.

Shortly Mrs. Howell returned with a fresh glass of water, and a few minutes later, she appeared with the thermometer, taking Fubby's temperature first, then sticking the thermometer in a glass of some solution. Then it was Georgianna's time. "Well I've got some good news. Neither of you has a temperature this morning. We will take it again later in the day. If you have no fever, then you may get up for a while."

"Fubby, you know what that means?"

"Yes, we go to the children's home. Is it the same as an orphanage?"

"I guess so, son."

Georgianna began to feel less homesick and was looking forward to meeting the other children that were going to be her family for awhile. They must be like her and Fubby, without a mother and father and separated from their families. She wished Dela could be there with them so she could look after her. Aunt Marilyn had two mean boys, and she hoped they would not hurt her dear little sister.

"This city is called Roanoke," Fubby spoke up. "I heard the conductor say that when we were still on the train. There are lots of houses everywhere."

CHAPTER 26

The Children's Home

The two awakened early to find fresh clothing placed on the foot of their bed and their other clothing placed by the front door. Mrs. Hopfield would be coming early for them. Mrs. Howell had given them each a toothbrush. Neither had one before. Mommy had taught them to break a dogwood twig and soften the end of it and brush their teeth, which they did occasionally. After breakfast they gave their teeth a good brushing, just in time to hear the door bell signaling Mrs. Hopfield's arrival.

Once again into the back seat of the black car they climbed, feeling some anticipation rather than so much anxiety. They looked around the town as they rode along and saw their first milk wagon, drawn by a white horse. There were many black cars, as well as carriages, wagons, and buggies. There were trees in the yards and sidewalks. The two thought it may not be too bad a place to live.

They drove up Patterson Avenue, turned at Eighteenth Street, and stopped in front of a large white house on the corner of Rorer Avenue. There were many children with coats on playing in the yard, some on swings, some on a sliding board, and some on a merry go round. Two big girls were rolling down the sidewalk on roller skates. It looked like they were having fun, and Georgianna thought they might like living here, when they got to know the other children and learned their names. There certainly were people to play with.

They followed Mrs. Hopfield up the steps, each clutching their box of clothing. After she rang the doorbell, a dark haired lady with dark piercing eyes and a frown on her face opened the door. "Mrs. Venable, I've brought you two more charges. This is Earl, better known as Fubby, and Georgianna Marlow."

"I've been expecting you. Come in. I'll summon Mrs. Jordan." A white haired, grandmotherly-looking lady entered the room. "Show these two around while I talk with Mrs. Hopfield."

"Come along, Grandma will show you where you will be sleeping." They went down a long hallway into the play room that was empty. "Nice weather is always playtime outside," Mrs. Jordan explained. Then they went into a long room with rows of beds on each side. "Now Fubby will be sleeping here with all the other boys." Then they went into a large kitchen, where several big girls were preparing food.

They proceeded into the dining room, where several tables would each seat twelve people, and there was a table by the window where the two matrons would be by themselves. They now went into the big hallway and up the stairs, seeing Mrs. Venable's own room, which she reminded them was off limits to the children. They walked by a door that was the sick room. Only one child was in bed near the window. Across the hall was a large bathroom with a big white bathtub like the ones Georgianna had seen in the Sears & Roebuck catalogue. They walked through another room that had six beds. "Now this is where the big girls sleep. They get to stay up a little later."

Adjoining this room, was the girls' sleeping porch. "This second bed is empty, and you, Georgianna, will be sleeping here." Many windows were all around the sleeping porches. "On cold nights, we place hot water bottles or jugs to warm the beds. We do not have any heat on the sleeping porches."

By the time the tour was over, Mrs. Hopfield had gone. Mrs. Jordan took the two children out to the playground, and everyone stopped their play to stare at the newcomers. "We will be ringing the dinner bell before long, and you two just come on in with the other children." She walked away, leaving them standing there holding hands.

After dinner everyone had to lie down and be quiet. Most took a nap. Fubby and Georgianna had not taken daytime naps for several years, and neither slept. After naptime was playtime again, and afterward, suppertime. They all lined up and marched into the dining room after washing their hands. Fubby and Georgianna had been assigned their regular place at the table, where they would sit as long as they remained at the children's home.

As darkness fell, loneliness returned. This was all so different. All the younger children went to bed at the same time, whether you were two or ten years old. The girls each had a bath in the big white bathtub in the girls' bathroom, while the boys did the same in the boys' bathroom.

Mrs. Venable came upstairs to make sure everything was going well for the new girl, and asked Georgianna, "Are you ready for bed?"

"Yes, Ma'am."

"Did you void?" At this the girl gave her a puzzled look and she repeated, "Did you void?" Georgianna was not familiar with the word, but thought it might be another word for pee. She meekly responded "Yes, Ma'am."

The following day was better. They learned some of the children's names. There was Genovee, who sat with her thumb in her mouth, with her forefinger hooked over her nose, while clutching her throat with the other hand. She was about the age of Georgianna, which was nine years old. John Norman, a little boy about four, wore glasses and was cross-eyed. Pete Parks was also cross-eyed. A girl named Frances had a lame leg. Most of the children were pretty normal. Poor Buster Lawson had the biggest mouth Georgianna had ever seen. Some of the children would make him laugh, and when he did, his mouth just about covered his face. Then everyone laughed.

The children liked Grandma Jordan and ran to her when she came into the room. It was not the same with Mrs. Venable. Georgianna was still shy around both of them, unless she needed something. Fubby had been to the hospital and been circumcised. He did not look like he felt very good for a few days. Georgianna hoped that she would not have to have that done, whatever it was. All the new stuff was not to her liking.

Fubby enjoyed his free time and blended in with other boys his age, and he did not pay as much attention to Georgianna. She felt very lonely for Dela. A day never passed that she was not missing the little girl with the golden ringlets that clung to her head when showers were on the way, the big brown eyes dancing when there was some excitement. Georgianna shed many tears after the other children had gone to sleep.

Georgianna had been at the children's home only a few days until she began feeling sick at the breakfast table. She left the table and hurried upstairs to the bathroom, barely getting there in time to throw up her breakfast. When she returned to the table, Mrs. Venable spoke harshly, "You are never to leave the table without being excused. Is that clear?"

"Yes, Ma'am," was the meek reply. The following morning, once again Georgianna was feeling sick, and didn't know just what to do. She knew she dare not leave the table, and she vomited all over the table, much to her dismay. She was led upstairs to be stripped, bathed, and put to bed in the sick room and a thermometer stuck in her mouth. By nightfall she was feeling short of breath and wheezing with an attack of asthma.

Dr. Phillips came to check on Georgianna. He left some pills that he thought might help. Several days passed, and Georgianna was no better, having to stay in bed propped up on several pillows day and night, so she could breathe. She was in bed for many months. Finally her wheezing stopped, and she did not cough as much. A pillow was removed each day until she could finally breathe normally with only one pillow under her head. Now maybe she could get out of bed and do something.

All the children were glad to see Georgianna again. No child was allowed in the sickroom unless they were sick. The small ones were especially glad to have her to read to them and give them more attention.

A fresh change of clothing was placed on each bed twice a week, on Sunday and on Wednesday. Seldom did you get the same clothes you had worn before.

Georgianna always had some work to do. Here all she did was eat, sleep, and play. She saw some of the older girls helping with the dishes, and she got up enough courage to approach Mrs. Venable, the head matron, asking, "May I help with the dishes? I have been washing dishes for years, so may I?"

"Well, we will give it a try. You can start tomorrow. Now I warn you, I can't have broken dishes."

Georgianna felt happier than she had for awhile, and she felt quite grown up working with the big girls. She liked hanging out the pretty white tea towels. She had never heard them called tea towels. The first week she was there when saw them hanging on the line, her thoughts were, "That must be what they use to make that white hot drink that we have every morning for breakfast." She soon learned it was only hot milk, but it tasted different to any hot milk she had back home.

Mrs. Jordan complimented her on the good job she was doing in the kitchen and asked her, "Would you like to have another job?"

"Yes, Ma'am."

"You can dust the hallway. Report to me tomorrow after you have finished helping with the dishes."

Georgianna was pleased to have another job to do and looked forward to the following day, when she would have something more to keep her occupied. Meanwhile, Fubby was enjoying his free time, not especially wanting any responsibility.

Georgianna reported to Mrs. Jordan just as soon as she finished helping with the breakfast dishes, knocking softly on the door and hearing Mrs. Jordan's soft voice, "Come in, please." Meekly she opened the door. "I've been expecting you. I'll show you what needs to be done," and she showed her where the dust cloths and dust mop were kept and explained just what was expected of her. Mrs. Jordan walked back into her office, leaving Georgianna with the dust cloth in her hand. She started at the top, as instructed, and wiped every piece of furniture, the lamps, the banister, the newel post, the downstairs tables in the big hallway. Then quietly she used a small dust mop to clean each step carefully and a large dust mop to do the downstairs hallway, and felt very proud as she surveyed her work.

The temptation to open the door marked "Nursery" was too great. She opened the door a tiny crack to see baby beds, two with babies sleeping in them. It was then she decided to do her very best job in the hallway, and just maybe she would be permitted to help in the nursery.

Some mornings the hallway would be finished early and the nursery door would be open. While Mrs. Jordan was finishing the babies' daily baths, Georgianna always stood at the door and watched for a while, not daring to venture in unless she was invited. This continued for several days, the child finishing her work hurriedly, hoping that Mrs. Jordan would notice that she was interested and would invite her in to help with the babies. Before long she was asked to come in and help arrange the bath table, putting the baby soap, powder, towel and washcloth in a convenient spot. She was getting really excited just thinking maybe she would be allowed to help bathe and dress the babies sometimes.

Her first job with the babies was being a sitter for them after they were bathed, dressed, wrapped warmly, and placed in two baby carriages on the front porch for their morning airing, when the weather was quite cold. Fresh air was important for good health. When they were fussy, Georgianna quieted them with gentle movement of the carriage. Mrs. Venable caught her doing this and, with the big frown on her face, ordered, "Don't do that; it will spoil them. Do you understand?"

"Yes, Ma'am," was the reply as she dropped her head, unhappy to have done something forbidden.

Mrs. Jordan had observed how capable she was with little Beatrice and Tommy, and she was soon allowed to help dress, feed, and change diapers, as well as supervise their daily airing. This made her feel very important. Georgianna was much more content being kept busy most of the morning.

On one occasion, while she was sitting with the babies, the front door had been left open, and she could hear what was being said in the office. She overheard Mrs. Venable on the telephone telling someone that Jackie Lawson was being adopted and was leaving the following day.

The babies were rolled into the nursery and placed in their beds. Georgianna was eager to spread the news, and, having her morning chores completed, she headed for the playground. The news spread like wildfire. Soon everyone knew that Jackie Lawson was leaving. Just before dinner, the girl was summoned to the office, quaking in her black high top shoes, knowing she must have done something wrong. No one had to go to the office unless they had broken a rule. She dreaded Mrs. Venable's piercing eyes and sharp voice. She was in no hurry to get there but go she must, not knowing what to expect. Maybe they were going to send her away just as she was beginning to like the place.

Mrs. Venable had that usual big frown on her face as Georgianna entered the room and was commanded to sit in the big office chair that practically swallowed her. She really felt small and helpless as Mrs. Venable spoke, "If you want to sit with the babies for their airing you need to understand something, you are never to repeat anything that you hear said in this office. Is that clear?"

"Yes, ma'am."

"You may go now, just do not forget."

"I'll be very careful, I did not mean to cause trouble."

Anyone leaving for a new home was never told until the last minute when their going away clothes were laid out and all arrangements made for their departure. Most of the children were excited and happy to be going to a new home and a real family. Georgianna had decided that she would be just as happy to stay here. She had become fond of the many children and knew she would never be with her family again. Since Fubby was here, she felt fairly content. She longed for the day when they could be together again.

The day came when Georgianna was told that the next day a man and woman were coming for her, wanting her to be their little girl. She felt that lump come in her throat. This would mean that she would be leaving Fubby, the last link in her family.

She made a comment that she was going to play sick. Really she did not intend to play sick, but someone heard the remark.

Georgianna awoke feeling terrible with a really bad headache and a churning stomach. Mrs. Venable came to check on her after hearing she was sick. She had also heard that she was faking sickness and with that constant frown she stuck the thermometer in the child's mouth and searched in the medicine cabinet for medication. She then read the thermometer to discover an elevated temperature. Showing her anger at the child for getting sick, she certainly could not give this couple a sick child. She took a large bottle of castor oil from the shelf, mumbling to herself over the dilemma. No one liked to take caster oil. The matron poured a large spoonful and shoved it into Georgianna's mouth. "This will teach you not to play sick again."

"You must stay in bed and you will get no breakfast."

Georgianna really did not feel like eating, so it made no difference. She lay quietly wondering what would happen when the couple came for her. She wished Fubby could come to see her, but the boys were not allowed on the second floor. Mrs. Venable made hourly checks on her temperature which continuously stayed above normal. She looked very exasperated.

Mr. and Mrs. Brown arrived mid-morning. They were disappointed that the child they had selected was unable to go home with them. "Would you like to look over the other children? They are all still in the playroom."

"Yes, please, we are ready for a child."

A brown haired girl about Georgianna's age named Louise caught their eye. Mrs. Venable followed them into her office and took a folder of papers from the drawer, looking it over carefully. She made a phone call to her superior. Readying her typewriter and typing the necessary information and re-reading it and placing it in the envelope, she then summoned Mrs. Jordan to have Louise dressed and ready to leave within the hour.

The Browns sat and reviewed the papers, and she gave them as much information as they needed. "It'll be a year before the final adoption is complete, and if things are not compatible by the end of the year, the child can be returned. We will be making a home visit unannounced every few months to review the progress."

Louise appeared at the door all smiles, happy to be going to a real home. Mr. Brown picked her up and placed her on his shoulders as they bid the matron goodbye and strolled down the walk.

Georgianna was relieved that she would not have to go to a new home, meaning that she would have at least one more day with Fubby, her only link with her family.

Two of the older girls attended school outside the home. The younger children had a little schooling in the playroom, led by an older girl. Georgianna was having her first experience with something called arithmetic. She wanted to just call it numbers. She learned to add, subtract and multiply. She felt like she was ready for something they called high school. She could read and spell and write, and now she had arithmetic. She decided that she would just take care of babies instead of going to high school. She didn't care much for school.

Georgianna was sympathetic to the thirty-five children, knowing they had been separated from family and familiar surroundings and felt lonely at times. She read to them and tried to comfort them when knees were skinned or feelings were hurt.

Whenever a new child arrived, everyone gathered around to make them welcome. One day three new ones arrived: a girl named Mildred, who was nine; a boy Billy, five; and one younger than Dela. The little one spent a lot of time crying and asking for titty, apparently not having been weaned from the breast. Georgianna tried to pacify her by rocking her in the rocking chair. She still cried for titty, and her older sister just ignored her. Little Billy looked pale and was sickly. After a few days he was put to bed in the sick room, where he spent several days and was then taken to Roanoke Memorial Hospital, never to return to the children's home. The children heard that he had died. His sister didn't pay attention to this news.

Georgianna was staying almost as busy as she had back in the mountains. A new job had been added. She was helping to bathe the younger children every night before bed time. The soap smelled better than what she had bathed with back home. When everyone had finished bathing, she then scrubbed the tub clean before going to bed.

The skates looked like so much fun but usually the older girls kept them busy. The nine year old girl was keeping her eyes open for a chance to give the skates a try, hoping the big girls would tire of this sport and leave the skates where she could try her luck. The first time she spotted one skate, she latched onto it, thinking one skate is better than none. She sat down on the step, carefully buckled it on over her black high top shoe and feeling like a queen, she rolled down the sidewalk, feeling lucky to have gotten her hands on even one skate. She felt like she was really living it up and called to Fubby to watch her. As Fubby turned to look, down she sat on the hard concrete. Fubby laughed along with the other children. Ole mean Pete Parks laughed hilariously, and Buster Lawson spread his big mouth even wider. All this did not damper her enthusiasm. She took advantage of her every chance. Never did she have the opportunity to use two skates.

The days were getting warmer, and Georgianna was looking forward to barefoot time, when she could shed those black high top shoes and long black stockings and feel the soft grass on her bare feet. She knew it would be soon. Some of the children were talking about a place called Lakeside, where you could ride, and a pool where you could swim. She remembered the good times when she and her siblings played in the creek back in the mountains, and how much fun it was.

Barefoot time came, but not for Georgianna. Mrs. Venable decided that after having asthma and spending part of the winter in bed, Georgianna would have to wear her shoes and stockings all summer long, hopefully to prevent another attack. Georgianna longed for the carefree days in the mountains when she had light attacks of asthma but never had to stay in bed or wear shoes all summer long.

CHAPTER 27

Fubby Leaves the Home

It was May 17, 1928, early morning, before the seven o'clock whistle had blown. Daylight had come and everyone was awake talking about different things and laughing, just having fun, when Mildred Cook spoke up, "I know a secret, I know a secret."

"What is it? Come on tell us," they pleaded until she could stand it no longer.

"Someone from the boys' sleeping porch is leaving today, but I can't tell who," as she cast a glance in Georgianna's direction.

Georgianna's heart sank and her stomach turned over. She knew it must be Fubby and she didn't know how she could stand to be left alone. He was the last link to her family, and she always looked for him the first thing every morning, when she entered the big playroom. Mildred continued to look at her.

Before the seven o'clock whistle sounded, she saw Nora Napier, one of the older girls, coming thorough the door followed by Fubby, all dressed to go away. She was truly devastated. All she could do was cover her head and begin to weep. She could not uncover her head to give him a hug. She knew she could not let loose of him. Her day was ruined as were a lot of successive days. She did not know that it would be seven years before she would see her beloved brother again.

She kept her head covered and wept uncontrollably until the seven o'clock whistle sounded. See knew she would have to get up and appear at the breakfast table. How would she swallow anything with this terrible lump in her throat? She knew everyone would notice her red swollen eyes, and she just wanted to stay in the bed for the rest of

123

her life. All of her family were gone, and she felt so alone. Life held no joy for her.

One of the smaller girls, that she loved dearly, came to her bed and hugged her, and she held onto this child for comfort, thinking maybe she could survive after all.

It was Wednesday when everyone had a fresh change of clothing. She began dressing, wishing that she had some of her own clothes to wear. Maybe the matrons didn't want you to have anything to remind you of your past.

Georgianna mostly just sat at the breakfast table eating very little but drinking her milk. You were usually required to eat all your food, but Mrs. Venable did not say anything, being understanding of her feelings. Georgianna was thankful not to be fussed at.

The day was long and lonely. Georgianna was glad that she had some work to keep her busy most of the morning. Part of the afternoon was spent in rest time on a pallet, so as not to muss up the beds.

Georgianna had her own special spot away from the children, and from this day on while the children slept, she shed many tears at nap time, wondering why this had happened to her. She had tried to be a pretty good girl and not give anyone too much trouble. Here she lay with a very broken heart and a longing for her family that would never end. She would forever miss her dear brother Fubby. Her heart was indeed heavy, and she felt she would never be really happy again. Summer had always been the happiest of times. Now she felt so desolate.

The warm days of June arrived quickly, and all the children spent most of the time outdoors, except for rest time. Georgianna would be happy to skip that part, when all she did was cry and think about her family and cry some more.

Lakeside day finally arrived. All the children were excited as they entered the gate. The pool house and pool were nearby. Nora Napier, and the other older girls who were in charge, issued out bathing suits. Georgianna stood expectantly by, waiting for her bathing suit, when Nora said "You cannot go in the water. You may sit on the bench and watch the other children, and then you can ride some of the rides."

The swimmers were having fun as Georgianna looked around at all the interesting things: the giant Ferris wheel that was so high it looked like you could touch the sky if you were at the top, and the hobby horses that went round and round as the music played. There were even airplanes. She had never known there was a place like this. The smell of popcorn was in the air, and as she sat on the bench watching the people in the water, she hoped they would soon get out so they could get on a horse.

The smell of popcorn reminded her of the evenings back home. Thoughts of Dela came to mind and the vision appeared of the little girl walking down the road in the white dress. That vision would probably remain with her forever. Dela had probably forgotten her by now. Her thoughts were interrupted by Nora calling the children from the pool to dress and turn in their bathing suits.

The rides were fun, especially the hobby horses which were Georgianna's favorite. She was enjoying it all and learning that there was a lot she had to learn about the world. She was eager to explore. Her mind was inquisitive, as she realized she had much to learn.

The hot summer days dragged. Georgianna missed and thought of Fubby every day, wondering where he had gone, what he was doing, and if he missed her as much as she missed him. Never a day passed without thought of the family, especially Little Dela.

A new baby girl arrived, and that was something to be excited about. Having three babies to help care for would fill a little more of her time. Little Tommy was standing alone and had his airing in the play pen. Georgianna enjoyed her private time, sitting on the big wrap-around porch, keeping an eye on the little babies. No other children were allowed on the porch, and it seemed such a waste. When it rained, they all had to stay in the noisy playroom.

This private time kept her busy with her thoughts. Noona's little girl would be about the size of Beatrice, with her pretty dark hair and sky blue eyes, and she wondered where she was. The wild flowers would be blooming in the mountains, and the beautiful rhododendron would probably be blooming. It grew like trees along the road to Granny's house and all around Mountain Lake. It looked like a fairy land. She made up her mind that she would find all of her siblings when she grew up and could go places by herself. She would find them even if it took forever. One day she would go to Mountain Lake.

Georgianna was uncomfortable wearing her long black stockings and high top shoes all through the hot summer days, and she was glad when September arrived, and the early mornings were cool. Always before she had never wanted the summer to end. Things were so different now.

The older girls went to school, while the younger ones had a few hours of school in the playroom. Georgianna could out-read and out-spell them all. Only her arithmetic was not so good.

September became October, and just after breakfast on October 4, 1928, Georgianna was summoned to the office. Quaking in her high top shoes, she slowly made her way to the office, that she had become quite familiar with, going through every day for the babies' airing. "What have I done now?" she thought, dreading those black piercing eyes that looked clear through you. She knocked softly on the door. When she was invited in, she saw a slight smile on Mrs. Venable's face. This puzzled her even more.

"Well, well, sit down." Mrs. Venable motioned to the big chair, the one she had sat in when being corrected for letting out a secret. She could not think of anything she had done. Mrs. Venable shuffled through some papers. "Would you like to go to a real home, with a mother and father who have two children?" Georgianna just dropped her head. Fubby was gone, and it really did not make much difference to her. She knew she would have to go anyway. She loved all the children here, having spent the past eight months with them, and she did not like changes too well.

"I am sure you will like this nice home in the country, where you will be a member of the family and go to school," Mrs. Venable explained. "Mrs. Hopfield will send for you just after you have an early lunch. You will ride the train to Lynchburg. Someone will meet you there and take you the thirteen miles out into the country."

"May I tell the children goodbye?"

"Yes, as soon as you put on the new clothes that have been provided and have an early lunch. Just keep quiet until I call you."

Keeping quiet was hard to do. She ventured back into the playroom, pulled three year old Lily up into her lap and read her a story, while everyone was waiting for the time to go to the playground. She knew she would miss the children that had been her family for the past eight months. She was instructed to go to the kitchen, where her lunch had been prepared. She didn't feel much like eating.

Mrs. Jordan appeared in the doorway as the children were getting play things from the closet to take outside. "Georgianna, it's time to dress." The girl followed Mrs. Jordan through the big hallway that she had dusted for the last time.

The new blue dress that matched her eyes was on the bed, with a petticoat and new white bloomers. This was the prettiest dress she had since coming to the children's home. She thought about the beautiful white Hamburg lace dress that she had tried so hard to grow big enough to wear, knowing now she would never get to wear it. She must have been in a trance. Mrs. Jordan asked," Why are you dawdling? Don't you want to have a new mother and father?"

"I guess so."

"Well get your clothes on if you want time to bid your friends goodbye. Mrs. Hopfield will be here before too long."

Looking in the mirror and approving of her appearance, she went downstairs. As she entered the playroom, she saw the children lining up to go outside. All eyes were on Georgianna, and they knew she was leaving. She went down the line, giving each one a hug and a kiss on the cheek, knowing that she would never see them again. Little Becky Sanuer held on tight and didn't want to let her go. She loosened the child's grasp, and with tears in her eyes, she slowly walked to the office before she wept, having kept her promise to Mrs. Venable that she would not upset the children.

There was only a short wait until Mrs. Hopfield appeared at the door, wearing her navy blue coat suit. After a short conversation with the matron, she was handed a sheaf of papers. Mrs. Venable gave Georgianna an awkward hug, something she seldom did. Definitely she was not a very warm person. The young girl didn't think she would miss this matron. She would miss the kindly white haired Mrs. Jordan and the sweet babies, as well as all the children.

Carrying the brown bag containing a gown and a change of clothing that had been given her, Georgianna slowly followed Mrs. Hopfield down the walk to the same black car she had arrived in.

Conversation was very brief as they made their way downtown to the Depot where trains were puffing smoke, train bells were ringing, and black porters were carrying luggage. Lots of people were coming and going, some in line to buy tickets. "Where could all these people be going?" she asked herself. She remembered the many times she had sat on the store porch back home and watched the trains. The big arms that moved the wheels always fascinated her as did the big black engine with huge puffs of smoke and the red caboose at the very end with a trainman who always waved to her.

She knew she would enjoy the train ride even if it was taking her away from familiar people and places.

The all-aboard signal had been given for the second time. The train began to move slowly, and the conductor came through the train, "Tickets, tickets, have your tickets ready."

Before they were totally out of the city the conductor called, "Vinton, next stop, Vinton." This was a short stop, with only one passenger getting off and two boarding, and a mailbag was put on. The all-aboard was sounded and the train began to move once again.

Neither Mrs. Hopfield nor the girl was very talkative. They just sat and watched the scenery, with an occasional remark. "I think you will like this nice home that you are going to." Georgianna said nothing.

"Next stop, Montvale, Montvale." The mailbag was unloaded and two passengers boarded. "All aboard, all aboard," and the big steam engine moved out once again.

The leaves were changing, and Georgianna remembered her last train ride from Goodwin's Ferry to Roanoke. Fubby was with her then, and she wished he were with her now. It had been about a year since she had seen Dela. She would be a big three year old and had probably completely forgotten all of her family. She hoped she was happy and that Aunt Marilyn, cousin Marie, and Violet were taking good care of her.

The train sped along. The hills were pretty with the fall colors deepening. Then the train began slowing, and its whistle sounded. As they rounded the curve, the conductor came striding through the car, yelling "Bedford, next stop, Bedford." Several people gathered their belongings from over head.

Several people were standing on the platform waiting to board the train, as these got off. A mailbag was ready to be loaded. A lady wearing a pretty red hat and holding a small girl by the hand entered the car and sat down in front of Mrs. Hopfield. Once again the all aboard was sounded, and once more they were on their way. "When are we going to get to Lynchburg?"

"Well, Georgianna, we are about half way there. I know it seems like a long way. Each stop takes time. I think there are only two more stops, and we will be there. Your new mama will be waiting for you."

Once again the conductor strode through the railroad car, loudly announcing, "New London, next stop, New London." This was a small place, with few buildings not much higher than those back home. They were moving once again, the engine belching black smoke and cinders flying in the window and laying on the brown bag on Georgianna's lap. She had not cried like she did on the way to the children's home. She had enjoyed the scenery and, with apprehension, was looking forward to meeting her new family. Mrs. Hopfield would be getting the train back to Roanoke.

Another stop was announced, "Next stop, Forest, Forest."

"Now, Georgianna, the very next stop is where we get off. Are you excited?" Georgianna just dropped her head.

The train moved on. Not much conversation was evident. Some folks were reading newspapers and some just relaxing. An occasional whistle of the train was heard.

Buildings began to appear on both sides of the train. The uniformed conductor walked through the train. After reaching the last car, he turned and walked back, as he announced the next stop. "Lynchburg, next stop, Lynchburg."

Finally they were almost there. Georgianna's heart began to pound. "What if they don't like me?" she thought. The whistle had sounded, and the train bell was ringing, as they slowed to a complete stop. Mrs. Hopfield took her by the hand and helped her down the steps, hanging onto her bag of clothes. They walked across the platform where there was a pretty young woman with dark hair pinned in a bun at the back of her head, and standing by her was a young man. "Mrs. McDonald, this is Georgianna. I know you two will get along just fine. Say hello to your new mama." Georgianna managed a weak smile and tucked her head. "I will be in touch in a few months. My train is due in a few minutes, and I must visit the ladies' room." Saying goodbye, Mrs. Hopfield was gone, leaving the young girl with two complete strangers.

CHAPTER 28

The New Home

Georgianna assumed the man with Mrs. McDonald was to be her new daddy. She later learned that he was the hired man at the chicken farm where she would be living. As they rode along in the Model A Ford, Mrs. McDonald asked questions to which Georgianna just nodded her head and kept quiet. Her new mother pointed out the school that she would be going to with her new sister, six year old Bethany, who was in the first grade. Georgianna was not excited about going to school, but she knew she would go. The reason she was placed in this home was so Bethany would not have to go to school alone.

As they turned off the main road onto a dirt road, Mrs. McDonald showed the child a log cabin to her left, that Gramma lived in when she was in Virginia. "She is in Chicago going to school."

"Now why in the world would a Gramma be going to school?" thought Georgianna.

"Look at the goats by the goat house." After leaving the goat house they passed the cherry orchard and then lots of trees. "We call this the second grove." After the second grove on the right was the bare garden spot across from the pine grove, with a swing made from an automobile tire hanging from a limb. A huge yard surrounded a pretty white house, with chrysanthemums of various colors growing beside it.

The car stopped in front of the house. Bethany came out, holding her little brother, Bobby, by the hand, while he clutched a biscuit and jelly in the other hand. He was about Dela's age, and a wave of sadness crept over Georgianna. She just wanted to hide and have a good cry, knowing she would never see her little sister with the golden curls.

She looked up to see three black girls peering from the doorway. She had never been close to a black person in her life, having seen them only as porters around the train. She wondered if they also lived here.

Mamma and Bethany led the way to the room she was to share with Bethany. It was a pretty room with pink walls and white ruffled curtains at the two windows. One was called a dormer window because of the way it was placed sitting out from the roof. Mamma looked in the brown bag and took the nightgown and placed it under the pillow. Georgianna's eyes filled with tears. Mamma picked her up, sat her on the dresser and tried to cheer her up. She still had a good cry, and then she felt better.

Bethany brought her a doll to cuddle and said, "Let's go outside and look around."

"Go to the bathroom first." They went through the pretty dining room with a big round table and chairs, a huge sideboard and a pretty glass china cabinet filled with pretty dishes, then into the living room, where a piano was near the fireplace and a radio with a big speaker sat on a table.

All this made Georgianna think they must be rich. They ventured into the kitchen which was quite small. Bethany introduced her to the black lady who was ironing with irons like back home. "Georgia, this is my new sister, Georgianna."

"How do you do, Miss Georgianna." Bethany explained, "She has three girls, Minnie, Christine, and Frances, that help with the work."

"Do they live here?"

"No, silly, just in the daytime during the week after school, and on Saturday."

Georgianna wondered what Mamma and Bethany did and what her chores would be. Back home everyone worked. She soon learned that Mamma gathered flowers and fixed bouquets for the house, did a little dusting, played the piano, and embroidered dresser scarves and pillow cases. Bethany and Bobby just played most of the time. Mr. McDonald came from working on the pipeline. He gave Georgianna a friendly pat on the head and sat down to read the paper, while dinner was being placed on the table.

All the plates were stacked at the head of the table, and as they sat down to eat, Mr. McDonald served each plate and passed it around the table. This was new to Georgianna. The food was a little different too. Black folks must not cook the same. They had something called Jell-O that shook when it was on your spoon. That was dessert.

When the lamps were lit, Georgianna wondered who cleaned the lamp chimneys, probably the black girls. She hoped there was some work that she could do, never having spent all her time playing.

CHAPTER 29

The New Clothes and the First Day of School

Wen Mrs. McDonald saw that Georgianna only had one change of clothing, she knew something had to be done about that before she began school. She certainly could not wait until Gramma, who always did the sewing, came from Chicago. Georgianna had already missed the first month of school but was glad for a few more days until she had clothes to wear.

Mrs. McDonald contacted some of her friends who sewed. A group got together at Ruby Dillon's house, worked for two days and completed several dresses with matching bloomers. Georgianna liked the one with blue and orange flowers with the string tie at the neck. Now that she had a change of clothes for each day of the week, new petticoats and more black stockings, everything was ready for school on Monday morning.

Georgianna would be just as happy staying home, entertaining Bobby and helping Georgia with the housework. Monday morning found her and Bethany dressed and ready to walk down the road to the main highway, where they had a ride with Mr. White and his sister, Millie. He let the three girls off at school on his way to work in Lynchburg. Georgianna tried to feel excited, even if she was really was not.

She assumed that she would be in the first grade with Bethany since she had never attended school. After being introduced to Miss Ethel Tinsley, a very tall lady with jet black hair, Georgianna stood, awkwardly, wondering if she met Miss Tinsley's approval. She was not feeling exactly pretty, with her mousy brown hair that she wished had stayed blond, as it was when she was small. Even at this age she was conscious of her heavy legs, as Miss Tinsley looked her over from head to toe. Seeing all the small children in the room certainly made her feel out of place. "We need to talk to the principal. You look like a third grader to me."

After a short conversation with the principal, Georgianna was taken into a room with third and fourth grades. There she was introduced to a nice blond haired teacher, Mrs. Mildred McIvor. In her raspy voice, she introduced Georgianna to the class and seated her at a desk near the front of the room. She felt very shy and self-conscious.

A friendly girl named Mary Mills sat across from her, and Mary was asked to guide Georgianna throughout the day, showing her just what they were doing. After reading class, Mrs. McIvor commented on how well she read. Her shyness was a handicap when it came to making friends. She had made a start with Mary Mills, and she thought maybe school would not be so bad after all.

At the end of the school day the bell rang, and everyone lined up to march out of school, then scattered in all directions.

Bethany and Georgianna walked a short distance to the Elon General Store that was operated by Barney Campbell and his brother Percy, two kindly men about the age of Bethany's daddy and now hers. She was still not real comfortable calling the McDonalds Mama and Daddy. Never having called anyone Daddy, it would take some practice. Mostly she just didn't call them anything, having known them less than a week.

There was a couple hours' wait at the store until Mr. McDonald came from work and took them home. The first day of school was bearable, but not exactly enjoyable. Her new daddy gave her an affectionate pat on the head as they got out of the car.

CHAPTER 30

Adjusting

B ethany soon let Georgianna know that she was number one in the household, and even being three years younger didn't deter her from showing that she was the boss, or thought she was, and Georgianna was expected to do as she said. Nobody but adults had ever bossed her around, and Georgianna was unsure how to deal with it. Even though she was a passive child, she could not see being bossed by a girl who was only six years old. She decided to just ignore it and obey the adults, like she had always done. Bethany pouted over this and was continually threatening to tell Mama every little thing Georgianna did that was not to Bethany's liking.

Bobby was a sweet little boy and adored by the cook, Georgia. He followed her around like a puppy, and she catered to his every whim. Whenever he happened to step in the chicken manure, he ran to Georgia, "Clean it off, clean it off."

It became easier to call the McDonalds Mama and Daddy, but still very hard to accept the family as being really hers.

Before long Mama began to find little jobs for Georgianna. This pleased her to have something to do. She noticed that Bethany never had anything to do but play when she was not in school or doing homework from her books.

Georgianna was adjusting, things were going well in school, and she was making some friends. Report time came and the students were excited. Reports came out once a month. You were required to take it home, show it to your parents, have them sign it, and bring it back the next day. If you did not, you must stay in after school or at

135

recess, if you rode the school bus. Receiving hers and opening it up, she found she had an A in reading, an A in spelling, a C in arithmetic, and a C in writing. Mary Mills had told her an A was good. She wasn't sure how to take the C. Mama would know if it was good or bad. School wasn't so bad after all.

The autumn days had gotten colder, and Mama began talking about Thanksgiving. Georgianna had not seen any hogs. She knew there was not going to be any butchering. Then Mama said they needed to get a turkey. She wondered just what was going on. Then Mama was checking with Georgia about what she needed to get for the Turkey dressing. Now Georgianna was puzzled. Who would want to put clothes on a turkey? There was talk of cranberry sauce and baking fruit cake and pumpkin pie.

Georgianna assumed company was coming, but there was no party, only a big family dinner. Georgia had the day off, and Georgianna had all those dishes to wash.

As soon as the Thanksgiving holiday was over, everyone started talking about Christmas. Now this Georgianna knew a little something about, for they had oranges and candy back home at Christmas. When Mama began making a Christmas list, Georgianna wondered why she needed a list. Every few days, Mama went to town Christmas shopping after asking what everyone wanted.

Georgianna wanted a doll. She remembered the dolls her brother Billy used to bring her and she grew excited over the prospect of a doll. Bethany had several, but did not want Georgianna to play with them.

Gramma, who always had money, sent Mama money to do her Christmas shopping. Mama warned everyone that the green room closet was off limits to everyone but her. Every time she came from a shopping trip, she hurriedly made her way up the stairs with her arms loaded and headed for the green room closet, warning everyone not to open the closet door. There was lots of temptation to open that door and find out just what was in that closet.

CHAPTER 31

Georgianna's First Real Christmas

It was Christmas Eve, and excitement was high. A light snow was falling as Daddy came in from looking after the chickens and announced they were all going to look for a Christmas tree. Georgianna had never seen a Christmas tree and did not quite know what to expect. Everyone put on their warm clothes, and Bobby stayed at the house with Georgia. It took a while to find the right one. Mama said it had to be shaped just right, and Daddy said it had to be tall enough to touch the ceiling. Finally Mama spied the perfect one, Daddy wielded the ax, and it fell to the ground. It was getting dark and the snow was falling fast as they trudged back to the house with Daddy dragging the tree that left a pretty pattern in the snow.

Bobby was watching through the window when Daddy drug the tree onto the front porch to dry. No one dawdled over dinner. They wanted to settle down early and wait for Christmas. Mama read "The Night Before Christmas" and the Christmas story from the Bible and ushered the three children off to bed to get to sleep before Santa Claus came. Now Georgianna knew there was no real Santa Claus. He never came to see them back in the mountains.

She and Bethany had a hard time getting to sleep. They were both excited. They could hear a lot of activity going on downstairs, the rustling of paper and things being moved. They got out of bed, looked out the window, and saw the snow still falling and the ground and shrubs covered with snow. Before falling asleep Georgianna's last thoughts were of Dela, and she wished they could be sharing this Christmas together.

Before daylight when all was still quiet, Bethany began shaking Georgianna by the shoulder saying, "Let's get up, let's get up." Quietly they slipped to the window and found the snow had ceased falling and everything was covered with a soft white blanket of snow. They did not wake Bobby, but crept silently down the stairs in their long nightgowns, hoping the creaking of the stairs would not waken anyone. The reflection of the snow made the house light enough, and they felt their way through the dining room, trying not to bump into anything and wake the household.

They entered the living room. Georgianna's blue eyes grew wide. They could see the big tree in the corner. Furniture had been moved to make room. The tree was covered from top to bottom with pretty ornaments and shiny tinsel that glistened even in the dimly lit room. An angel in a white robe and golden hair adorned the tree top. Once again Georgianna thought of Dela and wished she could share this moment with her.

There were lots of packages under the tree. Georgianna began to wonder if there really was a Santa Claus. They crept quietly back up the stairs and climbed back in bed to wait until it was time to get up, whispering quietly, hoping Bobby would soon awaken.

They did not have long to wait for Bobby to appear at their door as the day dawned. They knew they couldn't get up, not until Mama and Daddy were awake. Daddy shouted, "Merry Christmas," as he headed for the bathroom, and Mama appeared in the doorway in her pink flannel nightgown. "I put the clothes out that you are to put on, and then you can all go downstairs at once." They hurriedly dressed, with Georgianna helping Bobby. It was a scramble to see who would be completely dressed first. Bethany had trouble tying her shoes. All three were ready about the same time. They let Bobby lead the way, since they had already had a sneak preview.

The tree was more beautiful now that daylight was here. Georgianna gazed wonderingly at all the things under the tree. She knew all of these things could not have been in that green room closet. There were two beautiful dolls, one dressed in white and one in pink, a blue doll cradle, and a red tricycle. Turning around, she saw three stockings hanging from the mantle. They were stuffed and running over. Georgianna had never seen anything like this in her whole lifetime. Thoughts of her other family members were with her once again.

Mama spoke up, "Aren't you going to see what Santa brought?" Georgianna joined Bethany, who was already into the packages. The doll in the white dress caught her eye, and she looked to find her name on it and picked it up, folding it in her arms. "I am going to name her Dela, and she can sleep with me every night." Looking at the blue cradle that also had her name on it, she felt this was enough Christmas for her. She didn't want to let loose of her doll, afraid it would disappear. Many other packages also had her name on them.

The three children were ready to see what the stockings held. They found candy, nuts, crayons, pencils and other items. Mama mentioned, "You are not to eat any candy until you have had your breakfast." Everyone helped to get breakfast ready, so they could open the rest of their packages and eat some of their candy. None of the children wanted to take time to eat. They were eager to get their packages unwrapped after they helped clean up the dishes.

Packages were unwrapped to find doll clothes, books, hair ribbons, and blocks for Bobby. Each child had a new sweater that Gramma had sent from Chicago. Bethany's was the prettiest, since she was Gramma's favorite. That did not bother Georgianna one bit. She was very content with all the lovely gifts. A tinge of sadness was with her when she thought of Fubby and Dela and wondered if they were having a nice Christmas.

By evening everyone was tired and just relaxed by the crackling fire in the fireplace, having had a big turkey dinner with dressing, gravy, and candied yams, with mince pie for dessert. Everyone helped to clean up the dishes. Bedtime found them tired and content.

The two girls had a whole week off from school, and they planned to make the most of it. They both enjoyed playing house with their dolls. Bethany had a table and chairs and a tea set, so they visited back and fourth, dressed their new dolls, and had tea parties, inviting Bobby to join them. Bethany wanted everything done her way. Georgianna did not always go along with her and set some of her own rules.

The time off from school went so fast, and it was soon time to be back in school and be doing home work. There was still play time after the homework was taken care of. Georgianna still did not have a lot of chores to take care of, and her thoughts often dwelled on Dela and her other siblings.

CHAPTER 32

Entertainment at the General Store

The days back in school seemed longer. On many cold days when no one could play outside at recess, they had some quiet games in the classroom and were excused to go to the outhouse located in the edge of the woods. Sometimes Georgianna had a hard time pinning her bloomers together at the waistband with a safety pin, her hands being stiff from the cold weather. She didn't like sitting in school all day and would be just as happy staying home. She was relieved when the school bell rang at the end of the day.

The wait at the General Store for Daddy or a bus going their way was rather interesting, with people coming in making purchases and swapping stories. Usually several people sat by the pot bellied stove, just staying warm and talking and laughing. Sometimes Bethany and Georgianna would join in a game of some sort. Often someone played a harmonica. Georgianna loved to dance and was cheered on by the folks sitting by the stove She often danced for their amusement.

Bethany said something to Mama about the dancing. Mama thought it was sort of showing off but didn't forbid the dancing. Georgianna continued whenever someone played the harmonica, and everyone applauded her.

Sometimes they had guessing games and the girls joined in. On one occasion different persons gave their initials and the others tried to guess their name. Mr. Percy spoke up, "My initials are H. P." It didn't take Georgianna long to pick up on this, and she announced in a clear voice "Handsome Percy." The room rocked with laughter. Percy

was not handsome. After things quieted down he said, "My name is
Herring Pidget, but I like Percy better."

The girls arrived home and Bethany immediately related the
incident to Mama, who was not at all pleased and commanded
Georgianna not to flirt with the men at the store. Georgianna did not
exactly know what flirting was. From then on she kept pretty quiet
while at the store. She did dance once in awhile, if someone was
there with the harmonica. Mama soon put a stop to that. This put a
damper on any self-expression.

Bethany appeared to delight in trying to get Georgianna into trouble,
one way or another always bringing up every little thing that happened
during the school day.

Georgianna was developing an inferiority complex, thinking
because she was an orphan maybe she was inferior to Bethany and to
the other children in school. Every time she had any fun, she ended
up being scolded. Many times she went to bed with a heavy heart.

Bethany had a birthday in January with a cake with seven candles
on it. Being seven years old, she was sure she did not need any advice
from ten-year-old Georgianna, who was not about to give her any
even when she needed it.

Georgianna kept firewood on the porch for the fire that burned in
the fireplace continually, mostly for that cheerful effect. A furnace
kept the house comfortably warm with radiators in every room.
Bethany never had any work to do. This made the ten year old feel
less like a member of the family and more like a servant. She was
often asked to sweep the porch or take care of some other chore around
the house.

CHAPTER 33

Gramma Comes Home

A letter had arrived from Gramma that she would be home in two weeks, and to have Hattie and Henry Bunton get the two hundred year old cabin cleaned up and have wood in, ready for her occupancy. She had given the big house to Mama, and when she wasn't traveling or in school, she stayed at the cabin.

There was much activity going on for the next couple of weeks. The big house got a thorough cleaning, so everything would be in order when Gramma came. The floors were all waxed and shining, and the furniture was given a high polish. Silverware had to be polished, windows and mirrors washed, and fresh scarves put on tables.

Mama had given Georgia a menu to follow for a good supper. Gramma liked good food served elegantly. The table had been set early, using the best tablecloth and the good dishes. The daffodils made into a pretty centerpiece for the dining table.

Dalor Ramsey, the hired man, had gone into town to the depot to meet the train bringing Gramma into town. The Model T was heard about the time it reached the second grove. At this time all six dogs began to bark, giving Gramma a noisy welcome. As the car pulled to a stop Mama, Bethany, and Bobby rushed out to greet Gramma, while Georgianna stayed on the kitchen steps with her head down. She was still very shy around the strangers.

Gramma lifted Bobby up for a big hug, and there was a lot of hugging and patting for Bethany Girl, as Gramma called her. Mama called to Georgianna, "Come and meet Gramma." Georgianna was in shock and could not believe this was Gramma. The only grandma she had known was her small grandma with the gray hair pinned in a bun, a large goiter in her neck, and wearing a long dark dress. This Gramma had short wavy hair, pink cheeks and rosy lips, and was wearing a dress that was up to her knees and a fur piece around her shoulders. She looked more like a Queen than a Gramma, as the ten year old walked slowly to her and received a hug and a fake smile. "I am glad to meet you. I've read about you in the letters."

Mama spoke up, "I see you have cut your hair. You didn't tell me." In the twenties only fast women cut their hair, and Mama was a bit shocked. Georgianna thought she would like this Gramma, having noticed how good she smelled when being hugged. She later learned that her perfume cost sixty dollars an ounce.

"You must stay overnight here. We have a lot of catching up on our visiting. Now Mama, I know you will want to freshen up before supper. Get what you need and leave the rest of your luggage for Dalor to take to the cabin." Gramma selected a satchel and as they walked into the house, she said, "I have something to take care of first." As she began to open the satchel, Bethany danced around, "I knew you would bring me something," as she reached for the package Gramma offered, yanking the wrapping off and looking disappointed that it was only a book.

She handed Bobby a round object. He was pleased it contained a ball. Bethany spoke up, "I told you she wouldn't bring you anything, because she didn't know you." Gramma reached into a bag and handed Georgianna a few pieces of candy. "Save it until after you have had supper." Georgianna was pleased that she was not totally left out.

Mama walked in the kitchen and spoke to Georgia. "Mr. McDonald will be late. We will have dinner, and he can eat when he comes."

"Yes, ma'am."

"Mrs. Crowe will be ready in half an hour." Georgianna had a hard time thinking this was a Gramma. She was nice and often gave Georgianna that little fake smile. The girl got the idea she did not think too highly of Grandpa. When talking to Mama in an irritated voice, Gramma said, "Your father this" or "Your father that," and Georgianna wondered what he was like.

Georgia soon announced dinner, and it was about like Christmas again, with the good dishes and lemon pie for desert. When dinner was over the two girls were instructed to get their homework done. Bobby followed Georgia to the kitchen, and Mama and Gramma went into the living room and closed the door. This habit of theirs continued for many years.

After breakfast Gramma made arrangements to have most of her meals at the big house, not enjoying eating alone. "I'll walk to the cabin as the girls leave for school. Henry Bunton is to meet me there, I want to put out a small garden. Peas need to be in the ground as soon as it is plowed and prepared." She was pleased to have this faithful black couple. They had worked for her many years. She paid them well and gave them many useful items that she no longer needed.

Georgianna was pretty shy around Gramma. They did not have much to say to each other, and the girl was not sure if Gramma liked her, even if she did give her that little fake smile often. She often talked to Bethany Girl, though, while just ignoring Bobby.

One day when she was sent to the cabin with a message for Gramma, Georgianna found her working in the garden, all dressed pretty and smelling good, and she thought that Gramma must be rich. She wore such nice clothes and kept her hair waved, her fingernails polished, rouge on her cheeks, and lipstick. She used a lot of big words this girl had never learned or knew what they meant. She talked about Chicago and studying dietetics. Georgianna learned this was about foods people eat. Back home, they just ate what they had and didn't do much talking about it. The girl began to realize that she had a lot to learn.

By late spring, Gramma was carrying a basket of fresh vegetables up to the big house a couple times a week. She walked from the cabin up the mountain three times a day, rain or shine. She always carried her flashlight in the evening, going to the cabin after dark many times.

CHAPTER 34

Spring 1929

Spring arrived on the mountain. Everywhere you looked, there was life. A litter of puppies attached to Bobby's long coat. It was a comical sight to see the little boy with six or eight puppies clinging onto his coat. Ducks were hatching, and many died. Funerals were held in the pine grove, with Bobby's makeshift hearse hooked to his tricycle to carry the corpses, which fell off at least a dozen times before reaching the grave site. Georgianna and Bethany carried the flowers and walked behind, helping to reload the corpse each time it fell off the board attached to the tricycle. As Bobby threw dirt over the tiny creatures, Bethany and Georgianna sang a couple songs, then placed the flowers on the grave and marked it with a head and foot stone.

Mama was occupied with her flowers and embroidery and a few small tasks. The black folks did the cooking, the laundry, ironing, and other household chores. Mama had not been taught to work while she was growing up, being a doctor's daughter. Maids had always done the work. She played the piano some, read quite a lot, did some embroidery, helped with school work, and looked through the seed catalogue to see what was new in flowers, looking forward to the day when she could get her rock garden underway, with the fish pond of goldfish.

May found Georgianna studying for the final exams that occurred every year just before school closed for the summer, and the grade that you made decided whether you should be promoted or failed and had to stay in the grade for another year.

Mrs. McIvor sent a note home with Georgianna to Mama, telling her that Georgianna had done so exceptionally well in third grade, that if she reviewed fourth grade material during the summer, she could probably go into the fifth grade in September when school began. Mama bought second hand fourth grade books, and the two spent time nearly every day studying.

Georgianna had a little problem when it came to geography, having made her own pronunciation for Africa and Europe when she was much younger. She still wanted to say Af raka and E rope. By the end of July she had things pretty well under control and looked forward to going into the fifth grade in September and being with older students, getting a little more ahead of Bethany who would only be in second grade, but who acted so superior and did not always want to share her belongings. That made Georgianna feel like she was not a real part of the family, and so she longed to see her siblings every day of her life.

What was happening to Dela was her greatest concern. Dela would soon be four years old and probably was not aware that she had a big sister who really cared about her. Once again her eyes filled with tears as she wept silently.

One evening at supper, Gramma remarked to Mama, "I think these girls could use some new dresses, don't you agree?"

"Well, they will need some before school starts in the fall."

"When I go to get my hair done on Saturday, you can go along and shop for material." It appeared that Gramma liked to stay busy and get things done.

The Saturday shopping produced material for two new dresses each. Bethany was to have a blue checked one and Georgianna a pink one, both made by the same pattern. Naturally, Bethany's was made first, and then it was Georgianna's turn. She didn't know it was going to be so complicated. Mama had always made her dresses without a pattern or much fuss made. With Gramma, it was a different story. First she had to fit the pattern on you, pinning it together. After getting the dress partly together, you tried it on, and she pinned it here, and she pinned it there, all the while saying, "Stand up straight. Quit fidgeting. Put your arms down. This has to fit right, if you want to look nice." She was very precise in everything she did. When the dresses were finished, they did indeed look good, with a row of three buttons on each side. "Now you just wear these dresses for Sunday until school starts. With each new dress it was a repeat performance. Nothing but a perfect fit suited Gramma. She always put deep hems in, so they could be lengthened as one grew.

Georgianna now had the job of helping take care of the chickens, and she was having some problems with Daddy that she could not talk to anyone about.

On Gramma's weekly trips to town, she always came back with several bags of candy from the dime store. All three children brought this special dish, and she issued out candy. Georgianna always thought that she sneaked a few extra pieces into Bethany's bowl, since she was her favorite. Each child tried to see who could make things last the longest and bring it out after the other two had emptied their dish and gloat a little bit.

Before the days had gotten cold, Mama began wearing a sweater over the big apron she had recently started to wear. It looked to Georgianna like she was going to have a baby. No one had mentioned anything about a baby, and she had not seen any baby clothes around. Only time would tell. She knew quite a lot about babies by now.

September arrived, and the school bells rang again. Georgianna felt proud to be going into the fifth grade with children more her own age and to making some new friends. Betty Mae Hudson was so nice to her and tried to explain things that were not clear to her. Arithmetic gave Georgianna a problem, and she would just as soon skip that part. However, at the end of the month, when report cards were given out, Georgianna rated some As and some Bs, but a C in arithmetic. Mama was pleased that both girls were doing well in school.

Mama helped Georgianna with her homework and tried to make her arithmetic easier to grasp. One evening as they were finishing up, while they were alone, Mama said, "I am going to tell you a secret. You are not to mention it to anyone. Next month there will be a new baby." The eleven year old girl was pleased at this news and looked forward to the baby's coming, hoping she could help care for it.

October days dragged and another favorable report card had been brought home. Georgianna still thought of Dela every day and missed her. Maybe this new baby would fill up her time, and she would not have much time for thinking sad thoughts.

The early fall days were warm. Knee socks had become in fashion. Georgianna was glad to be free of those horrid black stockings. Most of the girls were rolling their socks down to their ankles. Georgianna did the same and enjoyed the comfort of her bare legs, until Mama, after a visit to town, stopped by just as school let out, and with an angry look, questioned, "What are you doing with your socks down? Pull them up immediately. I don't send you to school to look like a tramp!"

This scolding really took the joy out of her day. School just wasn't any fun, and she didn't have much time to study, gathering the eggs, and doing the dishes. She knew she had to stay in school until she was old enough to quit.

CHAPTER 35

The New Baby and More Chores

On November 30, 1929, the children awakened to find that a baby boy had been born during the night. Mama named him Jimmy. The girls were so excited, they did not want to go to school. Gramma bathed the baby every day and took care of Mama for several days.

Georgianna now had another job. She was assigned the task of washing the diapers twice a day, before going to school and on returning in the evening. Mama had told her that she could not hold Jimmy until he was able to sit up. She could change his diapers, though, while he lay in the crib.

By the time school was out Jimmy was sitting alone. Georgianna was soon taking care of him, almost full time, giving him a daily bath, dressing him, and carrying him around, just as she had Dela. On one occasion at bath time, he began moving around and turned the box of baby power over in his face. This upset the eleven year old. Quickly she cleaned the powder from his face, his eyes, and around his mouth. He coughed a few times and continued to cough occasionally throughout the evening. Apparently he had a little powder in his air passages. Georgianna was too afraid to tell Mama what was causing him to cough, knowing that she would be scolded severely for letting it happen. Mama had been in a bad mood quite a lot and was forever finding fault with Georgianna. Nothing the girl did seem to please her. Bethany just continued her play and took delight in seeing Georgianna scolded.

School had begun, and this gave her several hours a day that she was not being scolded. Saturdays were busy, and her main chore was looking after Jimmy, who was a light sleeper, if you could even get him to go to sleep. You rocked him, you danced around with him, and when you thought he was fast asleep, you placed him in the crib, and he immediately let out a cry that would wake the dead. Then you started all over again.

Mama often gave the baby a pan and a spoon, so he could hit the pan and entertain himself. Today he decided to chew on the edge of the pan, then began crying. He had caught his teeth under the rim of the pan. Mama removed the pan to find blood around his two lower front teeth. Mama was furious. "I'll teach you a lesson you will not forget." Marching Georgianna into the dining room and shoving her into a chair, she picked up the girls' jump ropes and tied her hands to the chair and behind her back. Taking the other rope, she tied her legs to the chair. Georgianna sat there for hours, wondering why she was being punished. Mama had given Jimmy the pan.

This certainly was not Georgianna's best week. A few days earlier, she had lost a button off her pretty pink dress. Mama switched her until blood ran down her short chubby legs. She was in trouble no matter what she did. Everything was getting very confusing.

School was closed for two days for teachers' meetings, and Mama was in such a bad mood, she instructed Georgianna to take a note down to the cabin for Gramma. It was written on a sheet of paper and folded. Georgianna didn't see any harm in reading it. She was surprised to read, "Mama, will you keep Georgianna for a couple days? I can't stand the sight of her." On reaching the cabin, the girl smiled at Gramma, who was looking nice, and handed her the note. Gramma opened the icebox and gave her a treat. Then she sat down to write Mama a note, folded it, and handed it to Georgianna to deliver to Mama. The inquisitive girl opened the note and read these words, "Don't be so mean to this child. She is so much help. You could never find another like her." This made her feel better. At least Gramma appreciated her. She arrived at the big house and handed Mama the note, never mentioning that she had read both notes.

Georgianna had been given another job of gathering the eggs, and she knew it was trouble, if it was a day Daddy was off from work, and she had to go to the huge barn, made into a hen house.

Twice a week after everyone had gone to bed, she spent a couple hours in the basement washing and crating eggs. Daddy had been coming home late, and they waited dinner on him. Georgianna would entertain Jimmy until Mama was ready for bed, and then would take him to her. Then she would clean up the dishes and go to the basement. She was continually tired and felt like nothing was going right. Her alarm clock was set for four a.m. so she could check and make sure the lights were on in the hen house. Since Daddy had put in a Delco system, they now had electricity, and more light made the hens more productive. That meant more eggs to sell and more work for her.

Jimmy had begun to walk, and the door knob was removed from the door leading to the basement, so Georgianna had to go outside to get into the basement. Daddy usually slept in the chair awhile before going to bed. Usually he was still there when Georgianna finished crating eggs. This particular night he awoke. She could hear that he was locking the door that she needed to reenter the house. She called to let him know she was still in the basement. She could not make him hear her. When the eggs were finished, she took an old coat from the basement, curled up in the wicker rocker on the front porch, and managed to get a little sleep. Morning came, and as soon as she heard someone up, she pecked on the door. Mama opened the door. "What are you doing out there in the cold? You don't have the fire made." Georgianna explained what had happened and was made to feel as if it was all her fault.

Things were just not going well at all. A sharp eye had to be kept on Jimmy. Georgianna didn't know what would happen to her, if she let him get hurt. He was climbing on chairs and up the stairs, and had to be watched carefully.

Dinner was a little later every night, and tonight it was extremely late by the time the young girl took Jimmy upstairs. She wished she could go to bed, only there were the dinner dishes to do. Everyone but Daddy had gone to bed. After getting about half of the dishes washed, she took a coat from behind the door and spread it on the pantry floor to take a short nap. She had done this before. She was so tired, she went sound asleep.

When she awoke and looked at the clock to see that it was four o'clock in the morning, she was petrified. First she looked to see that the lights were burning in the chicken house. The fire had gone out.

Her dishwater was cold. The first thing she needed to do was build the fire to heat the water. She knew you could build a fire fast if you poured kerosene on your wood before striking the match. She picked up the kerosene can and poured some over her wood and turned to get a match. Boom, boom! Several eyes popped off the stove, and black soot went everywhere. A spark had ignited the kerosene.

All of this mess had to be cleaned up in addition to finishing the dishes. The fire was burning, and her dishwater was heating. She was going to have to hurry, if she was to have everything done before the family came downstairs. She worked fast and finished up and had oatmeal on cooking when the family got up. She dared not mention the night's events. She was hoping she could get to bed early tonight. She surely needed the rest.

Christmas was on the way, and there was much activity getting ready for the big yearly event. All she had asked for was clothing for her doll, Dela. She would be a lot happier if her sister Dela were able to share Christmas with her.

Gramma and Grandpa had come in bringing gifts and were going to be at the cabin for a week. After all the hustle and bustle and all the preparations, Christmas morning arrived. Georgianna didn't feel like getting out of bed. Her head hurt. She had butterflies in her stomach and felt weak when she stood up. She could not feel much excitement for this morning. Bethany and Bobby were dressing and making a lot of fuss. She put on her clothes and hoped she could make it down the stairs. The girl never mentioned to anyone that she was sick, knowing it would be her fault.

The tree was beautiful and lots of packages were stacked under it. She saw the new doll clothes but couldn't get excited. Mama said, "Go get some wood for the fireplace." She just stood still as a wave of nausea and dizziness came over her. Then Mama spoke harshly, "Go get the wood." Georgianna could not move. She crumpled into a heap on the hearth. That caused a lot of confusion. Someone wiped her face with a wet cloth, and she came to her senses and went for the wood.

Most of this Christmas day was spent doing only what she was asked to do. When Grandpa came up from the cabin with Gramma for dinner, Mama asked him to check Georgianna, telling him she had a fit that morning. Grandpa, who was a doctor, looked her over briefly and pronounced her to be all right.

With the big Christmas dinner over, there was a mountain of dishes to be washed. Georgianna was feeling terrible, but she managed to get the dishes cleaned up and was permitted to go to bed as soon as she finished. She knew she probably had flu and just fainted instead of having a fit, as Mama called it.

Her Christmas holidays were not good at all. She felt bad the whole time. She still had to watch after Jimmy and keep his diapers washed, as well as all the other chores she had to perform.

Georgianna felt better when school opened the day after New Years, and everything seemed to be getting back to normal. They had been in school for two weeks, when Mama spoke to Georgianna, "Mrs. Hopfield is coming for you later this month. I cannot keep you any longer." Noting the questioning expression on Georgianna's face, "Well, you are a thief and a liar, and you had that fit at Christmas. I just cannot keep you."

Then Georgianna remembered borrowing Grandma Lucy's tiny pen and then returning it, saying she didn't have it, which was the truth. She had already put it back where she had borrowed it from. This girl didn't quite know whether to be sad or glad. She really hated to leave little Jimmy, but she would be glad to get away from the abuse she had put up with.

The next week she kept busy getting all of her things together, stocking her doll clothes in her doll cradle, along with her two dolls, while she wondered what kind of a home she would be going to.

On January 22, 1931, Mrs. Hopfield arrived in a black car. She looked nice in her navy blue suit and white blouse. She was not an especially warm person, but appeared trustworthy, and Georgianna felt comfortable with her.

Georgianna was instructed to get all her dolls into the back seat, and place her clothing beside them. Georgianna was dressed and ready. Mrs. Hopfield had notified Mrs. McDonald of her arrival time.

Mrs. Hopfield followed Mama into the living room, and the door was closed. Shortly the two women came through the door, sad good-byes were said, and Mrs. Hopfield opened the car door for Georgianna. She walked around to the driver's side, sat under the steering wheel, started the motor, and they were on their way. There was very little conversation.

The landscape was dreamy looking, it being mid-winter, and Georgianna felt rather dreary herself. The twelve year old girl wondered what was in store for her now and what her new home would be like. Her heart was heavy, being separated from her second family and going she knew not where. She did know that it would not be with her brothers and sisters, who were scattered around goodness know where. Georgianna once again vowed that as soon as she was old enough, she was going to find them all and know something about what had happened since they had been separated for over three years. Mostly she was concerned about Dela and Russ and if they were being taken care of and treated right.

Chapter 36

Another New Home

It was late afternoon when Mrs. Hopfield pulled into the driveway to the Bardy home, where Georgianna would spend the next eighteen months before being moved again. "Mrs. Bardy, I have brought you another fine girl."

"Fine, always room for one more, I have always been partial to girls, and these girls make up for the ones Mr. Bardy and I did not have."

After introductions, Mrs. Bardy spoke, "Georgianna, what a pretty name. Ellen, show her the room, so she can put her things away. By the way, all the girls call us Aunt Lou and Uncle Jim, and you can call us that, too. Uncle Jim will be in from the barn for supper in a short while."

This was called a boarding home, where girls stayed until a more permanent home was found for them. Ellen had been there nearly a year, and Bertha Mae only a few months.

Georgianna liked it here immediately and thought she would just like to stay. All the girls were treated the same, and she felt happier than she had since having been separated from her family. The other two girls had been separated from their families, too.

Just before dark Uncle Jim came from the barn. Georgianna noticed he had only one hand. He explained to her that he had lost the hand in a corn picker many years before.

Having a room to herself was something new for the twelve year old, and she planned to enjoy it. Each girl had her own room.

The Bardy home was in the country on a busy highway and in sight of some other nice homes. The home had electricity but no running water. A bathroom had been built but was never used. An outdoor toilet stood upon the hill back of the house.

The three girls were joined by three others as they left for Clearbrook School, about a mile away, where first through seventh grade was taught, only one grade to a classroom. The girls talked a lot as they walked along the highway, being joined by other children on the way to school. Georgianna liked her new teacher, Mrs. Whitlock, and her school year went smoothly.

The girls helped Aunt Lou and Uncle Jim with the spring planting. They raised vegetables to take to the Roanoke City Market. Aunt Lou had butter customers that she supplied every Saturday when they went into town. The three girls looked around town for lunch. They could buy two delicious giant cinnamon buns for five cents at Michael's Bakery on the corner of Church Avenue and Market Street. She had never been allowed to do much looking around in Lynchburg. The previous summer the children had not allowed in town due to a polio epidemic. This new-found freedom was very unexpected as well as enjoyable.

Aunt Lou had a mother, two brothers, two sisters, and several nieces and nephews who lived a very short walk away. All had built on Aunt Lou's father's property they had inherited when he died. There was a well beaten path through the field between the homes after daily visits were made. Once again Georgianna felt like she was part of a real family. She called the folks Aunt and Uncle and felt like all the children were cousins. She loved them all, but felt very close to Aunt Lou's two nieces, Ruby Miller and Catherine Campbell. Ruby was her age. Catherine was a couple years younger. They shared their secrets, and spent lots of time together.

Overnight stays were frequent.

Aunt Lou and Uncle Jim attended Red Hill Brethren Church. Footwashing was practiced there. Aunt Lou had mentioned that she never felt satisfied until she was in a church where she could wash feet. She was a very humble person. Aunt Lou's sisters and brothers, with their families, attended Red Hill Baptist Church. Aunt Lou's girls preferred the Baptist Church and rode with Aunt Margie. Sunday morning and evening found most of the community in one or the other church.

The teenage boys and girls were taking notice of each other, and Georgianna was no exception. She began taking an interest in her looks. Not having money for make up, the girls used whatever was convenient to make them look better. They found that red crepe paper, when wet and applied to the lips, was a great substitute for lipstick, and a little soot from underneath the stove lid did a good job of darkening the eyebrows. Your hair could be curled by rolling it on rags and leaving it overnight.

At the beginning of summer, Bertha Mae and Ellen Taylor had been placed in another home, and Vergie Vance and Mildred Hartman had replaced them. They were both older than Georgianna.

Georgianna had been noticed by a boy by the name of Grover Harrison, who was sixteen years old. The other two girls had also found boy friends. The three guys would show up at the Bardy home on Sunday afternoon, and they all sat in the parlor and talked, doing more sitting than talking. Aunt Lou would offer them leftovers from the Sunday dinner. All were too bashful to eat at her house. They would walk to church for the evening services. That was all the courting that went on.

Georgianna had eyes for others. One was the Baptist preacher, who was twice her age. She really had a crush on him and called him her brown sugar from his tanned complexion obtained from farming in addition to preaching. She really felt in love. Occasionally she and the other two girls would be permitted to ride with him in his convertible, when he had been invited to Aunt Margie's for Sunday dinner. Aunt Margie was an old maid, who worked for the Silk Mill and lived with her mother. She always cooked a big dinner early Sunday morning and always invited someone from church to have dinner with her.

Georgianna claimed Aunt Margie as a close friend and enjoyed helping her mow her lawn and tend her garden. When going to the garden, they would carry a knife and a salt shaker and enjoy cucumbers and tomatoes fresh from the garden.

Georgianna still kept in touch with the McDonalds, writing them once in awhile. She still missed her siblings and wanted to find them all. However, she felt really comfortable here in this home and hoped she would never be moved. Eighteen months had passed and she felt fairly secure. Mrs. Hopfield visited the Bardy home every six months to see if there was any problem. The girls had been granted an allowance of fifty cents a week. That was a nice allowance in 1932. Her third visit brought bad news for Georgianna. She was devastated when Mrs. Hopfield excitedly exclaimed, "I have found a new home for you and will be coming for you next week. I'll phone Mrs. Bardy, so you can have all your things ready."

She had looked forward to this second summer taking walks with friends and all the other things she had done the summer before. She had taken care of Uncle Lloyd and Aunt Alice's young children, while Alice went berry picking, taking her older ones.

The decision had been made by the authorities, and there was no choice but to comply. Still, she secretly hoped something would change and she could stay where she was.

The phone rang, and Mrs. Bardy answered, "Hello," Mrs. Hopfield was on the other end of the line. Their conversation was short. Georgianna heard the words, "I'll see that she is ready on Thursday," and she knew immediately what that meant. Someone had given Georgianna an old suitcase, and she sorrowfully packed as many things in as it would hold and put the rest in a bag. She had washed her doll clothes and dressed her dolls and placed them in the blue cradle, along with all her doll clothes. She no longer played dolls, but wanted to keep them forever.

On June 28, 1932, Mrs. Hopfield arrived early in the morning, looking fresh and neat as she always did, still driving the black car that Georgianna had been in many times. Once again her belongings were placed in the back seat of the car, and she sat in the front seat after saying her sad farewells, wishing that it was Virgie or Mildred who were leaving instead of her.

Mrs. Hopfield explained, "You will be in a home where a nice couple have four children. One is about your age. They live in a mining camp. I hope you will be satisfied there and enjoy your new school in the fall." Georgianna said nothing, afraid if she tried to talk that she would begin to cry and look like a thirteen year old baby.

The black car rolled into a parking spot at the depot, and the two got out. Georgianna sat her battered suitcase down and placed the bag on top of it, as she pulled her doll bed with dolls out. "No, no, you cannot take all that on the train. You will have to leave it here. We will send it to you later." Georgianna was unhappy over this. That was the last time she saw her dolls or her blue doll cradle.

Georgianna was to make this train trip alone. Mrs. Hopfield saw her safely on the train and into a seat near the window. "Mr. Onkst will meet the train in Norton, Virginia, and take you to Bonnie Blue. I will keep in touch." With these parting words she was gone. The thirteen year old wondered what would be next as the "All aboard" was heard and the train began to move.

CHAPTER 37

A New Experience

The train moved out of the city and began to pick up speed. It stopped many times to discharge or take on passengers and pick up mail bags. The woodlands along the tracks were lush and green. The dogwood and red bud blossoms had faded and dew was visible.

The train ride was quite long. Eventually the train man came through the railroad car and announced, "Norton, next stop, Norton," and Georgianna gathered her things together, not knowing what to expect when she departed the train in this new town where she knew no one. She walked up the steps to the platform feeling very forlorn.

A gentleman in a business suit approached her. "Georgianna Marlow?"

"Yes, sir."

"I am Walter Onkst. I came to give you a ride. You are to live with my family."

Georgianna had always been warned of strangers and not to speak to anyone you did not know. She had no choice but to go with him. They entered a car with a driver, and he drove away from the railroad station the forty miles to Bonnie Blue, Virginia. They passed through a small community called Pennington Gap, stopping at a small restaurant for lunch. Another small place about twelve miles from Bonny Blue was called Saint Charles. As they drove into Bonnie Blue, Mr. Onkst pointed out the office where he worked and other places.

Georgianna wondered how people found their house. There were hundreds all built alike on the hillsides. Some were painted different colors. She had never seen anything like this before.

The driver took them to the gate. Mr. Onkst carried her bag into the house and called to his wife. "Bertha, she is here. I am going to the office for a couple hours."

"So you are Georgianna."

"Yes, ma'am."

"You are going to share a room with Janet and Lelia, who've gone to visit friends for the afternoon." They walked through the living room, where fourteen-year-old Freda was reading a book and scarcely noticed that anyone was there.

Mrs. Onkst was a slightly built, plain, dark-haired lady who appeared to always be in a hurry. It did not take the girl long to find out why. There was always work to do. "I hope you can milk. We have six cows and supply a lot of the camp with milk and butter. Milk is delivered every day."

"Yes, ma'am, I can milk, if the cow does not kick."

Mrs. Onkst had supper ready when Mr. Onkst and the three children came in. Janet was eleven, Emil was nine, and Lelia was seven. They were all friendly. Freda was fourteen and not too friendly.

The milking was done, with Georgianna milking two cows while Mrs. Onkst milked four. Every morning dozens of quart milk bottles were filled and capped and placed in carriers. Janet and Emil had the job of making deliveries. Churning was also done every morning with a churn that was connected to the washing machine, thereby saving some work. The butter had to be washed, printed and wrapped. Then the buttermilk was bottled and capped, ready for delivery. Needless to say the refrigerator stayed full of milk. There were always empty bottles to wash and milk utensils to clean. By the time you had the mess cleaned up it was time to cook lunch. Mr. Onkst came home everyday for lunch.

There was laundry to be done for seven people. Freda never did anything except try to be bossy and sort of stuck up. Georgianna mentioned this to Mr. Onkst, and he explained, "She had rheumatic fever when a small child, and it left her with a damaged heart. We just spoil her and don't expect her to do anything."

Staying so busy didn't leave much time for the girl to think about her feelings. Mr. and Mrs. Onkst were kind. Freda continued to be snobbish and hateful to Georgianna, never having a nice word to say to her. Mr. Onkst had received word that his sister had died in Kentucky.

Mr. and Mrs. Onkst left for the funeral and were gone two days. The first night they were away, Freda ran a high fever and had swollen joints. She had been instructed to stay in bed anytime this happened to lessen the strain on her heart. A makeshift bed pan was fashioned from an old cake tin, padded with a towel. Freda was glad to have Georgianna there to give her help when she needed it, and for once was pleasant to her. There was no real emergency.

The Onksts returned home carrying a three month old baby girl who was left without a mother when Mr. Onkst's sister died. Finding Freda still running a temperature, Mrs. Onkst phoned the doctor for instructions.

Georgianna was delighted to have this small baby to care for, and she became almost entirely in her care. No baby bed was on hand, and she spent the nights in Georgianna's bed. During the day she occupied a pallet in the middle of the floor. Caring for Dorothy Fay was almost like caring for Dela again.

Janet, Emil, and Lelia were in school, and Georgianna was supposed to be in school. She saw no way that she could be in school and take care of all the work that was expected of her. She did not attempt school. Mrs. Onkst did not pressure her. She really felt like the hired girl, but with no pay, only room and board.

Georgianna had developed teenage acne, that really detracted from her looks. Mr. Onkst was kind enough to make an appointment with his barber to give her a treatment once a week that greatly improved the condition.

School had been in session about six weeks when Georgianna received a letter from Mrs. Hopfield, expressing her disappointment that Georgianna had not enrolled in school as planned, and that it had been her decision.

Mrs. Hopfield drove down the following week to see what she could do. Georgianna explained, "These people do not want another family member. They want someone to do the work that needs to be done. I am really not at all happy here."

"Do you think that I could go back to the McDonalds?"

"Well now, I can contact them and find out how they feel about it. That may be a good idea."

Georgianna began to be excited about going back to the home

where she had spent two years. She had not called anyone else Mama and Daddy. She had been away almost two years. She hoped things would be different and that the Daddy had changed.

When night came and she snuggled up to little Dorothy Fay, her thoughts turned to Bethany, Bobby and Jimmy. She knew Bobby would be in school and that little Jimmy would not even know her.

Before a week had passed, a letter arrived from Mrs. Hopfield saying the McDonalds would like for Georgianna to come and make her home with them. She was making arrangements for Mr. Onkst to put her on the train in Norton, and she would meet her in Roanoke.

Partings were always difficult for the girl who had recently passed her fourteenth birthday. Leaving this baby girl that she loved would make her sad. Leaving the milking and other things would be a welcome change.

Once again, her clothing was put into the battered suitcase and the remainder in a box, and she was ready to leave. Mr. Onkst did not own or drive a car. He hired a taxi to take them to Norton, forty miles away, where he bought her ticket and her lunch and waited with her until train time. As the train chugged into the depot, Mr. Onkst spoke gently, "I am sorry to see you leave and hope you will be satisfied at the McDonalds." She stood awkwardly, not knowing what to say. He gave her a slight hug, helped her onto the train, placed her suitcase overhead, and sat her box at her feet. She managed to wave to him after he descended the train steps.

The train ride to Roanoke seemed much shorter than the one to Norton four months earlier. Lee County where Bonny Blue was located was not a very pretty place, consisting of several coal mines, and in the fall it looked quite desolate. Georgianna felt better the closer she came to Roanoke and some familiar sights. She would really like to be going back to Aunt Lou and Uncle Jim's, but she knew this was not the plan. Anyway, she would not be going to a group of strangers, and that was some comfort.

Mrs. Hopfield was waiting for her as the train slowed to a stop. The porter helped Georgianna from the train, Mrs. Hopfield carried the battered suitcase to the black car, and once again the items were placed in the back seat. They stopped in a small restaurant for lunch before leaving for Lynchburg.

CHAPTER 38

Return to the McDonalds

They arrived at the McDonalds' home a short time before Bethany and Bobby returned from school. Mama greeted them with all smiles and appeared to be genuinely glad to see them. Little Jimmy came running, his golden curls bouncing and glistening in the sunlight. Spotting strangers, he slowed his pace and ducked behind his mother. Mrs. Hopfield and Mrs. McDonald walked into the living room, after Georgianna was told to take her things to the room she had shared with Bethany before.

Bethany and Bobby returned from school just as Mrs. Hopfield was slipping under the steering wheel. They were excited and glad to see Georgianna. Georgia, the cook and laundress, had the day off. She no longer worked full-time.

Georgianna helped Mama to prepare dinner. This just happened to be Daddy's birthday. A special dinner was planned. While they were working together, Mama halfway apologized for sending her away, saying, "After you left here, we really missed you. It was just as if someone died. We did have another girl here, named Thelma. All she did was cause trouble. Everyone was excited that you wanted to come back."

Georgianna had not thought about it being Daddy's birthday when she arrived on the mountain. It was November 7, 1932. When he came home from work, he gave her a bear hug. "What a great birthday present this is." Now she began to think that it may have been a mistake to come back.

The following day, after Jimmy reluctantly settled down for a nap, Mama invited Georgianna into the living room for a private conversation. "I am so glad that you have come back. Mrs. Hopfield and I agreed that since you have missed two months of school, you will stay out of school this year." I am glad that you have come back at a real important time."

Before Georgianna could think what was so important, Mama continued, "There is going to be a new baby here by the end of March." This was a delightful surprise. Nothing pleased this girl any more than caring for a baby. She hoped the winter would fly by.

Very few weeks had passed before Georgianna knew her foster father had not changed at all, and that constant dread was always gnawing at her. She still felt she had to do whatever was asked of her, and there was no way to escape.

Christmas came with the usual excitement. Georgianna was happy with some new clothes, dusting powder, and tangee lipstick.

No one mentioned that a new baby was coming. There was no shopping for baby clothes. Mama was wearing a huge apron and always a sweater to conceal her condition.

In the twenties, people were very discreet about private matters, even among family members. Georgianna knew that Bethany and Bobby had been told. Everyone was just keeping their own secret. Mama never went anywhere.

Gramma had come home after spending time with Grandpa. Mama prepared a list for her, and she made a trip into town and came back laden down with many bundles. She and Mama walked into the living room and closed the door. Later Mama carried the packages upstairs and put them away without showing anyone. Georgianna assumed they contained baby needs.

CHAPTER 39

Pegatty's Arrival

Blustery March arrived with gusty winds, snow squalls, sunshine, and showers, and each day kept one wondering when the new baby would arrive. When only one week was left in March and still no baby, Georgianna was sure something must be wrong. She continued to keep Jimmy entertained. Often Mama just asked her to go and amuse him when she was halfway through washing dishes. She complied and finished the dishes later.

The four children were excited on awakening on March 25, 1933, to the cries of a newborn baby. Eight feet headed for the room from which the cries came, only to be stopped by Virginia Shirey, a practical nurse, who had moved in earlier to await the baby's birth. "You will have to wait awhile to see your new sister." Everyone was pleased that it was a girl.

Miss Shirey stayed until little Pegatty was ten days old and Mama was out of bed and ready to do little things around the house.

Mama liked children when they were old enough to take for a walk, but did not enjoy taking care of babies. By the time Pegatty was two weeks old, she had been placed in the care of Georgianna, much to the girl's delight. The baby was being breast fed and had to be taken to her mother every four hours to be fed. Georgianna had been cautioned to support the baby's head, something that she already knew.

Pegatty grew sweeter every day, and her caretaker was in seventh heaven, bathing and dressing her every day and keeping her clothes washed. She also performed chores when her charge was napping.

Mama was a great lover of flowers and many shrubs bloomed in the spring. The lilacs scented the air with their fragrance. The apple orchard was a sea of pink and white. Georgianna would carry a quilt and spread it under the apple tree, place Pegatty on the quilt and sit by her for hours, sometimes weeping for the sister she had lost, but never giving up the idea of finding her. She tried to be cheerful as she listened to the birds chirping, the bees humming throughout the orchard, and sweet little Pegatty cooing by her side. It was a mixture of sadness and happiness. She knew the day would come when she would locate all of her family.

Pegatty was small and fair, with dark hair that curled easily, and by summer's end, she was sitting alone and sporting a few curls with a ribbon. She was a delightful, quiet child, and very easy to care for. Georgianna took great pride in this precious little girl who filled a void in her life. She was much happier than she had been in a long time, never losing sight of the fact that the time would come when she would go looking for her beloved sister.

CHAPTER 40

Measles Strikes the Family —
Fall of 1933

O nce again school started and no one mentioned that Georgianna should enroll. She did not mention it either, being content with what she was doing and not about to volunteer.

Nearly every day when Bethany and Bobby returned from school, Bethany reported who was out of school with the measles. The McDonald children had escaped them the previous year. Georgianna had not had the measles either.

It was no surprise when Bobby came home from school with a flushed face, watery eyes, and a runny nose, saying, "My throat is sore."

Mama came up with a favorite expression, "Ah me, let me see your throat. Say 'Ah'." Bobby spread his mouth, as Mama took a good look. "You are coming down with the measles. Go upstairs and get in your pajamas." The following morning he was feeling worse, and by the third day he was sporting a very red rash.

Just as Bobby's rash was fading, Bethany awoke calling, "Mama, I don't feel good. My throat hurts."

"Ah me! I expect these measles will spread through the whole family," Mama sighed.

Georgianna tried to keep Pegatty away from the sick ones. She was so little, and Georgianna herself never remembered having measles. She had heard that you were much sicker when you were older, and she was already fifteen years old.

168

Jimmy was next, and being somewhat spoiled, he claimed a lot of Mama's attention, not wanting her to leave him for a moment. Needless to say, Georgianna was continually busy with the many extra things to be done when there are sick folks.

Before Jimmy began to feel better, little Pegatty felt warm and was beginning to be fussy, not wanting to drink her orange juice, waking from a short nap very fussy, not at all like her usual good-natured self. Georgianna had waited on Bethany after Jimmy had demanded Mama's time and was afraid she may had carried the germs to the baby. She had been careful to wash her hands good, hoping Pegatty would not have measles at such a young age.

Little Pegatty was cranky and not sleeping well, very feverish and having to be held and rocked a lot. She had developed a rash and now was sleeping a little better. Georgianna awoke with a sore throat, headache, and just feeling terrible all over. She dragged through the morning's work, washing Pegatty's clothes and hanging them in the pantry to dry, trying to keep Pegatty comfortable and quiet, while Mama devoted her time to Jimmy. Georgianna had not mentioned that she was sick.

After she rocked the baby to sleep, and Mama had lain down with Jimmy, she quietly slipped down the stairs to get a cold drink of water to ease her burning throat. As she entered the kitchen, Georgia took one look at her and said, "You got it too."

"I am afraid so. I need a cold drink." She filled a cup with water and started through the dining room to go upstairs and lie down. Georgia heard the noise as Georgianna crumpled to the floor in a dead faint, spilling her cup of water.

"Mrs. McDonald, Mrs. McDonald, Georgianna fainted." At all the commotion, both children were awakened and began to cry. Mama came down the steps just as Georgianna was coming out of it. "What have you done now? Just when things were quiet!" Mama was very angry with her for waking the children and for getting sick.

The old feeling of not belonging returned. Mama had not gotten angry at the other children for getting sick. She certainly did not plan to be sick and had no control over it, and knew she was just a nanny for Pegatty and not a real member of the family.

Mama was certainly in a bad mood, because she had to look after the two young children, as well as do some things for Georgianna who was very sick for several days. Measles could cause some trouble if you were not careful. Blindness from too much sunlight, ear infections, and sometimes deafness.

Georgianna was glad to be feeling better after four days in bed. Both small children had fully recovered, and Bethany and Bobby were settled back in school. Things returned to normal.

Thanksgiving was over with and the Christmas rush was on. When Georgianna was asked what she wanted for Christmas, her only desire was a guitar. She had always wanted to play one and loved string music. December was, as usual, a busy time with shopping, and baking fruit cakes and other goodies. Then everything settled down for the drabness of mid-winter.

While Pegatty napped, Georgianna kept busy. The front porch had to be kept stocked with wood for the fireplace, that burned constantly. She kept her own as well as Pegatty's clothes washed and their shoes polished. And she took care of the evening meals, since Georgia was not in real good health and usually went home by mid-afternoon.

February had arrived, and it was very cold. However, the Jasmine was sporting its yellow blossoms. You knew spring could not be far behind and the forsythia would burst forth in a sea of golden colors. Mama's tulips and daffodils would be filling the rock garden with varied colors, and along with spring, there was renewed hope that Dela would be found before the year was gone.

March was ushered in on a gale of wind and would bring with it Little Pegatty's first birthday. She was already standing alone. Georgianna knew the easy time of caring for her was over. She would constantly need to be on guard to ensure this child's safety when she began to explore and climb on everything in sight. Remembering what had happened a few years ago, when she was tied to a chair for the day after Jimmy's episode with the cook pot, she surely did not want to go through that again.

Everything was going along quite well. While Pegatty napped, often Jimmy needed to be entertained, and that job fell to Georgianna. Some of her work just had to wait until everyone else had gone to bed for the night.

Mrs. Hopfield had discontinued her yearly visits. She did correspond occasionally with Mrs. McDonald, who assured her that everything was going well and that there was really no need for her to make the trip, unless they needed to discuss a particular problem. Georgianna did not tell everything that she knew, not wanting to be moved again now that she had little Pegatty to fill the void left by Dela. She was feeling a lot happier with this time-consuming responsibility. Caring for this child was a real pleasure, and she surely did not want to move again.

Mrs. McDonald received a letter in early summer from Mrs. Hopfield, bringing up the subject of Georgianna getting back in school for two years. Georgianna hoped Mama would just forget about that. Why should she go to school? She could read, she could write, she could sew, cook, and care for children. She could wash and iron. What more did one have to learn? She knew that she would have to do whatever she was told.

CHAPTER 41

The Unsuccessful Venture
and More Work

Shortly before school began, Mama suggested that Georgianna return to school, and Georgianna agreed, even if it would mean she would be the oldest one in the eighth grade. She had managed to catch up before and probably could again, if she had the opportunity.

The family was excited about the new school year, and every morning the three rode to school as Daddy went to work in Lynchburg. He had started his own feed store on Colling Street, in addition to the chicken and eggs business, and more money was available.

The first week of school went very well, but Georgianna was not able to spend much time with her books. Every evening she had Pegatty's diapers to wash and to look after the one year old and help with Jimmy. The alarm was still set for four a.m., so she could check on the lights in the hen house. The new girl that had been hired to help Georgia was no cook, and Georgianna often had to prepare the evening meal which was often served about nine o'clock. The dishes then had to be washed. Bethany was supposed to help, but invariably had to go to the bathroom, and by the time she returned, Georgianna had everything done.

The short nights and the busy schedule were catching up with Georgianna, and she was constantly exhausted. Mama was a continual grouch, having to look after both young children all day, and things were just not pleasant.

Georgianna found it impossible to earn good grades with lots of hard work at the McDonalds'. After a month of school, Mama and Georgianna agreed that she should discontinue school and look after Jimmy and Pegatty. Mama's disposition improved immediately, and things ran smoother. Georgianna noticed that Mama did not enjoy caring for small children like she herself always had done.

Thanksgiving and Christmas came and went with the usual hubbub of the holiday season. The days were busy, and three times a week eggs had to be washed and crated after everyone had gone to bed. Seldom did Georgianna have any time to herself. There really was not much time to dwell on whether she was happy or unhappy.

February brought some extra work. The nanny goats were having their kids, two at a time, and as Gramma came by the goat house on her way to the big house, she noticed the nannies were not feeding their kids. She reported, "The baby goats are starving. They will soon die in this cold weather without food."

Mama decided to let Georgianna handle the situation. The next day, when Pegatty was put to bed for her nap, Georgianna filled the wheelbarrow with straw and made her way to the goat house, where she found eight very weak kids. She gently placed them on top of the straw, noting one appeared to have a neck injury and could not hold his head straight. He was dubbed "Ole Side Neck." The girl had to struggle to push the wheelbarrow, with its heavy load, a good half mile to the barn, where she placed them in a warm shelter.

Pegatty awoke from her nap just as Georgianna finished filling quart gingerale bottles with warm milk, using old nipples to cap them. She dressed Pegatty in warm clothes and borrowed Bobby's red wagon. When the baby and the bottles of milk were in place, the two headed for the barn to feed the kids. Pegatty enjoyed watching the hungry kids devour the milk. This procedure was repeated twice daily for several weeks.

"Ole Side neck" always had some extra attention and was able to keep up with the rest of them. This project kept them busy and got them out into the fresh air regardless of the weather.

Pegatty had her second birthday and was chatting like a magpie, always wanting to know the why of everything. Georgianna sadly remembered that Dela was just this age when she had last seen her such a long time ago. Once again she resolved to find her this very

summer. Daddy had promised that when she grew up, they would go
to look for her, and she felt like she had grown up. He really owed it
to her. She was going to hold him to this promise. A feeling of happiness
enveloped her.

The kids had grown enough at green up time for them to be put
back in the goat pen to graze with the big goats. Georgianna felt like
it had been a worthwhile project when she saw them scamper over
the hillside, enjoying their freedom.

Mr. McDonald's feed store was doing well, and the family could
afford more material things. He had hired a builder to add to the
house a new bedroom, a new kitchen and an addition to the basement.
The present dining room was expanded as partitions were removed
from the kitchen and pantry, making one huge dining room with all
new flooring that was waxed often. The young folks tied rags on their
feet and skated to polish it. This made a terrific dance room, and with
the local musicians playing string music, a dance wad held
occasionally. Georgianna had learned to dance many years before and
enjoyed dancing with the older men. Few young men were present.

Now that Daddy was making more money, the family had a washing
machine and a pyrofax gas stove was in the new kitchen. One early
spring evening, the family thought they were getting company when
a pretty gray car drove up the road. Taking a second look to see who
it could be, Mamma was surprised to see Daddy's smiling face as he
got out of the car and headed for the house.

"How you like it?"

"It's pretty. Whose is it?"

"It's mine, of course." By that time everyone had gathered around
to join in the excitement. It was indeed a pretty metallic gray,
streamlined DeSota. Daddy offered everyone a ride around the small
community. It took little encouragement to get them all in the car,
with Jimmy sitting up front with Mama and Daddy. They stopped at
Franklin's store to proudly display the new car. Daddy bought everyone
a bottle of pop. The first few days, everyone offered a name for the
new car. The suggestions were Grey Mist, Silver Streak, and others.
Eventually it just became "the new DeSoto" that Daddy took great
pride in.

Georgianna put her thinking cap on and came up with the idea that this might be the perfect time to ask to go search for Dela. Daddy was always wanting to give someone a ride. She was sixteen and felt like she was grown up enough to begin looking for her family. After talking it over with Mama and asking Daddy about making the trip, a date was set, and Georgianna excitedly wrote Aunt Marty in time to get a reply.

Aunt Marty's letter arrived stating that it was all right to come on the specified Sunday in June. Georgianna tingled with excitement and could hardly keep still. The excitement kept her awake late at night.

Saturday evening found her navy eyelet dress ironed and her shoes polished. Her hair had been rolled up. She wanted to look nice for Dela.

CHAPTER 42

The Search for Dela

Georgianna was surprised to learn that Gramma decided to go with them. She had thought that it was just curiosity to see how Aunt Marty lived and just how poor she was.

Sunday morning was bright and sunny. The cow was milked, and Pegatty was fed and dressed. Georgianna had donned her navy blue eyelet dress and had brushed her hair and applied her tangee lipstick. She thought her reflection in the mirror looked nice, not exactly pretty, but nice.

Mama and Bethany were excited that Georgianna was going on a search for Dela.

Daddy and Georgianna picked Gramma up at the cabin, and Georgianna moved to the back seat. Gramma was immaculately dressed, as usual, having had her regular Saturday appointment with the hair dresser and manicurist, as well as the palm reader.

Georgianna kept her thoughts to herself as they drove over roads that she could not remember having been on before. Daddy was using a road map and she felt like she could find Aunt Marty's house whenever they arrived in the area. It appeared that it was taking forever to get where they were going. Daddy had never been in that area before, and he just took his time enjoying the scenery.

Georgianna's excitement mounted as she recognized the road across from the little country store in Newport. "There's the road, there's the road."

"What road?" was Daddy's quick reply.

"The road through Spruce Run and on to Goodwin's Ferry."

"Ok, here we go."

Over several miles of dusty road, Gramma complained about road conditions and all the dust, remarking, "These folks sure live out in the boondocks. All the houses sit on a hill. I don't see how they even keep from falling out of the yard. I surely hope that it is not much farther because my girdle is killing me. I'm not used to sitting so long."

After driving a couple more miles, they saw a man leaning over the fence dressed in bib overalls and a tattered straw hat. Daddy stopped to ask, "Are we on the right road to the Meredith's?"

"Which ones? There's right many live in the area," and he rambled on about which ones lived here and which ones lived there. "You must be a stranger in these parts."

"Yes, I am, but I have a passenger that was in the area several years ago."

"Sure a fancy car you got, Mister. Hain't never seen one like it."

"Ell Meredith's is the place that I am looking for. Do you know him? He's an uncle of my passenger."

"I've known him from way back. You ain't too far from his place. I grew up with good ole Ell. They live in the little white house on the hill overlooking the New River—a small white house on your left. You can't miss it."

"Thanks for your help."

Gramma was fidgeting, "I don't know why we are on this wild goose chase anyway; looks like a lot of foolishness to me. What are you going to do when you find this girl?" There was silence as Gramma cleared her throat. "This dust certainly is hard on your throat."

They drove a few more miles more. Daddy remarked how rough the road was, as the small white house came into view, looking much smaller than Georgianna remembered. "I see the house! I see the house!"

"I see it too, but how in the devil do you get to it.?"

There were houses on each side of the road all sitting on a steep hill. "The horse and buggy always went up this next road on your left," Georgianna said. The DeSoto shivered a little as it moved on over the rough road that appeared not to be used very much, and Daddy could not make much speed.

They came to a road that Georgianna recognized as the road that led up to the house. "This must be it, since you can see the river from here," she said, as they came to a narrow road leading up the hill to the small house.

As they approached the house, Georgianna thought it really looked small but was recognizable. She eagerly opened the car door and was met by an old brown hound dog, who wanted to be a little too friendly. Uncle El came out of the door onto the porch, calling the dog and eyeing the car suspiciously, never having seen one just like it.

Daddy got out of the car, as Gramma was opening the door on her side. Mr. McDonald spoke, "Is this the El Meredith residence?"

"I reckon so. I been living here near about twenty two years."

"I've brought you a visitor."

"Oh, that stubborn youngun. Youse come in the house. The old woman is sick in the bed."

Georgianna eagerly rushed to her Aunt's bedside, expecting a loving hug. She had waited so long for this moment to see some of her family, only to be greeted coldly without even a warm smile. She was truly let down. Uncle El spoke up, "This is one stubborn girl, don't you agree, Mr. McDonald?"

"Well, frankly, I do not," Daddy said.. "If all were as good as she, I would like to have them all."

"Well she was stubborn the few months that she stayed here."

Gramma kept quiet after being introduced, having very little to say the whole time and acting a bit grouchy, like she thought it was nonsense for Daddy to be going to all this trouble to help find Dela. She had been an only child, so could not possibly know how much this meant to a girl who had waited so long to locate her family. Georgianna knew she would not find the two year old with the dancing golden curls, but a girl who would be nine years old and would net even recognize her. The terrible thought came to her, "What if they could not find her?"

After a bit of small talk, Mr. McDonald spoke up, "The real reason we are here is to try to find the baby sister, Dela, and maybe locate some of the other siblings."

Aunt Marty was sick and kept pretty quiet, letting Uncle El do most of the talking. She only answering a question if one was required.

Good smells were coming from the kitchen, where Midge and Elsa were busy getting a company dinner. Georgianna hoped Midge's good caramel cake was on the menu.

Uncle El spoke up, "Dela stayed with Marilyn for a couple years and was here for awhile. After she left here, I think she was put with a woman at Bane."

Mr. McDonald asked, "Where is Bane?"

"Oh! it's not far. I think Midge has dinner about ready, and after dinner, I'll go with you so you won't get lost in these hills. Hey Midge, is that grub ready?"

"In just about fifteen minutes, Poppy." Shortly Midge appeared with a tray of food, which she placed on a chair by Aunt Marty's' bed. She announced, "Dinner is ready," as Elsa swatted at a fly.

Uncle El said, "Just take a chair and make yourself at home," as he helped himself to a generous piece of chicken and passed it to Daddy. Mashed potatoes and green beans followed, as did sliced tomatoes and cucumbers and onions. Everyone was too busy to talk, and just as everyone was about full, Midge appeared with her cake with the caramel icing and dishes of sliced peaches.

As Uncle El pushed his chair back from the table, he remarked, "I reckon we better get going, lookin' for that youngun." Georgianna was more than ready. Her excitement was almost more than she could handle. After all these years her dream of finding Dela was about to come true, and she was eager to be on the way.

As they drove down the hill, Georgianna spied the railroad tracks that ran along the New River at Goodwin's Ferry. In the distance across the river, high on a hill, stood the Sanuer's house. She remembered that they had wanted her to come live with them, and she refused to leave Aunt Marty's and Fubby. All this familiar scenery brought many memories and much longing to fulfill her dream of finding her family.

A cloud of dust rose behind the DeSoto as they traveled along the country road, which seemed long because the anxiety was so great. Eventually a sign was spotted: Kimbalton 1 mile. "Now I think Bane is not far away," Uncle El wryly announced. "The woman's name was Mrs. Boggs, and I think she is the only Boggs in these parts. I'll just have to look for a mailbox, so drive slow, Mr. McDonald, and we should find it soon."

A large white house stood on a hill, and they approached a mail box along the road with the name Boggs crudely written on it. "Well now, this must be the place, so just drive up the hill and see." Uncle El slowly made his way to the front door of the large neat frame house. After knocking loudly several times and getting no response, he ambled back to the car. "Nobody home. We'll check at the house across the road. I saw some folks on the porch as we drove by."

The gray DeSoto parked near the front porch, and the dogs began barking as El got out of the car. "Ma'am, call your dogs off. I just want some information. Do you know where I could find Mrs. Boggs?"

"Yes, sir, I expect you could find her in the county jail in Pearisburg. She was arrested for beating that little girl up that she was keeping for the welfare."

"Where is the girl now? I think they took her to a lady in Narrows, a Mrs. Chambers, who keeps children sometimes."

"Well thank you kindly."

Talking as he got in the car, El said, "She is at the Nars," his pronunciation for Narrows. "A small place. We will have no trouble finding it." Georgianna was getting fidgety. Time was passing, and they still had not found her. Georgianna was getting very uptight. What if they did not find Dela after getting this close? Her tension mounted.

After driving what seemed like a long time, but was really less than twenty miles, a sign beside the road read Narrows. "Well, here we are at the Nars," spoke Uncle El. "Stop at the next house on your right, and they can probably tell us just where the Chambers live. Everyone here knows everybody."

Gramma cleared her throat, and was probably thinking, "What a dump!"

Georgianna thought her heart would sure pound right out of her chest, she was so excited, as the lady on the porch gave directions to the Chambers home which was easy to find. Everyone got out of the car and approached the door, as a young child scampered into the house.

Uncle El rapped loudly on the door, and a middle-aged lady in a blue dress and a friendly smile on her face answered the knock. "Howdy, ma'am, you Mrs. Chambers?"

"Yes sir, I am. Can I help you?"

"Do you have a girl about nine years old living here by the name of Dela Marlow?"

"I certainly do."

"Well, I am her uncle, and this girl is her sister and this is her foster father, Mr. McDonald, and this is her granny, Mrs. Crowe." Georgianna knew Gramma didn't liked to be called granny and was probably feeling huffy.

"Well, come on in. She is out playing. I'll send someone to find her." They entered a simply furnished room, where a young girl about fourteen years old was feeding a baby on the breast. Mrs. Chambers introduced her as her daughter, then said, "I didn't know that Dela had any family. She was surely in a pitiful shape when Rhetta Johnson brought her here. She is looking much better now."

The sound of several feet running across the porch announced the fact that Dela had been located. She came into the room with a pleasant smile that showed the dimples that Georgianna remembered so well. The golden curls had darkened, and her hair was cut in a short bob. Both eyes were still black and blue and bruises were on both arms.

"Dela, this is your sister, Georgianna."

"I don't have a sister." Georgianna slipped her arm around Dela's shoulders, not knowing whether to laugh or cry. She hadn't expected to find Dela in this shape. "Yes, you do, and I have been wanting to find you for all these years, and now I have." She could contain the tears no longer, as she brushed them away with her hand. Dela did not respond, having no bonding with any of her family. She had seen Russ a few times, but really didn't think he was her brother.

The visit was short and not too fulfilling. Georgianna had a hard time realizing that this was the same Dela that she had so lovingly cared for many years ago. Georgianna's Daddy spoke up, "Why don't we just take her back with us." Mrs. Chambers said, "I can't let you do that. She is in my care, and I am responsible for her. You need to contact Giles County Welfare Department before you can take her anywhere. You are welcome to visit anytime."

The visit was over, and after dropping Uncle El off at his home, everyone was very quiet all the way home. By the way Gramma cleared her throat once in a while, one could tell she wasn't too happy about the whole day.

Georgianna kept turning things over in her mind. She knew she really needed to do something about Dela. She was so unhappy to have found that Dela had been so badly abused, and she knew that she really must do something soon.

Darkness came before they arrived back home. "Mrs. Crowe, do you want off at the cabin?"

"No, I'll just go on up to the house and visit with Ellen, I always carry my flashlight in my handbag."

Everyone was excited and eager to hear all about Dela. "Is she pretty?" was Bethany's first question. "And did she like you?"

"Yes, she is pretty, and I don't know if she likes me. She doesn't know me yet. I'll make her like me."

"Well how was the trip? And what do you think of Dela?" asked Mama.

"She's a real cutie, and I think we should consider bringing her here so she and Georgianna could be together."

Gramma cleared her throat loudly before speaking. "I think this family is big enough. Of course, I do not have anything to say about what you do, but I, for one, am against it."

"Yes, Mama, I hear you," Ellen spoke up. "We are just talking about it."

Georgianna was thoroughly excited but kept quiet not wanting to cause any problem."

"Come, sweetie pie, it's time for bed," as she led Pegatty up the stairs, feeling more lighthearted than she had in a long time, finding an address for Fubby and finding Dela all in the same day, and knowing that Russ was still with the Hutchinsons. Georgianna was on her way to locating her siblings. She still had seven more to find. She knew Lancy was in the Giles County area but not exactly where. She was already dreaming of a big family reunion.

Before falling asleep, Georgianna thought of all the things she wanted to share with Dela and ways that she could convince Dela that she was her sister, and that she had never stopped loving her. And, what if she liked Bethany best?

The following day was about as usual, with Georgianna caring for Pegatty, Bethany and Bobby in school, Mama working in her rock garden and fish and lily pond, Jimmy loading his wagon with stones and wood, pulling them a short distance and unloading, getting dirty as usual. He could be cleanly dressed one minute, and in ten minutes, he was one big mess. Getting dirty seemed to be one of his hobbies.

Apparently, Mama and Daddy had discussed Dela after everyone had gone to bed last night, because after lunch, while Jimmy and Pegatty were napping, Mama called Georgianna into the living room. As she proceeded to the living room, she was thinking, "What have I done now?" She was surprised to find Mama in a pleasant mood, but a bit serious.

"We need to talk."

"Okay, what about?"

"Your sister, Dela. Would you like for her to come here to live? Daddy thinks it would be a good idea, and I am agreeable."

"Oh, Mama, could she really? I would so much like that. We could make up for lost time. We have been apart for so long. I would love having her here, where I could see her everyday. I want her to learn to love me and accept me as a sister."

"You may go now, but do not say anything."

Georgianna slipped quietly out of the room, thinking about Dela coming probably after school was out. She really felt lighthearted and happier than she had been in a long time; and she wondered how Daddy would treat her little sister, remembering that she had been Dela's age, when she had come to make her home there she was hoping for the best.

There was no mention of Dela the next couple weeks. Georgianna noticed that Mama was doing a lot of writing, and she assumed that she was working on the plans for her to come. Georgianna often took Pegatty and Jimmy with her to get the mail, if Gramma did not bring it with her when she came for lunch. Today had been one of those days, and she noticed a business looking envelope with the return address of Giles County Welfare. She knew this must be about Dela.

At dinner Mama made the announcement that Rheta Johnson from Narrows was coming to visit on Friday of that week, and they would discuss Dela's future. Everyone was pretty excited, except Gramma, who was not in favor of increasing the family size.

Friday was slow in coming. Mama and Georgianna had dusted and polished furniture, and a fresh bouquet of spring flowers had been placed on the dining table, as well as on the piano. Everything looked presentable as Mama awaited the visitor, who arrived shortly after noon. Pegatty and Jimmy had been put to bed for a nap. Georgianna stayed out of the way, while the conference was held in he living room. Mama later called for her to come and meet Miss Johnson, who was a pretty young woman.

"So, you are Georgianna, Dela's big sister."

"Yes, ma'am."

"Would you like for your little sister to make her home here?"

"Oh yes, I really would."

"Are you happy here?"

"Yes," she had to answer. What else could she say when Mama was sitting there. She would be much happier when Dela could be there with her.

"Well I just wish that I could place more children in homes like this. You are a lucky girl, Georgianna," Miss Johnson remarked as she rose to leave. "Mrs. McDonald, I will be contacting you very soon. If all goes well, you should be having another daughter shortly after the closing of school. Dela will have the summer to adjust, and it will be good to know that she will be in the same school for the entire year."

The warm spring days were bright and beautiful. The forsythia had begun to fade, and the multicolored tulips had taken their place. The lawn was like a fresh green carpet. If only her Daddy would just act like a real Daddy, she would be a lot happier. Georgianna hadn't had one, so she did not know exactly how they were supposed to be.

She was looking forward to the blossoming of the May apple trees in the orchard, when she would take Pegatty and the two would have a picnic while the bees hummed and the birds chirped overhead. She had done this since Pegatty was six weeks old and had a favorite spot. Now she could bring Dela here sometimes. She knew that it could never be the same as when they lived back in the mountains when Mommy was alive and they were much younger. Georgianna had made up her mind that she was going to do her part to make friends. Everyday she checked the calendar to see how many days before school would be out.

Bethany and Bobby were studying for their final exams, and the time was getting near. Georgianna was glad that she did not have any of that school stuff to do. She loved to read and did a lot of that when she wasn't busy.

The last day of school had arrived. Bethany and Bobby came in plopping their books down on the table singing, "Schools out, schools out, teachers let the fools out." Everyone loved all that free time. Assuming that Giles County Schools had also closed, the family was eagerly looking for word from Rhetta Johnson. Surprisingly a letter arrived the day after. It said, "I will be bringing Dela to you on Friday of next week. If this is not a convenient time, please notify me promptly. I will be there in early afternoon."

Mama had already decided that Dela would room with Bethany, since Pegatty was sleeping with Georgianna and that was working well. Georgianna just knew this was the longest week she had ever spent. She was so full of anticipation she couldn't eat, couldn't sleep, and was full of anxiety. Friday finally dawned a bright sunny day, and all were eagerly awaiting early afternoon. Even Georgia, the cook, and her girls were excited.

CHAPTER 43

Dela's Arrival

Georgianna had shampooed and curled her hair, dressed in her blue dress with the rickrack around the collar and pockets, and had dressed Pegatty in a pretty play dress. Everyone was ready for the new arrival.

The dogs began to bark, and Georgianna tingled with excitement. She knew the car must be up to the second grove and would be coming into view any second. She didn't know whether to laugh, to cry, or to grab Pegatty by the hand and run. Instead she just stood watching as the black car came to a stop. Mrs. Johnson stepped out of the car, brushing the dogs away as she walked around the car and opened the door. Out stepped a pretty little girl in a pink dress with a pink bow in her hair. She was smiling, displaying the dimples in her cheeks, and her eyes were once again dancing. Gone were the black eyes and the bruises that were prominent a few months before.

Everyone felt a bit awkward. Then Mrs. Johnson and Mama greeted each other. "So this is Dela? I have certainly heard a lot about you from your sister. It's been Dela this and Dela that all these years that I have known her." Dela just grinned broadly and showed her dimples.

"I must get the car unloaded and get back to Narrows," Mrs. Johnson said. Everyone proceeded to help unload the pretty red tricycle, a wagon, and some dolls and other playthings, along with a substantial amount of clothing. Georgianna thought she must have been living with rich folks to have all those things. She remembered all she had when she came here the first time was a nightgown, an extra dress, and an extra pair of black sateen bloomers.

Bethany took Dela by the hand and said, "You want to see my things?" All carried in some baggage and up the stairs they went, while Mrs. McDonald and Mrs. Johnson entered the living room after Georgia had been instructed to bring some lemonade and cookies.

Pegatty was at Georgianna's heels as she carried Dela's belongings up the stairs. Bethany and Dela had gone to their room with Bobby following them. Already he had begun picking at Dela, who wanted to know if the black people lived here. Bethany laughed and said, "They are the servants and go home at night." Dela had not known any black folks in Giles County. No one had servants. Families did the work, with every one doing their share. Dela wondered what Mrs. McDonald and the children did all day.

While Georgianna put Dela's clothes away, noting that she had many pretty dresses as well as other clothing articles, she was hoping with all her heart that she would be accepted as a sister and that they would be close and love each other.

Mrs. Johnson was soon on her way back to Narrows after saying goodbye to Dela. "I hope you will enjoy living here. Having a sister should help. I will be visiting you in a few months." Dela appeared to be perfectly at home and was eager to get on with playing with Bethany, as Bobby continued to pester her.

Dinner was on the table at the appointed time, and Daddy had gotten home eager to see how Dela was making the change. "I passed your mother at the cherry orchard, so she should be along shortly." He greeted Mama, "Did our other daughter get here?"

"Yes, they're all washing their hands for dinner. She's much more lively than Georgianna ever was. She makes herself at home."

The sound of many feet on the stairs greeted Gramma as she entered the dining room door. As everyone sat down at their usual place, Dela took the remaining place between Bethany and Georgianna. After Daddy said grace, Gramma gave Dela one of her little fake smiles as Mama mentioned that there was an extra member in the family. It was plain to see that Gramma was not happy about it.

Mr. McDonald served all the plates and passed them around. Everyone began to eat but Dela. "Where are the beans? I do not like anything on my plate." She ate very little and certainly was not enjoying it at all, while everyone else was thoroughly enjoying the good dinner. Mama had a puzzled look on her face. The children usually were required to clean their plates before being excused. This time was an exception.

None of the meals seemed to suit Dela's taste. Mama bluntly asked her, "What do you like to eat?" The reply was "beans and onions and corn bread," as she flashed that big grin showing her prominent dimples. Beans were not a staple in the household. Eventually Dela learned to like many other foods and forgot that beans and onions were her favorite food.

One of Georgianna's past Christmas gifts had been a guitar which she had been trying to learn to play. Dela spotted it and announced that she could play one. Of course, her sister would not refuse her the privilege, wanting so much for them to be friends. Dela sat on the steps leading upstairs and began singing at the top of her lungs. It was evident that she could not really play the guitar, but she could sing quite well. The words did not come out just right, it sounded like she was singing something about a big eyed buzzle. Georgianna finally decided that she was trying to sing the song containing the words, "I Want God's Bosom to Be My Pillow," a recent gospel song that had become popular. Dela soon tired of the guitar and went on to other things.

It was soon evident that these two sisters were very different. Georgianna had always been quiet and submissive, always obeying and doing what she thought was expected of her without question. Dela was quite different. In fact, she was a bit sassy and talked back when Mama gave her an order. On one occasion she was ordered to go sit in the living room as punishment for talking back. She nonchalantly parked herself on the sofa and enjoyed leafing through the Ladies Home Journal, not at all disturbed that she had been sassy. Mama was slightly confused about how to mete out punishment to a child of this nature. Dela seemed very content, and Mama accepted her just the way she was. In fact, Mama appeared to admire her spunk and liveliness.

Georgianna still felt left out and not a real part of the family. She was just Pegatty's nanny and a little like a servant without pay. There was not the closeness that she wanted with Dela, who accepted Bethany more as a sister. At least she knew where she was and that things were better, and that was some comfort. The only thing they seemed to have in common was the fact that they were biological sisters, and Dela ignored that. It was certainly not the way Georgianna had hoped. However, she tried to accept the fact that she was past the age of a playmate, and that she was kept busy always doing something for Pegatty.

They remained a little like strangers. Georgianna was not about to give up on them having a closer relationship, even if it took fifty years, hoping that she could live that long. Maybe as Dela grew older, she would be more responsive to Georgianna's affection. She certainly was seeking this in the daily prayers. She knew God answered prayers. If He didn't, she would never have found her precious baby sister. She had waited this long, and she knew that she could wait even longer. One day it would happen even if it took a long time.

CHAPTER 44

News From Fubby – 1933

Georgianna and Fubby had been corresponding occasionally. It had been several months since she had heard from him. None of her letters had been returned so he must be getting them. There was nothing to do but wait. Gramma was away visiting Grandpa everyday the weather was nice.

Georgianna took Jimmy and Pegatty to pick up the mail. Today a letter arrived addressed to her with a Lexington postmark. She didn't know anyone in Lexington, and she could hardly wait to get to the house and open it.

> Dear Sis, I have been much too busy to write to you before now. I found the girl that I want to spend the rest of my life with. Her name is Evie. We were married in June and are living with the folks that I lived with after I left the children's home. I hope to get a friend to bring me to see you after the harvest is all taken care of here on the farm.

Georgianna wrote back immediately that she was eagerly awaiting the time when they would come.

When Dela came in from school, her sister relayed the happy news to which she replied, "I don't even know him." She did not share Georgianna's enthusiasm, just one more disappointment, but she had come to expect this rejection and was not surprised.

Georgianna had struggled through these eight long years since the morning Fubby had told her goodbye on the girls' sleeping porch at the children's home. She was very excited that she would not have to wait eight more years. Mama appeared to share her excitement, finally realizing how much her family meant to her. Hearing what a nice brother Fubby was, she would finally see for herself.

School was in full swing. The cider barrel was full. Everywhere you looked there was a basket of apples. Everyone delighted in sticking a lone straw from the straw stack into the cider barrel and having a good long sip while it was still sweet. Later it would be hard and eventually vinegar.

Bethany and Dela usually played house after school, and Bobby spent his time riding the billy goat and training it to jump by turning two pails upside down and placing a pole across. As he and the goat approached the pole, Bobby reached back and yanked the goat's tail and over the pole he went. This would continue as long as the goat didn't balk. When the two tired of this sport, Bobby would look for other ways to use his excess energy.

Halloween passed and harvest time was about over. Daddy announced that they were going to visit his mother, Grandma Lucille, at Thanksgiving. This created a lot of excitement. Trips were few and far between. A trip to Lynchburg, twelve miles away, was about as far as the family traveled, and that was not often, so it's easy to see why a long trip would be exciting. They were to leave the day before Thanksgiving.

All bags were packed and in readiness two days early, when a letter arrived from Fubby saying, "My friend has agreed to bring me to see you on Thanksgiving Day."

"Oh, no," Georgianna said to herself as she stuffed the letter back into the envelope and approached Mama excitedly. "Mama, Mama, we can't go to Ohio. Fubby's coming." This was more exciting than the trip to her anyway.

"That's too bad, we will not be here. They probably just want a good Thanksgiving dinner." Georgianna didn't speak up. Her joyful anticipation for the trip was gone. It was too late to write a letter, and she did not have a telephone number to phone. She had no choice but to go on the trip, thinking often about Fubby finding her gone, and probably he would think that she didn't want to see him.

The trip to Ohio was long, and Pegatty was restless as she sat on

Georgianna's lap. Jimmy sat up front with Daddy and Mama, while the other five crowded into the back seat.

They arrived late at night to be happily greeted by Grandma Lucille and her other son and his wife. They were hurried into the living room, where a big wood stove with a glass front gave of a warm glow. A pot of hot chocolate sat on the coal stove in the kitchen. This was a different atmosphere than back home, very homey and informal. It reminded Georgianna a little of her first home, only much nicer. Grandma Lucille made a big fuss over Pegatty, since her middle name was Lucille, this being the first time they had met.

Everyone was up quite early on Thanksgiving Day, and good smells were already coming from the kitchen. Much preparation had been done in advance. After a good breakfast and the dishes were washed, everyone did their part to help get the big dinner completed.

Daddy's two sisters and their families would be arriving to share in the festivities. So much was going on, Georgianna didn't have time to brood about missing Fubby's visit. She gave Grandma Lucille all the help that she could and hoped that Grandma Lucille had forgotten all about the time she had borrowed her little pen and carried it to school without asking.

The brothers and sisters and cousins enjoyed spending time together. It was a very successful day and no one was glad to see it come to an end.

The McDonalds were leaving much before daybreak on Sunday morning to get in for a good night's rest before getting back to work and to school on Monday. As they neared home before dark, Georgianna could see a paper on the door, and she knew Fubby had been there. Mama beat Georgianna to the door, and taking the paper from the door, she read it so all could hear. "We had a hard time finding the house, and then no one was here. We will come back another time. Love Fubby, Evie, and Frankie.

"I knew he would come back," piped up Georgianna, "and I am going to be sure that I am here when he does."

The week was cold, and by Friday a light snow was falling. Galoshes and gloves, scarves and anything to keep warm were in evidence as Daddy went to the feed store. Georgianna was glad to be staying in to

watch after Jimmy and Pegatty and to just stay warm, even if she did
have to get several loads of wood for the fireplace and keep the furnace
fired up. That was her regular chore now that Georgia didn't come
every day. Georgianna did most of the cooking and helped when
Georgia was there also.

Georgianna had written Fubby and explained why they were not
at home for Thanksgiving and how sorry she was that he had made
the trip for nothing.

All week long she took the two children with her to the mailbox
after putting coats, scarves, and mittens on them and hoping that
they would be tired enough to go to sleep after lunch. No letter arrived
from Fubby by Friday, and Georgianna was certainly disappointed.

Bethany, Dela, and Bobby arrived from school dropping their books
on the dining room table and grabbing an apple from the basket.
They were glad another week of school was out of the way. They
had reviewed for the six week test and were ready to relax for the
weekend. They checked out the kitchen where Georgia was paring
vegetables for the evening meal and a pot of soup for the following
day. Georgianna helped plan the meals and instructed Georgia on
what to prepare. Mama preferred to read, embroider, and arrange
flowers or visit with Gramma when she was here, and she more or
less just left the cooking to someone else.

CHAPTER 45

Fubby's Arrival

By Saturday morning the snow had stopped, but it was cold and everyone stayed inside. Georgianna always polished Pegatty's and Jimmy's shoes, along with her own, and shampooed hers and Pegatty's hair, so things would be in order for Sunday School. As Georgianna wrapped her head in a towel, the dogs began to bark, and a car could be heard chugging up the road. Georgianna peered out the bathroom window to see a gray Ford car with three people in it. They were hesitant about getting out of the car with the dogs yapping furiously. Mama opened the door from the dining room and quieted the dogs, as two men and a woman got out.

"It's Fubby! It's Fubby," shouted the usually quiet Georgianna, as she draped the towel around her shoulders and flew down the stairs and out the door, looking like a drowned rat with her stringy wet hair. She threw her arms around Fubby's neck before anyone could be introduced.

Mama reminded Georgianna that she should not be out in the cold with her wet head as she invited the visitors in. Everyone was ill at ease. "So this is Fubby, I have heard good things about you for years. This must be your wife?"

"Yes, this is Evie, and this is my friend, Frankie Lowman." Mama shook hands with them as the remaining family members traipsed down the stairs. Georgianna took Dela by the hand and pulled her over beside Fubby, announcing, "This is your big brother." Dela just smiled showing her dimples. Bethany and Bobby were much more friendly. Jimmy and Pegatty were shy but pleasant.

No visitors had been expected, and Mama excused herself and went to the kitchen to see if the soup pot was adequate and bread for sandwiches on hand. It was nearing lunch time.

By this time Georgianna was feeling somewhat embarrassed by her long stringy wet hair. She went upstairs to comb and pin it up and make herself look more presentable. She had noticed Frankie looking at her sort of strange. She looked a mess with her long stringy wet hair. There was quite an improvement when she came downstairs with her hair combed.

Mama instructed Georgianna to set the table for lunch and, "Don't forget the napkins." She proceeded with this job, as the butterflies flopped around in her stomach. She was so happy that she was a nervous wreck and hoped that it did not show. She felt really awkward and a bit like an "Ugly Duckling," never having been around many young men. She didn't know just how to act around Frankie who was dressed in a gray suit and looked really nice with his dark curly hair that sported a "widows peak." He didn't have much of a chin and it had a big dimple, but he was very polite.

Sitting down at the table before steaming vegetable soup and crackers, the visitors were a bit unsure which spoon to use. Picking up first one and then the other and taking note of what everyone else was using, they chose the soup spoon. Georgia had made sandwiches and chocolate pudding. Dishes were removed from the table, and all sat around the table to visit awhile.

Jimmy and Pegatty asked to be excused while the rest decided to play a few games. One game was played by one being "it" and instructing another what he wanted another to do. Bethany volunteered to start by being "it." Her request was a big surprise, "I want Frankie to kiss Georgianna." He must have been bashful. Instead he walked around the table and kissed Evie, who blushed. Fubby clearly showed his displeasure, but kept quiet, and the game soon ended. Fubby tried to hug Dela, but she only pulled away from him and didn't want to have anything to do with him. She did smile, showing the deep dimples in her cheeks.

Georgianna's happiness was evident, and she was not embarrassed to let people know how pleased she was that her brother had come, even unexpected, and she hoped that he would visit often. The afternoon passed swiftly. As usual, Bobby was up to his tricks, picking at Fubby and Frankie and being somewhat pesky.

Good-byes were said, the three entered the '32 Ford sedan, and Frankie drove around the circle drive to head back to Lexington. Georgianna waved as they pulled away, hoping that someday they would give her a ride. She noticed how nicely Frankie handled the car.

During dinner that evening all Georgianna wanted to talk about was Fubby, until everyone was tired of hearing her.

After Georgianna put Pegatty to bed, she and Bethany did the dishes together—for once, Bethany didn't have to go to the bathroom—and discussed the events of the day. Bethany agreed that Fubby was a nice brother.

Sleep was slow in coming for Georgianna. All she could think about was her family. Three had been together for the day after eight years of separation. She was seeing her dream slowly coming true. Fubby had said he had seen Cory and Corbin before leaving his home in Paint Bank, and she was hopeful that she could soon get in touch with them. Snuggling Pegatty close to her, sleep finally came.

CHAPTER 46

The Christmas Explosion

The next few weeks were busy with the usual Christmas shopping, wrapping, cleaning, and baking cookies, fruit cakes, and other goodies. Gramma had returned home and was going shopping often. She provided many treats at Christmas, seeming always to be endowed with that necessary staple, money. Christmas would certainly not be the same without her.

Georgianna mostly requested sweaters, skirts, or other clothing items as her Christmas gifts. Bethany, Dela, and Bobby were eager for the long holiday between Christmas and New Year's Day. Pegatty and Jimmy were forever asking, "Is Christmas tomorrow?" The answer, of course, was no, until the day to select the tree, when all the family wrapped warmly to go looking for the tree. After inspecting a dozen or more trees, a near perfect one was found and cut down. As Daddy pulled the tree to the house, the needles left a pretty pattern in the light snow.

Christmas morning arrived again, snow covered the ground, the air was cold and crisp, a great day to stay inside. The tree was beautifully decorated when the family arose, very early as usual on Christmas morning. Georgianna was pleased with her new clothes. Her navy skirt and burgundy sweater with white trim around the collar made a nice outfit.

Georgia, the cook, was off for the day taking care of her own family, so Georgianna had the job of preparing and cooking the turkey. She just hoped she knew what she was doing. This was her first experience with a turkey. She followed the instructions that had come with the new pyrofax kitchen range. "Pre-heat oven at 350 degrees."

"Okay, that's done," she said to herself as she struck the match to light the oven, then proceeded to wash the turkey and stuff him with the stuffing that had been prepared. Tucking his wings in just so and placing the huge bird in the roasting pan that was almost too small, she forced the cover on tightly to keep the moisture in and placed the roaster in the oven.

Shortly the smell of gas was evident, and knowing something was not right, the girl checked and found the fire was out. She did not think about turning the oven off and opening the kitchen door to air the place out before lighting the oven. As she opened the oven, the odor of gas took her breath away. She hurriedly took the match from the matchbox and brushed it across the box. "BANG," and Georgianna found herself across the room into the pantry against the wall with her hair on fire. The family came running after flower pots fell from window sills in the dining room and shook the whole house.

Mama took one look at Georgianna and calmly asked, "What's the matter?" By this time Daddy was there and picked Georgianna up and smothered her burning hair. She was a pitiful sight with her eyebrows and eyelashes gone and part of her hair burned off. After being carried upstairs and placed in bed, she began to have severe chills. Mama said it was shock. Piles of blankets covered her before she stopped shaking and felt comfortable. Daddy drove to the neighbors and phoned for Dr. Sandig, who was out on a call and never did come.

Mama had to complete the dinner and was not too happy about it. Georgianna began to feel better and took her place at the table. Afterward she cleared the table and cleaned up the dishes. Pegatty said, "Georgianna looks funny," and she already knew that, with no eyelashes, no eyebrows, and half her hair gone. The hair she had left smelled scorched. This had not been exactly her kind of Christmas day, and she hoped her hair would grow fast. There was really nothing that she could do to make herself look any better.

Bethany, Dela, and Bobby proceeded to enjoy their time off from school. Christmas was on Monday, and that left the whole week to enjoy the toys and games that they had received. A new game, called

Monopoly, was among the family gifts, and that could be played by all but the youngest ones.

The children counted the days and savored each one until they would return to school on Tuesday. The snow had stayed on the ground, and except for a few sleigh rides on Bobby's new sled, the time was spent indoors. Saturday arrived cloudy and cold, looking like more snow. The Christmas tree was still up, and everything still looked good. The weekly cleaning was delayed.

CHAPTER 47

Fubby's Return and Other Things

Late morning the dogs began their constant barking and everyone knew someone must be coming, but couldn't imagine who it would be at this hour in this cold snowy weather. Everyone began watching as a gray '32 Ford car pulled up and stopped. Georgianna's mouth fell open. "Oh, no, they can't see me looking like this." Mama opened the door and quieted the dogs as Georgianna flew up the stairs and wrapped her head in a turban and put on some lipstick in record time.

She wished Fubby had written that they were coming. She realized that she looked even worse than when they were here before and found her with the wet stringy hair. On her entrance to the living room, Fubby took one look at her and asked, "What in the world happened to you?"

"The stove exploded Christmas Day and burned my hair off. Why didn't you let us know that you were coming? I could have at least made me a dust cap."

Fubby said, "It will all grow back. We just decided to come this morning, hoping you would be here, so here we are. With all this snow, we just knew you would be home."

Mama was glad to know that some Christmas goodies were still on hand. She went to the kitchen to check on what was available for lunch, and found that there was no problem.

When lunch was over, the games were brought out, and a lively game of Monopoly began and kept going for sometime, until everyone grew tired if it. Mama spoke up, "Georgianna, why don't you fix ingredients for some pineapple ice. I know things to prepare it, with all this snow to freeze it. Frankie and Fubby can take turns cranking the freezer." Everyone agreed, and Georgianna quickly prepared the ingredients with sugar, eggs, and the last cans of pineapple on the shelf. Bethany and Dela put the games away, while Bobby took Frankie to the basement to get the ice cream freezer. With a huge bucket of snow ready at the kitchen steps, along with the bag of salt, the cranking began. The young men's hands were freezing, along with the pineapple ice which did not take long to freeze. Jimmy and Pegatty argued over who got to lick the dasher, which Mama convinced them to share.

Everyone agreed the dessert was really good, and the guests said they had never eaten this before. They always had ice cream. The nicest thing about it to Georgianna was that everyone seemed to forget all about her eyes and hair, and the day was pleasant. The visitors left in time to arrive in Lexington before dark.

When Daddy arrived, late as usual, and was told about the day's visitors, his first words were, "I think that fellow is stuck on Georgianna." Bobby and Jimmy had already been teasing Frankie, much to Georgianna's embarrassment.

Georgianna wrote several letters to Fubby but heard nothing from him all winter long, and she wondered what had happened. Gramma had gone back to visit Grandpa, and things were a bit dull. The McDonald family managed to get to the little Methodist church for Sunday School and preaching twice a month, and other than that, Georgianna was mostly on the mountain. There was not much socializing in the community in the winter time. She longed for a little more excitement in her life.

The early spring flowers finally made their appearance, the tulips and daffodils were in bloom, and the smell of lilies was everywhere as Georgianna and Pegatty skipped down the road to pick up the mail, only to discover that the postman had not arrived. They busied themselves gathering violets until they had a nice bouquet. They sat on a log to wait, and the wait was short. The mail truck pulled in by the mailbox, and the postman shoved a fist full of mail into the box.

As he pulled away Georgianna lost no time in getting the mailbox open, hoping she would hear from Fubby. On the top was a fat letter from Gramma, addressed to Mama. Looking through the remaining pieces, there was a letter addressed to her in Fubby's hand writing. "Well, it's about time," she said as she excitedly opened the letter after tucking the other mail under her arm. Pegatty carried the bouquet of violets and asked, "What does it say"? Georgianna was too busy to even listen to her, as she read the letter.

Dear Sis, I have a big surprise for you. I am going to be a father in July, and we are so excited! Evie is staying at Frankie's house, so as to be near the doctor. She is also helping take care of his mother who has asthma, and his maiden sister, who has arthritis.

I am still on the farm with Andy and his family. His three children keep me entertained. I go to visit Evie on Saturday and back to the farm on Sunday evening.

We would like for the McDonalds to bring you up on Sunday, and you could stay for a week and visit Evie, and we can take you home at the end of the week.

Love, Fubby

CHAPTER 48

Georgianna's Visit to Lexington

Georgianna was really excited and hurried home to talk it over. When Mama heard the news, she said, "You'll have to talk to Daddy when he comes home. You can't go until school is out and Dela is here to look after Pegatty."

Georgianna was eager to hear what Daddy would have to say. He was even later than usual coming in from the feed store. Dinner was usually kept until he came home. The dogs began to bark, and Georgianna knew it was time to re-warm dinner, which had been ready for sometime. She heated the ham and fried potatoes and peeled the hard boiled eggs to slice over the fresh homegrown spinach. Dinner was soon on the table, and everyone was seated in their usual spot. Jimmy wanted to ask the blessing, which always came out, "Lordy, Lordy, Lordy, Amen."

Daddy served everyone's plate and then Georgianna spoke to Mama, "Are you going to ask him?"

"Yes."

"What do you think about Georgianna going for a visit with her brother's wife? You could take her to Lexington, and Fubby says they will bring her back."

"I suppose you mean when school is out?"

"Sure, Dela can look after Pegatty."

"I don't see why not."

Georgianna beamed. This would be like a real vacation for her— one whole week, all her own! Of course, that was two months away, but she was already planning what she wanted to pack to take with her, wanting them to know that she could look better than the other times they had seen her. She would certainly take the two new dresses that Mrs. Bedford was making for her, and of course the navy blue and white checked with the pearl buttons, which was one of her favorites. She thought, "Why am I planning all this now? I have lots of time—two whole months!' Georgianna's nature was such that she liked to get her plans together well in advance, and she knew things would be ready when the time came.

The tulips and daffodils had faded, along with the lilacs, and the many apple trees were taking their place and filling the mountain air with their delightful fragrance. Her memory shifted back to the days in the mountains when the laurel were blooming all over the place, and she would like for Dela to go with her. After all, Fubby was her brother too. Dela appeared to have no special feeling for Georgianna or Fubby and gave Bethany all her attention.

The time had come to pack her belongings for the week long vacation. By Saturday night every thing was in her battered suitcase except the tooth brush. On awakening early on Sunday morning of June 16, 1936, she grabbed the milk pail and stopped to smell and admire the Dr. Von Flete roses that adorned the trellis outside the dining room door These were her favorite rose, such a soft delicate pink. Hurriedly she went to milk the cow and wondered who would take care of this job while she was gone. Maybe Bob, the hired man. She wasn't going to worry about it. Someone would do it. She strained the milk and put it in the ice box when she returned to the house.

She joined the other family members at breakfast and cleaned the dishes. She dressed Pegatty and fashioned her hair in long curls, then checked that she got dressed and fixed her long hair in a smooth knot at the nape of her neck.

Daddy yelled from downstairs, "Is everyone ready? We should get there an hour before dinner time so we can get acquainted with the family. You know I haven't seen any of them."

"You'll like them, I am sure, " Mama replied.

The drive seemed long and Pegatty was constantly squirming as she sat on Georgianna's lap. "Sweetie, could you please sit still. My dress will look like I slept in it last night. There will be a yard that you can play in when we get there."

Daddy announced, "We will soon be in Buena Vista, and it's only about eight miles from there." Mama got the directions out of her handbag so they could find the house without getting lost.

"All of you keep your eyes open for Scott's Service Station on your right. Just beyond that, we turn right at Barger's Stone Quarry." Georgianna was all eyes and was first to spot Scott's Service Station, and in the distance, Barger's Stone Quarry.

"Make a right turn here, Will, and drive slowly, so we don't miss the house." They passed one small house setting on a bank and another one that was built on a large solid stone. There it was the big white house with green shutters and Frankie's car parked in the driveway. Daddy pulled in behind the car, and all eight scrambled out, glad for the opportunity to stretch their legs. Five in the back seat had been crowded.

They approached the front door quietly, knowing about Frankie's sister not being well. A small lady dressed in a gray print dress, with a sweater draped around her shoulders sporting a string of safety pins dangling from the front, answered their knock on the door. "You must be Georgianna's family. I am Cora Lowman, Frankie's mother. Come into the parlor."

They entered a room with a leather sofa, three rocking chairs and some straight chairs, not enough room for everyone to sit. Frankie, Fubby, and Evie entered the room from the hallway, followed by Frankie's two sisters, Glady and Edwina, who was walking with crutches. The room was really crowded. Mama asked if the children could play in the yard "Yes, as long as they don't bother the flowers." And they were glad to get out of the crowded room.

The ladies excused themselves to complete the dinner, and Frankie went back to the ice cream freezer to finish his job that had been interrupted. Fubby and Evie stayed to visit. Evie was a very quiet person, and everyone was ill at ease. Daddy began to ask Fubby just what he did on the farm with Andy. And light conversation proceeded. Evie was wearing a pink smock to conceal her pregnancy. This condition was not highly publicized in the 1930s.

Yummy smells were coming from the kitchen, and Glady appeared at the door occasionally to interject a bit of conversation.

Dinner was announced and Georgianna was asked to summon the

children from the yard, where they had been enjoying themselves. They were sent to the back porch where a pail of water and a wash pan sat, and instructed to wash for dinner. Then, most families had dinner at noon instead of evening.

The younger ones were seated at the kitchen table, while Georgianna ate in the dining room with the older folks. Edwina preferred to sit with the young folks in the kitchen. They were served crisp brown chicken, gravy, potatoes, corn pudding, and fresh garden peas, and when dessert time came, large bowls of delicious strawberry ice cream made from real cream and fresh strawberries from the garden, served along with cake. Everyone enjoyed the delicious meal. The children returned to the yard to amuse themselves, while the rest returned to the living room after helping clear the table.

Andy and his family arrived to visit for awhile, with their children, two girls five and seven years of age and a boy three years old, who were a bit shy. Andy's wife, Ada, was a fat jolly person. Both she and Andy looked old to have such small children. It was plain the children adored Fubby and Evie. Andy spoke up, "Where's K.B.?" who also lived with his Grandmother Lowman.

"He is at his Aunt Beulah's for a few days. He and Lynny like to be together once in awhile."

Daddy decided they had better be heading back home and reminded Georgianna to get her bag out of the car if she was going to stay. They rounded up the brood and said their good-byes. They were soon on their way, leaving Georgianna feeling a bit lonely among all these strangers who she didn't know very well yet. Even Fubby was still new to her. They had grown apart all the years of separation.

When Andy left a short time later, taking Fubby with him to help with evening chores, she really felt lonely. She had been so excited that she had not given much thought about not seeing much of Fubby, but seeing Frankie and Evie every day. Now she really felt pangs of loneliness. Evie was part of her family now, and they had plans to go to the farm to visit them later in the week. She supposed she was going to be all right.

Glady and Frankie went to work every day. She was a dental assistant for Dr. Russell Engelman, and Frankie was doing electrical work, since he was not at the VMI laundry, where he worked during school months.

Georgianna helped Evie with the house work, and they took walks together. One occasion they visited Frankie's sister, Beulah, who lived in town. She was a pleasant person, who laughed a lot and served them tea and cookies.

Supper was usually not started until after the folks came in from work. Frankie milked the cow, while the women fixed the meal. When supper was over and the dishes done, the front porch was the favorite place to relax. Georgianna enjoyed the swing, and usually Frankie sat on the other end of it, while others occupied the porch rockers, until they decided they had something else to do and left Georgianna still in the swing.

Some folks may have called it courting, but it really was not. He sat on one end and she on the other. They just talked about various things until Mrs. Lowman would tell Frankie that it was time to come in. And soon everyone was in bed, the radio had been turned off, and all was quiet.

Evie talked to Fubby on the phone each evening after his chores were finished. Frankie suggested the family go to the farm on Wednesday to see Fubby, and Evie was delighted that they could have a little time together in mid-week. Since she had been at Frankie's, she only saw him on weekends, and they really missed each other.

The farm had been the homeplace of the Lowman family for a long time, Cora and William's father before them, now Andy's family.

Georgianna was eager to see Fubby again.

After the milking and supper were over with, all but Edwina, who preferred to stay home, journeyed the ten miles to the farm. Ole Shep, the sheep dog, lay curled up asleep just inside the gate. They were met by the three children, Vera, Lorene and Andy, who had acquired the nickname of Cedric from Fubby.

Visiting was done in the back yard where Ada served cookies and lemonade. They stayed there until the mosquitoes began biting. Ada went into the house and lit lamps, and Fubby and Evie went upstairs. Others followed into the house, leaving Frankie and Georgianna sitting in the big swing between the large maple trees.

CHAPTER 49

Frankie's Proposal

A full moon was shining through the trees, and Frankie moved closer to Georgianna, who didn't know whether to move or stay where she was. Shortly his arm encircled her shoulder, and he asked, "Are you cold?"

"A little." He moved even closer and she felt a little scared. Having only had one boyfriend for awhile when she was thirteen, and they had only walked to and from church with several others and sat in the Parlor, she had never really been this close to a boy. She was panic stricken. She felt like running into the house, then thought how silly that would look, for a seventeen year old girl to be acting like a small child, so she just sat, neither one saying anything. Then Frankie asked her if she liked poems. "Yes, I do."

"I have one just for you. I hope that you will like it." Then he began to recite, "Forget the Chances, Precious. Adopt a Ruse. Let me be the one you choose." Things were quiet for a time and he said, "I am asking you to marry me." At this point he kissed her for the first time and the second and the third.

Finally, she stammered "I don't know." He kissed her again. Still she said, "I don't know."

"Don't you think I can make you happy?"

"I guess so," came the weak reply. She never really said yes, but he thought she meant yes. He wanted to get married immediately. They were sort of semi-engaged. She knew she would have to talk to Mama, and she didn't know if she wanted to get married.

The rest of the week she spent much of her time alone, complaining of a headache. She just really felt disturbed, not knowing if she cared that much about this fellow to spend the rest of her life with him.

The two continued to sit in the swing in the evenings, while Frankie kept insisting that they get married immediately. Georgianna was just not ready for this, not really sure if she loved this man enough to commit herself for the rest of her life.

Saturday morning found Fubby at the Lowman's home, ready for Frankie to take Georgianna back home. Georgianna had enjoyed the week but was eager to get back to dear little Pegatty and the rest of the family. She already had everything in her suit case and was ready to go.

On arriving on the mountain, Frankie got out of the car and opened the door for who he now considered his girl, chasing the many dogs away. Approaching the dining room door, they were met by the family. Pegatty grabbed Georgianna around the legs. "I thought you were never coming back." Georgianna gathered the small child in her arms, and was thinking, "I don't know if I can leave this little girl for a man. It would be almost like leaving Dela again, and she knew a lot of thought would have to be given to Frankie's proposal."

This young woman knew that she really wanted to have a family of her own, with lots of children, and thought this may be her only chance. She didn't have the opportunity to meet young men, staying on the mountain most of the time. She was just going to think about it for a while.

As soon as everyone had settled down for a visit, Frankie came alive and announced to Mama that he and Georgianna wanted to get married right away. He really meant that he wanted to get married right away. Georgianna didn't know what she wanted.

"Isn't this sorta sudden? Why, you hardly know each other," Mama retorted.

"I just know what I want. I want to make Georgianna my wife and make her happy."

"But she is only seventeen. We will have to think about it for awhile."

Frankie began twitching his hands and moving his jaws like he was having a lot of frustration, and everyone was quiet. Georgianna was not saying a word either way, because she didn't really know what she wanted. She had really never had anything to say about the direction of her life, and she supposed Mama would take care of everything and work things out for her.

Georgianna was just glad to be back with Pegatty sitting on her lap. She could tell her hair needed shampooing and combing and would take care of that later in the day. She had really missed this little girl.

CHAPTER 50

Decisions, Decisions

The next few weeks brought many letters that made Georgianna happy but still in doubt about what she wanted to do. She really didn't know this man well enough or if she cared enough to marry him, not really knowing much about love itself. Her life had been so mixed up.

She was very fond of Bob, the hired man, who treated her with kindness and respect and playfully gave her the nickname of "Pete" She wondered how you defined love or knew if it were real. Frankie declared his love for her in his many letters, always ending with these letters, I L U P M A M E D, explaining they meant, "I love you, Precious, more and more each day."

At the end of the first month of being semi-engaged, Georgianna was still troubled about what to do and only wrote friendly letters, never declaring her love or committing herself in any way. She still did not know her heart and was thinking that she had better discourage Frankie.

Before she could get the next letter off to him, she had a surprise visit from Frankie who had brought Fubby and Evie for moral support. The family were just leaving for "Jimmy's swimming hole" on the Peddler River and invited the guest to go along. They had not brought swimming suits, so they just sat on the rocks and watched. Georgianna wished they had not come. She had already made up her mind to write and put everything on hold. After swimming was over the group went to the house and made sandwiches and lemonade.

The time came for the guest to leave for Lexington. Georgianna walked to the car with them, and Evie told her, "The next time you see me, you will be an aunt. Our baby is due within two weeks."

Georgianna said, "As far as I know this will be the first baby since Noona's little girl. I can't imagine Fubby being a daddy."

Frankie gave her a long hard kiss, and another, and another. This made her feel guilty, knowing she was writing that letter this very night, and she just wished he would go. The younger members of the family were behind the dining room door, peeping out and giggling. Frankie got in the car and then right back out for one last kiss. She was so embarrassed, and ran to the steps and waved them goodbye.

Early on Monday morning when Georgianna had finished her early morning chores, she began her letter to Frankie, "Dear Frankie." Here was a long pause because she didn't know just how to say what needed to be said. She started several times, trying to get the right words together, then crumpled the pages and dropped them in the waste basket. She decided she would just have to be truthful and say it like it was.

> Dear Frankie,
>
> I have been giving a lot of thought about your proposal, and I feel that it is best to just put things on hold for the time being. I need more time to think about it. I am not sure that I love you enough to marry you. We both need more time, and I hope that you will understand.
>
> Yours Truly, Georgianna

Georgianna watched the mail closely later in the week, expecting a response to her letter. None arrived. Bob had been giving her a little more attention, and she liked that.

Sunday afternoon found everyone in their swim wear and ready to go with Bob to Jimmy's swimming hole for the afternoon, only to see the '32 gray Ford pull up onto the driveway. Frankie was alone this time and carried his swimming trunks. Georgianna explained that they were headed for the swimming hole, and invited him to go along. Everyone piled into the back of the truck. Frankie sat by Georgianna who was blushing with embarrassment. None of the family knew about the letter. Frankie announced that Fubby and Evie had a little girl, and he had the honor of naming her "Colene." Georgianna was pleased with this news.

All afternoon she tried dividing her time between Bob and Frankie and just mingling with other family members. Frankie finally got her alone and remarked, "That was a very nice business letter that you wrote."

Almost at a loss for words, but knowing that she had to say something, "Well, that is the way that I feel, and I do not know what I can do about it. You will just have to wait for me to make up my mind, and I do not know when that will be." Frankie's jaw began to twitch, and she knew he didn't like what she had to say.

Nothing more was said about it, and Frankie left as soon as they returned to the McDonald home. Georgianna thought she might never see him again.

No letter arrived the following week or the next. Georgianna missed his letters, and wished that he would write her after all.

Mr. McDonald offered Bob the use of the truck and encouraged Bob to take Georgianna to the movies to cheer her up. He was really trying to break up the relationship between her and Frankie. Liking Bob a lot, Georgianna was eager to go out with him, anywhere he wanted to go, and twice a week he took her out, seeing her to the door when they returned.

Tonight she had felt very close to him and was becoming more and more confused about her feelings as they stood on the dining room steps. She was just the right height as he kissed her on the lips. She didn't want him to stop as she threw her arms around his neck and held him close.

"This is goodbye," Bob said. "I am very fond of you, but I don't love you like a man should love a wife. This tells me that you do not love this man like you should."

She felt fully crushed and slipped quietly in the house and upstairs to bed, where she lay awake for hours. She felt even worse when she learned that her Daddy had asked Bob to try and break up the friendship. She felt betrayed by Daddy and by Bob pretending to care for her when he was only following orders from her Daddy. Her confusion was getting out of bounds.

She thought of taking Pegatty and running away, but where could she go? Immediately she put that thought aside.

Georgianna continued to go about her daily chores, with a long face, feeling more dejected each day as no letter arrived.

Mama was becoming aggravated with all the indecision, one who was sure he was in love and the other unsure of her feelings. She secretly wrote Frankie a letter and explained Georgianna's unhappiness on not hearing from him, that he owed her some explanation, or was this the end of their friendship.

Meanwhile Frankie's family in Lexington had noticed his unusually quiet and brooding manner, and that no letters were arriving for him, and that he was not writing any. Then the letter with the unfamiliar handwriting arrived. They were puzzled. Frankie was thinking, "My plan worked. She found out that she missed me, so she must love me after all."

He was up and through his morning chores early and appeared before his mother, dressed to go someplace, and announced that he would be back in time to do the milking, not mentioning where he was going or why. She had a pretty good idea.

Georgianna was totally surprised and sort of happy to see the gray Ford coming up the road to be met by the barking dogs, and she immediately greeted Frankie warmly at the car. She really was glad to see him.

Frankie answered the question as to why he didn't write, "I thought this was a good way for you to decide if you loved me." Georgianna still was not really sure she had missed him. Maybe she did love him even is she didn't see stars or hear bells ringing. Possibly this was love, and she just didn't recognize it. She had always had someone to decide for her what she was to do.

Mama eventually spoke up, "I am tired of all this fooling around. I think that you had better just go on to Amherst and get that marriage license and get it over with."

Georgianna agreed reluctantly, thinking, "Probably this is my only chance to get away from the abuse and have a family of my own."

"Now, Georgianna, you know you cannot be married under the McDonald name that you have been using for the past years. You will have to use the name you came here using."

"Why?"

"Well, it's not just done that way." Georgianna put up no argument and went upstairs to get ready, not being very excited about it, still wondering if she was doing the right thing. Mama dressed to go with them. She needed to sign for Georgianna and seemed very relieved that decisions were being made, even if she was making them.

During the ten-mile ride to Amherst Courthouse, the three discussed a date and decided on the Sunday before Labor Day, which was ten days away. This would give time to shop for a wedding outfit and a few things.

The car was parked, and the two young people stood before the county clerk, both experiencing butterflies. "May I help you?"

"We would like a marriage license." replied Frankie very meekly. "Are you both over eighteen?"

"I am, but Georgianna's mother will sign for her."

The procedure was soon over with, and they walked out of the courthouse and Frankie stuck the license into his breast pocket. Georgianna still wasn't quite sure what she was doing. Mama thought it was all right, so it must be.

The next thing to take care of was to contact the Reverend Earl Collie to see if he would be able to perform the ceremony on the set date. And they found he would be free just after church on that date at the parsonage at Monroe, Virginia.

Frankie left for Lexington later, flying high and saying that he would be back on Saturday, shop for a ring and take Georgianna to the movies. This would be their first date, and they already had the marriage license. Everyone was more excited than Georgianna, who was still in a state of indecision, but it looked to her that she was really getting married and she didn't know whether to be happy or sad. There was a very mixed feeling, happiness at the thought of having her own children that no one could take away from her and a great relief that she would no longer have to endure the abuse that she had endured for such a long time.

There was sadness about being separated from precious little Pegatty whom she dearly loved as much as she loved Dela. She would not be seeing Dela very often. There had not been the closeness between the two the past two years that had existed when they were much younger, so maybe this would work out. Mama thought it was a good idea for Georgianna to get married. Dela could take over the care of Pegatty and she would have no need to worry about that.

Needless to say the whole family was excited, that is until Daddy came home. Learning the news he was furious and stalked out of the house to the car and drove off to calm down. He really did not want to accept the fact that Georgianna would be leaving to make a life of her own and would no longer be at his beck and call. She felt better then about the plans for getting married.

CHAPTER 51

The Ring

Saturday was a beautiful day, and Georgianna was excited about Frankie bringing her a ring and taking her to the movies. She spent lots of time in front of the mirror, trying to get her hair to behave. Mama promised her a permanent before the wedding and that pleased her. She was becoming somewhat excited about the upcoming events.

Finally getting her hair like she wanted it, she descended the stairway just as Frankie drove up to be met by Bobby and the dogs, followed by Jimmy and Pegatty. Georgianna waited inside for him to come to the door. She was a very shy person and had been taught not to be forward when it came to persons of the opposite sex. And she did want to do what was proper, so Mama would be pleased with her. Things were confusing enough, and she surely did not want anyone upset at this time in her life.

Frankie sauntered jauntily into the dining room with Jimmy clutching his hand. He headed directly for Georgianna, who was still hesitant about the whole thing, threw his arms around her and kissed her lingeringly, to the laughter of all the other children. She felt embarrassed and blushed. Mama entered the room with a pleasant hello.

Frankie went on to explain that he had been in Lynchburg all morning shopping for rings and had also bought a charcoal gray suit to be married in. He reached in his breast pocket and pulled out a small black case, placed it on the dining room table. He then opened it for everyone's benefit and displayed a diamond ring with a matching wedding band.

Georgianna would have liked for him to have waited and shown them to her first when they were alone. It appeared that was not the way Frankie did things.

Everyone was in a jolly mood at the evening meal, that is, everyone but Georgianna who remained pretty somber. She was thinking, "It's too late to back out now," since the time was near for her to be married.

Time for the first real date with Frankie was finally here. And when the dishes were finished, Georgianna slowly ascended the stairs to get ready for the movie starring Connie Francis, not really very excited about the whole thing. She was wondering when Frankie was going to put the engagement ring on her finger so maybe then she would feel engaged.

Frankie was eager for them to go, so she had little time to primp. She combed her hair and pinned it up and applied fresh lipstick. She fastened the strand of pearls around her neck.

She was ready to go when Bethany ran up the stairs, out of breath. "Frankie says you better hurry or you will be late for the beginning."

"I am ready," and the two girls walked down the stairs together. Frankie stood beaming at the foot of the stairs.

Everyone watched as the two walked to the car and Frankie gentlemanly opened the car door and closed it after Georgianna was seated. After he had sat down and closed the door on the driver side, he reached into his breast pocket and pulled out the ring case. He took the diamond out and paced it on Georgianna's ring finger. "Now we are really engaged, and I wish we were getting married tomorrow."

Everyone waved as they drove off, while the young woman wondered if this was real, or was she in a dream. She had not been alone with Frankie except while sitting in the swing on the front porch and then in the big swing at the Lowman's homeplace when Frankie had proposed to her.

The movie was enjoyable and a beautiful full moon was aglow, as they rode the thirteen miles back home. It was a night for romance. However, Georgianna didn't know a lot about what romance was. Frankie pulled her close to his side as they rode, and she felt a little fear of men in general.

On arrival at the house, Frankie wanted to sit in the car. Mama had told her many times that nice girls do not park in the car with boy friends. Since she was engaged, she thought it was all right for a little while. They were in sight of the house, but even so she felt uncomfortable.

After what seemed like hours, Georgianna told Frankie that Mama would be very angry with her if she did not go in the house, so reluctantly he got out of the car and opened the door for her. They slowly walked to the door and entered the dining room. He wanted to stand at the door and cuddle, until she insisted that she must go in or Mama would be really mad.

In parting he said, "I'll be back on Wednesday and we will go to see that Shirley Temple movie. Would you like that?" Georgianna agreed it would be all right and immediately stepped inside and closed the door, feeling a little breathless. After that last kiss, she assumed that Frankie must love her, and that marrying him would not be a big mistake.

CHAPTER 52

The Shopping Day

Mama informed Georgianna that they would take the next Friday to shop for luggage and a suitable wedding dress. Friday morning arrived bright and clear, and with a certain amount of anticipation, Georgianna took care of Pegatty's needs for the morning. She brushed her long hair till it shone, then fixed it into pretty long curls, all the while wishing she could take this little girl with her when she married and left the mountain. She knew she would miss her terribly.

Then she knew she could someday have her very own little girl. Knowing she would be living with Frankie's mother and sister, plus a niece and nephew for awhile, she hoped they would be in an apartment or place of their own when they had children. The time was really drawing near, and she couldn't back out now.

Mama called up the stairs that Daddy was ready to go, and they had to ride in and stay at the feed store until other merchants opened later in the morning. They were off on Georgianna's first real shopping trip. She and Bethany had gone hat shopping one Easter when they had selected hats in poor taste. Gramma or Mary Bedford had always made her dresses and there was no need to shop for that.

There was indeed a little excitement in the air as Mama and Georgianna left Colling Street and walked up to Main Street, then past Grant's, Kresge's, and Woolworth's to some of the fashionable shops, and walked in Leamens Ladieswear. There were many beautiful dresses hanging on the racks, but none that really suited Georgianna.

Shop after shop was explored before something was found that pleased both the shoppers.

After entering Mildred's, a nice department store and riding the elevator to the dress department, the two spent quite a lot of time looking at the many new fall styles that had recently arrived at the store. They found a deep green two-piece dress with a Mandarin neckline and tapered sleeves, braided trim, and two decorative buttons at the neckline. "Goodness me, Georgianna, it's lunch time. We have spent the whole morning and only brought a dress. We'll go in Woolworth for a sandwich and ice cream soda, then we have to look for shoes, handbag, hat, and a piece of luggage."

"Has Frankie mentioned a honeymoon?"

"No, he hasn't. I don't guess we will have one. He said he had promised to take Fubby and Evie to Paint Bank the day we are married, so I guess that will be our honeymoon."

"That's no honeymoon," Mama remarked, while they waited for their sandwich. "You need to go somewhere by yourself."

"But Mama, I don't think Frankie has any money. He said he borrowed the money to buy my rings. He is to get some soon, but will have to pay back what he borrowed."

Lunch was soon over, and more shopping had to be done. As they neared Leamen's Ladies Shop, Georgianna spied a pretty peach colored nightie in the window and pointed it out to Mama. It had tiny white stars all over it. They immediately went in and asked the price, which was unbelievable for such a pretty gown. The saleslady smiled as she rung up the sale and placed the gown in a bag. Georgianna thought to herself, "Two more days and I'll be wearing this," and she felt a tinge of excitement.

Soon a green hat was found that matched the dress perfectly. Many pairs of shoes were tried on. Georgianna had a short wide foot and was hard to fit. Finally a pretty pair of green shoes with squares of suede and squares of leather fit perfectly. Mama pulled the dress from the bag and held it close to the shoes. "Um, a perfect match. Georgianna, you will be a pretty bride." The two felt good to have found matching items.

Now, one last thing, a piece of luggage. Mama spoke up, "Where is that shop that handles inexpensive luggage?" Georgianna had never owned a piece of luggage, always just putting her clothes in a paper bag or a box when she moved from place to place. She was beginning to feel important, and it was a good feeling. "Oh, here is the luggage shop. A good thing, our time is going fast."

They were met inside the door by a nice young gentleman. "May I help you"?

"Yes, please, we need a piece of luggage. This girl is going to be married on Sunday, and we need a small piece of luggage."

I think I have just the thing, if you want black." He pulled a small black bag from the shelf and opened it to reveal a deep green moiré lining. "Look, Georgianna, a beautiful green inside that matches your outfit. "It's perfect. We'll take it."

On arrival back home, the whole family had to inspect the purchases. Bethany held the green dress up to herself in the mirror and admitted it was pretty. "I am going to have a long white dress and a veil when I get married."

"I hope you get it. This suits me just fine, and I know Frankie will like it, because I will be inside it." And the whole bunch gave a hearty laugh.

Georgianna had an appointment to get her hair cut and have a permanent the next day, and that would be another full day. Getting a permanent was an all day job, taking a good four hours. The hair was wound on metal rods, and then each rod was inserted in a cylinder, attached to a big machine that generated a lot of heat. You had the feeling that your head weighed a ton. After you fried for awhile, the rods were disconnected, the hair unwound and plastered with a setting gel and set in your favorite style. Then you sat under the dryer for ages, before it was dry and the pins removed and finishing touches were made. Georgianna was tired, but after one look in the mirror, she felt that it was worthwhile. She looked better that she had in her whole life. In fact, she thought she looked almost pretty.

Georgianna felt it hard to believe that by this time tomorrow she would be married, and she didn't know whether to laugh or cry, so she did neither, only feeling like she was still in a dream.

CHAPTER 53

The Wedding Day and
Brief Honeymoon

September 6, 1936, could not have been a more beautiful day for a wedding, plus it was Mama's birthday, so there was much celebrating to be done.

Georgianna awoke extra early so she could take care of her chores, plus go to Sunday School at Mount Tabor before they traveled to Monroe for the high noon ceremony. As she milked the brown Jersey cow, Bossy, talking to her all the time, she was glad she would not be having to do this every morning.

Bethany was supposed to milk part time. Lots of times she just skipped it, and many times Bossy went unmilked. Bethany was pretty lazy for fifteen years old. Georgianna never ratted on her when she neglected her chores. Mama would probably accuse her of being a tattler. Anyway she would not have to worry about that anymore.

Pegatty was up when Georgianna reached the house with the steaming pail of milk. The little girl was eager to get the day going and pestered Georgianna while she was trying to strain and put away the milk. "Don't be so impatient, Pegatty. You will be pestering Dela to do things for you after today."

"I wish you were not going away to live with Frankie. I need you here with me," and she grabbed Georgianna around the knees and held tight. "I know, sweetie pie. I really do not want to leave you, but it's the only way that I can have my own little girl. You can come to visit and I will come back to visit you, I promise." Dela will look after you and take good care of you. Everything will be all right.

223

When breakfast was over, Georgianna washed the dishes, the same as usual. She dressed Pegatty in her white crochet dress and put a pink ribbon in her hair and warned her to stay clean while she prepared herself for Sunday school and the wedding afterward. She had plenty of time, and for once she was not in a big rush. Her bag had been packed the night before, and most of her other belongings were in a box ready to place in the car. She would be going to a new home, only this time things were a lot different. No one would be moving her again.

When the grooming was completed, Georgianna liked what she saw as she placed the green hat over her golden hair that really looked good, after the permanent. She picked up her black suitcase and her new handbag and strode proudly down the staircase, really feeling like somebody.

Everyone at the small Methodist church was really excited about the coming wedding, and Georgianna was getting compliments from every side. All of this really boosted her ego, and she began to feel important. It was indeed a good feeling. And about time, since she had always felt like nobody really cared other than Pegatty, who did not want to let go of her hands and was a little pouty about the whole thing.

Georgianna knew that she would not be seeing these friends for sometime. She had to hug everyone and especially her friend, Dorothy Franklin, who also expected to be married soon.

When Sunday School was over and all the good-byes were said, the McDonald family climbed into the car for the ride to Monroe, Virginia, where the wedding was to take place at the parsonage. Daddy was very quiet, while the rest of the family chattered like magpies. Bethany asked Georgianna what she thought about sleeping with Frankie, to which the bride-to-be replied that she really hadn't given it much thought.

On arrival at the parsonage, Frankie's car was already parked. He, Fubby, and Evie sat in the car, Evie holding the new baby, Colene, that Georgianna had not seen. When Georgianna spied the pink bundle she became excited, knowing one day she would have her own pink bundle to carry.

Frankie's mother and three sisters arrived with a brother-in-law and his two sons, a car really full. After greeting one another, all waited in the cars until Reverend Collie's car drove up. He had delivered his morning service at a nearby church. He stepped from the car and opened the car door for his wife and ten-year-old daughter. By this time everyone had gotten out of the cars.

After introductions, they followed the preacher into the large white house. Frankie was getting more jittery all the time, and Georgianna had a good supply of butterflies in her stomach but appeared as cool as a cucumber and in control of her emotions.

Everyone was very quiet, and it was almost like a funeral. The preacher spoke, "Shall we begin?" Frankie reached into his breast pocket and retrieved the marriage license. Georgianna clutched the ring for Frankie in her right hand which had become somewhat sweaty. She hoped it would soon be over with.

"Let us pray," came the soft voice of the preacher. It was a very impressive prayer, and Georgianna listened to every word very carefully. She truly hoped they would keep their commitment to each other and have a happy marriage.

"Do you, Frankie, take this woman to be your lawful wedded wife, to have and to hold, for better or for worse, for richer or poorer? Will you cherish her and love her all the days of your life, as long as you both shall live?"

"I do."

"Do you, Georgianna, take this man to be your lawful wedded husband, to have and to hold, for better or for worse, for richer or poorer... Will you love him and cherish him all the days of your life, as long as you both shall live?"

"I do."

Just as Georgianna said I do, Pegatty, who was being restrained by Dela spoke up loudly, "Quit it." There were smiles around the room as the ceremony was continued with the double rings exchange. Once again, a prayer to seal this marriage. "I pronounce you now man and wife. You may kiss the bride." Georgianna was blushing, shy and bashful, as Frankie kissed her swiftly.

Congratulations were offered, and a few photos were snapped, as the bride and groom walked into the front yard, on this extremely beautiful day, to begin their life together.

Into the automobile, everyone took their place, only Georgianna sat in Frankie's car, beside him for the ride back home to pick up her belongings.

On the arrival home, Georgianna was surprised to see Georgia had baked a cake, and had the punch bowl out for a little celebration. Mama had secretly planned this, and Georgianna was pleased thinking, "I guess Mama likes me after all."

There was not much time to linger. Frankie had promised to take Fubby and Evie to Paint Bank for a short visit. On arriving in Lexington to pick up Fubby's suitcase, there again was another surprise. Glady had arranged a small reception for them, with a cake, punch, and goodies. Frankie's brother and family had arrived and felt slighted that they had not been invited for the wedding. Frankie said, "I just didn't want too many people around."

Frankie announced to Georgianna that they were going to Washington, DC., for a short honeymoon after leaving Fubby's family at Paint Bank. The drive to Paint Bank was quite long, and it was very late in the afternoon when they arrived there.

Georgianna held Colene, while the others retrieved their items from the car. Georgianna looked down to see a stream of water trickle down the front of her wedding dress. Evie grabbed a clean diaper and hastily brushed the dress dry before it has a chance to soak in. This incident provoked a lot of laughter from the bystanders.

Soon the married couple were on the road again, finally by themselves. Frankie urged his bride to move closer to him, which she shyly did. "Now we may get to Crowes where we can find a room to spend the night."

They had not gone far before spotting a service man, thumbing a ride. Frankie slowed and stopped and invited the gentleman to sit in front seat with the two. Georgianna thought, "What kind of honeymoon is this? It's being shared with so many people." A light conversation followed and soon the soldier was fast asleep on Georgianna's shoulder, and was awakened when they reached his destination. "Thank you sir, and God Bless you in your new life together."

Alone once again they began the search for a room for the night, stopping at several places to find 'no vacancy' signs. Labor Day travelers had filled all the rooms. Finally stopping at a small run down place, they found that a room was available. Frankie paid for the room and was given a key with the room number on it. On opening the door, Georgianna's mouth flew open, "We can't stay here." Frankie agreed, and they went to the office to get their money back, only to find they did not give refunds.

After traveling and looking to no avail, Frankie spoke up, "We may as well go on back to Lexington, I know there is room there, and we will start out tomorrow morning." Georgianna, never having made her own decisions, agreed that it was all right.

They arrived at the Lowman's home about midnight and found a dark house with everyone in bed. Not having a key, Frankie rapped on the door and awoke the family who wondered what was wrong. Frankie's mother said, "Thought you two were going to Washington. What happened?"

"All the tourist homes were full up, and we could not find a room. We will start out early in the morning." Frankie's mother led them into the room where Evie and the baby had been sleeping.

"You can sleep in here. Goodness, sonny boy, you must be worn out."

Georgianna took her suitcase into the bathroom, washed her face, and put on the peach colored nightie with the stars on it. She shyly went back into the bedroom to find Frankie in a pair of tan pajamas sitting on the side of the bed. It was a little scary crawling into bed with a man she hardly knew. He pulled her close to him and smothered her with kisses, and the marriage was consummated awkwardly while the rubber sheet crackled underneath them. It had been put on the bed to protect it from six week old Colene who had been there with her mother Evie.

Everyone was in a good mood on arising, and Glady was busy with breakfast. Edwina, who used crutches because of arthritis, was cheerful. Frankie's mother was short of breath, having asthma. Frankie went to milk the cow. Georgianna set the table, already knowing where everything was from her previous visit in June.

When they sat down to breakfast, Glady kidded the new couple about the rubber sheet being on the bed especially for the bride and groom. Georgianna blushed shyly.

It was evident that Frankie was very close to his family. Georgianna began to wonder if she would ever really be first in his life. She saw how his mother wanted to baby him and tell him what to do. Georgianna felt that his mother would keep a grip on him while they lived in her household. Mrs. Lowman had been a widow for eleven years and depended on her children for many things.

Dropping Glady at her place of employment by eight o'clock, the couple were once again headed for Washington D.C., another beautiful day for travel. Frankie pulled a twenty dollar bill from his wallet and handed it to his bride. Georgianna had never had a bill of this size, and she assumed it was hers to keep. Before the day was over, Frankie asked for the money back to buy gas. Georgianna was beginning to wonder if Frankie knew much about handling money since he had lost the room deposit the night before.

They drove Route Eleven through Fairfield and were in the small town of Staunton before noon, stopping in Harrisonburg at a small restaurant to have lunch. They sat and talked for awhile and Frankie was in no hurry to get to Washington. Georgianna had never been in this part of the country before and was enjoying the beautiful scenery.

After leaving Harrisonburg, Frankie spotted a small airport where plane rides were featured at a reasonable price. "How would you like to take a plane ride?" To which Georgianna replied, "I'd love it, if you would." He drove in, parked, and bought two tickets and they walked across the field toward the planes. Georgianna had to walk fast to keep up. As they reached the plane, Frankie's pace slowed and he took a long look at his new bride and said, "I don't think we had better do this, I do not want to lose you now that you are all mine."

The young couple turned around and walked back to the ticket booth They hoped for a refund but heard, "We do not give refunds." That was more money down the drain.

Their next stop was Endless Caverns. Neither had toured a cavern, and they decided it would be fun. Driving into the parking lot, they found it quite full because of the holiday. Frankie took money from his wallet and bought two tickets, after Georgianna said, "You are not going to back out of this, I hope." And he gave a little laugh.

They were awestruck by all the beauty that was underground. The tour was quite long and when they exited the caverns, it was plain to see that the sun was getting low in the west. Frankie was ready to eat again, and by they time they had found a small restaurant and had ordered and been served, the sky was dark. They were nowhere close to Washington, and the whole day was gone.

After once again entering the car, they continued driving for a few miles and stopped at a service station for gas. After paying for the gas, Frankie took a second glance into his wallet. Georgianna had the feeling he was running out of money. Goodness knows, she could not help. All she had was the five dollars her Daddy had given her after she asked for it, wanting to have a little money in her pocketbook.

Getting into the car, Frankie sat quietly for a few seconds and remarked, "We probably can't find a room for the night. I think we better just go on back to Lexington." Georgianna was very disappointed but said nothing, always having let someone else make the decisions and going along with whatever they thought was the thing to do.

On arrival at the Lowman's', Frankie got a lot of teasing from Glady and Edwina about getting homesick and coming back home. Thus ended the short honeymoon.

CHAPTER 54

The Dance

G eorgianna was delighted and somewhat surprised to receive a letter a few days after the brief honeymoon. She became excited as she read,

> Dear Georgianna,
>
> We all miss you, especially Pegatty, who continues to ask where you are and when are you coming home. Dela doesn't quite give her as much attention as you did. It's hard for her to understand that you have another home now, and do not live here anymore.
>
> The real reason for this letter is we have planned a dance and shower in honor of you and Frankie on Saturday, September the twenty fifth, so make your plans accordingly. We will be expecting you early for dinner at five thirty.
>
> Love, Mama

This was very unexpected, and gave Georgianna some serious thinking. Maybe Mama did love her a little after all, to go to the trouble to plan this dance in her honor. She also was remembering the many previous dances that were held in the homes of various neighbors and the barn dances that were held in new barns before the livestock took over. Those were joyous times when daughters danced with daddies, and anyone else who asked them. Small children would curl up anywhere they could find an unoccupied spot and sleep until the local musicians played Home Sweet Home at midnight. Then everyone knew it was time to congratulate the host and hostess, gather up their children, and head for home.

Georgianna really loved these times and was just getting warmed up when Home Sweet Home ended the party. Part of her time was spent tending to Pegatty until she was safely asleep in the middle of a feather bed, surrounded by many pillows to keep her safe. Then an occasional check was all that was necessary. Simple refreshments were usually served. Lemonade, cider, cookies was all anyone needed. Of course some of the men may have had a bottle stuck somewhere handy, but nothing ever got out of hand.

Georgianna remembered the Halloween parties, especially the masquerade ball that was held at the McDonald's home when Mama and Daddy dressed as George and Martha Washington. They were so handsome. Things were great until a bee of some kind found its way under George's mask, and he rushed outside to remove his mask. No one removed their mask until midnight, when Home Sweet Home was played. That was one of the most memorable times.

Georgianna was eager for Frankie's return from work so she could give him the good news, hoping that he would be as excited as she was. She kept one eye on the clock and another on the front gate. She just knew something must be wrong with the clock. The hands moved so slowly.

Eventually the gray Ford pulled in the front gate, and Georgianna lost no time getting to the car by the time Frankie retrieved his lunch bucket from behind the driver's seat. He hadn't had time to get rid of the wad of tobacco. Georgianna didn't care much for tobacco kisses. She turned her head and got a smooch on the cheek. They stood by the car as she pulled the letter from her pocket and read it to Frankie, whose mouth began to twitch. Then he spoke, "You know I always go help my brother Andy on the farm on weekends." After seeing her crestfallen face, he had second thoughts. "I guess we can manage to go. I warn you I am not much of a dancer."

Saturday the twenty fifth was a bright beautiful day. All that was on Georgianna's mind was the evening ahead of them and wondering who would be there and if Bob would be in attendance and just how she would react to seeing him again, knowing that she was a married woman now and would need to behave like one.

Frankie was not too excited about the whole thing. He took care of whatever he needed to do and they left in time to get to the five-thirty dinner hour. Georgianna had her white organdy evening gown carefully spread over the back seat of the car and was eager to see the family again. Fubby and Evie had moved from Andy's to the McDonald's and converted the garage into living quarters. It would be good to see them again.

After the delicious dinner, the kitchen was hurriedly cleaned up and all the furniture moved to one end of the large dining room. The sideboard was cleaned to hold the gifts guests would be bringing. Soon all was in readiness just waiting for the guests to arrive. Georgianna felt very important knowing that all of this was in her honor and that Mama was doing it for her.

Harry Keith and the local musicians were the first to arrive with their stringed instruments and their wives and children. They bantered among themselves, in a jovial mood as they tuned their instruments.

Bethany who was fourteen but thought she was twenty one, insisted she looked the best. Georgianna felt satisfied that she looked pretty good in her white organdy evening gown. Her self-image had improved since she had married. Frankie had gone to visit Fubby for a few minutes while the guests were arriving.

Georgianna felt very well satisfied as she descended the staircase and met a couple fellows coming up to the bathroom. One of them whistled, as the other said, "There's another prima donna." Things were getting a little noisy as the musicians tuned up for the beginning. Mama met Georgianna at the foot of the stairs. "Where's Frankie? You two are to lead the dancers onto the floor."

"He is at Fubby's. I'll send Bobby for him right now." The two arrived out of breath, with Frankie somewhat irritated that his visit was interrupted.

"We are to lead the dancers onto the floor." Mama gave the signal to the musicians, and the strains of "Golden Slippers" filled the room as the bride and groom moved onto the floor, followed by others. Georgianna liked this evening. Even if Frankie was a bit awkward, he smelled good and looked good in his charcoal suit he had worn for the wedding.

Georgianna's heart flipped as she saw Bob enter the room and head straight for her. He tapped Frankie on the shoulder, "May I dance with your wife?" Frankie's mouth began to twitch as he walked away without saying a word. "Are you happy, Pete?" Bob asked. He had given her this pet name a couple years earlier.

"I guess so," was her reply. She was relieved when the music ended, unable to sort out her feelings.

The sideboard was laden with gifts prettily wrapped. At intermission as refreshments were being served, Georgianna was instructed to open the gifts with Frankie's help. There were many pieces of pink glassware that was in vogue at the time. An abundance of towels, eighteen in all. Someone remarked, "That is how many children you will have," which brought a blush to Georgianna's face.

The musicians had been refreshed and were tuning up again for some square dancing, announcing the Paul Jones, a favorite square dance that you had to follow instructions. Frankie kept getting confused and going the wrong way. While Daddy was dancing with Georgianna, who had more or less avoided him, he said, "You're going to have to teach that husband of yours to dance. He doesn't know right from left."

"He's just nervous, that's all," Georgianna replied.

All too soon the strains of Home Sweet Home were heard, as the hands on the clock were on twelve, and guests gave their thanks to the hostess and good wishes for the bride and groom. Soon everything was lots quieter. The gifts were packed into the car, and the couple headed for Lexington.

When they arrived, they saw the lights still on in the house. They were met at the door by Frankie's mother with her shawl around her shoulders. "I've been worried to death. Do you know how late it is?" She could not realize that Frankie was a married man. An adult could make his own decisions. Georgianna felt like she had just traded mothers and would never be able to be really grown up and make decisions on her own. Someone else always was in charge of her life, and she wondered if her whole life was going to be like this, with someone else always making the decisions that affected her.

CHAPTER 55

After the Honeymoon

As with every marriage there is a period of adjustment, so it was with Frankie and Georgianna. She had to adjust to living in a new household in addition to a husband.

Frankie's mother still wanted to control him as if he were still a child instead of a married man. It was "Sonny, do this," and, "Sonny, do that."

Georgianna did not know just how she was to fit into this family of four adults and one teen age boy, Frankie's nephew, Kyle. The first few weeks were difficult, while Frankie and his sister were at work, but were more pleasant in the evenings. Glady and Georgianna worked together preparing the evening meal, which was still "supper." Frankie worked in the laundry of Virginia Military Institute, while Glady worked as a dental assistant for Dr. Russell Engleman.

There was late garden produce that had to be canned, and Georgianna did her share of whatever needed to be done. Mrs. Lowman was slow, even though she was just in her sixties. She was bothered with chronic asthma. Edwina had rheumatoid arthritis and used crutches but could sit and pare vegetables. Georgianna was very fond of her and knew they would be good friends.

Frankie's nephew was called by his initials, K.B., and when he came in from school, he and Georgianna spent time tossing the football before Frankie and Glady arrived from work. Frankie often brought cubed steak from the VMI commissary, where he kept an account that took quite a bit of his monthly check of fifty dollars. The balance he handed to his mother to be used to help pay bills.

Georgianna did not feel much like a married woman, only a servant in a household where she made none of the decisions, but was expected to do her share of the work. Frankie often went to the farm on the weekend to help his brother, Andy, who would give him a bag of flour or some garden vegetables for pay. Andy and his wife Ada had three children, ages three, five and seven. They lived at the Lowman homeplace, where all the Lowmans as well as Mr. Lowman's father had been born. Frankie still had an interest in the farm. A portion was to come to him eventually, and he felt it was his duty to help take care of the farm. His father had died in 1925, when Frankie was twelve years old. Mr. Lowman evidently was a very shrewd man and good with money, having bought the nine acres where Frankie's mother moved part of the family after his death. The parcel of land and house were close to the town of Lexington, Virginia. The farm of 200 acres was at Kerr's Creek.

K.B.'s father married for the third time after being widowed twice, and he decided K.B. should live with him. Georgianna was sad to see him leave. They had become good friends, and the after-school play time came to an end in late November.

Georgianna had been doing some sewing with Edwina's help, and when Frankie mentioned going to the Fireman's Christmas Ball to be held in the Washington and Lee College gym, she was indeed excited. They never had any social life. Frankie, she and Glady took in a movie once in a while, and they attended Manly Memorial Baptist Church. They had both been baptized there in late November, he having come from a Presbyterian church and Georgianna from a Methodist.

Now where to get enough money to sew a gown was the big question. After a furtive search, enough change was found to buy royal blue moiré taffeta to make a backless gown with a jacket. In spite of being made by an amateur, it turned out well, and even in 1995, it still occupied a spot in Georgianna's cedar closet, along with the green wedding dress.

The ball was exciting even if Frankie was not the best dancer. Georgianna remembered the many dances that were held while she was growing up when some new barns were built and a barn dance was held to celebrate the occasion. The whole family had attended, and the children curled up and went to sleep whenever they could find a spot. These were some of the best memories Georgianna had.

The harvest at the farm was finished, and Frankie had a little more time on the weekend. Georgianna was lonesome to see Pegatty and Dela, also Fubby and Evie, who had moved to the McDonald's shortly after Georgianna's wedding to take care of the several hundred head of cattle. A day to go back home was set, and Georgianna realized how very much she had missed them all.

CHAPTER 56

Going Back Home

Sunday morning was bright and beautiful with a cool brisk breeze. Frankie took his mother and sister to their Presbyterian Church in Lexington, and he and Georgianna were alone in the car. This was a rare occasion. Most of the time they were alone only after retiring for the night. She felt more like a married woman having Frankie to herself and being on the way to see her family. She was excited, this being only her second trip back home, to be able to see Fubby and Evie's little girl, Colene. And she could get the few belongings that she had left, a few odds and ends of dishes, whatnots, etc. She wondered if they had missed her and how she would be received.

The waiting was not long. As they came to a stop in front of the familiar house, the several dogs met them at the car and had to be chased away. Mama, followed by the children, excitedly came out of the dining room door to affectionately greet Georgianna and Frankie like they were honored guests. She knew now they had missed her. Pegatty held onto her, inquiring if she was going to stay? Of course the reply was, "Just for the day, sweetie." The three-year-old was crestfallen at this news. Dela had taken charge of caring for Pegatty but was away at school every day and did not have the time to devote to her that Georgianna had always given her. She missed that close companionship, and she stuck close to Georgianna for the entire day.

Bethany couldn't wait to get Georgianna alone and boldly ask her, "How do you like sleeping with a man? What's it like? Do you like it?" and any other question she could think of.

Georgianna meekly replied, "It's all right," not knowing a better way to say it.

Everyone treated her sort of special, and it gave her a good feeling. She now felt more closeness to this, her second, family.

Before leaving, she went to the attic space under the dormer window where she had left her few belongings. She looked in every nook and cranny. They were nowhere to be found. She approached Mama, "Where are my things that I left in the attic?"

"Oh, those, I thought that you did not want them, so I gave them to Georgia."

Georgianna tried to hide her disappointment about her belongings and made no big deal over it, but it sort of spoiled the day for the married girl. She did indeed want them and felt betrayed that they were given away without her permission. Once again she felt as if her feelings never mattered to anyone. She decided then and there to have several children, and knew her feelings would be important to them. They would fill a void in her life, and her family would be a very important part of her life. This she vowed, she would never give their possessions away without their permission.

Frankie had gone to Fubby's place, since they were more like brothers than brothers-in-law. Fubby had made the garage into living quarters for him, Evie, and Colene, and they were adjusting well after the move to the McDonalds. Fubby was a good steady worker and knew how to look after the cattle. Georgianna soon followed, eager to see them and to hold little Colene. She had not been there long before Evie confided that she thought she was pregnant again and was hoping for a boy, since Fubby really wanted a son.

Mama started talking about Christmas shopping and how much she had done and still had to do. Georgianna kept quiet, knowing she didn't have money to shop for anyone, and on leaving, she wondered what her first married Christmas would be like.

On the way home Georgianna asked Frankie about getting a job. She knew how to do many things and could learn easily and really wanted to have some money of her own. "Why do you want a job. I need you at home to look out for Mom and take care of Edwina and do the housework. And besides, I do not want my wife working. A wife should stay home. One of these days we can start a family for you to care for."

Georgianna assumed that was the end of it and resigned herself to the fact that someone else always made the decisions for her, and it was up to her to abide by them. Whether she like it or agreed to it didn't seem to be important. This was the way it had always been, and getting married had not changed things that much. She wondered if her life would always be like this.

Georgianna had been feeling sort of blue and was not looking forward to Christmas, which was about six weeks away, knowing it would be very different from previous ones. She continued to do whatever was required of her. Edwina needed help with her daily bath. She and her mother didn't get along too well, so this job fell to Georgianna.

November the fifteenth Georgianna awoke with a severe pain in her side. She went to see Dr. White, who announced, "I think you had better see Dr. Leech. I think you have appendicitis and need surgery. You can see him at Jackson Memorial Hospital. I'll phone and see when he can see you." He phoned. "I have a patient I want you to see... All right, I'll send her right over."

Georgianna walked the two blocks, and was examined by Dr. Leech. "I'll schedule surgery for tomorrow morning. You can report to the hospital this afternoon."

It was a short walk to the dentist's office where Glady worked and Frankie always picked her up. "What did the doctor say?"

"I gotta have my appendix out tomorrow."

Georgianna spent a week in the hospital.

CHAPTER 57

Georgianna's First Married Christmas

This Christmas held no excitement as the previous Christmas had, since there was no money for gifts for anyone. She had saved a few cents and hoped there would be enough to buy a new necktie for her husband's first Christmas. She had seen some pretty ones at Rose's in Lexington and would like to replace the gray and black one he always wore. Something bright would go well with his gray suit and the charcoal one he had bought to be married in.

Glady had just bought herself a new winter coat to the tune of $79. "How in the world can you afford an expensive coat with a fifty dollar a month salary?"

"Oh, I just put it on my Adair Hutton charge account, and I'll pay some every month and eventually I'll have it paid for. I really needed a nice winter coat for church. These folks at the Presbyterian Church all dress nice, and I don't want to look out of place in my coat I wear to work. And anyway it's almost Christmas, and my circle is having a special meeting, and I need to look good."

"Well, I guess the Baptists will just have to look at my old coat that I have worn for a couple years and like me as I am," remarked Georgianna, really feeling a twinge of resentment that she couldn't have a new coat. She had never let clothes worry her a lot, and she felt thankful that she had a coat to wear. Georgianna heard Mom Lowman talking about ordering some things from the Sears and Roebuck catalogue. She heard her mention galoshes and Frankie say, "Okay, what size?" The young woman thought, "That's not going to be my first Christmas gift from my husband," and she dismissed the thought from her mind, and was counting on a necklace or some piece of jewelry, something romantic.

A few days before Christmas, Georgianna checked the change in her purse, and to her delight she found, after counting it for the second time, that she had one dollar and fifteen cents. She hurriedly dressed to go shopping. The weather man on the radio was predicting snow flurries for the next day, but today was an ideal day, bright, sunny, and crisp. She could be back before Frankie and Glady arrived home from work, and she had picked a perfect spot to hide her purchase.

After announcing that she was walking into town and inquiring if anyone needed anything, which they didn't, she walked briskly the mile to Lexington and gazed into the windows at the pretty things. She entered Rose's and headed for the rack where she had seen the neck ties. She looked at every one before she settled on an attractive dark tie with a red stripe. The price tag said 79 cents. "I wonder if they have a box to put it in," she mused, as she approached the clerk. "I would like to have this tie, and do you have a box I can put it in?"

"Yes, I think I have the perfect box, but it will cost you a nickel."

"Good, I have the money," she said as she proudly counted out her change to pay for the treasure. Placing the package under her arm, she briskly retraced her steps back to the house in time to hide the package and set the table before Frankie arrived home.

A few days passed and a package arrived from Sears Roebuck addressed to Frankie's mother. Georgianna was curious about what the package contained. Mrs. Lowman laid it aside as she said, "I'll open it later."

Christmas was just a few days away, and Frankie's sister and her husband were coming in for Christmas. Georgianna had not met them, but they were mentioned often. The house had to be cleaned from top to bottom, so the next two days were really busy. Frankie went to the farm and came back with a small cedar tree, much smaller than the ones at the McDonalds. Glady, who seemed to be the leader in the household, located a box of Christmas decorations, and as soon as Frankie had the tree in place everyone, including Edwina with her crutches, took part in decorating the small tree. Now it was beginning to smell like Christmas, as cedar gave off its fragrance.

Georgianna was hoping Frankie would like his new tie on Christmas morning.

Christmas eve was a cold cloudy day. Andy and Ada brought their three children to visit. Andy slipped out and dressed in his Santa Claus suit and appeared at the door ringing his sleigh bell, surprising his children. He sauntered in and reached into his gunny sack and pulled out a small bag for each child. Oh, my, they were excited. Each bag contained a tablet, a pencil, an orange, and a few pieces of candy. The children were thrilled at this meager Christmas.

Georgianna didn't really know what to think. She had been accustomed to more elaborate ones than this the past nine years. It seemed to make these three children very happy. Georgianna was surprised to learn that this was their total Christmas other than a family dinner.

As Georgianna settled in for the first Christmas as Mrs. Frankie Lowman, she was a bit puzzled and wondered what the next day would bring. Frankie always wanted to snuggle until the bed warmed. Having no heat in the upstairs, it took a while to adjust to the cold sheets and be comfortable enough to fall asleep.

Daylight arrived with everyone greeting each other with a "Merry Christmas" and the usual morning chores. Frankie requested pancakes for breakfast, which were made ready while he did the milking and brought coal from the old house that was used as a storage shed as well as a stable. Frankie came in with the warm milk. His mother always took care of the straining and putting the milk away. "Are those hot cakes about ready. I need to split some wood."

Glady spoke up. "You know it's Christmas. We do not need to be in such a hurry. After breakfast, we have our gifts to unwrap. Ramona and Lanny will be here for dinner. You can split the wood tomorrow."

"Andy expects me to help him at the farm tomorrow."

Georgianna felt left out. Frankie never had any time for her. It was always something for his family.

The sizzling sausage and golden pancakes were ready with the hot syrup and a pitcher of molasses on the table. As Edwina came through the door with her crutches, Georgianna moved her chair with the cushion, so she could sit comfortable. Then she took her seat by her husband.

Breakfast was soon over and preparations were underway for the midday meal before the guests arrived. Georgianna was not very excited about this Christmas. She had only sent her family, the McDonalds, a Christmas card, not having money to buy gifts. Mama had always let the children do a little shopping, small things like a box of handkerchiefs, scarves, or a decorative pin. It was nice to have something to wrap and put under the tree for Christmas morning. She knew there was a lot of excitement back on the mountain.

Conell the dog let out a yelp as Ramona and Lanny arrived. This livened things up a little. Ramona was a bright cheerful person, giving Frankie a big hug with, "Hi, Sugar Tit," one of her expressions. She warmly greeted everyone as she sat a bag of packages on the nearest chair. "Lanny's family sent their regards. We are to spend the night with them. All the family plan to be together tomorrow."

"Ramona, this is my wife, Georgianna. I got a good deal. Fubby is now my brother-in-law, as well as my nephew, and she is a good worker, too. She also takes good care of Mom."

Georgianna managed a cordial "hello," not knowing what else to say. She went back to potato peeling, while Glady took their coats and hung them in the hallway. Ramona followed her husband into the sitting room/bedroom to greet Edwina, who had stretched out on the bed. "Hi there, Toots, you already for Santa?"

"As ready as I will ever be. I hope he brings me a new body that doesn't have arthritis."

"Well, Sis, I wish he would, too. You have had it for three long years, and that's long enough."

After finishing the dinner preparations Glady, who usually took charge, picked up a bell and walked through the house ringing it while singing, "Here comes Santa Claus, here comes Santa Claus. It's time to open your gifts."

Edwina retrieved her crutches from the side of the bed and, grimacing with pain, was soon on her feet. She followed the others into the parlor where the small tree stood with a few packages neatly wrapped, quite unlike the huge tree with the mounds of gifts that were always at the McDonalds' house on the mountain.

Glady took charge and started handing out items from under the tree. Ramona hurried to get her bag of gifts from the kitchen.

Georgianna watched Frankie as he opened his gift from her. "Oh, a pretty tie, but I already have two, what I really need is a pair of pliers. Thank you, lady."

The large package was handed to Georgianna and she knew without opening it what it contained. She carefully unwrapped the package and neatly folded the wrappings. Placing the bow on top, she tried to look excited as she took the lid off the box to see a shiny black pair of galoshes. "I hope you like them. Mom thought you would need them when you went for the cow, while I am at the farm."

Georgianna faked a little smile and said, "They will keep my feet dry," never letting anyone know how very disappointed she was. From then on every time she started outside, if it was wet or a skiff of snow lay on the ground, Mom Lowman came after her with the galoshes. Put these on or you'll catch cold."

Those galoshes lasted a long time. Georgianna did not wear them if she could get away with it which many times she did. They were good when the deep snow lay on the ground and she and Frankie would take his sled into the pasture where there was an excellent hill to coast down. Getting back up was the problem. You took three steps up and slid back two. This was one of the enjoyments the young couple had and it was free, whenever the Lord provided the snow. Frankie talked of a snow party they had the winter before when friends come by after sledding. They all went to the house and had hot chocolate and what fun they had. Georgianna had met very few of his friends. There was never a repeat of that fun time.

CHAPTER 58

The Four Seasons and Georgianna's Pregnancy

O ccasionally, enough money was available to take in a movie. Glady always went with them and a special treat was ice cream at McCrumm's Store where many of the town folks gathered after a movie or other events. Frankie was rather timid about introducing his wife. Georgianna was also timid and therefore she made few friends. All her socializing was at Manly Memorial Baptist Church in Lexington where she and Frankie were regular in attendance on Sunday, Sunday evening and midweek prayer service. This was very important to Georgianna. Her Sunday School teacher was a dear woman who had taught Frankie in school and had taught the Fidelis Class for many years. She was a real mentor for the young woman. Georgianna hoped that someday she would be able to follow in her footsteps and teach a class in Sunday School. Mrs. Lowman and Glady were let out at Lexington Presbyterian Church a couple of blocks down the street and were picked up after worship. Edwina no longer felt able to get out on Sunday morning. However, she sometimes did finishing touches to Sunday dinner.

The dreary winter dragged. Instead of taking care of Pegatty, she was caring for two older persons as well as doing the family laundry under Mom Lowman's supervision. Mrs. Lowman could not do much work because of shortness of breath due to asthma. The greater part of the housework fell to the young daughter-in-law who dutifully did whatever had to be done.

Washday was always a big job. The wash water was caught in barrels under their drain spout. In winter the water in the barrels froze. While Frankie did the milking, Georgianna used a hatchet to chop the ice, filling four square pails which Frankie carried in to place on the cook stove before he left for work. Most things had to be hung outside to dry, and what a hassle that was! Garments froze before you completed the hanging, and if there was a little breeze they slapped you in the face. It is easy to see why folks did not change clothes often!

Frankie spent many of his Saturdays at the farm helping Andy get ready for spring planting. During the week his time was taken up getting the garden ready. At his Mother's there was never any time for fun. When the garden was planted, Georgianna thought maybe they would have time to do something pleasurable, but Frankie became very excited about going prospecting for gold with an old codger he had been talking to.

For several months they left every Friday after work for West Virginia, coming back on Sunday with a handful of rocks which Frankie paid to send away to be assayed. They kept this up for about a year and Frankie was always the one to provide transportation and pay for the assaying, so money was shorter than ever.

Evenings were spent with all five in the sitting bedroom with the radio on. Some conversation was shared. Frankie's Mother and Glady usually soaked their feet. This was a ritual Georgianna was unfamiliar with. Frankie was urged to soak his feet. Sometimes he complied just to please his Mother, who was always concerned about taking care of yourself. Frankie was the youngest of eight children and had apparently been pampered by the whole family and it showed when he couldn't have his way about things.

Spring was busy for Georgianna who spent a lot of time in the large fertile garden which produced a good crop of lush vegetables. Canning began as soon as the peas and strawberries were ready followed by green beans, beets, cucumbers etc. One day you picked the next day you canned and some days you picked and canned the same day. Wash day was usually Monday and everything had to be ironed. Ma Lowman helped with canning but most of the work fell to Georgianna, who dreamed of a small apartment of her own and doing as she pleased, just she and Frankie, but he seemed very satisfied to stay with his Mother and sisters.

Georgianna was fond of them all but this was not her idea of marriage. As soon as school was out and VMI was closed for the summer, Frankie did odd jobs to make enough to survive. The cow provided the milk and butter, a few chickens produced the eggs, flour came from the farm and sometimes meat. Mrs. Lowman made a batch of yeast bread on Friday that usually lasted a week. There was always plenty of food.

Georgianna was excited to get a letter from Mama saying they were bringing Dela and Pegatty to stay for a week. This brightened her day. She had really missed them since she had married, always hoping for closer fellowship with Dela. It appeared that Mama really did not want them to be close and was always telling them how different they were.

Frankie's nephew Lynny came often and that kept the girls entertained with some card games. Mrs. Lowman didn't have much patience with children, and she slapped Lynny for some minor offense. She missed and hit Dela instead; she never realized what she had done. Dela just grinned and showed her dimples.

Pegatty occupied Georgianna's lap much of the time. Edwina seemed to enjoy the children being around and was more cheerful as she watched their antics. The week went much too fast.

Frankie had agreed that he and Georgianna would take the two back home, but neither of the children was excited about leaving and Georgianna certainly was not eager for them to go.

When they arrived at the McDonald's, Bethany met them at the car, "Did you have a good time?"

"Sure did!" piped up Dela, grinning and showing her dimples. "I did too," chimed Pegatty. "I wanted to stay longer."

"Mama, can Georgianna come back home to stay?"

"No Pegatty, she has another home."

"Well can I go stay with her? Well, can I?"

They made a short visit to see Fubby and Evie. Colene met them at the door. She was already walking. She was followed by Evie who was about to have her second child. They were doing fine and seemed happy. Evie gave them a jar of her fresh canned blackberries, knowing how much Georgianna enjoyed them. Bobby popped in to tell them lunch was ready and then the visit was over.

Mama had a nice lunch an the table, and they visited as they ate.

"Georgianna, why don't you come and stay for a while?"

"Lib Dawson comes to her Mother's and stays for a month at a time."

"Maybe I can sometime." Frankie didn't say anything. Georgianna knew that he didn't want her to go home for a visit and leave his Mother with all the responsibility. Georgianna had learned who came first with her husband and it certainly wasn't her. His family always came first. It didn't take long to realize that fact. As usual Georgianna continued to follow instructions and never spoke up for what she wanted to do.

The summer was busy with gardening and lawn mowing. When Frankie was between odd jobs he went to the farm to help Andy and came home on weekends. September arrived and the cadets returned to VMI and Frankie was back at his job in the laundry room. He was now earning fifty-five dollars a month which was much better pay than the odd jobs in the summer. September the sixth came and went with no big celebration for their anniversary. This was no surprise to Georgianna.

Manly Memorial Baptist always had a fund-raising oyster supper in October. The older ladies did the preparation and the Y.W.A, which stood for the Young Women's Auxiliary, did the serving. This was a pleasant experience for Georgianna, working with Christian ladies and being one of the gang. Ruth Hammic, a local jeweler's wife, brought her cook to fry the most delicate brown crisp oysters that were a big hit with everyone. This experience encouraged Georgianna once again to approach Frankie about going to work and increasing their income.

"Why do you want to go to work, you have plenty to do home helping Mom and looking after Edwina. One of these days we will have a baby. Then you will have enough to do, how about that?" Georgianna just shrugged her shoulders and gave up trying, wondering how would they have enough money to have a baby and take care of it.

Precaution was disregarded and month after month passed and Georgianna wondered if she was ever going to get pregnant. Maybe they would not have any children after all. The winter had been a cold one and a lot of cuddling had gone on with many opportunities to become pregnant. That seemed to be the only time Frankie was affectionate, whenever he had a need.

The springtime was beautiful, the lilacs and the hydrangeas were in blossom. Georgianna had been busy helping Frankie get the garden planted. The cow had given birth on the date Frankie had marked on the calendar after he had the cow bred. Plenty of milk had to be cared for. There were so many things to take care of. The strawberries were producing heavily and had to be gathered and preserved.

June 1938 had arrived before Georgianna began checking her calendar and discovered she had missed a period in May. She thought it was because she had been working so hard. Nearing the last of June she began feeling a little dizzy in the mornings and didn't really want any breakfast, which was very unusual. She strongly suspected that she might be pregnant. She waited a few days to say anything, continuing to stay busy. By this time the peas were ready to pick and she got really dizzy when bending over.

After going to bed, she said, "Frankie, I think we might have a baby after all."

"Why?"

"I have been feeling sorta sick and dizzy when I get up and when I bend over."

"Well you had better go see Dr. White. Do it tomorrow. You can walk into town and I can bring you home after I get off from work with the electricians." He was employed with them for the summer while the cadets had gone home.

"What will I say to the doctor?"

"You'll think of something."

Georgianna arrived at Dr. White's office at two o'clock to find a room full of people. Everyone waited their turn as no appointments were made. She found a seat and waited, growing more nervous by the minute. Finally, "Georgianna Lowman, the doctor will see you," said the smiling nurse in her crisp uniform. The young woman gave a big sigh as she arose and entered the Doctor's office.

"What can I do for you?"

"I need an examination."

"What for? Is it a question of pregnancy?"

"Yes, I have missed a period and have had some dizziness and feeling sick to my stomach in the mornings."

"Nurse prepare her for a pelvic." Georgianna wondered, what's a pelvic?

"Remove your underwear." The nurse sensed the young woman's apprehension and said, "This will not hurt, just relax."

After the examination she was instructed to put on her clothes and talk to Dr. White. "Well young lady, you are indeed pregnant, about six weeks and you should deliver about January the fourteenth. Take care of yourself, drink plenty of milk and watch your weight."

Georgianna's step was light as she walked around the block to Dr. Engleman's office where Glady worked to wait for Frankie to get off from work. Concern was in the back of her mind, how could they afford a baby? How could she get material to sew the tiny garments that would be needed, but she felt a happiness and thought "If the Lord is sending me this baby I know he will help me to provide for it." Faith calmed her fears.

Glady met her with a smile as she entered the dentist office. "What are you doing in town?"

"I just had something to take care of that's all."

"It's almost time for Frankie to get off from work, and I'll ride home with you two. We are taking care of our last patient. You can browse through the magazine rack."

Frankie had parked in his usual parking spot to wait. The small town was almost deserted with the VMI cadets and the W and L students away for the summer. When Glady had taken care of closing the office, the two women hurried down the steps to the waiting gray Ford. "Hi, lady, how did it go?"

"Okay" was all that was said, until Glady reported on folks that Frankie knew had been in that day and had asked about him.

The usual evening chores had to be taken care of. Glady and Georgianna tended the evening meal while Frankie did the milking and brought in the wood. Frankie and Georgianna spent some time in the garden before dark and mid-evening found all ready for bed. As Georgianna snuggled closer to Frankie he was eager to know what Dr. White had to say. "I am indeed pregnant and we should have a baby about the fourteenth of January and I have ordered a boy and we will name him after you."

"Wow!" That'll be a cold time of year. Are you happy about it?"

"Of course I am happy about the baby but I wish we had our own apartment."

"You know you need to stay here and look after Mom, and you will need her help with taking care of the baby."

"I know how to take care of babies, I've done it all my life, and I will not need any help except for your help."

"Well there is no way we can move and that is that. You'll just have to accept it."

As usual that's what Georgianna did. No announcement was made about the coming of the new baby, but after noticing Georgianna leaving the breakfast table suddenly several mornings and leaving part of her food, Glady walked over to the calendar where Frankie always wrote in the name and date when a new calf was due. She boldly wrote, "Georgianna January." Little did she know she had guessed the correct month.

Georgianna didn't admit anything and just went about her usual work everyday, looking forward to the fall days when she could begin sewing. She hung on to every cent she could get her hands on. After Mom Lowman found out about the expected arrival, she was forever reminding her, "don't do this," and "don't do that." Georgianna did whatever needed to be done and was fine after the morning sickness went away.

When Georgianna had only been married a few months and had had her appendix removed, an acquaintance of Mom Lowman had come to visit. After being there a short time she spoke, "Georgianna, may I see the baby?"

"What baby?"

"Heard that you were in the hospital."

"I've only been married three months, how could I have a baby?" The young woman was noticeably embarrassed and the lady apologized and left with a red face.

The garden had been cleaned and everything canned. By the end of September Georgianna had developed a very round belly and was feeling life within her. Her doctor had given her many booklets to read about baby care and she had just about memorized every word. She knew just what was needed, and that everything should be ready by the eighth month. Pouring over the Sears Roebuck catalog and wishing for some of the pretty things, she knew she could only afford the barest necessities. Georgianna kept busy selecting: some soft white material for two long dresses, outing for three gowns, three undershirts, three bands and two dozen bird's eye diapers. After she added this up she knew every cent she got her hands on would have to be put aside for the baby clothes. Quilting for three blankets was added to the list. Other items would be bought at Woolworth in town.

Georgianna knew that her winter coat was getting shabby and after taking it out of storage, she hung it in the sun to air. She hoped to get rid of the mothball odor before trying it on, only to discover that it was too small already and she had three months to go. Georgianna was getting bigger all the time. The subject was discussed at the supper table and Glady mentioned a Persian lamb coat that she saw in the catalog and offered to order that for her as a new mother gift. It was indeed a nice gesture.

As the days grew cold and Georgianna walked into town she looked somewhat like a black bear. On each trip she picked up a few needed items: safety pins, baby powder, baby oil, then stored them in a box in the corner of their bedroom. Edwina had helped her cover a box with wall paper and pasted baby pictures cut from magazines onto the sides and top of the lid. That made an attractive container for the baby clothes. Edwina was also a big help with the sewing. Georgianna smocked one dress in blue and trimmed the other in white and did some edge stitching on the gowns. She was feeling pretty good about herself.

By the middle of December nearly everything was ready for the expected baby. The Fidelis class had a surprise baby shower and was she ever surprised! So much so that she shed a few tears before opening the pretty wrapped packages. The first contained a darling crocheted blue and white sweater and cap. There were booties, bibs, undershirts, and a beautiful baby blanket like one she had admired in Sears Roebuck. All her Sunday School classes were offering many good wishes and she was filled with happiness that her child would have a little more than the bare necessities.

When Frankie came for her and she greeted him at the car with her arms laden with packages, "Hey, what's going on? You've been shopping?"

"The class gave me a baby shower now all we need is that brown eyed baby boy. I'll show you all the pretties when we get home. Everyone will be as excited as I was. Fredrieka is letting me have her bassinet, I'm so excited that I might have that baby this night."

"I think you had better wait until the due date of January the fourteenth."

"I will, I will."

Christmas cards were arriving and Glady was expecting one from a male friend who she was hoping would ask her to marry him, as she was almost thirty years old. Mrs. Lowman's granddaughter had come to stay with the family. Georgianna enjoyed having a young person seventeen years old. Nell crocheted things from the twine that some stores used to tie up merchandise. She also spent time keeping Edwina company as the two of them listened to "Aunt Jenny" and other stories on the radio.

A few days before Christmas a large bundle of Christmas cards arrived, among them was one for Glady from her friend. Georgianna stuck it behind the clock on the mantle and watched as Glady swiftly looked through the stack of cards. As soon as she and Frankie arrived she looked very disappointed. Georgianna reached up to the mantle and handed the card to her, "Is this what you are looking for?"

"Yes! I am almost mad at you," and they embraced. They were more like sisters than sisters-in-law.

Christmas came and went without a big to-do. Glady gave Georgianna a new gown to wear when the baby came and Frankie presented her with bedroom slippers, the first ones she ever had.

CHAPTER 59

The Joys and Trials of Motherhood

Georgianna had put fresh linens on the guest room bed that she would be using for delivery. Margaret Jones, a practical nurse, had been engaged to come care for the mother and new baby for ten days. Nell had polished Georgianna's fingernails, and the box containing the baby clothes and other necessities that the booklets had said were necessary for a new baby were ready. There was no doubt that the baby would be breast fed. Frankie had mentioned that she would end up like a brood sow and get skinny. Anyway, Georgianna hoped to nurse the baby for the many benefits and because of the economy. All there was left to do was to wait for January the fourteenth and that was only two days away.

Georgianna awoke on the fourteenth with a backache. Snow and ice covered the ground. After her feet hit the cold floor, which really woke the young woman up, she crawled back under the covers. Frankie hurried downstairs to build a fire in the cook stove and to fire up the one in Edwina's room. Since it was Saturday, no one had to go to work. Georgianna just stayed in the bed. About noon Mom Lowman came in to see why she had not gotten up. "I have a really bad backache and do not feel like getting up" Georgianna said.

"Have you had any pains?" Mom Lowman asked.

"No, only this nagging backache," Georgianna answered.

Mom Lowman asked, "Don't you want anything to eat?"

Georgianna answered, "No I am really not hungry, maybe later on." Georgianna didn't even get up for the evening meal.

As soon as everyone had settled in for the night, Frankie crawled in bed by his wife's side. "You have the bed good and warm by staying in it all day. I've laid the fire in the guest room ready to strike the match when we need to. Is your back any better?" he said.

"No, and I felt a pain a couple of minutes ago," Georgianna answered. Soon there was another pain and shortly after that another one. "I think we are going to have to make a call to Dr. White," Georgianna said.

"You mean I have to get that woman on a night like this?" I am glad I already have the chains on the car, I'd never get over those back roads without them. I'll get Mom to phone the doctor while I get ready to go. I'll also light the fire in the other room so it will warm up." Shortly everyone in the house was wide awake and the fires were burning.

Frankie was shaking like a leaf. He was trying to get his warmest clothes on so he could go get the nurse. "Mom, have you called Dr. White?" Frankie asked.

Mom answered, "No, I'm going to do that as soon as I get my warm sweater. That hallway is like an icebox. You get going for that woman."

"O.K, O.K," Frankie answered and out the door he went. After a few tries the car started and he was on his way.

"Glady, help Georgianna get settled in the guest room while I call Doctor White," Mom Lowman said. Mom Lowman picked up the phone and dialed the doctor's number. "Doctor White, this is Mrs. Lowman, I think the baby decided to arrive tonight. You better come and check things out. I'll leave the porch light on for you. Thank you."

By the time the doctor arrived, Georgianna was having pains about five minutes apart. "Well, young lady," he said, "you are indeed in labor but it will be a while, so I will go downstairs and take a nap. I was up late last night delivering another baby. I do need a nap before this one arrives." He proceeded to go downstairs, pull a rocking chair up to the kitchen stove and open the oven door. He took his shoes off, stuck his feet in the oven and leaned back in the rocker. Soon he was fast asleep, oblivious to what was going on upstairs.

Frankie returned with the nurse. He entered by the side door without waking up the doctor. He escorted the nurse upstairs to the room where the expectant mother was lying. The nurse ordered him to wait across the hall and said, "I'll call you if we need you." The nurse quickly took charge. Georgianna sensed that she was not a very warm person as she briskly set about getting things in order just the way she wanted. She was strictly business and offered no sympathy as Georgianna moaned in pain. All she said was, "It's going to get worse than that."

Mom Lowman wiped Georgianna's forehead with a cool cloth. That gave her some comfort. Georgianna said, "If Frankie could hold my hand that would help."

The nurse replied, "Well, this is no place for a man, he'd soon fall to pieces and someone would have to doctor him." The pains were getting closer and closer and by three thirty they were almost continuous.

Mrs. Lowman went downstairs and tapped the doctor on his shoulder and said, "You had better get upstairs and help this girl out."

"Where are my shoes," he asked. "Right beside you. Now get up there," she answered. Georgianna continued to moan in pain. "Now, now, young lady, it can't be that bad," the doctor said, "You'll have that baby in your arms in no time. Let's see what's going on."

"Now you have to really get down to work. As you feel the pain, push with all your might."

"I can't," Georgianna cried.

"Oh yes you can," the doctor said. "You'd better if you want a live baby." Georgianna followed the doctor's instructions. The nurse held a strainer with ether over her nose to deaden the pain.

Frankie Junior let out a lusty yell at four o'clock in the morning, on the fifteenth of January, 1939. Frankie stuck his head in the door and Mrs. Jones said, "Stay out until I get this baby cleaned up." The afterbirth was expelled after a few more pains.

Georgianna was comfortable but very tired after six hours of labor. She was almost too tired to appreciate the beauty of her perfectly formed firstborn son, with the beautiful brown eyes and soft brown hair. He was bathed, dressed and placed in the bassinet close to Geogrianna's bed. Soon he was fast asleep.

Doctor White gave instructions to the patient. "You may sit up on the eighth day and get out of bed on the tenth day. You are to stay upstairs for six weeks and then I want to see you and the baby in my office." He placed his items in his little black bag and with a warm smile, he left.

Little Frankie's bassinet was lined in white with blue ribbons. The bassinet was given to Georgianna by a good friend. Frankie was allowed to admire his son. "Well, lady, you did a good job. We better get some rest before it's time to get up." All was quiet.

Georgianna was determined to breast feed. The doctor put the baby on a four-hour feeding schedule, but her baby awoke every three hours. He cried for an hour and by feeding time he was too tired to nurse sufficiently to sustain him for four hours.

Georgianna had badly cracked nipples and she dreaded feeding time. A nipple shield helped some. Georgianna was happy when the ten days were up and Mrs. Jones was dismissed. Now she could feed her baby every three hours instead of letting him cry for an hour. Things were much quieter then and everything was running smooth. Nell brought a tray to Georgianna and was really good to her. Mom Lowman wanted to supervise the baby's bath. She acted like Georgianna didn't know how to care for a baby.

After three weeks of staying upstairs and doing nothing but caring for Frankie Junior, Frankie offered to carry his wife downstairs for the day. He then carried his son down and placed him in the large laundry basket that Ada had fixed up for a bassinet for her children. She loaned it to Georgianna. She kept one upstairs and one downstairs by the foot of Edwina's bed. Edwina adored Frankie Junior. She had given much care to Frankie when he was a baby and she sort of felt like a Grandmother.

Georgianna was carried up and down the stairs for a week. When she was up on her own, she was glad to be up and helping with the housework and helping with Edwina's bath. "Oh my, it feels good to get my back washed," Edwina said. "I haven't had a good bath since you had this baby."

"I guess everyone was too busy," Georgianna said. "Anyway, I am here and will be helping you every day. And you can watch after Frankie Junior when I am out of the room."

Mom Lowman was quite critical of the way Georgianna took care of her child. She was always reminding her to keep his feet warm or he would get colic and to keep him wrapped like a mummy. "Don't let him see himself in the mirror," she would say, "or he will have a hard time cutting teeth." And, "Always keep his face covered when taking him out."

It was gardening time and Georgianna worked in the garden. Mom Lowman would say, "Cool off before you feed that baby or you'll make him sick." Georgianna tried to comply on most things.

Frankie Junior started sucking his thumb and that really upset his Grandmother. "He'll have an ugly mouth and crooked teeth," she would say. Georgianna became somewhat upset on finding his hands wrapped in bandages. She was instructed to keep them that way. She left them that way for a short time until Edwina became sick.

While Georgianna was in the garden, Frankie Junior was often placed on the bed beside Edwina to give her an opportunity to play with him. He became fussy and cried when his hands were wrapped, so Georgianna calmly removed the bandages. All was peaceful when he could put his thumb in his mouth again. Georgianna loved the way he snuggled and nuzzled when feeding time came.

Edwina became weaker and weaker and on May eleventh she was unable to talk. Doctor White was summoned. After consulting with her Mother and informing her that Edwina's death was near, he asked permission to give Edwina a shot to lesson her discomfort. The family was notified. Many came and stayed until late afternoon when she passed away. Harrison's mortuary was called. After the body was prepared, it was returned to the home. This was the custom in 1939.

This was Georgianna's first experience with death since the death of her mother many years before. It brought back sad memories. She was glad she had her precious son to hold but knew she had lost a good friend. The funeral was held at the house and the burial in New Monmouth Cemetery. After everyone had left, the house was lonely. Edwina's bed sat empty. After her spending most of her time there, the room indeed looked lonely.

Glady had become engaged to Charlie and they had set the date for June the eleventh. They saw no reason to change it. It was to be a brief ceremony in the home with family.

Georgianna really missed Edwina. She missed having her to keep an eye on her four month old son while she worked in the garden and the yard. Mom Lowman, Georgianna and Frankie Junior were alone during the day.

On warm sunny days the baby was stripped and placed outside in the screened crib that Frankie had made. Georgianna was a great believer in the benefits of sunshine. Skeezix, the dog, would lay protectively under the crib as long as it was outside. The grandmother didn't think much of this sun bathing. Georgianna was determined, though. Her baby books said this was good for babies and she believed it. She was a firm believer in the sun and its benefits.

CHAPTER 60

Glady's Wedding

Plans were underway for Glady's wedding. She had chosen a long white lace dress. Glady and Georgianna designed a veil of net attached to a heart shaped headband and with ruffled netting. The matron of honor was Frances Eckert, a long time friend from Poughkeepsie, New York. A five-year-old great niece, Josie Wingate, was to be her flower girl. Jason Eckert, husband of the matron of honor, was to be the best man. He and the groom had been roommates in college and remained close friends. A record player was to provide the music.

The wedding meant the house had to be cleaned from top to bottom. Feather ticks were carried out and put in the sun, along with all the old coats and Frankie's father's suit, which his mother hung on to. His father had died fourteen years earlier. That suit was hung out to sun every year along with many old, outdated coats.

Things indeed were busy. When nighttime came, Georgianna went to bed very tired. She didn't find much time to play with her baby, except at feeding time. He was a good baby, seldom cried, and kept himself amused. Georgianna thought he was the most beautiful baby in the whole world. Frankie didn't give him a lot of attention, but you could tell he was proud of his son. He was not adept at baby care and never changed a diaper. He insisted that was woman's work.

When Glady and Frankie came home from work, plans were discussed about the wedding. "Frankie, you are going to give me away, aren't you?" Glady asked.

"I guess so," Frankie said, "what do I wear?"

"All the others are wearing white," Glady answered. "Charlie will be in a white suit."

"Looks like I will have to go shopping for a white suit," Frankie said. "Hope I can find one I can afford."

"I saw one in Adair Hutton's window that will be perfect," Glady said.

"I'll go look at it Friday after work," Frankie said. "I'm surely going to miss you, Topsy," a pet name he had given her, "who am I going to pick at, with Edwina and you both gone?"

"Just pick on Georgianna," she answered. "Georgianna, I want you to help me decide on decorating the parlor for the wedding," Glady said. "I think we can use roses from the yard."

"You know you can count on me," Georgianna replied, "I already have a couple of good ideas. I'm gonna miss you too. I'm glad you and Charlie are getting married. I don't want you to be an old maid."

"Well everybody doesn't get married while still a child like you did," Glady said.

"Don't rub it in. I know I was too young to know what I was doing," Georgianna said. "Anyway, I am married and I have a beautiful baby to show for it, and I hope to have some more before it's over with. That makes me a woman, wouldn't you say?"

"I suppose it does at that," said Glady. "Now let's get back to the business at hand and plan the decorating. I'm going to order my bouquet and one for the matron of honor. For Josie I'm ordering a nosegay. I'll leave the mantle decorations up to you."

"I'll handle it and hope everything meets with your approval," Georgianna said.

Everything was falling into place nicely. Frankie had purchased his white suit along with brown and white wing tip shoes. He tried everything on and strutted around the house. He thought he was hot stuff. He did look good. He was so tall and slim and his dark hair combed straight back was becoming. Georgianna felt proud that he was her husband and father of her child.

The immediate family was informed of the upcoming ceremony. Cora, Josie's mother, was making Josie a dress for the occasion. Josie was a tiny five year old with sparkling brown eyes, a sweet smile and was to be attired in pink. One distant cousin, that was close to the family, was invited along with her mother, husband, and daughter.

The big day was a beautiful, bright June day. Charlie had arrived the day before and was staying at the Donald's Tourist Home close by. The Eckerts were guests of the Lowmans. Cora and Josie had arrived the night before. The household was busy and no one made it to church. There were last minute things to do before the three o'clock ceremony. Georgianna was occupied with the last minute decorations and setting up the record player in the hall. She asked Cora to attend to the music when the time came.

All the available chairs were placed in the parlor, still many would have to stand for the short ceremony. The ceremony was to be performed by Dr. Murry, who a month before performed a funeral in the same room.

Charlie and Jason stood on the front porch. Glady was upstairs doing finishing touches. Frankie stood near the foot of the stairs waiting, visibly nervous, as the other family members took their seats in the parlor. Georgianna planned to stand in the hallway with her son. Glady waited at the top of the stairs while the record player played "I love you truly."

The two men entered the front door and took their places beside the Minister. The matron of honor took her place and little Josie calmly walked in and stood next to the matron of honor.

Strains of the wedding march filled the area as Glady slowly descended down the stairs. She took her brother's shaky arm and the two took their places facing the mantle.

Dr. Murry said, "Let us pray."

You could hear a scratching sound as Cora removed the needle from the record. After the prayer, the minister asked, "Who giveth this woman in marriage?"

Frankie softly said, "I do," and then he stepped aside. All the chairs were filled. The ceremony continued.

"Do you, Charlie, take Glady as your lawful wedded wife, to have and to hold, to love and to cherish, in sickness and in health, for richer for poorer, all the days of your life until death you do part?"

"I do." Glady was asked the same, then the rings were exchanged.

"I now pronounce you man and wife, you may kiss the bride," and then it was over.

Frankie immediately walked outside and lit a cigarette. Georgianna hurried into the kitchen to finish the punch. Dr. Murry declined the invitation to the reception. Andy's children were excited, this was the first wedding they had attended. The atmosphere was indeed more joyful than the funeral that had been held a month before. A birth, a death and a wedding had happened in this house in less than six months.

Charlie had a speech problem and occasionally stuttered. As he entered the dining room, he asked, "Where's my bri bri bride?" She had slipped out to fix her lipstick. "Oh, there you are."

Glady flashed her brightest smile at her husband. "Yes, you need to help me cut the wedding cake."

Everyone seemed to be talking at once. Georgianna took her place at the punch bowl and began filling the punch cups. The bride and groom cut and shared the first piece of cake, both all smiles and looking great in their white attire.

The guests soon left, some having evening chores to take care of. Ramona and Lanny were staying over. Georgianna slipped upstairs to talk to Glady, who was changing into her rose colored dress that was her going away outfit. They were not going on a honeymoon, just to the apartment Charlie rented for them in Chester, Pennsylvania. He was a chemist at General Chemical Company.

Glady wanted advice about birth control. "I don't want to get pregnant for a while," she said. Georgianna gave her the information that she needed and they embraced. Knowing they would miss their time together, tears filled their eyes. Georgianna felt a tinge of resentment, since she had not been able to have her own apartment. She wished Glady much happiness in her married life. A couple of pictures were taken and then the couple were off.

The chamber that Frankie and Andy had tied to the car made a noisy racket as they rode up the gravel road. Others left and you could already feel the void in the big house. Georgianna was glad that Ramona and her husband were staying overnight. Kyle and Ida had already left for Roanoke.

CHAPTER 61

Coping with Change

Georgianna knew there would be less income to run the household now that Glady was gone, along with her fifty dollars a month that had helped with expenses. She knew that God would provide a way for them to manage. Mom Lowman had a little money, that helped with the utility bills.

The young woman could sew if she just had some customers. She didn't have a long wait. Two young neighbors in their teens wanted summer dresses. The material was inexpensive and she had the time.

One day when the youngest came to pick up a gallon of skim milk, which cost ten cents a gallon, she saw Georgianna at the sewing the machine and meekly asked, "Would you make me a dress?"

"If it's not too fancy I could, do you have a pattern?"

"I do not think so but I know just how I want it made."

A money-making idea was born as Georgianna made several dresses for the young girls. The girls always wanted the length at the big part of their legs. Since the girls were both skinny, finding the big part of their leg was a puzzle. However, they were both pleased with their new frocks and Georgianna was pleased to have earned some pocket change.

Another neighbor, who was expecting, asked to have baby clothes made. That was a real pleasure. When the baby boy arrived, the mother, being very illiterate, named her baby Frankie Jr. The baby's father's name was George but she evidently liked the sound of the name or felt like she was honoring Georgianna by naming the baby after her son.

Frankie was working at odd jobs while the cadets were gone for the summer. With her sewing, caring for the baby, the housework, and working in the garden, Georgianna stayed plenty busy. She only had time to play with her baby at feeding time. When Georgianna came in from the garden and it was feeding time, Mrs. Lowman always admonished her, "Don't nurse that baby while you're hot, you'll make him sick. I know all about babies. I raised mine right. You need to cool off before feeding him."

Georgianna would calmly wash her hands, change the baby's diaper and sit in the rocking chair to feed him. Her mother-in-law would mumble low to herself and leave the room in a huff. Frankie Junior was never sick from an overheated mother.

The only social life was at the church on Sundays. Frankie's sister, her husband, and two sons came nearly every Sunday afternoon. They stayed for a snack supper with the leftovers from Sunday dinner. Mom Lowman usually baked bread on Saturday and Georgianna made cakes and pies so there was food for everyone and bread for the whole week.

With lots of work to do there was not a lot of time to miss Glady or the income she brought home. Things seemed to go along smoothly. Andy and Ada's daughter was school age and whenever you asked Ada what she had been doing it was always "getting Vera ready for school."

Andy had asked his mother if Vera could stay with her to go to school. This way she would not have to get out so early to get the school bus. The plan was given the go ahead and the day before school opened Vera arrived. Georgianna was eager to see the outfits that were in preparation for Vera's schooling. Mostly she wore blue coveralls. Georgianna expected some cute dresses and was disappointed. Andy brought a sack of flour, some corn meal and occasionally some meat to help feed the family.

Frankie Junior was a delightful baby. He seldom cried and kept himself amused. By October he had eight teeth but was not yet sitting alone.

Georgianna didn't believe in pushing babies to perform. She knew he would sit up when he was ready. Two days before he was nine months old Georgianna walked in to find him sitting ram rod straight.

He was playing with his toys. Two days later he was pulling himself up and standing on his feet. He was happy as a lark. From that time on, he was on his feet more than his seat.

Georgianna wanted to visit her foster family who had not yet seen her son. After all the canning was over with she approached Frankie. "What do you think about me going home for a few days?" she asked.

"If that's what you want," he said. "I can take you next Sunday and come for you the following Saturday. I think I can manage without you that long."

The next few days Georgianna gathered things together. She knew she would have to carry a lot of extras for the baby. She was still nursing him so she needed only to take juice and water bottles. She also took his food that she had pureed from the garden vegetables. Baby foods were in the stores but doing them yourself was less expensive.

On arrival at the McDonald home, Georgianna was treated like royalty. Everyone wanted to hold her baby. "He's cute," piped up Pegatty. Frankie beamed as his son was being admired. At the end of the day, Frankie left alone as everyone waved to him from the dining room stoop.

Alease, the young black girl who replaced Georgia, wanted to take charge of the baby. She waited on him hand and foot. Anything he dropped from the playpen or high chair she was on hand to retrieve it.

With no work to do, Georgianna felt like she was having a real vacation. Even Mama treated her so different. It was a nice change. Mama wanted her to stay for a month. "You know Lib Dawson comes home often and stays a whole month with her mother."

"Frankie would have a fit if I stayed a month and his mother had to do all the cooking," Georgianna said.

The week was soon over and Georgianna was back at the Lowman home and at her usual duties.

Glady and Charlie were coming for Christmas as well as Ramona and Lanny. Georgianna wondered what little trinket she could buy for the two favorite in-laws. She got an ash tray for Charlie and handkerchiefs for the others. That was all they could afford.

Georgianna was glad when the holiday was over and things got back to normal. The Lowmans had very few close friends and the winter evenings were long. The radio was a source of entertainment. Georgianna liked to read, which she would do if she had any spare time after the sewing and mending was taken care of. Mrs. Lowman was the "queen" of patches. She would patch a patch. Georgianna's mending seldom satisfied her and she would redo Frankie's items. This was a put down for the young wife and she just pretended she didn't notice.

Little Frankie celebrated his first birthday and was walking. He was not as happy in the play pen anymore. He had reached the age that all he wanted to do was explore the world. He was allowed out of the playpen when Georgianna could watch him. On days when the weather was good, his pen was placed outside. Georgianna could hang the laundry and work in the garden while keeping an eye on her son. He could watch the lambs frolicking in the pasture. Andy usually brought a couple of truck loads every spring in order to let his pasture recover.

Georgianna enjoyed her son. She would still like to be in her own apartment where she could relax and care for her child like she wanted, with no interference. Many times his grandmother wanted him punished for every little thing that he did. Whenever he plucked a flower for his Mommy or stripped grass seed from the grass, she would say, "What he needs is a good whipping." Many times Georgianna punished him just to satisfy his grandmother. Later she would regret her actions. The young mother always showed respect for her mother-in-law and seldom said anything that would cause hard feelings.

Frankie occasionally played with his son but left all the care to Georgianna. Frankie Junior received lots of love from his mother. She thought he was just about perfect. His features were handsome and his beautiful brown eyes sparkled when one spoke to him. His smile would melt a heart of stone. He was indeed a cherished child.

CHAPTER 62

World War II and Georgianna's Second Pregnancy

Frankie Junior had just passed his second birthday and Georgianna was considering a second child. She knew it was not the ideal time for another baby but it didn't appear things were going to get better any time soon and her child would need a playmate. Vera was no longer there during the school months. Her younger sister had started school and they could wait for the bus together.

The spring and summer were as busy as the previous ones. Georgianna was kept busy with the garden and yard work and keeping an eye on the adventurous two year old. He was growing fast and Georgianna was kept busy making outfits for him. She made those outfits from her brother-in-law Charlie's father's shirts that had frayed at the neck and were passed onto her. Many adorable outfits were made from these most welcome donations.

By mid-September, Georgianna noticed she had skipped her monthly period. She was exceedingly happy to learn that she was pregnant. The doctor bill had not been paid for the delivery of Frankie Junior. Since Frankie didn't worry about it, why should she?

A new young doctor had come to town and she would go to him without being embarrassed. After filling out the paper forms, she was ushered into the examining room. She was greeted by a very handsome, very young doctor, with coal black hair. After the examination he said, "Well, young lady, I see that you already have one child. You should have another one around the eighteenth of May. I'd like to see you once a month."

"Thank you, doctor," Georgianna said. Georgianna was happy at this news.

Georgianna left Dr. Brush's office eager to tell Frankie the news. She hurriedly made her way home for she didn't want to leave her son with his grandmother for too long. She hoped he took a long nap. With each step she took she tried to figure out ways to earn a little money so she could buy materials to make garments for the new baby. Most of the baby clothes were in good shape and there would not be a lot of things needed. She wanted to make preparations for a girl, who would be soft and pink with blue eyes. Thinking how she could care for her and dress her in lace and bows made Georgianna happy.

Bedtime arrived and Georgianna had waited for this moment to inform her husband. Hoping he was as excited as she was she said, "Guess what?"

"What?" he asked.

"You're going to be a dad again," she said.

"How did that happen?" he asked. "You know how it happened. You were there." They both laughed and cuddled closer. "I'm not telling anyone else for a while," Georgianna said.

A few days later Georgianna was picking the last of the lima beans when Frankie came home before quitting time. He calmly began helping with the bean harvesting. "What are you doing home early?" Georgianna asked.

"Oh, just taking a little break," he answered. Nothing more was said. Georgianna was a little suspicious but didn't question further.

Morning came and things seemed to go as usual. Frankie went to milk the cow while Georgianna packed his lunch and made breakfast. When Frankie finished eating he calmly went to the old house, which also served as coal shed and barn. "Something must be up, Mom Lowman, why isn't he going to work?"

"He may not be feeling well," she said.

Shortly, he came in the back door. "You're going to be late for work," Georgianna said.

"I thought I told you," he answered, "Miles and I got fired yesterday."

"What for?"

"The boss told me to do something and I told him I wasn't going to do it. Same thing with Miles," he answered.

Georgianna quietly walked away thinking, this is a fine how do you do. A new baby on the way and no job for the daddy. How could he lose his job just because he didn't want to do as he was told? This was a real dilemma that didn't seem to bother Frankie a great deal. He puttered around the house for a couple of months before looking for another job.

Georgianna encouraged him to apply for work at the rug factory that was in full swing in Glasgow. Glasgow was about twenty miles away. "I hear they make good money," Georgianna said. Fortunately he had no trouble getting a job as a rug weaver. He was to report the following day. A fellow worker was to share rides with him. What a relief this was. Maybe everything would be better.

Wages were more than at VMI laundry. There would not be a payday before Christmas. Dad McDonald had sent Georgianna a few dollars to help have Christmas for her young son. Frankie Junior was as lively as a kitten with a ball of yarn. He went around opening all the doors, drawers and exploring continually. Georgianna heard him going upstairs and by the time she got to the top of the stairs, he was coming out of the room where she had placed his red wagon. This was to be his Christmas surprise. Happily pulling it behind him he said, "Look what I found." Georgianna took it and hid it in a better place, hoping he would forget all about it by Christmas.

On December 7, 1941, Japan attacked Pearl Harbor and the nation was at war. Many of the United States troops had been sent to aid the war that was going on in Europe. Adolph Hitler was attempting to create a master race by destroying thousands of Jewish people. The United States had joined Russia in the overthrow of Germany. After the vicious attack at Pearl Harbor, and the loss of many lives and naval vessels, the President of the United States declared war on Japan.

Many fine young men were immediately called into service. Georgianna had five brothers in the service on foreign soil at once. They were Billy, Cory, Corbin, Lancy and Russ. Her foster brother Bobby was also there. Great was the fear that the United States would be attacked. Air raid sirens were installed and sounded at noon everyday. Everyone had to use black out drapes so no lights would be visible from the outside. The news was on the radio and Lexington had a weekly newspaper. There was much tension. Only single men were being drafted into service; Frankie would be exempt.

Most of the Christmas conversation was about the war. Ramona and Lanny had come and brightened the season. They were a joyous couple and were going to stay for ten days. Then they were going to go to Salem, Virginia, to visit Ramona's brother. They invited Georgianna and little Frankie to go with them. Lanny had a nice car and they kept a blanket in there. The fifty mile ride was comfortable. A light snow was on the ground and the temperatures were low. The visit in Salem was pleasant.

They were late getting back to Lexington only to find Frankie in the bed with a fever and an onion poultice on his chest. "Georgianna, you will have to get the cow and milk her," Mom Lowman said. "Frankie came home sick and was unable to do that."

Georgianna, four months pregnant, pulled on the hated galoshes, grabbed the milk pail and headed for the pasture to hunt for the cow. It was ten thirty at night. A full moon shone on the light snow as Georgianna carefully made her way to the old house. She was hoping the cow would be close by. She was in luck, finding the cow waiting patiently to be milked. Georgianna was a bit awkward, as she sat on the three legged milking stool, with her rounded belly.

She could feel the baby move within her as her thoughts shifted to her husband. She hoped it was nothing more then a light case of the flu. Frankie did not tolerate pain very well so at the urgency of his mother, he took good care of himself. He began doctoring at the first sign of illness. Georgianna did not pamper herself and tolerated pain well. She usually kept going when she was not feeling up to par. She was seldom sick enough to take to the bed.

The milk pail was soon filled and Georgianna walked carefully back to the house. She didn't want to risk a fall that would harm the baby. This baby was very important to her. Letting her mother-in-law take care of the milk, she took her son upstairs to put him to bed. It was very unusual for him to be up this time of night. She then checked in on Frankie. He was running a fever as well as having chills. She wondered if she should call the doctor. Mom Lowman said, "Wait until morning." And so it was.

Ramona and Lanny were going to his folks for the night before leaving for Maryland the next day.

Georgianna climbed in beside her husband for the night. There was not much sleep for her because of her concern for her husband. He had a restless night. Georgianna knew he must be pretty sick and that they needed to put him in a room with some heat. She had picked up a glass of water for a drink, only to find it frozen solid. She placed another blanket on her son who was kept covered by an old robe of Glady's that Georgianna had fashioned into a sleeping bag that tied on the sides of his crib.

Dr. White was summoned the first thing after daybreak. Georgianna carried wood and kindling to the spare bedroom upstairs. Mom Lowman built the fire while the young son was being fed. Soon the fire had warmed the spare room, and Frankie was moved into it by the time Dr. White arrived. The doctor made a through examination and with a few hums and haws, he reached into his black bag and took out a bottle of pills. "We have a case of pneumonia here," he said. "He is to have one of these pills every three hours until all are taken. I will be back the day after tomorrow before I have office hours." Frankie's mother followed him to the door.

Georgianna attempted to make her husband as comfortable as possible, before dressing Frankie Junior. While replenishing fuel in both coal and the wood stoves and taking care of the morning milking, she asked herself, "Just how serious is pneumonia?" She had heard that some people had died from it. But Frankie was young and in good health. She knew he would be all right in a few days.

Dr. White came for his second visit to find the patient greatly improved and wanting to get up. "You can sit up by tomorrow, continue your medicine and take it easy for a few days before going back to work," the doctor said. Mom Lowman would be sure that he took care of himself, hovering over him like a mother hen. He was ready to go back to work the following week. As he left, his mother reminded him to bundle up good, cover his mouth with his scarf and not to breathe the cold air.

Spring arrived and Georgianna was getting more round everyday. She kept busy helping plant the garden, caring for her son, sewing in her spare time, and making plans for the new baby's arrival in May.

World War Two was in full swing and many young men were being sent to war. Frankie was still working at the rug factory. He occasionally spoke about joining the armed services. Everything was running smoothly. The pay from the factory was good and the family were able to have more.

Georgianna packed his lunch and he waited on the porch for the ride he knew was not coming. He remarked, "He must have forgotten about me." The next morning when Georgianna started to fix his lunch she was surprised to hear, "Don't pack me any lunch. I am not going to work today."

"Why not?"

"Well I, I," he stammered, "I got fired."

"You what?"

"Got fired"

"For what?"

"I just didn't want to do what the foreman asked me to do."

This could have been the couple's big fight, but Georgianna kept quiet. She knew he would walk away and ignore anything she had to say. Without a paycheck, what had been saved needed to be used to take care of current expenses.

Frankie puttered around the old house and garden when, out of the blue, he announced, "I think I will join the Army. It would be steady pay and I could see other parts of the world."

"You mean you want to go away just before the baby's born?" Georgianna asked.

"There are not many jobs here and we need money," he replied.

The following day found Frankie at the recruitment office for his examination. Georgianna was thankful that he was classified as a 4F, which meant that he was physically unfit for the service. He was notified of his status a week later.

Georgianna's time was running out and she was glad the baby would be born before the hot weather. She had made arrangements with a neighbor, Mrs. McKenny, to assist the doctor when the time came. Glady was to come and help for two weeks. By then the young mother felt that she could care for the children. New ideas about birth were more relaxed and mothers were allowed to be more active earlier than when Frankie Junior was born.

Frankie was not very verbal about what he was thinking. This kept Georgianna wondering what would come next, as week after week there was no paycheck. The small savings were almost gone. With only a few weeks until the baby's arrival, the young woman was kept in a dilemma. God had always provided and she assumed that He would make a way for them to survive.

Many of the local men had gone to work in the Newport News Shipyard and other places to aid in the war effort. There was a scarcity of some items and you heard much talk about rationing. Many items like sugar, meats, gasoline, as well as automobile tires, were rationed. Georgianna stayed busy and did not dwell on the war. She wrote to her brothers and occasionally heard from them. Corbin wrote that he had made her the beneficiary of his ten thousand dollar life insurance policy. She greeted this news with this thought, "Please come back all right. We've lost too many years already."

CHAPTER 63

Katherine's Arrival

The merry month of May arrived with many spring blossoms adorning the large yard at the Lowman home. A new calf had been born. Andy had bought a truck load of lambs along with three mothers and had put them in the pasture. A few chicks had hatched, and everywhere you looked there was new life. Peonies were at their peak, and Georgianna thought what a great time for a new bundle from heaven.

On May nineteenth Georgianna had a very busy day weeding the garden. Finishing the dishes from the evening meal and putting Frankie Junior to bed, she began some unfinished sewing. She was startled by the telephone; Glady was on the line. "I'll be getting the bus first thing tomorrow, so just wait to have that baby till I get there."

"I'll try, but I'm already a day overdue, and I'm anxious to get this over with." No sooner had the receiver been placed on the hook, when two longs and one short were heard again. "Hello, this you, Georgianna?"

"Yes ma'am."

"This is Mrs. McKenny. I just wanted to let you know I just helped deliver a strapping nine pound grandson, and I am free whenever you are ready for me- just give me a call."

"Thanks for calling; I'll call when I need you." Georgianna relayed the message to Frankie and his mother and returned to her sewing.

When bedtime came around, Georgianna took a look into the spare room that she was to use while confined to see if everything was ready. Frankie had put a cot in the room for Glady to sleep on. Seeing that everything was orderly, she went to bed for a good night's rest. There was no need to put an alarm clock on since no one was scheduled to work.

Awakening to the gentle sound of her young son, "Mama its time to get up—I gotta go to the potty."

"Just a minute." The young mother sat on the side of the bed for a few seconds feeling a little queasy, and she felt a twinge of pain as she stood on her feet. Frankie Junior had crawled out of bed and headed for the night pail that sat behind the curtain every night. Another pain was evident while she selected her young son's attire for the day that she suspected was going to be a busy one. Traipsing down the stairs and hurriedly getting breakfast on the table, she announced, "We are going to have to call Dr. Brush, I'm having pains and it is time for the baby."

"Sh! Sh!" came from Frankie's mother. She was appalled that she had told the young child that they were having a baby, and she told Frankie, "You can take the boy out to the old house with you after breakfast and keep him out there until I let you know it's over."

"Okay, Mom, I'll keep him busy."

Georgianna phoned the doctor when her pains were getting regular and was informed that he would be there by nine-thirty. She then called Mrs. McKenny and said "Guess what? I've phoned the doctor and he is going to be in here by nine-thirty. You can come anytime and wait with me."

Leaving her mother-in-law to clean up the dishes, she went upstairs and put on the night gown that she had worn on her wedding night and on the night that her son was born and climbed into the bed, wishing that Glady had arrived earlier and could be here to hold her hand when the pains were the worst; what a comfort that would be.

Placing the delivery pads that she prepared on the bed, folding the spread out at the foot of the bed, she climbed into the bed after a sharp pain made her grimace, knowing they would be coming closer and closer. After having one child, one knew what to expect and she hoped that this birth would not be as painful as the first one. Mrs. McKenny arrived with a smile on her face as another pain hit. "I'm sure glad you waited till the morning. My daughter-in-law kept me busy last night. Both mother and baby are fine and the daddy is all right, too. Their first boy was born in a hospital, so he didn't know much about what goes on. He got an education last night."

"Where's Frankie?"

"His mom sent him out to keep Frankie Junior busy."

Georgianna groaned as another hard pain engulfed her. Hearing voices downstairs she knew the doctor had arrived. The handsome doctor with the black hair entered the bedroom and Georgianna was relieved to know that she was in good hands. After a brief examination he smiled and said, "Well young lady, you have been working hard and we should not have long to wait until this is over with. Just try and relax between pains. Mrs. McKenny delivered her grandson last night, and here we are again." They both laughed with amusement.

Only groans were heard from the patient, much different from her first baby's birth. Maybe she had conditioned herself to bear the pain better when she knew the rich rewards of motherhood. A few hard pains and Doctor Brush held up a plump, pink bit of humanity. As she let out a big squall, he exclaimed, "What a beauty!" and she was, plump and shapely with rounded calves in her pretty legs.

Georgianna watched with awe as the Doctor tied and cut the umbilical cord and handed the precious package to Mrs. McKenny. You take care of this while I take care of the mother. Mrs. McKenny reached for the baby while exclaiming, "You didn't make anymore noise than an old cow."

Mom Lowman had hoped to get a bouquet of peonies into the room to greet the new baby and was surprised when she walked up the stairs with the vase of flowers to know that she was late for the arrival. At ten o'clock her sixth granddaughter, Katherine Elaine Lowman, who the Doctor swore was the most beautiful baby he had delivered, was born. The mother could agree with him as she carefully examined the precious daughter who reminded her of her sister Dela when she was a baby. Her happiness was boundless, and she was eager to share her joy with her husband and son.

Mom Lowman waited until the Doctor had left before she summoned Frankie and Frankie Junior from the old house to come see what the doctor had brought. They excitedly came up the stairs. After looking at the baby and his mother, Frankie Junior asked, "Why are you in bed, Mama?" Mrs. Lowman was quick to inform him that she had to stay in bed to take care of the baby for a few days. She would have been very upset if the three-year-old was told that the baby did not come in the little black bag that the doctor brought. Georgianna just let it go at that, not quite knowing what else to tell her son.

Things about childbirth were not as freely talked about as in later years. Mrs. McKenny stayed for a while to be sure everything was all right and to give the baby an opportunity to nurse. Georgianna assured her that she could go home to get some much-needed rest. "I'll be all right with the bassinet by my bed and Glady will be here this afternoon, I am not tired like I was when Frankie Junior was born. When the next one comes I may not need a doctor."

Mrs. McKenny laughed. "Ah, yes you will. My last one was the hardest to get born, you just never know. I will be going; I need to check on my daughter-in-law and see how they are doing. Just phone if you need me. I like doing things for neighbors." No mention of pay was exchanged. A soft hug and Mrs. McKenny was on her way.

Mrs. Lowman phoned to find that the bus would be about an hour late and should be in by five o'clock. Frankie was instructed to peel the vegetables to help get the evening meal underway before going to meet the bus. Taking his young son with him he drove into the back parking lot behind McCrum's Drug Store that also served as the bus terminal and waited until the bus arrived. Spotting his sister descending the bus steps, he took his son by the hand and hurried to meet her. "Hi, Topsy" as she gave him a bear hug and stooped to hug her nephew.

"Well, Topsy, you missed the show."

"What do you mean?"

"I mean that I'm now the proud father of a beautiful baby girl."

"When?"

"Ten o'clock this morning. Give me your ticket and I will get you your bag. Hang onto the boy, he is like a bolt of lightning."

The arrival at the Lowman home was a joyous one. Mom Lowman was overjoyed to greet her youngest daughter who had spent her first thirty years living at home (other than the year she spent in Poughkeepsie, New York, going to dental school). Frankie Junior tugged at his Aunt Glady. "Come see what the Doctor brought Mama."

"What did he bring?"

"A baby, all wrapped in a pink blanket. I'm going to help take care of her when Mama gets out of the bed. Grandma said Mama had to stay in bed to take care of the baby."

Georgianna listened as the footsteps were approaching the door to her bedroom. The two greeted each other with a warm embrace, then Glady peeked into the bassinet where her beautiful new niece lay peacefully asleep. She said softly, "Why didn't you wait for me? I was supposed to be here when you arrived, Katherine." The baby squirmed and opened her big blue eyes as Glady picked her up and caressed her forehead. Georgianna smiled and said, "I think she knows that it is supper time, she has been quiet all day. What do you think of her?"

"You are already two ahead of me and I am ten years older than you."

"Looks like you need to get busy before you get too old. I am so glad you got here. Frankie put you a cot where you could be close if we needed you at night. You better go help Mom get supper ready. She is not used to doing it by herself. Just hand me my doll and I'll nurse her while you are downstairs."

Bedtime came early after the busy day. Glady settled in her cot in the corner after seeing that the baby was dry and comfortable for the night and was soon fast asleep. Georgianna kept a flashlight under her pillow to enable her to check on her daughter without getting out of her bed. At the first whimper, the young mother was wide awake and lifted the baby by the blanket and nursed her, changed her diaper and placed her back into the bassinet while Glady slept on. Every one had a restful night and was ready to greet the day, especially Frankie Junior who was already up early as usual and clamoring for the attention that a three-year-old expects.

"I'm hungry, what am I going to wear today?"

"Whoa, whoa, give your Mama a break, sugar. Aunt Glady will get your clothes, don't wake your sister, it's not time to feed her."

Glady stayed for two weeks, and the young mother was at her usual chores when Charlie came to take Glady back to Pennsylvania. One look at the new baby and Charlie remarked, "Well, Georgianna, you really put your heart in your work."

CHAPTER 64

Frankie Leaves For Out-of-Town Work

As they sat at the table for the evening meal, Frankie calmly announced that he and his brother-in-law were leaving for Newport News to seek work at the shipyard because "There's nothing around here to do."

Georgianna was somewhat surprised that he would be leaving her with the cows to look after, the big garden that had been planted, and grass mowing time was here. She had a two week old baby and all the responsibility was falling on her. She was not really surprised that her husband announced his plans at the last minute, never discussing things with her first. She knew she could handle her part if Frankie would just send the money home. He was not very good with money as long as he had any in his pocket. If he occasionally came up short, he spent it, not realizing that bills needed to be paid off. Every three months the bill for Frankie Junior's birth arrived in the mail and had been ignored for nearly three and a half years. It was only twenty-five dollars; but there never seemed to be twenty-five dollars on hand.

After the announcement, Georgianna survived the shock. "When do you plan to go?"

"We're going first thing tomorrow morning. I am packing my bag tonight, and I may be able to go to work immediately, so I will not be home for a couple of weeks. Lady, do you think you can handle everything?"

"I'll do my best, plenty of work will keep me out of mischief. Just be sure to send some money as soon as, and often as, possible."

"Okay, okay," he patiently replied.

   Mom Lowman just kept quiet, looking as sad as if he would be
gone forever. He was the youngest of a family of eight and had always
been home except for a few months that he spent with his sister
Beulah in Poughkeepsie. Apparently she expected him to always live
with her. Maybe this would be a good chance for the young couple to
eventually get to themselves.
   A few days passed and a letter arrived at the Lexington address.

   Dear Lady,

   We were both lucky. After filling out an application we
   were informed that we could begin work tomorrow so we
   went out looking for a room to share and a boarding house
   not too far away where we could get three meals a day at
   a good price. I am to be a welder and will have several
   weeks of schooling. I already miss all of you and will get
   back to see you as soon as possible. We will be working
   seven days a week for awhile, I'll send money as soon as
   I get paid.

   I L Y P M A M E D
   Frankie

   Little Frankie danced around as his mama read, and chimed in,
"When's Daddy coming back?"
   "It's no telling, sonny boy, he is going to work all the time but he
will be back before too long, I'm sure of that."
   Frankie sent some money the first two weeks that he worked.
Georgianna stashed it away waiting for more so she could pay for her
two children's births. Then she could know they were really hers.
She didn't like to owe anybody anything.
   By the end of the first month while both children slept, the two
women were startled to see someone at the front door late at night.
They were both surprised to see Frankie standing there with a big
grin on his face. "Surprised you, didn't I?"
   "You surely did," said his mother as she opened the door. He gave
her a hug and then embraced his wife who shed a few tears of
happiness. "I sure missed you, but I've kept really busy, there is always
something to do."
   "I'm bushed, let's go to bed," were Frankie's next words. He

followed his wife up the stairs, giving her a pinch on the rump, before they reached the last step. She knew what was on his mind.

He looked at his peacefully sleeping children. "I sure have missed the two as well as you. I hate to think of going back."

The weekend was short and sweet. Frankie Junior was delighted to have his Dad for a romp in the fresh green grass. They all walked to church on Sunday morning. With the war in full swing there was a shortage of tires and gasoline was restricted so the car sat in the garage. When Sunday dinner was over Frankie's ride back to Newport News was waiting at the front gate. He had readied his luggage while Georgianna finished preparing dinner. Hasty good-byes were said and the travelers were on their way.

Frankie had left a little more money and Georgianna felt happy that she could pay the two doctors who had delivered her babies. It was time for Katherine's six week check up and she could take care of both at the same time.

The children were settled in for the usual afternoon nap and Mom Lowman had settled for a nap. Georgianna stayed busy cleaning up the dishes before taking a break. Then she began to wonder what Frankie spent his money on. He was making quite a bit, but it took more for his expenses then he was sending for them to live on.

The children slept peacefully along with their grandmother while Georgianna cleaned the kitchen. Then she sat down to plan her week while all was quiet. Monday was always wash day, weather permitting, and Tuesdays were taken up with ironing, so Wednesday would be the first opportunity to get into town to the doctor's office. There were always many things to fill in the time and keep the young woman very busy. Diapers were done daily along with the many other duties that claimed daily attention.

Georgianna entertained thoughts of an apartment in Newport News so they could be together as a family. She had doubts that Frankie would agree to it but that didn't keep her from dreaming. While all was quiet there was time to scan the Lexington Gazette that was filled with news about the war and of course the young Virginia men who were killed in battle. Georgianna was relieved that all her brothers were safe as far as she knew. She exchanged letters with them occasionally and offered prayers for them daily.

CHAPTER 65

Catching Up with Expenses

Wednesday dawned bright and clear—a beautiful July day. The milking was over with, the children had been fed, the diapers were gently swaying in the soft breeze. Georgianna informed her mother-in-law that she was taking the children into town. "It's time for Katherine's six week check up and the weather is perfect for the walk into town."

"Be sure and keep the baby's face covered up in the breeze, we don't need a sick baby on our hands."

"I'll take care of her, Mom, no need for you to fret, she'll be fine."

The children were dressed in their best attire and Georgianna had on her favorite blue dress with the white collar. She felt quite confident as she rolled the wicker baby carriage down the front steps and placed her precious sleeping baby smelling of baby powder into the carriage. She followed instructions to cover the sleeping baby's face even though it was a warm July day. Frankie Junior danced around friskily wanting to get going and offered to help push the baby carriage. Mom Lowman's last words were, "Don't stay long and wear the children out."

"We'll be back by nap time."

Georgianna had a good feeling with money in her purse to pay bills and maybe buy a few items. Her first intent was to pay the bill for Frankie Junior, feeling almost too embarrassed to be three and a half years in paying it. Parking the carriage by the door, and taking the children, she meekly approached the receptionist and handed her the bill and the twenty-five dollars, apologizing for the long delay. "It has been a long time, hasn't it?"

"With the depression many folks have been late paying their bills. Thank you very much."

Georgianna gave a big sigh of relief as she placed her baby in the carriage to walk around the block to Doctor Brush's office, not feeling as apprehensive as when she entered Doctor White's office. She approached the desk and informed the receptionist that she was there for her and her baby's six week check up. "Just sign in and have a seat, we will call you when the Doctor can see you."

Finding a chair near a small child's table with children's books was a perfect place for them to wait. The room was occupied by strangers. Georgianna still didn't know many local residents, only the ones she attended church with. After a short wait, "Mrs. Lowman, the Doctor will see you now." Georgianna proudly entered the Doctor's office to see the handsome dark haired Doctor looking relaxed as he reached for the pink bundle she held in her arms.

"Any problems?"

"None at all. She is as good as gold and very little trouble."

"She's just about the prettiest baby I've taken care of and everything looks fine. She will need her shots in another six weeks so bring her back then." Handing Katherine to the nurse, he examined the mother and reported everything was okay. They discussed birth control, and Georgianna was fitted with a device that would help. The young mother paid her total bill proudly and announced, "We'll be back in six weeks for the baby's shots."

"Thank You."

With a light heart they proceeded up the street and around the block to McCrum's drug store when Frankie Junior announced, "I gotta go, I gotta go." They entered the ladies restroom, leaving the baby carriage outside the door. The young boy was dancing around in urgency, he knew how to take care of himself. Luckily a chair was provided, and Georgianna was able to nurse the baby while Frankie, Jr. used the toilet.

After washing his hands and leaving the room, Katherine was made comfortable in the carriage. Frankie Junior was eyeing the people eating at the round table. The many ads displayed on the wall were of interest to him and he boldly asked, "Can we get ice cream?"

"You've been such a good boy and a big help, I think you deserve a cone of ice cream, what flavor would you like?"

"I want the brown kind."

"That's chocolate, I am going to have the orange kind, that's orange pineapple." The orders were placed, and they walked over to a table near the window where they could see what was going on outside. It was lunch hour, and many came to McCrum's for a light lunch. Georgianna's spirits were lifted since she had taken care of the bills. Now her children belonged to her and she felt a certain amount of satisfaction as she watched the men in dress suits and the ladies looking nice in their career clothes. Many spoke and remarked about the baby in the carriage.

The family walked up the street to Rose's Ten Cent Store, bought some sewing items, stopped in the White Front Grocery Store for sugar and canning jar lids. They leisurely strolled the mile back home to find Mom Lowman pacing the floor. "What took you so long?"

"Well, Mom, we just took our time and enjoyed seeing all the people."

"Guess what, Grandma?"

"What?"

"We had ice cream."

"Did you bring me any?"

"No. we ate it all, we brought you a bag of sugar."

Georgianna hastily prepared a light lunch and settled her son for a nap before heading for the garden while the three slept, feeling comfortable leaving them. There were beans to pick, weeds to pull and the first ripe tomatoes to gather. The canning season had begun and it would be a busy week. The young woman was thankful that Frankie had time to mow the large yard while he was in, relieving her of one less chore to handle. She enjoyed the bright sunshine on her face as she busily took care of the weeds first, then filled the pail with beans, placing the tomatoes on top, and sauntered back to the house.

As she reached the back steps, she sat down just to enjoy the quiet all by herself, only to hear her mother-in-law say, "I see you out in the sun without a hat. You'll pay for it. I've told you time and time again to wear a hat when you are in the sun."

"Yes, Mom." Feeling like a small child, she picked up the pail of

vegetables and entered the house to find her daughter had wakened
and it was time to feed her. "Now don't nurse that baby, you'll make
her sick, sit awhile until you cool off"

"Yes, Mom." She washed her hands, changed the baby's diaper,
picked her up and began nursing her as the grandmother huffily left
the room mumbling to herself.

CHAPTER 66

Enjoying Motherhood and
Frankie Junior's Antics

The summer days were busy ones and everything was fairly stress-free. Georgianna managed to keep everything under control until the cow was in heat and needed to be bred. Not feeling comfortable talking to a neighbor who owned a bull, she approached her mother-in-law. "I am going to let you handle this problem, the cow needs to be bred, I just don't want to talk to Richard about it. Frankie always took care of that, but I will phone and have him take her to his place for a few days."

Little Frankie loved his baby sister and showed her a lot of attention— almost too much sometimes. One occasion, his mother walked into the room to see him standing by the bassinet with the salt shaker poised over the sleeping baby. She rushing to his side and grasped the salt shaker before any damage was done. "What were you doing?"

"Mama. I heard you say she was so good that you could eat her without any salt. I thought she would be better if I put salt on her."

"Don't ever do that again; that's not a good thing to do."

"I won't, Mama, I promise," looking at his mother with tears in his big brown eyes and hugging her around the knees. "I love you Mama."

"I love you, too, sweetheart."

Georgianna related the event to Mom Lowman. "I hope you gave him a good whipping." The young woman just walked away, not wanting to get into a discussion on punishment, feeling she did too much of that just to make her mother-in-law happy and was having guilt feelings about it. The young woman was enjoying mothering these two precious children but resented all the advice that her well meaning mother-in-law offered at every turn of events. She longed for the day when she and Frankie had a place of their own and she could raise her children without interference, but she doubted that Frankie would leave his mother alone.

Frankie's letters arrived weekly; most contained money and episodes of his boating, fishing with his two young single roommates who took their girlfriends along and what fun they were having. Apparently they were enjoying the freedom from weekend and evening chores. Needless to say, Georgianna felt like she would like to be enjoying some of these pleasures. Most of their time together was always work, work, work, very little time for fun things. The few times they took a Sunday afternoon walk he always asked his mother to come along.

Frankie Junior was becoming almost too helpful in helping care of his baby sister. After hanging the clothes on the line, Georgianna checked the room to see if all was well, only to find her young son had removed Katherine from the bassinet, placed her on the bed, and was undressing her. He knew he was doing something wrong as soon as he saw the shocked look on his mother's face and hastily spoke. "Mama, she needed a change."

"Son that is the mother's job, you are too small to carry her, you might drop her and hurt her bad. Please don't do that again or I will have to punish you."

"May I go out to play?"

"Just be sure to stay in the yard, and don't forget." The baby was dressed and put back into the bassinet and the incident was never repeated.

Sunday was always a special day, looked forward to with pleasure. The young mother polished shoes on Saturday, disinfected the high chair and other things the children come in contact with. Her baby book instructions were to keep all things as germ free as possible and that was what she tried to do. The children were healthy so it must have worked.

Sunday mornings the milking had to be taken care of while Mom Lowman cooked oatmeal for breakfast. The children were dressed prettily: Frankie Junior in his white and navy sailor suit and Katherine in her prettiest frock. Georgianna felt really proud as she and her mother-in-law walked into town. Little Frankie insisted on helping push the baby carriage over the graveled surface until he reached the sidewalk that went by the Washington and Lee Fraternity houses. Mrs. Lowman had asthma and couldn't walk very fast, so they strolled along, reaching the Presbyterian church first where Mrs. Lowman attended. Then they walked up Main Street to Manley Memorial Baptist where they were warmly greeted by other members. The nursery workers made a big fuss over the baby, ignoring Frankie Junior who announced, "She's my sister and I help take care of her." Georgianna took him by the hand and led him into the proper room, and kissed him goodbye.

"I'll be back after Sunday School."

"You can leave the children in the nursery during church."

"I'll just take them in church with me, they are no trouble."

Georgianna enjoyed her Sunday School class taught by Lula B. Tardy whom she regarded highly and hoped that one day she could teach a class as well. When the class dismissed, she took the children into the church and found their usual pew, with Senator Willis A. Robertson and his wife on the other end. Georgianna eagerly anticipated Schools opening and she could take the children out to watch the VMI cadets march up the street and stop at their particular places of worship. They usually filled the balcony. It was an inspiring sight to see the young men so stalwart and proper in their place of worship.

The last hymn was sung and the congregation filed out. Georgianna took her brood out the side door, where she had parked the baby carriage. While Frankie Junior danced around, she placed her precious bundle in the carriage and covered her with a light weight blanket. It was summer time and warm, but the grandmother strongly insisted that a blanket was needed.

Strolling down the street to the Presbyterian Church, she could hear them singing their last hymn. She watched the worshippers come out of the church and noticed that most of them dressed a little more fancy than the Baptists and did not appear to be as friendly.

"There's Grandma," said Frankie Junior as he spied his grandmother in her dark dress exiting out of the usual side door. They were a bit more formal at the Presbyterian church and sang unfamiliar hymns. "Grandma, did you sing ya, ya yup?" He had visited with her the previous Sunday and the hymn sounded this way to him. "No we didn't sing that, I do not know what you mean." The three retraced their steps back to the large empty white house.

Skeezix the dog met them halfway down the graveled road, begging for attention which was soon provided by the young boy. This episode was repeated weekly whenever the weather cooperated, even if light snow was on the ground. This ritual was an important part of Georgianna's life. She desired that her children partake of the good life. The best she could do was give them a good start in life, if she couldn't provide them with lots of material possessions.

CHAPTER 67

Frankie's Brother Dies

Georgianna planned a surprise party for her mother-in-law's seventieth birthday and had secretly invited a few of the neighbors, hoping to bring a smile on the woman's face. She seldom smiled and looked somber most of the time. Two days before the party was to be held a phone call from her daughter-in-law in Salem, Virginia, informed the older woman that her oldest son was ill and in a bad way in the Roanoke Memorial Hospital. Mom Lowman hung up the phone, then phoned the bus terminal to check the schedule. Finding that she could get a bus out that afternoon, she packed a small bag, got a cab and left Georgianna alone with the two children.

Georgianna had a party to cancel, which she took care of immediately. Some did not have a telephone, so neighbors were asked to pass the word. Two guests showed up, not having gotten the word, to Georgianna's embarrassment. She did enjoy getting to know the neighbors a little better, and they seemed to enjoy admiring the children.

Georgianna bundled up her young son and took him to the barn while she did the milking, knowing Katherine was safe in her crib. She needed to keep an eye on the lively little boy who was rather venturesome and not afraid to try new things. His help was enlisted to get wood for the stove while Georgianna carried the coal pail in one hand and milk in the other, saving a trip back later. The kitchen felt cozy after being out in the cold. Georgianna added fuel to both stoves, strained and put away the milk before fixing food for their evening meal.

Frankie Junior offered to set the table. "If you put the plates down, I can get the silver," he was a very helpful child. Georgianna rather liked having the house to herself with no one to tell her what to do, and she felt safe and comfortable handling it alone.

News from Roanoke reported that Kyle was seriously ill and was not expected to survive the night. On December the eighth, 1942, another phone call reported that Frankie's brother had passed away at fifty years of age, and there would be information about the arrangements.

When the message arrived about the arrangements, Georgianna sent a telegram to Frankie, and he arrived in time for the graveside service at New Monmouth Cemetery outside of Lexington. Kyle was laid to rest next to his first wife, who died from goiter surgery when K.B. was eighteen months old. His second wife, Clara, had died several years before from appendicitis. He was survived by his third wife, Ida, his three children, Cora, Nell and K.B., also four grandchildren.

Afterward the family gathered at the Lowman home where a neighbor had cared for Katherine during the burial. The fire had been lit in the parlor to handle the overflow from the kitchen and bedroom-sitting room. Ida looked like she would never smile again but managed to eat some lunch that had been prepared. The family left a few at a time, and the house became quiet with only Mom Lowman, Frankie, and his family. Katherine didn't want anything to do with her Daddy, choosing to cling to Georgianna. Frankie Junior was a bundle of energy informing his dad of everything that went on, "Mama let me milk. I squeezed hard, but no milk came out. I put feed for Jersey, and she ate it, I can carry wood in and set the table. Mama said I was the man of the house while you were away."

"I guess you are at that. I'll do the milking tonight, and I am off for a couple days, and your Mama can take a break from that."

Georgianna felt sympathy for her mother-in-law's loss of another of her children and tried to be really kind to her, thinking it must be terrible to have your child die. She never wanted to go through burying one of hers.

It was good to have her husband home, and a few things that needed to be done were brought to mind. "I'll take care of it tomorrow, but I think we should go to bed early and get a good night's rest. I think Jersey must have forgotten me; she had a strange look in her eye when she saw me with the milk pail; she didn't kick the pail over."

"Next time you can wear my dress; it'll be pretty short, and your long legs might scare her, so just let well enough alone."

The interlude was over, and Frankie said, "I'll try to get back for Christmas, it's only two weeks away." Georgianna had been so busy that she hadn't given much thought to Christmas. Now that she had more money, she could do more for Christmas and was surprised when Frankie said, "Can you spare a few dollars? I lost some in a poker game and need some to tide me over until pay day." Georgianna saw the light. This was why some weeks he sent so little home!

She thought that it wasn't fair that I am working hard and saving every cent, and my husband is gambling, fishing, boating, and goodness knows what else. She handed him part of her savings and kept some to provide a Christmas for the children, kissed him good-bye, and closed the door as she watched him disappear out of sight.

CHAPTER 68

Early 1940 and the New Cistern

Georgianna made much use of her galoshes, her first Christmas gift from her husband. The winter was a rough one and Frankie came home only once a month. Snow had to be shoveled from the house to the old house and barn. The stable had to be cleaned out daily. There was not much time to dwell on the things that should have been. The young woman had worked hard ever since she was a small child. Now she was caring for two small children and a mother-in-law. Her mother-in-law had frequent attacks of asthma, especially in the wintertime. Everything was more or less kept on a routine. The children stayed healthy and everything ran smoothly through the cold winter months. Laundry was hung in the kitchen on the coldest days. Many times, when the clothes were hung outdoors, they froze before one could get the clothespins on.

Wintertime was not exactly Georgianna's favorite time of the year, but it had some advantages. There was no garden to work and no grass to mow. This left some reading time and many stories were read. While holding Katherine on her lap and sitting by the large coal heater, she read stories to her four-year-old. These were special times for the mother and her children.

Georgianna was laying aside all the money that she did not need to use. She was hoping to save enough to start buying some bedroom furniture. She wanted to get rid of the boxes that held most of their clothing.

The garden had been plowed and seeds ordered to get the garden underway, when out of the blue, Frankie came home and announced, "I am taking a few weeks off to put in another cistern, so we can get rid of the rain barrels." Georgianna was not in favor of this and thought, "There goes the bedroom suite. It'll take all the money that has been saved." Since Frankie never considered her advice, she said nothing.

Katherine cried every time her Daddy came close to her. She became more familiar with him during this lengthy stay. The garden was planted and the cistern completed. The saved money was spent on a cistern that was not large enough to take care of the water needs for the household.

Georgianna was thankful that the new calf had arrived while Frankie was there. The cow had been dry for weeks and milk was purchased from a neighbor who lived across the highway that ran from Lexington to Buena Vista.

Frankie packed his bag and bid his family good-bye again. As he kissed Georgianna he asked, "Do you have any money? I'll need a few dollars to tide me over until payday."

Of course the young woman found a little money that she had hoped to keep, and gave it to her husband. As she gave it to him she said, "I'll miss you" and "you'll miss all the money you could have made while you were here working on that cistern."

"We'll make it lady," he said. "Don't fret, you worry too much."

"Well someone has to worry about our future," she said.

"I'll be back in a few weeks. Take good care of Mom and the kids."

"You know I'll do that," Georgianna said. "You take care of yourself and get in as much overtime as you can. The time you were off from work took a big chunk out of our income. I'm back to zero again. Watch out for those poker games." He picked up his hat and bag and left. The family watched until he was out of sight.

As usual, the late spring and early summer were busy times. The strawberries, peas, and beans had to be gathered and either preserved or canned. The lawn had to be mowed. The housework and child care kept Georgianna on the move. She took some time, every now and then, to let Katherine out of the pen. Katherine was now walking. She was totally potty trained at fourteen months. She had not tried the art of talking yet and just gave a winsome smile when spoken to. When needing the bathroom, her signal was to tug gently at her mother's dress and head for the bathroom. The children were indeed the young woman's pride and joy. They received plenty of love and affection. The grandmother was showing more respect for Georgianna's method of correcting her children and didn't interfere as much.

CHAPTER 69

The Visit to Maryland and Pennsylvania

Georgianna had been corresponding with her sister Noona and had seen pictures of her and her family. She had not seen her in person since shortly after their mother's death in 1927.

Ramona and Lanny came in for the fourth of July and stayed a week. They tried to entice Georgianna to go home with them to visit for a few days. Then they could go to visit Glady and Charlie. After that, they would go into Philadelphia to visit Noona. After much discussion, Frankie's niece agreed to stay with her grandmother, thus freeing Georgianna from some responsibility.

Getting their clothes together for a week to ten-day stay took some thinking. Everything fell into place and Georgianna was looking forward to spending some time away. Ramona and Glady were her favorite sisters-in-law. She was a little unsure how she felt about Noona, remembering the hanky that she wouldn't share at their mother's funeral.

The ride to Cumberland was pleasant and the visit with Ramona was a nice change. The couple loved children but had none of their own, and they gave a lot of attention to nieces and nephews. The train ride to Chester, Pennsylvania, was exciting but fast paced. It almost didn't give the two women and two children time to get off. Glady said to Charlie, "They didn't come." But at the last minute they exited the train, just before it pulled out.

There were hugs and more hugs before the group entered the car for the ride to their home. Charlie's mom and dad, having come from Patterson, New Jersey, for a visit, were waiting there for them.

Glady and Charlie had bought a French Tudor home and Georgianna really liked it. She wished that she and Frankie had a home of their own.

Sunday morning found them in the Swarthmore Presbyterian Church. Afterwards they had a leisurely dinner that had been mostly prepared ahead. They relaxed on the patio while the children played in the yard. Charlie had recently completed a stone walkway to the small garden. He was proud of his garden and showed it off. He pointed to his first well-developed eggplant saying, "It looks like the Bulls." Georgianna blushed.

Frankie Junior picked his little sister up and started up the walk. Just as Georgianna opened her mouth to tell him "no," he tripped and fell on top of Katherine. The mother hastened to pick up the limp child who had not let out a cry. Not knowing what to do, she handed the baby to Glady, who didn't know what to do either. The two entered the kitchen and threw cold water in her face. Katherine let out a wail that was music to their ears. She just had the breath knocked out of her. The little boy sat there with tears in his big brown eyes. As his mother gave him a hug he wept, "I sorry, Mama. I didn't mean to hurt her."

Charlie and Glady were taking Georgianna to Philadelphia, so she could stay a few days with her sister Noona. They drove into the downtown section of tall brick apartment buildings and found the address. Georgianna was homesick already. She had mentioned, "I may not like her."

Charlie's mother said, "But she's your sister." It had been fourteen years since they had seen each other. Georgianna nervously checked the mailbox inside, to find out that they lived on the third floor.

Georgianna looked at her sister-in-law and said, "She has children. Where can they play." Charlie carried the luggage while Frankie Junior kept up with the diaper bag.

They ascended up the stairway to the third floor. Georgianna meekly knocked on the door. A rather large woman with long black hair, looking rather gruff, answered and asked, "Is that you, salve head?"

"It's Georgianna. Are you Noona? I want you to meet my sister-in-law and her husband. They were good to bring me here."

They entered a very dull, gloomy apartment. Georgianna wondered why she had come. She was there and would stay the few days as planned, but she felt weird and uncomfortable. Charlie and Glady left and Georgianna felt worse than ever in this dreary place. There was no evidence of any children. This was a puzzle.

"Where are your children?" Georgianna asked. "Oh, they are up state in a home. We will get them as soon as we get a house in the country," she answered. This was still puzzling and Georgianna wondered why she had come. Noona had a gruff, mannish voice and was a bit bossy.

Footsteps were heard and then a man's singing voice reached their ears. Noona said, "Here comes my Dave." A jolly man walked into the room, kicked off his shoes, reached into the refrigerator, and pulled out a bottle of beer. He offered Georgianna one, which she refused. "You must be that little squirt your sister's been talking about," he said.

"I am Georgianna. These are my children." Dave had a friendly way about him but he was somewhat crude.

"I'll be glad when we get that house and get our children out of that home," he said. Georgianna didn't question why the children were in a home.

"Hey, Mike, what are we going to do tonight?" Dave asked. Georgianna didn't know why he called her Mike.

"We could go to the movies," Noona answered. "Hey salve head, would you like to do that?" Noona asked Georgianna. "I always put the children to bed early," Georgianna said. "I seldom take them out at night. Maybe we can celebrate tomorrow. It's been a long day."

Needless to say, Georgianna didn't sleep much. There was something disturbing about that place. Maybe it was because she had never been in a third floor apartment. She had never even been in such a large city overnight. There were lights and noises all night long. She wished she were back in the big white house in Lexington.

The city was awake early. Streetcars, buses, milk trucks, and taxis were all on the move before the sun was up. Frankie Junior kept busy by looking out the window. He was fascinated by all the activity.

Dave left early for work. Noona fixed breakfast and announced that they would go shopping when the stores opened. "I know you will like all the big stores we have here in Philadelphia."

"I don't have a lot of money," Georgianna answered. "I really just came for a visit. Maybe we can go to the park where the children can play. They like to play in the grass."

"We'll shop and then do the park later," Noona said. The shopping trip was a very hectic experience. Everything was rush, rush. Getting on and off the streetcars with two small children, the doors just about closed on you.

"Boy am I glad I got this harness on Frankie Junior or I'd lose him for sure," Georgianna said. Noona laughed. She was accustomed to all this rush. They went in many stores and Noona insisted on buying the children something. She bought Frankie Junior a cute sailor suit and Katherine a pretty, smocked, pink dress. They still lay in Georgianna's cedar chest in 1995.

Georgianna was glad to get back to the apartment. She put her sleeping baby to bed along with Frankie Junior. She needed to rest her arms. They had their lunch downtown. Noona had some ironing to do. Georgianna felt a bit more comfortable with her sister as the day drew to a close.

The following day they did visit the park. The two children played in the grass and watched the ducks on the pond. Charlie and Glady came for them when he returned from work. It was a big relief to be headed for a quieter place. The next day they would be on their way back home. Georgianna was anticipating the train ride back to Buena Vista. There was no station in Lexington.

Ramona was to get the train out of Washington, DC, to Cumberland, Maryland, while Georgianna was to continue to Buena Vista, Virginia. By the time they reached Washington, Ramona was adamant that she was not going to go by herself. Georgianna, against her will, traveled to Cumberland, and had to use the next day to get home. Ramona never liked going anywhere alone.

The next day Lanny took the young mother and the two little ones to the depot, before going to work. He worked as a mechanic on big trucks. Georgianna was informed that she would have a delay in Shenandoah junction. That junction was a small station where there was no place to wash the children or change a diaper. A wet wash cloth in the diaper bag was a help. It was a long and tiresome wait. If things had gone as planned she would have been home the day before.

She arrived in Buena Vista in the late afternoon. She phoned a friend to come pick her up. She was glad to be back in familiar surroundings. Frankie Junior was happy to be free in the yard. He related to his grandmother all the things he had seen and done. He even related the incident when he fell with baby Katherine. "I hope you got a good whipping for that," she said. "If you didn't, you should have." Georgianna kept quiet. She settled her precious, sleeping baby daughter in the screened crib on the side porch. She was glad to be back where things were quieter and more relaxed.

CHAPTER 70

Visiting Frankie and Pregnant Again

Frankie's niece was still with her grandmother when his sister Beulah suggested that she and Georgianna visit their husbands in Newport News. She said they could leave the children at home. Georgianna was hesitant about leaving them. Trusting Vera to take good care of them, along with the grandmother's supervision, she agreed to go. She would need to be back before school began.

After packing her bag again, getting the laundry done, and kissing her babies good-bye, the two women were off to get the bus. They phoned Frankie and told him to meet them at the bus depot. "Now do not tell Miles. Beulah wants to surprise him," Georgianna said.

Frankie talked to Miles and asked him to meet him at a small restaurant for supper. They were to arrive in the evening. Beulah lived in town and could just walk to the bus terminal. Georgianna called a cab to take her and her luggage to the bus terminal. As she left, Frankie Junior waved to her from the front porch. This was a difficult time for the young mother. She had never left her children overnight and only for a very little time during the day. She knew how much she missed them when she went in town for only a short time. Still, she was excited about seeing Frankie, who had not been home for a few weeks.

The two women kept up a lively chatter. They sat near the back of the bus. Beulah had a robust laugh and was very talkative. Georgianna noticed that when she stood up she was overcome with dizziness.

She felt a little nauseous. She thought it must be the fumes from the engine and dismissed it from her mind.

The Greyhound bus made many stops along the way and it appeared to be a long way to Newport News. The bus managed to be on time. Georgianna spotted Frankie on the platform looking for them. He had a big grin on his face. He watched them depart the bus and then walked towards them. "Hi, lady. It's great to see you," Frankie said. "Hi, Sis. Miles is meeting us for dinner. Will he ever be surprised to see what I have brought along. We'll get the bus to my place. I reserved a room there. We'll leave the luggage there and walk to the cafe where we are having supper. I can't wait to see his face when we walk in."

The meeting was a joyous one as Miles said, "Oh thunder!" That was one of his favorite expressions. Georgianna had eaten very few meals in restaurants and was at a loss as to what to order. She asked Frankie to order for her. "How about meat loaf, potato, a green vegetable and rolls?" Frankie asked.

"Sounds good to me," Georgianna answered.

"Miles, we will have to go to my room to get Beulah's bag," Frankie said. "I've reserved a room for us in the house that I am in. I couldn't take my wife into the room with Harry and A.T. I know you have a room all to yourself. We can show these girls around town while they're here."

"What I would really like to do is look for an apartment so I can move here and live with you," Georgianna interjected.

"Oh, no," Frankie said. "Who would look after mom and all the cows back home? Just put that idea out of your mind." Georgianna knew it was a lost cause when she saw his mouth start to twitch. He would never leave his mother.

After leaving the deli, Frankie walked into a bakery and bought an apple pie to take to the room for later in the evening. "I do this quite often," he said, "the boys and I enjoy a late night snack after we have taken in a movie or been out for a card game."

Beulah's luggage was picked up at Frankie's place. The older couple were giggling and behaving like teenagers. They left for Miles' room, which was a couple of miles away, and the young couple were alone. Frankie's next words were, "I'm bushed. Let's go to bed early."

Georgianna knew exactly what was on his mind and was not going to mention the feeling she had on the bus or what her suspicions were. She decided to wait until she knew for sure.

Frankie wanted to stay off from work while his wife was there. "Oh no you don't," Georgianna said. "You lost a lot of time in the spring and we are just catching up on everything. I'll get the bus and look around. Just tell me which ones take me where. You can take me out when you get off at three o'clock. We will have time together. I have two more days here and I want to see Bethany while I am here. You've been going there often."

"Okay lady, I'll work. But I really do not want to. I'd rather be with you," he said. He held her tight and whispered in her ear, "Let's eat some pie and get to bed. I have to get up early, at six o'clock, to go to the boarding house for breakfast before going to work. You can sleep as late as you want and go as late as you want. Just be back here before three thirty. That's when I get off from work. I'll be back here by four and we don't want to waste a minute."

The alarm woke them early and Frankie wanted to cuddle a while longer before leaving. After dressing, Frankie kissed his wife good-bye. She thought about going back to sleep. She had never been able to do this, except when she had a new baby. She stayed in bed but it was no use. The city was awake and noises floated into the bedroom. She did dwell on the idea of moving here to enjoy all the free time that Frankie had. All the time in Lexington was spent working. Now, he worked eight hours and had lots of playtime to enjoy himself. While she was in Lexington she was working most of the time. "It's just not fair," she said out loud as she plumped up the pillows. She gave them a good whack with her fist, then she felt better.

The young woman dressed and left the room. She walked down the street looking for a place where she could get some breakfast. As she was looking around, she was thinking, I could be happy here with the children and Frankie.

The day was spent riding buses to different areas of town and just enjoying the different sights. She made sure she was back in the room and freshened up in time to greet Frankie when he came in from work. "Hi lady. Did you have a busy day? I told Miles that we would meet them and show you two the shipyard where we work. We're working on one of the largest ships built."

"Yes, I had a very busy day," Georgianna answered. "I rode all over town. I like it here."

"Well you wouldn't like it here, if you were here all the time. It's too noisy."

The ship that the two men were working on was huge but could only be viewed at a distance. The men had to wear badges to get close to the ship. No one else was allowed.

The short visit was soon over and the two women were aboard the bus and on their way back to Lexington. Georgianna stood up for a few seconds and felt very faint. She didn't mention it but was thinking, I must be pregnant again. It's back to Dr. Brush again this week. After some counting, she realized she had missed a period and overlooked it. They had been careful and she was surprised. She wanted more children but not this close together. She vowed to pay for this one sooner than the other two had been paid for.

What a joy it was to greet her two children. When getting out of the cab Frankie Junior was hanging on to her and asking, "Did you bring daddy?" Katherine was a little shy about coming to her after only a few days of separation, but that didn't last long. Georgianna passed around little treats that she had brought for everyone. "Your daddy is coming in a couple of weeks."

There were a few things to catch up on. Laundry had accumulated and the lawn needed mowing. Georgianna decided she had better take care of that before seeing Doctor Brush. Vera would be staying the rest of the week and she could watch the children while the young woman went into town.

"Well, young lady, what brings you here?" the doctor asked. "How are those two fine children?"

"I've been feeling a little dizzy and I might be pregnant again," Georgianna replied. "That so. Nurse, prepare for a pelvic." After the examination, she put her garments back on and met with the doctor in the another room. "When was your last period?" he asked. "I've sort of lost count. It's been a busy summer."

"I'd say you are about seven weeks. We will give you a date of April the nineteenth for delivery."

"Thank you doctor," she said. "Come back in a month and take care of yourself," he told her.

CHAPTER 71

Winter 1944 and Frankie Quits His Job

F rankie came home just about every two weeks. Georgianna was glad to see him, but he was losing a lot of overtime pay plus the train fare home. The young woman stashed aside everything she could. She had put aside some money for Christmas expenses.

In early November Frankie had an accident and injured his knee when falling through a porthole on the ship. His letter stated that he would not be working for a while and as soon as he could walk without the crutches he was coming home for a while. He said he would probably just stay until after Christmas. Georgianna was happy that he had not been hurt badly in the fall. She thought, "Here goes the money saved for Christmas." It would all be needed to keep up with the expenses.

Frankie arrived in early December and they celebrated Christmas without a lot of gifts, but were happy to be together. Frankie was fully recovered from his injury and left for Newport News two days after Christmas. This had been a break for Georgianna, to have a period of not having to do the outside work the past few weeks.

The new cistern was not adequate to supply water for the laundry. Georgianna was right when she told Frankie that he was wasting time and money when he built such a small one. It was the same as previous winters, chop the ice from the rain barrels. Georgianna now had to carry the five-gallon pails and lift them onto the kitchen range. This was a tiresome chore, with her belly getting larger every day and in the way when she occupied her place on the milking stool while the water heated. She was not afraid of hard work but concerned that she may harm the baby she was carrying. She knew her mother had worked hard and had healthy babies, so it must be all right.

The winter was a hard one and many Sundays the family missed church because of the bad weather. No unnecessary work was done on Sundays. Georgianna had time to play with the children and they listened to a church service on the radio. Frankie Junior would get a little restless when he couldn't go outside. He was such an energetic little fellow and kept himself amused with ABC blocks and other toys that had accumulated over the years. Reading to him was a favorite pastime. Georgianna delighted in sitting with both children on her lap, close to the large heater. She wished Sundays would come twice a week so she could spend more time devoted just to her most prized possessions. Katherine was getting more beautiful every day and sported a ribbon in her blonde hair almost daily. Frankie Junior was a devoted big brother and proud of his sister. She was admired whenever they took a trip into town or at church, which was their only recreation.

Frankie's mother had asthma attacks in the winter and didn't get out in the cold air much. Often her time was spent in bed, with her head elevated on two or three pillows. These were tense times. Georgianna had to leave the five-year-old and the twenty-month-old unsupervised while she did the milking and outside work. Fortunately they stayed safe.

The year before young Frankie had started a fire in the wood box. It was discovered before damage was done. Georgianna spanked him soundly, then sat on the stairway, and did her own crying. She felt so bad about having to punish him but that was a dangerous act on his part. What if she had been outside and the children and Mrs. Lowman were trapped inside? Some anxiety was always felt when the young woman had to leave them alone. She did the outside work as fast as possible.

Frankie had been home once in January. The middle of February he arrived bringing all his belongings. He gave Georgianna a warm greeting and some affection to the children. Katherine was still very shy with her daddy when he first arrived. Georgianna thought he was about to tell her something when he started to scratch his head and his mouth began to twitch.

"I know, you got fired didn't you?" she asked.

"Not exactly," he replied, "I quit."

"You what?"

"I quit. I was tired of being away from you, Mom, and the kids. I'll find something here."

"Like what?"

"Don't worry there should be a job somewhere."

Frankie piddled around the house for a couple of weeks before looking for work. Their resources were dwindling. Georgianna knew she may as well keep quiet, her advice never seemed to have any effect on him.

While having breakfast one Monday morning in March, Frankie said, "I suppose I had better see if I can find a job here around Lexington."

"Good luck," Georgianna said, "You probably will not find one making very much money."

"I'll find something," he said. He was gone most of the day and came home with a smile on his face. "I got a job! I go to work the first week of April."

"Good. How much does it pay?"

"Not very much but we can manage."

"What do you do?" Georgianna asked. "Baggage man at the Greyhound Terminal. We had better get potatoes and peas out before I start work."

"Mom can watch Katherine and you and Frankie Junior can help me in the garden the next few days."

"Well sonny, I'm glad you are staying home. Maybe you can keep this boy in line," Mom said. "Georgianna lets him get away with too much."

The first Monday in April Frankie began his job at the bus terminal. He had time off between bus schedules so he came home for lunch and went back by mid afternoon.

CHAPTER 72

Ellen's Arrival

Glady had her first child, a daughter, in November. She named her Mary. Georgianna was looking forward to her own baby's birth and would miss her sister-in-law's help with this baby. Two other sisters-in laws offered their help when the baby came. The young mother felt confident that between them everything would come out all right. Vera had started school in town and was there in the evenings. She could be a big help with the children.

Glady and Georgianna exchanged letters often and Glady's last letter reported that Mary was sitting up and was teething. "Maybe your baby will be born on my birthday," which was very close to the delivery date of April nineteenth, that the doctor had given. Glady celebrated her birthday on April eighteenth. On Sunday, April seventeenth Georgianna felt draggy. When she came through the kitchen door, Mom Lowman remarked, "It looks like the baby has dropped. You better not go to church today." Vera took the children to Sunday school. Frankie had to work so the three of them walked together in the bright sunshine. They took turns carrying Katherine.

Mrs. Lowman was wheezing so she and Georgianna leisurely prepared the Sunday noonday meal. They made sure to fix enough to have leftovers for the evening meal. Beulah's family usually came every Sunday, bringing their leftovers, and they shared a meal together. Beulah, with her boisterous laugh, always added a bit of flavor to the gathering. Sometimes she and Miles would get into an argument and they both always wanted the last word.

Georgianna remembered years before, when their son Ronald was small, and they were visiting. Ronald would ask questions of Miles, who was reading the paper. He would always say, "Go see Mama." Many times she was busy doing something in another room and didn't have time for him.

Her response was usually, "Go see daddy." They kept the child busy going from room to room, never getting his needs met.

Dinner was prepared for when Frankie was on his break and the three arrived home from church. After the usual clean up was taken care of, the children were settled in for an afternoon nap and the grandmother settled in for hers. Frankie took off for the old house for some tinkering. Georgianna settled in for some quiet time of reading while Vera was busy with her schoolbooks. The Lilac bush was in full flower and a few tulips were sporting their beautiful colors.

Beulah and her family arrived about the usual time bringing a little humor to the placid afternoon. Beulah had her teeth extracted. Georgianna missed seeing her prominent teeth when she laughed. When their leftover snack was over and it was time to leave, Georgianna cautioned Beulah to keep her week free. "I may be needing you before the week is over."

"I'll keep an ear open for the telephone," Beulah said, "Just be sure to call me as early as you can."

Monday morning was a bright beautiful day. It was perfect for getting the laundry done. Much heavy lifting was done on laundry day and Georgianna was exhausted at day's end. The baby she carried had been restless, probably wanting to get out.

Tuesday was another bright day. Georgianna put the ironing board up. Beside it sat the large laundry basket chock full of items to be ironed. After several hours of ironing, walking back and forth to the stove, where the flat iron heated, and keeping a look out for the children, Georgianna occasionally felt a quick pain. Lunch had to be ready by twelve o'clock when Frankie had his break from the bus terminal. While preparing lunch, there were more pains. Frankie came in for lunch and Georgianna greeted him saying, "I think I'm in labor. I've been having a few pains. I have another day until the due date. I'm going to give Beulah a call while you and the children have lunch."

She put a bib on Katherine and sat her in the high chair. Katherine needed no help feeding herself. She was a very independent little girl for twenty-three months. She was not very talkative but often gave that charming smile.

Georgianna made the phone call to her sister-in-law. She said she would be there in a couple of hours and hoped Georgianna could wait that long. Lunch was over. Georgianna left the dishes for her mother-in-law to take care of and put Katherine and Frankie upstairs for an afternoon nap. She took the bassinet and the box of baby things downstairs. Frankie tinkered in the old house until it was time to go back to work. He calmly went back to work.

Georgianna was surprised that he didn't stay at home and phone his employer that there was an emergency. She would really have liked him to stay and comfort her at this time. However, she said nothing. She finished the ironing and placed her delivery pads on the bed downstairs. That was the bed she was to use while being confined. Mrs. Lowman phoned Dr. Brush and informed him he would be needed. "I'll be right out before my office hours begin at two o'clock."

Beulah arrived just before the doctor and was on hand when the examination was taken care of. "Well, young lady, I don't believe you want to see this baby before dark."

"Will I have another day?" Georgianna asked. "I am going back to the office and will drop by after office hours," he answered. He picked up his little black bag and left, leaving Beulah in charge of the situation. Beulah had assisted at some births and was good at the job. She coached Georgianna, who needed little coaching this being her third child. The pains were getting closer and harder. It didn't appear that Georgianna could wait until the doctor's office hours were over. Beulah phoned the doctor's office and told him he had better get himself out there quickly.

After dismissing his patients by telling them to come back another day, he was on his way. Georgianna gave one big push and there emerged another darling daughter. The doctor's car stopped in front of the house and he leisurely strolled up the sidewalk with a cigarette in his mouth. Beulah walked to the door, "Throw that cigarette away and get in here and take care of this baby," who by now was crying lustily. Mom Lowman was having her hands full trying to handle Frankie Junior, who wanted to find out what was going on.

Doctor Brush took the situation in hand, as he tied and clipped the cord and held the squalling baby by her feet. "Well you've done it again. A beautiful baby girl." He handed the baby, wrapped in a towel, to Beulah and said, "get her cleaned up while I take care of the mother."

By five o'clock everything was taken care of and the doctor left. Beulah telephoned Frankie to inform him that he had a new baby girl, who was born on Glady's birthday, April 18, 1944. She weighed seven and a half pounds, with small-defined features and plenty of hair. Georgianna mentioned that she heard all poor babies had lots of hair.

Frankie Junior was overwhelmed and asked, "Where did the baby come from?" His grandmother lost no time telling him that the doctor had brought it.

Frankie beamed when he viewed their new daughter. "What are we going to name her?" he asked.

"I was thinking of calling her Ellen after Mom McDonald. Do you want to give her a middle name?" I was thinking of calling her Clarice."

"Okay," he said, "It's Ellen Clarice."

CHAPTER 73

Frankie's New Venture and
Mrs. Lowman's Death

Frankie soon tired of work at the bus terminal and its irregular hours. He decided he would go visit his sister Glady in Pennsylvania. There was plenty of work there. She had told him he could stay with her.

When Ellen was three weeks old, he packed his bags and rode the bus to Chester, Pennsylvania. He left Georgianna with three children and his mother, who seemed to be in failing health. She was more short of breath everyday. There was also a large garden to handle as well as a new calf that had just arrived. Milk still had to be bought from a neighbor and it had to be gotten twice a week.

Unable to locate Frankie Junior, Georgianna searched everywhere. She searched the house, the old house, the garden and began getting panic stricken. Just then the five-year-old appeared carrying a gallon jar of milk and almost out of breath. "Hi Mama, I know you have a lot to do so I got the milk. Mrs. Moses was surprised to see me."

"I was scared when I could not find you," Georgianna said, "Don't do this again. It's too dangerous for you to cross that highway. You could get killed. Please, please, do not do that again."

"I was just trying to help," he said. "I know sweetheart. I love you for wanting to help." Tears came to his eyes as he hugged his mother around the legs.

Frankie Junior always wanted to be of help. Sometimes his helping spirit backfired on him. On a particular day he decided to play cowboy and lassoed the calf. He almost choked it to death. He came running in the house saying, "Mama, come quick. The calf's tongue is hanging out." Georgianna hurriedly followed him to the stable where a calf with a rope tightly around its neck was indeed in trouble. All the young woman could do was phone a neighbor, Richard Moses, who immediately rescued the calf, avoiding a fatality.

Frankie was fortunate to get work at the Sun Oil Company, which paid very good. The two exchanged letters often. Georgianna always gave glowing reports on the children. Frankie was enjoying his sister and her baby, Mary, who was six months old.

The job at Sun Oil was more demanding than Frankie liked and he soon tired of it. Charlie got him a job at General Chemical, where he was employed. That didn't last long. The fumes from the chemicals bothered him and in a few weeks he was back home without a job. He puttered around the old house for a few days and took over the yard and garden work. That was a relief for Georgianna but that was not bringing in any money. After a short vacation he decided to look for work. He found an opening with the telephone company's linemen and went to work immediately.

The summer was a stormy one. Many times Frankie was out in bad weather, especially when there were wet cables that interfered with communication. Sometimes it lasted into the night. His mother was still very protective of her youngest son. Many times she would phone the manager's wife asking why Frankie was not home. This happened quite often and the manager dismissed him. Once again he was jobless.

Beulah's husband left his job at Newport News and was looking for work. The two traveled to Baltimore looking for work to no avail. They hit upon the idea of going to Connecticut to see what they could find there. Taking their luggage, they left in early September. They were fortunate to get work at Chance Vaught aircraft plant in Bridgeport, Connecticut. Once again he left Georgianna to cope alone. Frankie was to be an inspector and needed some training before actually going to work. He didn't start out with high wages but they would increase after his training was over.

Everything went fairly smooth until early October. That's when Mrs. Lowman came down with a severe case of asthma that confined her to bed. Vera had come to make her home at her Grandmother's during the school year. Georgianna was thankful that she didn't have to bundle up two children and take them with her when she did the evening chores. More wood and coal was used since they had to keep a fire in the sick woman's room. Her room had been moved downstairs.

Georgianna was often up late at night watching after her mother-in-law. The doctor came every other day. He was concerned to see Georgianna looking so haggard and worn. He suggested placing Mrs. Lowman in Stonewall Jackson Hospital where she could be better cared for and Georgianna could get a good night's rest.

Making the arrangements fell on Georgianna. She phoned Glady and Frankie and they agreed that was the best solution. Both said they would arrange to come the next day. This was a comfort knowing there would be someone else to make the decisions and relieve her of the responsibility.

Andy and Beulah visited their mother in the hospital before coming to see Georgianna. Immediately Beulah asked, "Who put her in the hospital?"

"It was the doctor's decision," Georgianna said, "I guess you can say he put her in there."

Glady, Charlie, and baby Mary arrived ahead of Frankie. Glady took one look at baby Ellen and remarked, "My, you just have a little peanut." Mary was a large built baby while Ellen was very petite. "She's a sugar coated peanut and a good baby," Georgianna said.

Frankie arrived shortly and visited his mother in the hospital. "She looks very sick to me," was his comment. "You'd written that she was sick. I didn't realize she was that sick."

Glady decided that she and Georgianna would stay at the hospital, leaving the men to watch out for the children. The children would be put to bed before the women took their bedside vigil. Everyone was looking pretty glum. The two women were taken to the hospital at ten o'clock. They sat at the bedside softly talking while the patient lay sleeping in a semi-conscious state. The nurse visited the room every hour and found everything satisfactory.

The women dozed off and were awaken by noises from the bed. "We better ring for the nurse. I think Mom's in trouble." The nurse arrived immediately and asked the women to step outside the room.

They followed the instructions. They embraced each other, both having the feeling that things were not going well. The two shared a closeness like sisters instead of sisters-in-law.

The nurse left the room. "You two wait here while I call the Doctor." Doctor Brush followed the nurse into the room, ignoring the two women waiting outside the door. The doctor was in the room a very short time before stepping out and informing the two women that Mrs. Lowman had died. It was November 5, 1944. "I'll phone the funeral home," he said. "Which one do you prefer?"

"Harrison has buried all our people so call them."

"I'll take care of it. You two go home and get some rest before making the arrangements."

Charlie was summoned to come for the women. They checked in on their children then went to bed for a short while. When they got up, they made the phone calls to the other family members. They planned a meeting to finalize plans for the funeral. The body was prepared, brought back to the home, and placed in the living room until the funeral.

This was the day that Georgianna realized that men use sex for comfort in any situation. Her husband had been gone for six weeks. She had no desire for sex, she only wanted the closeness of her husband.

The funeral was held at the home. It was mostly attended by relatives. The burial was in New Monmouth Cemetery in the Lowman's plot. On the way back from the cemetery, Georgianna faced the fact that the woman she had lived with for eight years was gone. She was dealing with loneliness, now that it was over. They had not been real close but being connected to Frankie, they had respect for each other. Georgianna now knew that the saying, "no house is big enough for two women in love with the same man," was a fact. Georgianna wondered what the future held and where they would go when the home was sold.

CHAPTER 74

1945 and Frankie's New Job

Frankie announced, "I'm not going back to the aircraft plant. I'll look around here for work. There should be something, all the young men have gone to war." Several times a week he searched for work, to no avail. The saved money dwindled rapidly.

Ramona and Lanny came in for Christmas and made a suggestion, "Hey, toots, you can go home with us. You could probably find a job there. You can stay with us as long as you like."

Frankie answered, "I just might do that. There's nothing here."

Once again, Frankie packed his bags, bid his wife and children goodbye, and left with his sister for Cumberland, Maryland. He was searching for the pot of gold that had been very elusive.

The second week, he landed a job with the city as a garbage man helper. This was not a very glamorous job but one that was quite demanding, regardless of the weather. Frankie soon tired of this unpleasant job and quit. He found another job doing odd jobs, but soon tired of it. The weather in Cumberland was terrible in the wintertime. He packed his bag and was back home in Lexington in time to put out a garden.

Georgianna made a suggestion, "Why don't you get a job in Roanoke? You could come home every week and maybe we could move there. You know this house is going to be sold and we will have to move somewhere. May as well be Roanoke."

"I'll think about it," Frankie said. "I guess I could stay with my niece Cora and her husband Wallace, while I look for a place to buy.

When we get our share of Mom's estate, that would make the down payment."

Andy, who was overseeing his mother's estate, planned a meeting of family members to divide his mother's household items. The day of the meeting found Georgianna nursing a very sick child. Ellen was running a fever and had an upset stomach. The mother spent the day caring for her child. Frankie sat in on the meeting and didn't speak up when all the others were expressing their desires.

Connie, the daughter that had done the least for her mother, seemed to ask for the most. She got it, including a chest of drawers that Frankie and Georgianna had spent many hours refinishing. Georgianna expected Frankie to ask for that. After allowing his sister to take it with her, he requested it back. Of course he didn't get it and fell out with his sister for years. Finally, Georgianna told him it was time to visit her and make friends. Which he did.

Frankie and Georgianna became the owners of the old kitchen cabinet and a table in the kitchen that had several layers of oilcloth tacked to it and looked worthless. Later, Georgianna stripped it of the oilcloth and found a solid cherry, drop leaf table. It sits in Georgianna's living room in Roanoke, years later.

They were also the owners of a desk, which they prized, the dining room table and an assortment of chairs. Before the day was over, Beulah asked, "What happened to all Mom's new towels?" sounding very accusing that Georgianna had taken them. The towels had been given to Georgianna and Frankie at their wedding shower. The dishes and glassware were divided. With Frankie letting everything get away from him, they were given one blue plate from the set that his mother had started housekeeping with.

Georgianna was glad to see the day end. The house was pretty bare when they all removed their inheritance from the home. Only the few possessions that the young couple had, were left in the eight-room house. Georgianna was eager to get settled in a place of their own. Her own memories of this house were not exactly all pleasant. She and her mother-in-law had disagreed on child raising and proposed punishment for the children. The young woman was eager to relocate. She hoped Frankie would decide to look for work in Roanoke. She had some friends there that were like family to her. Having made few friends in the Lexington area, only her church friends, it would not be hard for her to leave the area and start a new life for her family.

Saturday morning found Frankie mixing a batch of pancakes, which was one of his specialties, for breakfast. Little Ellen was placed in her high chair and was good at feeding herself. Georgianna fried the pancakes while Frankie and the children devoured them. Then she fixed a plate for herself and sat down opposite of Frankie.

She noticed his mouth begin to twitch. She knew he probably wanted to say something. Evidently, he had a problem with communication and usually waited until the last minute to inform his wife of any decision he made. Eventually, he pushed his plate away and took his last sip of coffee. "How about me getting the bus to Roanoke tomorrow?" he asked.

"I've been trying to tell you to do that," Georgianna answered.

"I have the garden planted and you can get Frankie Junior to help keep the weeds out. I can mow the lawn on weekends, if I can get home."

Frankie left for Roanoke and was welcomed by his niece Cora, her husband Wallace, and their three daughters, Jo, Ann and Adele. Frankie was very fond of this niece, having been babies together. He tried his luck at the Greyhound bus terminal. He hoped he could meet the requirements of a bus driver. He found out that he was too lightweight for that job. He was offered a custodial position, which he refused. After several attempts to find work failed, Cora's husband, who was a paint contractor, spoke up. "Do you like house painting?" he asked.

"I can do it, if that's what you're asking," Frankie answered.

"I could use another man," Wallace said, "Of course there are times when bad weather or the fact that I have no contract, means no work."

"Okay, I'll take it," Frankie said.

The painting career began. Frankie came home nearly every weekend. When the weather was good, Georgianna dressed her children in their best attire, put Ellen in the carriage, and they walked proudly into town for church service. The young woman loved having her children noticed and beamed with pride when friends made complimentary remarks about them. Of course Georgianna thought that they were the prettiest children she had ever seen.

Chapter 75

Summer and Fall of 1945

Frankie was doing very well with his job of house painting and began looking for a house. He borrowed a vehicle from Wallace and spent several weeks looking. He found a couple of good prospects. Georgianna arranged to have a caretaker for the children and rode the bus back to Roanoke with Frankie on Sunday evening to cast her approval. The Lowman home was under contract and, if approved, they had to be out within six months.

Borrowing a station wagon from Wallace, the two rode all around town looking at houses for sale. Finally they stopped to look at an eight-room house. It was occupied but appeared to have lots of possibilities. It was located in the North West near a good school, a grocery store, a drug store and a beauty shop, not that Georgianna ever went to one. The churches were within walking distance. It seemed an ideal location for a family without a car. Their car had been sold. Frankie jokingly said to a fellow, "I'll sell this car for fifty dollars." The gentleman took him up on it. The car was worth much more than that but Frankie sold it anyway. After making the offer, Frankie didn't want to go back on his word. Frankie was no whiz when it came to money.

The two agreed on the purchase of the house. Thirty eight thousand dollars was the total cost. They had to pay a down payment and thirty dollars a month. It was signed and sealed in August, 1945. This allowed the present occupants four months to move.

Frankie Junior was due to start school in September and was enrolled in Bordens Run, a small, two-room school where a friend of the family, Ethel Malsted, taught first and second grade. Only two other children were enrolled in the first grade.

Frankie came home nearly every weekend and the two discussed what had to be done before moving to Roanoke. The walls were all covered with dirty wallpaper. The best solution was to paint over the wallpaper so it would be clean. Then room by room they would remove the wallpaper.

Frankie usually romped with his son on these weekend trips. On one occasion, with Georgianna's disapproval, he roped the yearling calf, handed the rope to Frankie Junior, and swatted the calf on the rump. The calf took off like a bullet and Frankie Junior was hanging on with all his might. The calf fell flat, with the six-year old boy still hanging onto the rope, while his father was bent over with laughter. His mother held a very different view. "You know he could have been hurt," she said.

"Gotta make a man of him," Frankie answered.

"Well, he is only six years old. He has time before he becomes a man," Georgianna said.

The first day of school arrived and Frankie Junior was excited about the new experience. He was confident enough of his ability to go by himself and cross the busy highway. Georgianna was very apprehensive about allowing him to go by himself. She watched him with his book and lunch bag until he was out of sight. She was thinking, "He'll never be the same again."

Georgianna was forever canning, washing, ironing, sewing, and trying to keep everything taken care of. At the same time she cared for her three young children, who were her pride and joy. She was looking forward to the move to Roanoke. There the milk would be delivered to her door and maybe life would be easier. She felt like she had been working ever since she was two years old. Finally they would be a real family, in a home of their own, with her husband home every night. A thrill ran through her body, just at the thought of it. She could renew old friendships and make some new friends. Her dream was finally coming together.

The tenants moved out of the house in late November. Frankie was staying in Roanoke every weekend to paint the rooms and to get the house in condition to occupy. Georgianna stayed very busy packing the canned goods for moving.

Frankie Junior was learning very well and writing cursive. He was not quite as adept at reading but he knew his numbers. With only three first graders, the teacher gave them much attention. Frankie Junior was happy to be getting out every day.

Christmas arrived. Georgianna seldom missed an opportunity to give her children pleasure. Many Christmas programs were held. Manly Memorial Church was having their children's program. In spite of the cold and the mile walk into town, Georgianna set out with her brood to visit Santa Claus. Katherine meekly climbed upon his lap, looked into his eyes, and exclaimed, "You've got boo eyes like mine."

CHAPTER 76

The New Home

The big move was to take place on New Year's eve. Georgianna made arrangements for Katherine to stay with Andy and Ada, while Beulah volunteered to care for Ellen for a week. Frankie had not been able to get all the work done on the house. This allowed them time to get things orderly without the little ones under foot. Frankie Junior would need to get settled in his new school.

The thirtieth of December, nineteen forty-five, Frankie and Georgianna, with their two little ones in care of relatives, loaded the most used items on the station wagon. Their neighbor helped. The cat was secured in a box, so they thought, and they left for Roanoke just before dark, stopping at Fancy Hill to eat. While the family was eating, the cat was working his way out of the box and meowed contentedly from the front seat when they entered the car. Quickly they got him back into the box securely, so they thought, only to see him out within a few miles. Out of desperation, back into the box went the cat, with a sheet wrapped around the box. This cat was really delaying the move.

Arriving late at night, they took the time to set up two beds and fire up the furnace. They waited until morning to unload. Frankie Junior was excited about the house and eager to look around before the three were settled in bed. They were looking forward to a busy day in the morning. It was Sunday, New Year's Day, and Georgianna felt content. Finally her dream was materializing. Their very own home at last. She snuggled close to her husband and was soon peacefully asleep. She was dreaming of a happy new year, being her own boss, and starting a new life.

Many a hard day's work needed to be done before they could really get settled. Frankie managed to get the living room, the hallway, two bedrooms, and the kitchen painted. It would be a rewarding experience, since it was to be their very own. The furnace with a single register in the downstairs gave off quite a bit of heat to warm the whole house. The upstairs stayed chilly. This was no big deal for the family was accustomed to a cold house.

New Years Day was a hustle, getting everything into place. They put the canned goods in the basement. Locating food to eat, they used a small hot plate to cook with until they could get a gas range.

Frankie Junior was eager to meet the boys that lived next door after having seen them in the yard. "May I go outside," he asked, "there are two boys out there."

"Wait a while then I will take you to meet them and find out about school," Georgianna said. "One more day and you will be in a new school with a new teacher."

After she finished unpacking a box Georgianna said, "Get your coat, Sonny. Let's go check on school. Only one more day and that's it." The family next door was friendly. They were the parents of three boys. Richard was the oldest and in third grade. Georgianna was glad that Frankie Junior would have someone to walk to school with. She asked Richard if he would take him the first few days. "Yes Ma'am. I'll see that he gets there and back," Richard said.

"Thank you Richard." Georgianna really should have taken him and met the principal and his teacher.

It was a much larger school with twenty-five students in each first grade class. This was a big change from the small school with only three in first grade. Later she realized this was a very traumatic change for her young son.

The week passed quickly and it was time to go for the rest of their things and to get the two little girls that had been sorely missed. Andy brought the girls, having to pass Beulah's house along the way. He helped load the station wagon. The family was once again whole and on their way back to Roanoke to settle in their new home.

The winter was busy indeed with the family scraping the wallpaper from each room. Frankie Junior was a good helper. Some days Frankie was off from work. Things were looking better all the time. However, every day lost from work meant a day's loss of pay.

Georgianna found that living in the city was more expensive and their four quarts of milk a day were costly. The young woman was having many decisions to cope with and it was not an easy task. Frankie left most things up to her. The many years that her life was directed by someone else had finally come to an end. Decisions had to be weighed before being finalized. This was a slight problem for many years. She sometimes asked Frankie for his input and it was usually, "Whatever you think."

CHAPTER 77

Frankie Junior Plays Hooky
and the New Shoes

The family appeared to be settling in nicely with their new location. Miss Bennet, Young Frankie's teacher, was very impressed with his writing skill and considered placing him in the second grade. None of her students had begun cursive writing. After reviewing his reading skills, she decided to have him work on a different style of writing, printing. All of these changes were a bit confusing to the young fellow.

The family had found a church in the locality where Cora and her family attended. Frankie and Georgianna moved their church membership and began to make some new friends. Katherine and Ellen were both placed in the nursery during Sunday School, and afterward all the family assembled in church for the worship service, sitting near the back so a quiet exit could be made if it became necessary. Few problems arose. Sometimes Young Frankie would get restless, but a slight pinch on the arm by his mother usually worked. Sometimes you could hear "Ouch, don't pinch me." Georgianna hoped no one took notice of this and thought she was abusing the child.

Young Frankie was not exactly happy about having to learn a new style of writing and often developed what his mother called a nine o'clock stomachache. If there was no fever or cold symptoms, he was usually encouraged to go on to school. Many of the school children lived close enough to go home for lunch. Young Frankie liked this time away from school. Coming home each day for lunch gave him a little break. Measles were spread throughout the school. So far the Lowman household was not affected.

Arriving home from school one day, Frankie asked his mother what hooky was. She explained just what it meant and didn't dwell on it, but informed him that it was not allowed. He began arriving home for lunch very quickly every day. "You must have run all the way home."

"I just walked fast." When he arrived home after school, it was "Didn't I get home quick?" Georgianna just dismissed it from her mind until there was a knock at her door. "Mrs. Lowman, I am the truant officer from the school. I need to know what is keeping your son out of school."

"He is in school."

"No, he isn't, has not been for two weeks. The teacher thought he may have the measles until one of the students said he had been in Sunday school the day before." Georgianna was astonished and did not know what to say. The truant officer said, "I suggest you take him to school tomorrow and talk to the principal and his teacher."

Shortly, Frankie Junior arrived home, plopped his book on the table and remarked, "Didn't I get home quick?"

"Yes, you did, a little too quick. We are gonna have a little talk. Why haven't you been in school the past two weeks?"

The young boy hung his head and started to cry. "It's too hard, Mama. Miss Bennet doesn't like me."

"You do have to go back. I'll go with you tomorrow. You will have to stay in the yard for the next two weeks to remind you that this is unacceptable behavior. Maybe you can have a different teacher. I want you to like school and learn everything that you can."

Georgianna enlisted a next door neighbor to watch the two little ones while she walked Young Frankie to school and met the principal, Mrs. Farmer, and Miss Bennet for the first time. They agreed on a plan that whenever he was absent they would notify the home if they did not get a message that he was going to be absent. As far as his mother knew, he never played hooky again. His two weeks' confinement, along with his embarrassment, was evidently effective.

Young Frankie was outgrowing his shoes. Georgianna was busy

caring for the two girls who had been battling a cold for a few days so she entrusted Frankie with the job of taking his son downtown to be fitted for a new pair of shoes. They arrived home a couple hours later, the young boy proudly sporting a pair of shiny clodhoppers that were three sizes too long. Georgianna thought she would surely faint. "Why did you get those ugly shoes?"

"That was what he wanted."

"They are too big for him and you let him wear them home. We can't take them back or afford another pair." Georgianna was blazing mad. She always tried to make their money do all that was possible and now she would have to look at those horrid shoes for a long time.

Wearing them to school on Monday and returning home beaming, Young Frankie said, "Miss Bennet liked my shoes. She kept looking at them." Georgianna felt the embarrassment all over. Miss Bennet was a very stylish lady and Georgianna could just imagine what she was thinking. Who would put shoes like that on a little boy? Georgianna hoped they would wear out fast, and they did, with him playing in the creek and catching crawfish which he called crawdads. Georgianna never trusted Frankie to go shoe shopping again.

CHAPTER 78

Summer of 1946 and Georgianna's Fourth Pregnancy

The Lowman home faced a busy street with lots of traffic. The child-ren spent much time playing in the yard. Sometimes they played out front. At those times Georgianna would take her hand sewing and sit in the yard where she could keep an eye on the two girls, ages two and four. The home was not far from the railroad that was still using coal. The girls needed to be bathed twice a day when they played outside, before nap time and again before bedtime. The neighbors were concerned that they would be washed down the drain.

Usually two changes of clothes a day made laundry and ironing day a big chore. The water heater was connected to the coal furnace. In summer the water was heated on the gas range and carried upstairs for bath time. Georgianna was still having to put in many hours of labor to care for her family, but it was a labor of love. The small garden produced fresh vegetables for the table and tomatoes for canning. Help from the children lightened the work. Georgianna believed in children having responsibility at a young age. Her responsibility had begun early and she felt that she had profited by it.

Frankie Junior had the job of keeping the front porch clean while complaining many times, "What if my friends see me doing this?" This comment just fell on deaf ears. Katherine could set the table for dinner and little Ellen was good about picking up her toys. The family had adjusted to city life very well. Frankie put swings, a sandbox and a see saw in the backyard and continued to make improvements on the house He was working pretty regular. Georgianna often could smell alcohol on his breath. This disturbed her greatly, knowing they really didn't have money to spend that way and knowing what alcohol could do to a family.

Frankie had had a few drinks when they lived in Lexington. Georgianna would not have married him if she had known that he drank. This she found out after the wedding. His mother asked her not to let her family know that he drank. When off from work, he often rode around with some painters. It appeared painting and drinking went together. Many Sunday mornings found him reluctant to go to church with the family who walked or got the bus. They still had no car. Coming home and finding a half-empty liquor bottle behind his chair gave Georgianna much concern. She knew there was no use in saying anything and hoped this would come to a peaceful end.

September the sixth would be their tenth anniversary and Georgianna planned a dance in the home for a celebration. She counted on Frankie's sister, Beulah, to bring some musicians from Lexington. Beulah and the musicians never showed. Georgianna stuck a record on the record player and danced a few numbers with her husband. The neighbors milled around, refreshments were served and every one went on their way. Georgianna was very disappointed that things did not go as planned.

The following week, Georgianna realized she had missed a period. She really wanted more children, but later on! She was feeling a little down when Frances Cole from next door came into her kitchen, as she usually did after her four children left for school. "What are you looking so down about? You need some loving."

"I think I've had too much of that already."

"You're kidding?"

"I've missed a period and I am usually regular so you know what that means." The two women drank a cup of coffee while sharing some woman talk.

Frankie was very aloof when his wife mentioned her possible condition. "I am going to see Dr. Davis tomorrow, then I'll know for sure." Georgianna had a neighbor girl to watch the children while she made a trip to the doctor several blocks away. When the examination was completed, the doctor confirmed her suspicions that she was indeed pregnant and told her, "I do not deliver babies. You'll have to find another doctor for that."

"Thank you, doctor."

After retiring for the night, Frankie asked, "Did you see the doctor?"

"Yes, I did and I am about six weeks along."

"Is that all?" Georgianna had the feeling that another baby was not welcome as far as Frankie was concerned. He expected her to have an abortion which was illegal unless there was a problem concerning the mother's health. Georgianna would never consider that procedure.

Life was not pleasant for the young woman during this pregnancy. Her husband just seemed to pull away from her and spent more time away from home, bringing in less money and paying less attention to the children. He mostly ignored his wife unless he had a need to be filled.

Dela was married and living in Charlottesville when her baby boy was born and was quite ill with a kidney condition. Georgianna left Frankie in charge of her son and baby Ellen while she made a bus trip to Charlottesville, taking Katherine with her. It was a very long ride and on arriving at the hospital, she found that Dela had been discharged. Hailing a cab and giving the driver the address, they arrived to find everything was going well and under control.

Since Georgianna needed to get back on Sunday night so Frankie could go to work on Monday, the visit was short. Dela's baby son was adorable. Georgianna took care of some laundry and mopped the kitchen floor while there. Cal, Dela's husband, was good at helping around the house and would keep everything under control.

The bus trip home seemed long, and on the stop in Lynchburg, who should board the bus but Georgianna's foster grandmother. She said, "I am going home with you for a few days. I get pretty lonely in the cabin by myself."

"That's great. The children will keep you entertained and you can stay as long as you like."

The family was very surprised on the visitor's arrival and happy to see their mother. Gramma enjoyed the children, sitting in the porch swing and watching the traffic. She stayed for a week.

Georgianna had great admiration for the precise older woman who could be sort of picky at times. They had a pretty good understanding of each other.

Most of the baby clothes were pretty well worn out after three babies. Money was very short and some months there was not enough to pay the note on the house. Georgianna was treasurer of her Sunday school class and occasionally had to borrow out of the till to put coal in for the furnace. She promptly replaced it.

There didn't appear to be funds to buy baby clothes. Fortunately Frances Cole had a baby shower for her that produced some of the necessities along with some crocheted items which were greatly welcomed by the young mother.

Georgianna was quite unhappy about the attitude of her husband who just didn't seem to really care about her. Many days she felt as if it would be better if she and the baby died at birth. Then she knew she had to live to care for her children.

A few weeks before the baby was due, Georgianna told Frankie just how she felt. He apologized and was more affectionate with his wife. Life was more pleasant after that.

Frances Cole had agreed to come and assist Dr. Richards, who had been recommended by a neighbor, when the time came for delivery. Georgianna had done the usual preparations for her baby's birth.

Two of their upstairs rooms were rented out for $25 a month to bring in a little more income. Ernest and Myrtle Tyree were the current renters. Often, one could hear them having a domestic spat. The family just tried to ignore it. They did not get very loud. Georgianna and Frankie had moved their bedroom downstairs in what was to be their dining room.

Early in June Georgianna was awakened by a piercing scream from Katherine. Of course Frankie could not be seen without his trousers on. While he was fumbling with that, Georgianna hastily made her way up the stairs to find a very distressed little girl. "Mama, there was somebody on my bed."

"There's no one here. You must have had a bad dream." Georgianna crawled into bed with her two little girls and stayed until morning.

Georgianna thought she heard the rattle of milk bottles on the front porch when she went upstairs. Upon examining the screen in the window over the front porch, it appeared that it had been pried open. Possibly someone had been in that room after all. The family had their suspicions as to who it might have been, a neighbor boy who was let run loose all the time. Since no harm was done, no report was made to the police. They made sure the window was kept locked at night after that incident.

CHAPTER 79

Lila's Birth

E veryone was settled in for the night, but Georgianna just couldn't settle down and go to sleep. After getting up several times and tidying up the downstairs, she checked on the children, and got back in bed beside a soundly sleeping Frankie. Sleep eluded her. As the child squirmed within her she felt the first pain. In about ten minutes there was another one.

"This must be it," she mused. Quietly she got out of bed again and looked through her box containing baby needs to be sure everything she needed was in place. Delivery pads were inside the pillowcase and everything that would be needed was ready. Sitting quietly in the rocking chair in the hallway, she began to watch the clock. The pains were getting very regular. The teakettle was filled, the large wash pan washed out with Clorox, and clean towels were placed on the kitchen table before she woke Frankie at two o'clock in the morning. "You've got to go over to the Keenes and call Dr. Richards." Frankie nervously dressed and went two doors away to make the phone call. Arriving back home, he said, "Dr. Richards said to call him back later."

"You get back over there and tell him to come now, then get Frances."

Georgianna had put the delivery pads in place and lay back down, hoping the Doctor would get there in time. She had requested that Frankie stay with her through this birth, hoping that he would not faint or start vomiting. He agreed to stay and she felt good that he would have the experience and know what a woman went through to birth a baby.

Dr. Richards arrived shortly with his little black bag. He was a tall wiry older man with very kind eyes. Frances came in the back door, her usual point of entrance. The Doctor was pleased with the way Georgianna had everything arranged. "If everyone had things ready like this, you would never want to take a woman to the hospital. I've delivered babies in the back woods on old coats in conditions you would not believe. It's a good thing that you didn't wait any later to phone me. We're going to have a baby here any minute."

The Doctor handed a strainer with a piece of gauze over it to Frankie and gave him a can of ether. The last thing Georgianna heard before her child's cry was "soak the strainer." Another little girl joined the family June 19, 1947. They named her Lila. Frances carried her to the kitchen while Dr. Richards took care of Georgianna.

Frankie came through in good shape, saying, "So that's the way it is done? I guess I will not go to work today. I'll call Ada and see if she can come up for a few days and give you a hand. We're supposed to start that job out of town."

Ada arrived and took charge. Katherine had been spending time with her Aunt Ramona along with Cora's daughter, Josie, and was to get back that day. After a phone call to Cumberland, the five-year-old was excited and eager to get home and see her little sister. Josie reported that every half-hour it was, "Are we almost there?" Ada was probably glad to get away. She was a buxom body with slender arms and legs and was a cheerful hardworking woman—helping run the farm. She would relish the change.

Frankie left for out-of-town work when Lila was three days old. Ada had to get back to her duties on the farm, so before the week was up Georgianna was up and caring for the family. The children were a big help. Georgianna could send three year old Ellen to the basement for potatoes and she would come back with the correct number and size for baking. She saved her mother many steps. Frankie Junior kept the porch clean and made trips to the store. Katherine took on the job of house cleaning, and everything went along smoothly. Georgianna proudly displayed her new daughter to the neighbors who dropped in and admired her.

Lila began having colic when she was about six weeks old. The doctor called it intestinal indigestion. Every evening about five o'clock she began crying and often spit up her milk. Eventually she was taken off the breast and put on formula after formula until one was found that worked.

These were trying times. Georgianna finished the evening meal and did the dishes with Lila over one shoulder while working with one hand. By one o'clock in the morning Lila was peacefully asleep. During the day this baby was a perfect angel and eventually the colic came to an end and all was peaceful.

CHAPTER 80

Mama McDonald Moves in and
Mrs. Leedy Joins the Family

Georgianna's foster parents had separated a few years after Georgianna's marriage and had both remarried. Mama had gone to Atlanta, Georgia, to work in an airplane plant. Never having worked outside the home before, this was quite a change. While there she met a man who was divorced and had custody of his five children. They eventually married and moved back to her home in Virginia. At middle age she became the mother of another son whom she named Fred.

The marriage just didn't work out and the woman filed for divorce. She brought her eighteen-month-old son to stay with Georgianna, keeping her whereabouts secret while the divorce was in progress. She found a job downtown in Leggett Department Store and left her small son in the care of Georgianna during the day.

Things ran along very smoothly. Georgianna turned the downstairs bedroom over to her mother and moved back upstairs after giving the renters notice to vacate the two rooms. Things ran rather smoothly during this time. Pegatty had been staying with her grandmother during school. When school was over for the year, she asked if she could join the Lowman household. At this time she was receiving five dollars a week from her father and agreed to donate this for household expenses during her stay. Georgianna coped very well with the increase of the family and fixed nutritious meals for them. Mama remarked, "Frankie is certainly a good provider," not realizing what a good manager Georgianna had to be to cope with the usual shortage of money to keep the household running smoothly. The family now consisted of nine people, four of whom were adults. Pegatty seldom assisted with the housework, spending her time reading while Georgianna washed, ironed, cleaned, and cooked. She would watch the children if Georgianna needed to go to the store. It was a help not to take them along.

The divorce became final and the houseguests returned home.

While Georgianna was pondering what to do next to bring in a little income, she was approached by a lady from the welfare department asking if she would consider caring for a lady who had lost a leg in an automobile accident and was dependent on welfare for her care. An acquaintance had recommended Georgianna. The social worker explained, "It only pays $50.00 a month, but she can take care of herself. You will need to do her laundry." Anything to bring in a little income was of interest. "I'll talk with my husband and see what he has to say about it."

The first of the month found Mrs. Leedy settled in the spare room upstairs. She used a pillow to scoot down the stairs, pulling her crutches along with her. The children watched her with amusement. Ellen who was five was fascinated by the way she rolled her hair up in pin curls and began pinning hers up also. Mrs. Leedy did some embroidery. Ellen took this up also, drawing on a scrap of cloth, threading her needle, and turning out small swatches of embroidery. An Easter egg was especially pretty.

Mrs. Leedy would take a walk around the block handling her crutches really well, usually coming back from the drug store with ice cream on her face. Georgianna felt that it was good for her children to learn from people who had a handicap. An acquaintance enticed Mrs. Leedy to come live with her, giving her the advantage of a telephone which the Lowmans did not have.

Georgianna had to devise another way to earn some money while still being home for her children when they arrived from school.

CHAPTER 81

The Motor Vehicle and Other Things

The out-of-town job was steady work, and when it was finished Georgianna had been able to put some money aside every week, hoping their dream of having their own car would become a reality. Frankie began searching the used car lots for something they could afford. Eventually he drove up the driveway in a dilapidated green wood paneled station wagon, smiling as he came up the front steps. "I've always wanted a station wagon."

"It surely is not much to look at."

"I am going to replace the paneling with those cedar strips that I have in the basement.

A lengthy project began with Frankie spending lots of time rebuilding the body of the station wagon. That turned out really well and it certainly was one of a kind. Now that there was transportation, the family visited the city parks. Tinker Bell Park had a swimming pool that was enjoyed by all. An occasional out-of-town trip was a real treat.

Georgianna delighted in caring for her brood who were a real pleasure. Frankie Junior was an independent young fellow with an I'll-take-care-of-myself attitude. Picking up every empty soft drink bottle he saw, "I'll get two cents posit for this." He really meant deposit. Always a deposit was made on soft drinks if you did not return the bottles. He spent lots of time with the neighbor boys at the hut on the hill where he had spent his time when playing hooky in the first grade. He saved his change, found wood scraps in the basement and fashioned a shoe polishing kit. He visited the beer joint behind his

338

home and polished shoes to make spare change for comic books and other trinkets that he desired.

Occasionally, Georgianna borrowed money from him for a loaf of bread. He always reminded her to reimburse him. Eventually he opened a store under the front porch, set up a display of used comic books, toys (some with a wheel off), fruits from a neighbor's yard, and anything else he could find to sell or trade to the neighborhood children. He seldom was without a little change to jingle in his pocket.

Lila reached her first birthday. She ran everywhere when she was allowed out of the safety of the playpen where she spent most of her time unless Georgianna was free to keep an eye on her. Katherine was being outfitted for school, which kept Georgianna at the sewing machine many hours of the day.

Georgianna was pleased that she had a responsible son to see his sister to and from school. They both came home for lunch. The school year went nicely and both children progressed with their work. Every P.T.A. day found the young mother in place after getting the two older ones from their classrooms. All were nice and quiet. Only one other person was accompanied by children. The P.T.A. president began talking about opening a nursery during P.T.A. meetings to allow the mothers a bit of freedom. This was eventually set up in the library with some of the most responsible six graders helping an adult. Georgianna scarcely knew how to act without a child on her lap and others beside her.

Spring arrived and the family spent much time outside. Muffy had a new litter of kittens that Katherine delighted in playing with. Many times she carried the mother cat over her shoulder. The cat, impatient to get down, left a deep scratch on Katherine's neck. With a quick swab of alcohol and paint with Iodine, the wound was soon forgotten. Two weeks later the six-year-old awoke with a fever and swollen glands and was kept home from school. The problem didn't go away and a visit to Dr. Davis was made. After checking her over, he asked "Has she been around any rabbits? It mimics Rabbit Fever."

"No, could a cat scratch have caused it?"

"I don't think so. We'd better put her in the hospital 'til we discover what it is."

Georgianna arranged for care of the children while she took

Katherine to Roanoke Memorial Hospital. They were reluctant to admit her without a one hundred-dollar deposit which the family did not have. The hospital phoned Dr. Davis and she was admitted. Frankie was furious when he arrived home and discovered his daughter was in the hospital.

"How are we gonna pay the bill? I don't see why you didn't wait and ask me."

Georgianna slept very little that night. Katherine had not been away from home among a group of complete strangers before, and Frankie's attitude disturbed her also. The following day a diagnosis of Mononucleosis was pronounced and after another day she was home again. The hospital was reluctant to discharge her without the bill being paid until they talked to the Doctor who asked them to discharge the patient immediately. A few days in bed and good food and she was back in school catching up on her school work under Miss Bennet who had been Young Frankie's first grade teacher.

The school year ended after a chicken pox outbreak. The Lowman family thought they had escaped until one by one the four children began breaking out. None of them were sick enough to stay in bed. Lila only had about a dozen lesions. Last to get the disease was Georgianna who never knew whether she had them when she was a child. Lila awoke, "I go potty."

As Georgianna arose to take care of her needs, the room began to swirl around her. She woke Frankie with, "Take Lila to potty, I can't get up."

"What do you mean you can't get up?"

"I must be sick, maybe I have the chicken pox. You'll have to fix your own breakfast and lunch. Just go on to work, we'll manage."

Katherine really surprised her mother at how well she took charge of the situation with the help and cooperation of Frankie Junior and Ellen who was five. Food was far from Georgianna's mind who just felt like she would like to crawl into a hole and pull the hole in after her. She knew she had to try to at least supervise running the household.

The seven-year-old just amazed her mother with her maturity, taking charge of everything. Lila was kept in bed, not because she was sick, but just for her safety. Georgianna could at least keep an eye on her. When she started the evening meal, Katherine had everything under control. "Mama, I am going to put Lila in the high chair. She's tired of the bed. She can watch me do supper." Georgianna soon fully recovered from her bout with chicken pox and was back at her usual duties.

Late afternoon usually found the three little girls gathered around their small table that their dad had fashioned of scrap lumber, with a tea party in progress consisting of graham crackers cut into small squares and chocolate milk or some other healthy beverage. Seldom were they allowed carbonated drinks.

CHAPTER 82

Young Frankie's Adventures

Young Frankie had requested a bicycle for the previous Christmas, desiring Schwinn, a famous make which was not affordable, and receiving a Sears Roebuck instead. The boy was probably allowed more freedom than he should have. He and that bicycle toured the city of Roanoke. Every time Georgianna heard a siren, she expected to see an officer at her door to tell her that Young Frankie had been hit by a car. He managed to escape harm, however. His guardian angel apparently rode on his shoulder and protected him.

Two of the neighbor boys were old enough to caddie at the Roanoke Country Club, which was three miles away. The starting age was twelve years. Frankie Junior just could not wait, so before his twelfth birthday arrived, he left home early on a very rainy Saturday morning and headed for the County Club. He hoped someone would need a caddie for the day. Apparently it never rained too hard for the golfers to stay off the course. The eleven-year-old arrived home at dusk soaking wet, with the brightest smile anyone could imagine. His mother greeted him at the back door. He, excited and out of breath, eagerly began to give his report on his earnings. "Guess how much I made?" he asked as he began pulling wet crumpled bills from every pocket. He counted it up. "Thirteen dollars," he excitedly hugged his mother. Thirteen dollars in 1950 was a nice sum for an eleven-year-old.

After that, there was no stopping this young fellow. Every Saturday found him at the golf course, apparently making a good impression on the professional men who played and requested his help. Often on retiring his last words were, "Wake me up early. My man tees off at seven o'clock." Many times on returning home, he would announce, "I carried a triple today."

"A triple, that's too much." Georgianna inspected his shoulders to find them red and irritated and she felt like crying. She had worked hard since a small child but was not expecting her children to be compelled to follow this pattern.

Frankie Junior had joined the junior high school band as a drummer and used the landing on the stairs as a practice for his street beats. This was heard throughout the house. Georgianna attended all the parades, taking the girls to watch their brother march. He was handsome in his blue and red uniform with his highly polished black shoes. Usually he paid one of the girls, who were eager to earn a dime, to keep his shoes shined. He left the band after a couple of years to play sports that had conflicting schedules.

Young Frankie always had a girlfriend from the first grade on. By the time he was in junior high school he apparently was deeply in love with Susie, a young girl who lived several blocks away. Dressing in his best attire and grooming his hair to perfection, he would strut proudly down the street. The two would get the bus for a downtown movie and stop in Kress for an ice cream soda.

Young Frankie reached the age of fourteen and persuaded his parents to allow him to hitch hike to Florida. They agreed reluctantly. Hitchhiking in the fifties was a reasonably safe way to travel, and this young fellow had a charm all his own. He reached Florida and located his Uncle Fubby who lived on an orange grove in Zephry Hills. Fubby's wife proceeded to phone Georgianna, assuming that Young Frankie had run away from home. She was surprised he had permission to undertake the journey.

CHAPTER 83

Georgianna Goes to Work
and Lila's Illness

Frankie no longer worked for the paint contractor and had taken a job with the city schools, helping keep schools painted. The work was steady but with a small salary. His hours were from three o'clock until eleven o'clock. With the fourth child starting school in September, Georgianna began looking for work to help out with expenses, expecting Frankie to see to the safety of the children in the morning.

After several early morning trips to Kenrose Manufacturing Company, who made ladies' dresses, she was put to work at a sewing machine in a very large noisy room with material scraps everywhere you looked. Lots of ladies of various ages sat at sewing machines. Georgianna felt very uncomfortable seeing all the material on the floor and wondered if she could work in this environment.

The floor lady, Ethel Underwood, greeted her warmly as she instructed her on the operation and care of her machine that must be oiled daily. "Have you ever done any sewing?"

"Oh, yes, I make all our children's clothes, but not on a machine like this. I use an old treadle machine."

"I'll be back to show you just what to do," Ethel said. She returned in a few minutes with a huge bundle of skirts to be hemmed. The ticket on them had ten dozen on it, showing just how it was done. Ethel walked away while Georgianna felt like she had just swallowed a swarm of butterflies, afraid to begin. Eventually, she made it through the day and caught the bus home at three-thirty.

The children were unsupervised for a short time before Georgianna arrived home. The extra money that was brought in helped with expenses. The time away from home gave Georgianna a busy time in the evenings and on the weekends. Things were being kept on schedule with the children's help.

Lila started school in the fall with big sister, Katherine, helping get her hair done.

Christmas came, and the cold days of winter kept the family inside. Georgianna didn't settle down until Frankie came home after eleven o'clock. Her workday started at seven. She had secured a ride back and forth with a neighbor, leaving Frankie to see the four children off for school each morning.

Everything appeared to be going smooth until Lila began running a fever and complaining of a sore throat one day. Georgianna's last words to Frankie before she left for work were, "Take Lila to see Doctor Davis as soon as office hours begin."

"Okay, I'll do that. Your ride's out there." When she arrived home after work, Georgianna was upset that Frankie had not taken Lila to see the doctor. His excuse was that Lila didn't want to go. She did seem to be feeling better and after two days at home, she was back in school in Mrs. Griener's first grade.

In early March Georgianna was awakened to the call of her youngest child, "Mama, I've wet the bed." Georgianna pulled the covers back to find her child lying in a pool of blood. The family had acquired a telephone and she immediately phoned Doctor Davis who was always "Johnny on the Spot" for a sick child.

He examined the young child but could not find anything he could put his finger on. "I think we had better put this child in Roanoke Memorial Hospital and have a kidney specialist check her out. I'll phone first thing and have her admitted."

Georgianna phoned her employers and informed them of her absence for the day. Lila was placed in a room with a girl about her age who had been burned and was having skin grafts. Georgianna reluctantly left her young daughter in the care of the hospital staff where she would spend the next two weeks.

Georgianna continued her job, and when three-thirty came she walked across the railroad tracks, caught a bus for Roanoke Memorial Hospital, and sat with Lila until her evening meal was delivered, encouraging her to eat. Then she would leave the hospital and transfer buses in downtown to go home to care for her family. She felt guilty at leaving them unsupervised for three hours in the afternoon. They were instructed to never have other children in the house at this time.

Georgianna asked for a leave of absence to care for Lila when she was discharged from the hospital. The request was not granted. The only way you could obtain a leave of absence was for your own illness.

Lila was finally diagnosed as having Nephritis, a serious kidney condition that required her to be taught at home for the rest of the year and to be kept off her feet. Georgianna signed her resignation and brought Lila home to care for her for the next few months. On bright sunny days Georgianna carried Lila out into the yard and placed her in a chaise lounge to get some sunshine. Some days the mother would barely get into the house before Lila wanted to come back in.

The homebound teacher came three days a week for a few hours to work with Lila, whose attention span was very short. Lila's kidney condition was caused by strep throat that she had a few weeks previously. Georgianna regretted that she had gone to work. Had she been home, her child would have seen the doctor who possibly could have prevented the kidney condition.

Lila made a good recovery and was seen by the doctor regularly. He cautioned her never to neglect a sore throat.

CHAPTER 84

Frankie Leaves the School System and Buys a Business

Frankie tired of having to go to work regularly. He quit his job with the school system and took up with two other painters that located their own work in a hit or miss fashion. Frankie liked having time off and enjoyed tinkering around in the basement. He didn't give much thought that a day lost at work meant a day's loss of pay. Georgianna always managed to see that adequate food was on the table and the children were dressed as well as possible.

Cora, Frankie's niece, passed her girls' clothing down and they were in turn passed on down to Nell who had a daughter. With Georgianna's expertise at the sewing machine, the girls were often accepting compliments on their attire.

One of Frankie's co-workers convinced him that he should buy a business that he owned and offered it to him for the sum of fifteen hundred dollars. Georgianna was totally against this. They still owed the hospital for Lila's confinement, and she did not feel they needed another debt. Frankie fussed and cussed and displayed other childish behavior until his wife finally agreed to their borrowing the money, including enough to pay off the hospital. The woman knew it would be up to her to see that the debt was paid off.

So it was in 1955 that Frankie became the owner of a waterless hand cleaner formula with a distribution area of two hundred miles that covered a large area. The seller offered to accompany Frankie on his first delivery to Pulaski to introduce him to the customers. On a Saturday Frankie loaded the station wagon with hand cleaner, and the two men set out for their destination. Returning home with a pleasant smile on his face, Frankie reported he had made ninety-six dollars in sales. "You see, I told you it was a money-making operation. I gave Monty half for going with me."

Frankie soon tired of spending time in the basement mixing the formula, and often customers phoned in an order that he was unable to fill. Ingredients escalated in price and the customers dwindled until it finally became more of a liability than an asset. It was just a plaything for Frankie who was definitely not a businessman.

This waterless hand cleaner called Speed could have been a moneymaker if it had been handled right. Everyone who used it praised its qualities. Because of the lanolin content, it kept the skin soft and was extremely good for auto mechanics and others whose hands come in contact with grease, paint, or other hard-to-remove substances. Georgianna pleaded with Frankie, who had many days off from painting because of the weather, to use this time contacting some of the old customers and rebuilding the business. Her words fell on deaf ears. Eventually there were two customers left, and Frankie managed to keep them supplied for a few years before the business ended.

CHAPTER 85

Georgianna Helps Out

Georgianna tried some mail order business selling "Wilknit hose" and "Fashion Frocks" while the children were in school. She walked many a mile canvassing the neighborhood and taking a few orders, not really making very much money. Deciding this small amount was not worth the trouble, she ran an advertisement for childcare in her home. This produced immediate results. A young mother came to arrange for the care of a three-month-old baby boy. Georgianna was delighted when this little boy with the blond hair and wrapped in a blue blanket was placed in her arms the following day.

This was a job that she enjoyed and she would be paid fifteen dollars a week for it. The children were pleased and a great help in entertaining the three month old.

When Johnny was eight months old, a neighbor who had an eight-month-old daughter had to have lung surgery. She approached Georgianna about caring for her baby twenty-four hours a day until she was able to care for her. Georgianna didn't hesitate to take on the job of caring for two eight-month-old babies and being able to help out financially.

School expenses were much greater with Frankie Junior in high school and Katherine and Ellen both in the junior high school band. Someone was always needing something that required money. Young Frankie was more or less self-supporting other than a large item such as a dress suit or a heavy winter coat.

The mother of the eight-month old girl recovered and resumed the care of her child. She moved to another locality. A young couple with a four-year-old moved into the vacated apartment. The four-year-old called Junior joined Georgianna's household while the mother worked.

The school had built on a nice cafeteria and Georgianna allowed her children to buy their lunch that was reasonably priced and nourishing. This allowed Georgianna a little more time to concentrate on her young charges who were just like her own children.

The clerk in the grocery store just back of the Lowman's yard made a strange remark that puzzled Georgianna. "I'll bet you treat them like your own." How else would she treat children, she wondered?

Before her childcare years were over, Junior started school and also had a baby brother called Anthony who joined Georgianna's household along with his cousin, Greg. Georgianna was now attending three different PTAs, taking the children with her and putting them in the nursery. The exception was the Jefferson High School PTA which was held at night when she and Frankie both attended.

Georgianna was pretty stressed out by the time five o'clock arrived and the mothers came for their children. Of course little Junior was back after going home for five minutes. He loved Lila and enjoyed being there. He was not Georgianna's responsibility after five, though, and children being around didn't bother her.

Childcare did not leave Georgianna much time at the sewing machine except at night after the evening meal when the clean up was left to the girls. They took turns at cleaning the table and washing and drying the dishes. Frankie Junior had a turn helping occasionally. He spent a lot of time with his many friends and played basketball that held practice often.

CHAPTER 86

Church Activities

The Lowman family was usually in their place every Sunday morning in the Baptist church and were active in varied organizations. Young Frankie was in the Royal Ambassadors and the girls were in Girls Auxiliary. Katherine and Ellen earned many badges in their Girl Scout troop while learning many crafts and having a camping trip in Dark Hollow occasionally. Lila never became interested in Scouts, probably because she was younger and had no buddy to go with her to the meetings. The whole family was active in the church Training Union that helped one to learn to speak before a group. Many social gatherings were planned for the families and held in Wasena Park. Tri-City City composed of the churches in the Valley held a meeting every three months in various churches when poster contests were judged. Katherine and Ellen always participated and invariably came away with the first place award since both were talented in art.

All four children made their profession of faith while still young and became full-fledged members, much to Georgianna's pleasure. Occasionally, Young Frankie would fake an illness to be allowed to stay home. At these times he was reminded by his mother, "You know what this means—no outside play today." Usually this prompted the young fellow to immediately feel better and join the rest of the family on their way to church. He stayed in Training Union until he was the only one left in his age group, others having dropped out one by one. However, this training was beneficial in turning out a young man with good values that would inspire him in his quest for success.

Every so often Frankie would stop attending church with the family, leaving the spiritual guidance to Georgianna who felt really let down. He was head of the house and needed to be a good role model for the children, especially for their son.

Georgianna quietly urged the family to be ready for the mile walk to church. They took turns pushing the stroller with its passenger, Lila. Georgianna had a class to teach and needed to be at the church to get her baby to the nursery and see the others to their department before going to her assembly. She strived to always be there on time.

Many G.A. girls attended summer camp at Massanetta. The Lowman family did not have the financial funds necessary for their girls to attend. This was depressing for the mother who wanted her children to have all the advantages that their peers had available to them. Katherine and Ellen took this all in stride, however, and seldom complained that they couldn't take advantage of all the activities.

CHAPTER 87

The Junior High and Band Years

Young Frankie was much more interested in girls and sports than in schoolwork and was compelled to repeat the seventh grade. Evidently he enjoyed his junior high school days. He attended all the dances that were held in the gym.

Special occasions called for a corsage for Susie. On one occasion while Susie visited the girls' room, she placed her corsage on a shelf. A jealous friend proceeded to throw it to the floor and smash it to smithereens, leaving Susie in tears and wanting to leave the school. Young Frankie was an avid dancer and all the girls wanted their turn dancing with him.

Black and pink was the "in" thing at the moment for males. Of course, Young Frankie had to stay in style, being sure to be well groomed. He purchased black trousers with a pink stripe up the side and convinced his mother to make him a pink shirt with black buttons and black stitching. With his hair combed in ducktail style, he felt like the king of his territory.

In years past, Georgianna had sewed numbers on his friends' jerseys or T-shirts and was often requested to do a bit of sewing of this type.

The change to junior high school was a big one for Katherine, having to go to six different classes. She took art and home economics in addition to her other studies. She stayed very busy after school, working on one project or another. She used broken glass to fashion mosaics for an art project and used an old dishpan, filled with broken glass of many colors, to work with. She learned from her mother that you needed to find ways to increase your finances.

The twelve-year-old began making lollipops that she sold at school. She came home every day with a long list of orders for different colors that kept her extremely busy. Many days found her painting a picture while making candy, running from the dining room where she made a few brush strokes back to the kitchen where she worked with her lollipops. She left every morning with a bag of lollipops to deliver. The principal intervened and put a stop to this practice, telling her it caused too much distraction in the classes. She was the only band student, however, that left on a band trip with two suitcases, one filled with lollipops that she sold before the bus got out of the city. This gave her change to spend on whatever she desired.

The students often sold greeting cards, candy, or some other item to make money for their band trips. Georgianna's children often scrimped on their lunch and saved their lunch money to buy something they felt they needed. This mother wished that she could provide more for her children.

Katherine, who had already learned much from her mother about sewing, began to make her own clothes. She did a fantastic job of it and proudly wore her own creations to school. All the while she tried to keep her grades up with much late night study. Many of the students were into steady dating. While Katherine liked the boys all right and dated occasionally during junior high school, staying busy with school, band, and church activities left her little time for dating.

By the time Ellen reached junior high school, Georgianna had turned two evenings a week over to the two girls who were to plan and prepare the evening meal while Georgianna did the clean-up job afterward. They learned much from this and Georgianna was able to continue at the sewing machine or whatever she was involved in.

Often one of the girls would announce, out of the blue, "I need a skirt for tomorrow or a white blouse." These times Georgianna came through with the needed item and met the emergency on short notice.

Ellen signed up for home economics and began making her own clothes. She often came home unhappy with the teacher's idea of sewing. "Mama, you know a lot more about sewing than that teacher does. I have to tell her how it's done and she doesn't like for me to tell her."

A neighbor who coached sandlot football and other sports kept Ellen busy cutting down uniforms for the small children. Ellen made money to add to her allowance. She also scrimped on her lunch and used the money for other things. Ellen was a quiet child who made the best grades with the least effort. The two girls were very close and stuck together through "thick and thin," sharing girl secrets with each other, but excluding Lila who was younger and had close friends who liked the same things.

The year Ellen entered Jefferson Senior High School, Lila entered junior high school and talked about trying out for majorette. Her attention span was not very long after she had the kidney condition in the first grade, and Georgianna thought she might not have the stamina for the grilling rehearsals. She discouraged her from trying out for it.

Lila was an animal lover from her early years and was always picking up a critter of some kind. Often, she came home in a different outfit than the one she left home in that morning. She would stop at her friend Sheila's house where they would change into each other's clothes. Other students didn't know what belonged to which girl. They were very close as were she and India who loved horses. For years they had ridden their stick horses over the Lowman's back yard. Lila was small while India was a tall, well-built girl. It was indeed a comical sight to watch them at their serious business of stick-horse riding.

Lila was very helpful with the children that her mother cared for, and often did the evening meal. Senior high school claimed the two older girls' time along with boys who presented themselves some evenings.

Lila came home one day with a six-week-old puppy in a cigar box. "Nancy gave me this dog; his name is Tippy." She added this puppy to her many chickens that Crobuck's Drug Store were giving away with each purchase. She sometimes made two trips a day to buy a small item and come home with another baby chick to add to her flock.

Unlike the other girls who forfeited their lunch to buy accessories such as a purse, Lila did without her lunch to buy chicken feed. She eventually sold them off when they were grown and used the money for dog food. Then, outgrowing the stick horses, she took up horseback riding with her friend, India, who had become part owner of a horse. Lila did not go for any extra-curricular activities. Having grown up with television, she spent some time being entertained while helping with the children at home.

Frankie and Georgianna shared the pride of having their two oldest girls in junior high school band. Ellen had reached concert band level when a fourth grader. Both girls were good musicians and played the flute. Before they entered the junior high, they had to be at the junior high school at seven in the morning for band rehearsal and then walk back to the elementary school. Often rehearsals were held in the afternoon, also. The band conductor, Alan Hall, ran a tight ship and everyone was expected to be in their place at the appointed time and in proper attire. The band played at all the football games in the city and often at out-of-town games. This provided social exposure for the girls that the Lowman family could not otherwise afford.

Every spring a sell-out concert was held. Georgianna sewed red taffeta evening dresses with a blue sash which all the girls wore, while the boys wore their uniforms. Frankie Junior had left the band by this time and was busy with sports and usually out on the town with his many friends.

One of the proudest moments was when Ellen soloed in a program that she was very shy about performing. "I know if I do not do it, Mr. Hall will kick me out of the band, so I've got to do it." Georgianna had bought some second-hand evening gowns from a friend. A white one with sparkling sequins was perfect for Ellen's debut. After it was all over, Katherine hugged her sister. "I was the proudest I've ever been in my whole life," she said. She wasn't the only one that was proud. The whole family beamed over her achievement.

The band traveled to Washington, D.C., every spring for the Safety Patrol Parade. Several adults went along as chaperones and helped to supervise and keep order. Sometimes they had to take care of a small repair job for one of the students. This band usually came back in a flame of glory for having taken first place honors. You can be sure that everyone stayed in step with their glistening black oxfords sparkling.

The band also took a trip to Baltimore every year where they were housed in the army barracks a short distance away. They came back to Roanoke gleefully sporting a first place award trophy. The Apple Blossom Parade in Winchester was a yearly event that also captured a first place award.

The efficient band director sought many invitations for his prestigious band to perform, and he beamed with pride at each report he gave. Participation in the band taught honesty, discipline and pride, as well as music.

Georgianna took her young charges along with Lila for every parade held in the daytime. Frankie's presence was evident at evenings or Saturday parades. The two girls went from junior high to Jefferson High where they both were in the band. The band had been invited to play in the Gator Bowl football game. Georgianna had to do a lot of scrimping and finagling to get enough money together to finance the trip. She wanted to provide every advantage that she could for her children.

Katherine reached her dream of becoming a majorette for the Jefferson High School band and proudly strutted her stuff at all the parades in the coldest weather imaginable. There were no pantyhose then, just bare legs with short skirts. Georgianna knew that Katherine was the most beautiful majorette in the band, but she hoped Katherine didn't freeze to death! It never seemed to be too cold for them to march. Probably when the girls reached the point of numbness they just didn't feel the cold!

For ten years Frankie and Georgianna were proud spectators at most parades their daughters participated in. This came to an end in 1962 when Ellen finished high school.

CHAPTER 88

High School and the Dating Game

Frankie Junior was a handsome young man by the time he reached high school, having matured at a young age. He had bought his own car with his golf course earnings and proceeded to customize it. He got only as far as stripping all the chrome from it because he was much too interested in sports and girls to spend time on his automobile. It sat in the driveway unadorned for some time.

Finally, the time arrived that caddying at the country club had lost some of its appeal. Young Frankie was fortunate to secure an after-school job at Rapho, a photofinishing outfit. Of course no respectable young man could go to work without first coming home to freshen up with a clean shirt. Then, after his work time, he again often needed a fresh shirt for a date. Many evenings found Georgianna still at the ironing board at eleven o'clock, ironing starched shirts that had to be exactly right. There was no doubt that Young Frankie wowed the girls and had no trouble getting a date. He was a smooth dancer and all the girls looked forward to their turn to be escorted onto the dance floor by him.

The fact that Young Frankie did not make a lot of high grades did not seem to bother him as much as it did his mother who never knew if he occasionally skipped a class. He apparently never played hooky again, or, if he did, it was a well-guarded secret.

The end of his senior year found him short a credit. That compelled him to attend summer school and graduate at the completion of summer school along with several other students. Georgianna was filled with pride as she sat with her three daughters and a sister-in-law, Glady, when Frankie Junior confidently walked across the stage, shook hands with the principal, and received his diploma from Jefferson High School, never having caused his parents any real problem during his high school days.

Katherine entered high school eager to join in as many activities as possible. She made plans to fit them in with the band schedule which was not as active as the junior high band but nevertheless took time for rehearsals, etc. Being an attractive girl, she was chosen as majorette soon after school began.

Joining the Youth Symphony became a priority, and she was elected as treasurer. After several concerts, when things were running smoothly, she and a friend left practice early to join in some other activity. The two were dismissed from the Youth Symphony. Katherine was devastated over this turn of events. Hopefully, she learned a lesson from the experience.

Always eager to be involved in any project that was available, Katherine joined Junior Achievement, an organization sponsored by local businessmen who allowed high school students to participate in craft projects that were sold She profited in many ways from this experience.

A bid to join one of the sororities was also high on the sophomore's list. These sororities were not sponsored by the school and were more or less social organizations that required a lot of nonsensical things to be performed before one became a full-fledged member. These consisted of having raw eggs broken over one's head full of curlers along with other silly things that girls could think of. Of course Katherine was determined to pass all the requirements for one called the "Jugs" that met on Sunday afternoon. They occasionally took on a small charity project.

The junior and senior boys always eyed the new sophomores, and Lee who was a saxophone player in the band and drove a snazzy black '57 Ford car soon was bringing Katherine home from school and hanging around every afternoon. Georgianna did not allow the girls to date on weeknights. Lee was visible nearly every afternoon and took Katherine out after the Friday night football game. It seemed impossible to chase him away. The young fellow seemed like a nice, well-groomed guy. Soon, the two were almost inseparable and feeling the pangs of first love. Katherine really wanted to date other fellows, but Lee had staked his claim and became furious at her intentions of dating anyone else.

Katherine had to work hard to keep her grades to the passing point and continue her other interests. She stayed up late many nights to finish a special art project between telephone calls. Georgianna attempted to limit the calls to a short period, but that was very difficult to enforce.

Mike appeared on the scene and was interested in Katherine, much to her parents' displeasure. They were almost hit by his car while he was showing off one night near the school. They really did not want her to go out with him, fearing for her safety.

Lee and Katherine had spat after spat. They were unhappy when apart, unhappy when together. When Lee would skip a few days without phoning, Katherine would phone him and they were at it again. Katherine finally told him, "It's over," and he pushed his fist through the car window and left. Lee graduated and Katherine thought she would have a year of school free to date anyone she wished, but Lee signed up for a post-graduate course and stayed in school, much to her displeasure.

Sock hops were held in the parks. Informal dress was the attire for these fun times and no one really needed a partner. Lots of fun was had by all.

Shortly after Young Frankie's high school graduation, he chose to fulfill his dream of going to California, on his thumb, so to speak. He was always fortunate to get a ride. (It was fairly safe at that point in time.) He packed his bag and fashioned a sign, "California, here I come." Frankie drove him to the main highway and waited nearby until a vehicle stopped. The young fellow waved as he entered the vehicle. He was on his way to "see the world."

Every few days a post card arrived. The first one said, "Haven't slept yet and haven't gotten wet." His stay in California was brief and then he was back on the road again, never having to pay for transportation. His return route was planned to come back through Kansas to visit his Aunt Beulah. She and her husband made their home out there after their son married and settled there.

Darkness had arrived when he knocked on their door. Peering

out, she was reluctant to admit him. She did not recognize him since he had matured. The visit was short. They lived in a trailer near the railroad tracks and it was not a very pleasant environment.

Young Frankie went on the road again. He arrived in Cumberland, Maryland, in the middle of the night for a stopover with Aunt Ramona. She didn't recognize him, either, and took the second look before opening the door.

When he arrived back home, he was ready for a long rest.

Ellen joined her sister in high school and was active in the school band. She enjoyed the activities the band participated in and was happy to be in the same school as her older sister. The two had always been like two peas in a pod. During their younger years they often dressed alike and were sometime thought of as twins, with their golden curly hair which they often wore in a similar style.

Ellen was a very quiet girl who made pretty good grades without a lot of work. The two girls continued to use part of their lunch funds to buy a new purse which seemed to be a status symbol. Immediately on entering high school, Ellen had a bid to join the "Jugs" and knew what to expect before becoming a full-fledged member. The two looked forward to the occasional weekend at Baldwin's Cabin, a rustic hideaway in the mountains.

On one occasion on parents' night, Frankie and Georgianna were distressed and tempted to take their two daughters home after seeing the security guard that had been hired to be on duty to ensure the girls' safety. He was staggering around, much too drunk to even protect himself. Being assured by a chaperone that he was being replaced immediately, the parents left the two at the cabin since they did not want to humiliate them in front of their peers.

Ellen was not eager to be involved in a lot of extra-curricular events. Both girls were making many of their own clothes but were reluctant to admit it. They preferred to let their peers think they had come from an exclusive shop such as Smartwear Irvin Saks. They usually just ignored the question, "Where did you get that beautiful skirt. I'll bet it came from Smartwear."

Ellen seldom asked for any help on her schoolwork. She had already surpassed her parents' formal education and knew they could not be of any help. A public library was near by and the two girls often went there in the evenings to complete their lessons.

Ellen dated many boys, some only once or twice, never latching onto any particular one. Being very quiet may have been the reason. Ronnie's mother made the remark, "I know you said she was quiet, but I was surprised by how very quiet she is." Being shy prevented her from having a lot of very close friends, but she had many casual friends.

After Katherine and Lee dissolved their friendship, Lee took Ellen out a few times. Lee decided to join the Air Force and pleaded with Katherine to go to the airport to see him off. She refused but watched from the back yard as the plane flew overhead. She was relieved to have that part of her life behind her so she could date whomever she pleased without interference.

Graduation day arrived in 1960 and was held in the beautiful American Theatre in downtown Roanoke. Katherine greeted it with a sad heart. She loved school and had missed very few days since entering junior high. She really wanted to go to college, but finances were just not available. With tears in her eyes as Georgianna hugged her, she said, "Mama, this is the saddest day of my life." Georgianna had tears in her eyes also. Frankie was not in attendance and she missed the support he could have given at this time.

Georgianna applied for a position with the city school board as food service assistant. She hoped to be relieved of the awesome responsibility of caring for young children now that her own children were older and expenses were climbing every year.

Katherine was not enthused about going to work and had to be encouraged to apply for employment. As she scanned the newspaper for opportunities, she viewed an ad for a dental assistant for a local dentist. She went for an interview with butterflies flapping in her stomach. She arrived back home with a big smile on her face. "I got the job, I got the job! Mama, I need money for uniforms and shoes. I go to work next Monday."

"Great, I knew you could do it—wasn't so hard, was it?"

"No, but I would rather be going to college to study commercial art."

"I wish I could provide a way for you to go." Georgianna felt pretty good to have seen two of her children graduate. Dela was the only one of her family to graduate from high school, and Glady was the only one in Frankie's family to graduate.

Ellen missed the closeness of the two girls being in school together. They still had their "Jugs" meeting together and their church activities on weekends. They continued to be inseparable, while Lila went her way with her animal-loving friends, horseback riding whenever possible, and helping with child care activities during the summer.

CHAPTER 89

Georgianna Goes to Work and Katherine's Engagement

Georgianna received a notice to report for work on the second day of school at Washington Heights Elementary School. She notified the parents of her charges that they would need to get a new caretaker for their children. As Ellen and Lila entered school, Georgianna also entered the school work force. She was met by a friendly manager when she arrived.

"I'm Virginia Peterson. Have you worked in a cafeteria before."

"No, Ma'am."

"I'll show you what to do. We only feed about a hundred people here and today is an easy menu. Mrs. Campbell is the principal and she runs a tight ship. No goofing off here. Don't buy uniforms yet, you may not want to continue this work. I may have some that you can shorten and use if you decide you want to stay."

The day was pleasant and Mrs. Peterson was a fun person. Georgianna thought that she would like it. The pay was not very good, but lunch was provided. Sixty-five cents an hour was lower than her child care fee, but it would be a change and she would get to meet some new folks, and she would be around children whom she loved, even if they belonged to someone else.

Katherine was taking care of her own needs by this time and buying what Georgianna thought were quite expensive gifts for friends' bridal showers. Georgianna, wanting her to be responsible for herself, asked that she contribute a small portion of her salary to living expenses.

You would have thought her soul had been required of her! However, she grudgingly contributed a small amount each payday.

Georgianna had a feeling of pride when she viewed her lovely daughter in her crisp white uniform boarding the bus to go to work. She knew some lucky man would someday claim her as his bride.

Georgianna continued working with the school system while Ellen and Lila kept busy with school. Frankie Junior worked and dated and fell in love. He gave Kitty a diamond and signed up for the Marine Reserves in 1962. Mixed emotions were felt as Frankie and Georgianna, along with Kitty's mother, awaited the plane's departure for Parris Island, South Carolina. It was evident that Frankie Junior showed the same feeling. Georgianna had been excused from work early to share in this, her first child's departure for a lengthy time away from home.

The family missed the usually cheerful young man who had been home for the evening meal most of the time. His infrequent letters conveyed his loneliness and his desire that the six months would pass quickly so he could join family and friends back in Roanoke.

Georgianna tried having family counseling sessions. Frankie just wanted to lay down the law and set curfew at ten thirty. There were objections from every side, including Georgianna. At this point Frankie pushed his chair back and went to the basement, leaving Georgianna to finalize the decision and also to take the blame if things didn't work out. Curfew was set at a reasonable time of midnight. Of course there were times the girls rebelled at restrictions, and there were times that curfew was not met. Georgianna never settled down for the night until all the children were safely home.

Frankie was not an affectionate father and seldom shared in the children's activities other than band performances. He left the job of raising the children to Georgianna who would have appreciated more support in some decisions that she had to make on her own. It was not easy, due to not making decisions when she was a young girl.

Family sex discussions were more or less taboo. Georgianna knew her children had grown up in the church and a Christian environment and trusted that to sustain her children in their behavior. Katherine continued working as a dental assistant and met new people. One of her friends wanted her to date a gentleman from West Virginia. She insisted on a date with a friend for him with these words, "I don't want to date a West Virginia hillbilly." Eventually, at the friend's insistence, she decided to give Malcolm the pleasure of taking her out. They dated often for the next few months. Occasionally, he joined her for Sunday morning worship service.

Easter time arrived and Katherine expressed a desire for Malcolm to join the family for Sunday dinner. Georgianna had reservations, not knowing if she should encourage this relationship. "Do you really want him to join us.?"

"I would not have asked if I didn't."

"There is always plenty of food, go ahead and ask him. I assume he is joining you for the Easter Service. I'll set the table before we leave for Sunday school and dinner will be about one o'clock."

Georgianna always had a presentable meal for Sunday dinner and some extra for special occasions. The yearly Easter cake with the lemon frosting and the nest of green coconut in the center filled with colorful jellybeans had been a treat at Easter time ever since Frankie Junior was a little tot. Easter egg dying was still performed on Saturday even if Lila was fifteen years old. Georgianna knew it would continue until the last child had flown the nest.

Katherine and Malcolm drove around and arrived just before the family was to gather around the table. Georgianna calmly greeted the guest. Frankie came from the basement and offered a warm handshake. "Malcolm, you may sit in Frankie Junior's seat, but you cannot fill his shoes."

"I don't intend to," said Malcolm. There was no doubt that Malcolm was enjoying the home-cooked meal and that he liked to eat and was not the least bit bashful.

The family learned that he was an insurance salesman and had been raised near coal mining territory in West Virginia. He had located in the Roanoke Valley after serving in the Merchant Marines. He had graduated from the Merchant Marine Academy in Kings Point, New York. The young man appeared to be quite mature, polite, and friendly, and it was evident that he was very attentive to Katherine.

The annual spring-cleaning kept Georgianna extremely busy after work and on weekends. Katherine's twentieth birthday arrived and Malcolm took her out to celebrate. The two arrived home early, which was unusual, and Malcolm came inside. They both looked a little smug and glanced at each other, each waiting for the other to speak. Finally, Malcolm came alive and said, "I've asked your daughter to marry me."

Georgianna covered her face and began to weep. "She's too young and immature." Katherine put her arms around her mother and said, "We are in love and both want to get married. Just be happy for us."

For a minute Georgianna forgot that she had been married for three years and had a baby boy by the time she was Katherine's age. "Malcolm, you will just have to finish raising her, and good luck."

"Could we have a church wedding?"

"I do not see how, but we will talk about it. You know I am scheduled for surgery next week to have those fibroids removed."

"Well, Mama, we are not going to be married until August."

"Just wait and see what comes up and maybe I can pull a rabbit out of a hat or make some magic of some kind. I still think you need to grow up."

The following week Georgianna bid her work associates farewell for the rest of the school year and left for the hospital where Dr. Lee was to do her surgery. A friend at work had mentioned, "Dr. Lee is knife happy. I have heard he will leave your hiney and your elbow. One will have a hole in it and the other will bend. He is thorough to be sure."

Georgianna was a little apprehensive because too many things were happening at once. Katherine's engagement to Malcolm Shane, her surgery, the wedding coming up, Frankie Junior coming in from his Marine reserve training—all this gave the woman plenty to think about while she recovered from surgery.

CHAPTER 90

Ellen's Graduation and Katherine's Wedding

Ellen finished her high school years with creditable grades, and Georgianna proudly watched her third child march across the American Theatre stage to grasp the principal's hand and receive her well-earned diploma. Frankie had not thought it important enough for him to take time off from work to attend. However, he had taken time off many times for much less important things. This puzzled Georgianna. Her children's activities were extremely important to her and she felt they should also be important to their father.

Katherine continued to work as a dental assistant. Ellen was glad to be through with school and knew there was no way she could go to college. Little help was available in 1962. Neither was she eager to go to work, preferring to help around the house, do some sewing for neighbors, and bake birthday cakes. Making spending money satisfied helping with the usual housework.

Georgianna knew she had to find money for the church wedding Katherine was eager to have. She had an opportunity for an Avon route and jumped at the chance, even knowing she would have to walk a lot to cover the territory.

Katherine was busy selecting her wedding party, adamant that she was not including her youngest sister, Lila, who did not always agree with her. Georgianna was unhappy about that, but realized it was Katherine's day. Ellen was to be maid of honor and Cousin Mary was to be one of the bridesmaids. Georgianna and Katherine shopped for material. Beautiful white brocade was chosen for the wedding gown and a soft green taffeta for bridesmaids' dresses. Katherine thought of making her own gown but then turned it over to her mother who had recovered from her surgery in the spring.

It was indeed a busy summer for Georgianna who sewed awhile then picked up her Avon attaché case and walked her territory, hoping to make a few sales. The territory was not a choice one, but she earned a few dollars.

An appointment was made for the sitting for the bridal photographs. The photographer welcomed the mother and daughter. When Katherine came from the dressing room he said, "Now this is the type of gown that I love to photograph. They turn out so well." After the camera session he asked, "Now what store does the gown go back to? I'll take care of that." He was quite surprised to learn that it was fashioned at home by the bride-to-be's mother.

Katherine stopped work a month early and just wanted to be a girl again. She and Ellen sat in the swings, played with the kittens and enjoyed being together and taking care of the house work. The two girls just seemed to want to make the most of their time together and were seldom separated. Katherine and Malcolm would be moving to Pennsylvania where he had secured a good position with an excellent company.

Katherine took care of her many charge accounts, some that Georgianna had closed out to keep her from getting so far in debt. When this was completed, her bank account was zero, not enough left to purchase new undergarments for her trousseau. Friends had bridal showers for her and she received many nice items. The fine undergarments were a welcome gift. Georgianna purchased what additional things were needed because she wanted her daughter to have a good start in her marriage.

Finally the big day arrived and guests began to come. Malcolm brought Mary with him to prepare for the rehearsal on Friday evening. He dropped her off at the Lowman home and checked in at a motel where he had reservations for his best man and ushers.

The conservative family did their own decorations with a good friend, Dora, who was adept at flower arranging. Dela treated the lady attendants to a breakfast at a local restaurant. Two other friends had agreed to take care of the reception to be held in the fellowship hall of the church. Malcolm's sister, June, had arrived at the Lowman home by this time and everything was falling into place.

Georgianna had mixed feelings about all this, joy at her daughter's happiness but a tinge of sadness at her leaving home and moving so far away. She also regretted that Gramma, who had died suddenly fourteen years before could not share all the festivities of the wedding day. This grand lady had taught Georgianna a lot of things that had inspired her to raise her family in a proper manner.

Mama would be there and that would help some. Her greatest regret was that Mommy Anna would not be there for her granddaughter's special day. Tears filled her eyes as once again she remembered the lonely march to the cemetery back in the mountains so many years ago. Brushing her thoughts aside, she continued with what needed to be done for the two o'clock vows to be said.

Georgianna arrived at the church in plenty of time, wearing the light green dress and hat that she had made. Ellen looked lovely in another shade of green taffeta, also made by her mother. Friends helped Katherine into her wedding gown and arranged her veil. Truly, she was a vision of loveliness as she waited to be escorted to the altar by her father who looked tall and handsome. When everyone was seated and the attendants were all in place, the wedding march reverberated throughout the silent sanctuary. Slowly the two walked down the aisle to be met by a smiling Malcolm with his best man at his side. Frankie responded almost inaudibly when the pastor asked, "Who giveth this woman to be married?"

The short ceremony was soon over, and after the photography session, all gathered at the reception where Dot and Jean had everything in readiness. Georgianna was in a daze and her thoughts were, "Is this a dream or reality?"

Some of Malcolm's family had missed the wedding but found their way to the house where a crowd had gathered. The bride changed clothes. After weeping on her mother's shoulder, she clutched her sister, Ellen, in a bear hug and gave a fond embrace to her big brother, Frankie Junior. "Where's Lila?" she asked.

"Up in her room crying." She had gotten upset at the reception and a cousin had taken her home.

Katherine flew to Lila's room to try to make amends for not letting her take part in the wedding. Then she bid her dad farewell and the two were off for their new home in Conshocken, Pennsylvania.

CHAPTER 91

News from Pennsylvania and
Other Things

Things more or less returned to normal in the Lowman home. Katherine was greatly missed, especially by her devoted sister, Ellen. These two had been inseparable since early childhood. Once, Malcolm mentioned during a phone call that when he returned home from work one day, he found his new bride in tears. When he inquired about the reason, Katherine said, "The strap broke on my red shoe," never admitting that she was homesick, especially for Ellen. No one thought that it would be a year before she would be able to return home to visit her family.

Having her Aunt Glady not too far away was a help, and some weekends found them sharing time together. They also located Georgianna's sister, Noona, and they spent some time together at the first Christmas away from home.

It was a big surprise to get a letter in January announcing that Frankie and Georgianna would be grandparents in late June. This was cause for rejoicing, but it would have been nice if the newlyweds had more time alone before a baby arrived. Katherine loved babies and probably could handle motherhood pretty well. Georgianna was excited at the prospect of having a baby in the family again. She kept many thoughts to herself while making plans to be on hand when the baby arrived and the new mother returned home from the hospital.

Ellen was somewhat moody and had not come to grips with the fact that she should be looking for employment. She continued to sew and do some baking and occasionally some ironing for a neighbor. She made a few dollars for her personal use and helped with household chores. This gave Georgianna more leisure time after her eight-hour workday.

Ellen was becoming an expert at the sewing machine as well as in the kitchen. She was seeing a lot of one particularly nice gentleman. They went sleigh riding and horseback riding. Dan usually had his sidekick with him for moral support. Often they just sat in the living room and Lila joined them. Lila also participated in the horseback riding.

Frankie Junior had rented an apartment downtown. He had become disillusioned when he came back from Parris Island to find that Kitty, to whom he had given a diamond ring before he left, had been having a gay old time dating other guys. He retrieved the diamond and pawned it, bringing an end to the engagement. Having his own apartment gave him the freedom and the motivation to succeed. His contact with the family was limited to a phone call or an occasional drop-in for Sunday dinner.

They were surprised when on a Sunday afternoon his green convertible stopped in front of the house with an attractive young lady by his side. "Dad, Mom, this is Hope. We have just been to visit her mother and now here we are to announce that we are getting married." Frankie smiled as Georgianna remarked, "Well, this is a big surprise. I've just gotten over Katherine's wedding."

"It'll just be a small wedding and Lila will certainly be a bridesmaid."

Two weeks later found the bridal party in the chapel at Calvary Baptist Church, pledging their troth. They left afterward for a short honeymoon and then settled into the apartment. They had to struggle to keep up with expenses, and the family saw very little of them.

The due date for the arrival of Katherine's baby was drawing near. Georgianna had her bag packed and was ready to travel. She was just waiting for the phone call announcing that she was indeed a grandmother. Every time the phone rang, everyone rushed to answer it, hoping to be the first to get the news. The call finally came, and the only one in the house was Georgianna. "Congratulations, you are now the grandmother of a beautiful baby girl. Mother and baby are fine and the proud Papa is busting his buttons. When can you come? They will be in the hospital only a few days."

"I can get the bus tomorrow. I'll inform you as soon as I check the bus schedule." She hung up the receiver and nervously flipped the pages of the directory to locate the number for the bus station. She found that Frankie could take her to the station on his way to work. This would put her in the Philadelphia bus depot just after Malcolm's work day was finished. She thought, "Oh boy! He can meet me and we can go to the hospital."

Georgianna made a quick call to Malcolm. "It's all set. Meet me at the Philadelphia bus depot and don't tell Katherine. Let's surprise her." Katherine was indeed surprised to see her husband followed by her mother. The two hugged and brushed away the tears of joy at their first reunion in ten months. "Where's the nursery?" Georgianna asked. The three walked down the hall to look through the window at the many bassinets full of squirming babies. They motioned to the nurse to bring baby Shane to the window for viewing. All three beamed as the tiny dark haired baby opened her eyes.

"Have you named her yet?"

"I'm not sure but I think it will be Amber Katherine."

"Sounds good to me."

"When do you go home?"

"Two more days and you will be able to rock her to sleep."

Malcolm took his mother-in-law to visit Glady until the mother and baby were dismissed from the hospital. This was a real treat. Mary was home from Vassar College and Sharlyn, her younger sister, was out of school for the summer. Glady's family had always been very special and Charlie was a lot of fun. The two entered the door of the French-style home and Malcolm received congratulations while Charlie said, with a grin, "Here, Grandma, you get the rocking chair." They all had a hearty laugh.

The two days passed swiftly, and the mother and baby were discharged. Malcolm arrived early so Grandma could accompany him to the hospital to bring his family home. Georgianna was elected to hold her granddaughter for the ride to the apartment. She thought, "I guess my daughter is finally leaving her childhood behind her now that she has reached motherhood."

Katherine wanted to make her mother feel like a guest instead of a helper. Early the next morning the new mother rattled the pans in the kitchen and wanted to prepare breakfast. Georgianna shooed her out of the kitchen. "What do you think I came for, to have you wait on me? Now get out of the kitchen. I'll take care of breakfast."

The new mother was glad to comply because she did not have as much strength as she thought. She attempted to breast feed her baby but soon gave up on that, not having a good supply of milk. The grandmother stayed until the new mother was strong enough to take care of everything. She delighted at the joy the new parents were experiencing and at the daily changes of the beautiful baby granddaughter.

Georgianna arrived back home to be warmly greeted by the family who had survived well without her. Things settled down to normal. They looked forward to the new parents' vacation in a couple of months when they would be bringing the baby to visit.

CHAPTER 92

Scott Joins the Family and Grandparents Again

When Frankie and Georgianna assumed their child raising was about over now that Lila was fifteen, they were blessed with a precious blond-headed baby boy they called Scott. He was a delight with a charming smile and beautiful brown eyes. The two grandparents began parenting all over again. Georgianna had not worked during her other children's early childhood, but knew that she would continue to work at the school. She had a responsible job that was paying much more than when she began.

During the school year the young fellow was enrolled in a local nursery school where the pay was adjusted according to the family's income. A station wagon came for him every morning and brought him back in the afternoon with everything running smooth.

Ellen and Lila adored this little guy and Frankie was better at giving him attention than he had been when the other children were small. They often sat in the lounge chair, side by side, with Scott doing the rocking while Georgianna prepared the evening meal.

Ellen had finally come to grips that she needed to find employment. She landed a job at a local hospital, working in a morgue. It had been too gruesome a job for the former employee and she had handed in her resignation. Ellen filled the spot and coped very well with it by ignoring the gruesome part of the job.

Hope announced that she and Frankie Junior were to become parents. It was exciting that the family was growing and the days

375

flew by. On a cold day in January, Hope visited the doctor who confirmed her suspicions that her labor had begun. Since her husband was at work, she walked back to their apartment, placed her toiletries and gowns in a small suitcase, and walked the three blocks to the hospital. She felt a lot of apprehension as she approached the desk and stammered, "I am pregnant." The nurse smiled and said, "Really? What can I do for you?"

"The doctor told me to come here because I am in labor."

Hope phoned Young Frankie and told him where she was. He was tied up with his work and could not get to the hospital in time for the arrival of his tow-headed son whom he named Frankie the Third. Eventually the baby became known as Trey.

The Lowman family had increased by three in less than two years. Frankie Junior was a devoted father and gave his son a bath every other day. Hope learned to cook, making their income cover inexpensive meals. She had not done much cooking while growing up so she was inexperienced when it came to managing a home on a limited income. The family did not see very much of them.

Hope's mother became ill, and Hope had to go out of town to look after her. Frankie took his six-week-old son to a sitter during the day and took him home to care for him during the night. He turned down his mother's offer to keep him over night for these two weeks. The baby-sitter lived close to the Lowman home and Georgianna was willing. The two guys made it through in good shape.

As the years went by Scott and Trey became good friends. The age difference between Scott and Frankie Junior kept them from ever being really close like brothers should be.

The two boys liked to spend the night together on Halloween so they could go trick-or-treating. Their mothers would walk with them through the neighborhood as they collected more candy than they needed. When they returned home, the boys quickly emptied their bags to see who had the most candy. The mothers examined all the loot to make certain the candy was safe to eat before they allowed the boys to devour several pieces. Soon Scott and Trey would be hustled off to bed where they talked excitedly about their adventures before settling down for the night.

CHAPTER 93

Ellen Leaves Home, Lila Marries, Graduates and Leaves Home

Ellen was moody and secretive and seldom shared her feelings with the family. Georgianna could sense that she was becoming bored and dissatisfied with her job at the hospital. She was not surprised when Ellen came home one evening, looking relieved, and announced that she had ended her employment. "Now what do you plan to do?" Georgianna asked.

"I've been thinking about going north to be near Katherine. I feel so lost not being able to talk with her often. Mama, you just don't know how hard it's been for me since she married and moved so far away."

"Oh, sweetheart, I know, but you still have the rest of us."

"It's just not the same," Ellen said.

"You're twenty-one and I can't tell you what to do, so be assured that your parents are here for you and will be supportive of your decision. I know Katherine has missed you and will be delighted to have you closer. I assume that you will stay with her while you look for employment?"

"That's my plan and I shouldn't have any trouble finding work of some kind. I'll survive one way or another, you'll see." Ellen lost no time in contacting Katherine who was ecstatic at the news.

Frankie took care of seeing that the car that had been purchased for Ellen to drive to work was checked out and readied for the long drive to Pennsylvania. It was natural that the parents were apprehensive about their young daughter driving that distance alone. A tearful departure saw her on her way to Conshocken where Katherine and Malcolm made their home while their new home was being built. They were also expecting their second child.

Rapidly Georgianna's nest was emptying with their third child moving out. Only Lila and lively baby Scott were left with their parents. Lila was in her senior year of school. Since she had missed some in her junior year because of illness, she could not graduate with her class. She had to attend summer school to make up a credit. She dated a young man, Lewis Collins, who was also completing his senior year. They were eager to be married in June. Lewis had no parent to sign for him to get married so they made plans to go to North Carolina where parental signatures were not needed.

Georgianna found herself fashioning a white satin wedding gown since they were to be married in a church. The only attendant was Lewis' teenage brother, Bill, who served as best man. Lila's parents and Scott were the only ones in attendance. Lila was a beautiful bride, and Georgianna was sorrowful that she was not having a conventional wedding at their home church with all of their friends and family in attendance.

The bride and groom had a brief honeymoon and moved in with Lila's parents. The two had jobs and Lila completed her school year. Georgianna was free for the summer and enjoyed young Scott who was a lively little three-year-old.

Summer school came to an end, and once again Georgianna proudly watched her fourth child walk across the stage to grasp the hand of her principal and receive her high school diploma. Lila's father chose to take time off to join his wife and son-in-law for this occasion. This was the first graduation he had attended.

The young couple soon tired of living at the Lowman home. Occasionally they were interrupted by young Scott who was not aware that a closed door required a knock before entering. They, too, decided to move north where employment was more advantageous, and they left to stay with Katherine and Malcolm until they were settled in their own apartment and had employment.

Georgianna had not previously given much thought about the changes that had occurred in four years' time. Four of her children had ventured out into lives of their own, and the large house was nearly empty. It would have been very lonely had Scott not added activity and liveliness to the home. He kept Georgianna busy and occupied and left no time for her to dwell on the changes that had occurred.

Frankie Junior and his family still lived in the area, and they visited occasionally. Scott and Trey were good friends.

Georgianna's fervent prayer had been that she be allowed to live to see her children grown. Now she prayed that she be granted life and health to see Scott grow to manhood. Losing her mother while a child had made an impact on her life. Many times her thoughts turned to her early childhood with her many siblings and her strong, strict Mommy to whom she felt a real kinship after all these years.

The years passed swiftly and Georgianna's family increased. Katherine and Malcolm were parents of two fine children, Amber, and Malcolm Junior. Ellen met and married a much older man. They were parents of Lisa, Darrel, and Allison. Frankie Junior and Hope bore two children, Frankie the Third, and Mary. Lila and Lewis became parents of Amanda and Lewis Junior.

Georgianna concentrated on placing a marker at her mother's grave. At the urging of her children, she contacted several siblings. A stone was ordered and a meeting time was planned for a gathering of several family members to participate in erecting the stone sixty-five years after her burial. Georgianna left the grave site with a feeling of sadness, but also a feeling of satisfaction that this woman who bore twelve children and worked so hard to care for them could now be recognized by the ones walking through the small cemetery where she had been laid to rest many years before.

CHAPTER 94

The Anniversary Party

There was no doubt that after fifty years of marriage there should be a celebration to honor their perseverance in hanging in there through thick and thin, hard times and difficulties, having respect and consideration for each other. It was assumed that Frankie Junior who lived locally would take the lead in making the arrangements. He had a heavy workload, however, so Scott volunteered to take over the job. It was gladly turned over to the young man who was capable of many things.

Scott searched for a suitable spot for the occasion. Many were turned down as not being elegant enough for the important occasion. Georgianna suggested a church fellowship hall. He inspected it and found that it was available for a fee. He returned home excited and all aglow. "Hey, Mom, it's perfect, and it's available, and I have had it reserved. What do you think of that?"

"It sounds good to me," Georgianna replied. Scott said, "I need your help in ordering the invitations. How many, the wording, and all that."

"I am available to give you all the help you need. I'll make a list first to confirm the amount to order. You'll need to consult with the others about what you can spend so no one gets upset if it's out of bounds."

Things began humming and Georgianna was enlisted to help with enclosures, stamping, and other minor duties to get the invitations out on time. The list was long for she had attempted not to miss anyone. Scott had done some catering, and he knew just what was the in thing for a party of two hundred plus. He was excited about pulling the plans together and arranging for the necessary equipment and serving items that would be needed.

Georgianna planned to wear the same dress, a long rose-colored satin, that she had made for her beautiful granddaughter, Amber's, wedding. She also had the matching satin shoes.

The family began arriving. Many stayed at hotels. Everyone arose early on the eventful day to spend a hard day's work preparing veggies and fruits, and taking care of all the many other things that needed to be done. While this was going on, the celebrities were staying out of the way and looking forward to an exciting evening with friends and family. Hope stayed busy doing all the flower arrangements as well as a corsage and boutonniere for the couple.

The family gathered for a photograph before the guests began to arrive. It was exciting to see old friends, some from school days, some from their former church. The friends from Georgianna's workplace, Loraine, Phyllis, Carolyn, Gladys, Bernice, and Era, had baked the most beautiful cake for the occasion. Some guests were from Frankie's workdays, and some were friends of their children.

The nine grandchildren, their parents, and two great grandchildren, all attired in eveningwear, added a lot of beauty to the occasion. A table was piled high with gifts from well-wishing friends and families. Some of them had traveled a great distance to help celebrate the occasion.

The next day was spent opening all the lovely gifts and reading the meaningful messages that the cards contained. Georgianna had never thought she would live this long. Now she had to get all those thank you notes written!

CHAPTER 95

Georgianna Retires

After twenty-five years in the work place, it was time to retire even though she could have worked another year. She had worked with a condition that had caused much discomfort for several years. She made plans to do some traveling while she was still able, and filled out her retirement papers. She looked forward to not having to arise early every morning. She felt satisfied.

The school's retirement dinner was held to honor several retirees. As they received their awards, most of the retirees made no comment. When Georgianna's name was called, she proudly and confidently walked to the podium, accepted her award, and proceeded to make a speech. She ended with a joke that produced hilarious laughter, and her joke telling career was launched.

She brought laughter to many gatherings, some on the bus tours that she and Frankie's two nieces, Cora and Nell, took together. One fellow traveler urged the tour guide to hire her to go on all the tours to entertain the travelers. That did not come to pass, but it would have been a fun job.

Now that there was free time and no small ones to look out for, she planned to do all the traveling that her purse would allow. She hoped that Frankie would join her, but he was satisfied to putter in the basement or to visit a relative. Other than accompanying her on a Bahama cruise before their anniversary celebration, his time was spent mostly at home.

Georgianna traveled to Canada where she was "Queen of The Thousand Islands" on the paddle wheeler. Nova Scotia was in her plans as was a cruise to the Virgin Islands. She also planned to visit her children and take many short visits to local events. She looked forward to painting classes with anticipation after her first lesson produced a painting that was suitable for framing. It was presented to her son, Frankie. This was something she had always wanted to try her hand at. Two of her daughters were gifted in this art form.

Eventually she produced many paintings that turned out well. She passed these to children and to the grandchildren. She thought maybe some day she would sell some to add to her income and to ensure more travel while she was physically fit to do so.

CHAPTER 96

Georgianna's Later Years

Georgianna felt blessed that her prayers had been answered. She watched Scott grow in stature and intelligence. He made a profession of faith, played the piano for the children's choir, and excelled in school. With a dear friend by her side once again, she rejoiced to see her fifth child parade across the stage, confidently grasp the hand of the principal, and receive his high school diploma. Frankie had fallen and was homebound with foot injuries. He was prevented from attending. He had retired and was free to use his time as he chose.

Scott went away to college for a couple of years and then dropped out, much to Georgianna's dismay. She envisioned him as an excellent student and knew that he had the intelligence to succeed. He was an adult, however and needed to make up his own mind.

One by one the grandchildren finished high school, three in one year. The grandparents were fortunate to attend their graduation exercises and to see some on their way to college.

Georgianna was now the oldest of her biological family. Noona passed away, then Russ, who was the youngest boy, followed by Corbin, Elva, Fubby, Cory, Billy, and Bidgy. The last links to her biological family or siblings, are Lancy who is in poor health and Dela who is a devoted Christian lady and very thoughtful of others. The two sisters have been very close for many years, and Georgianna is at peace and feels she has had a fulfilling life. She has been successful in raising five fine, law-abiding citizens who in turn have produced nine quality offspring. Some are still furthering their education. Three have married and are parenting seven beautiful children for their great grandmother to admire.

Georgianna has called her family together to join in the sorrowful celebration of the life and death of her husband, Frankie, with whom she shared fifty-eight years. He was the last of ten children born to the Lowman family. The grieving was done over a period of time while Frankie spent a lengthy time in a nursing home. He was unable to share his feelings as his family visited him often. The parting was hard for Lila and Scott for they had been unable to visit as often and had held hope for his recovery.

Georgianna sits alone with her many memories in the home that she and Frankie shared for nearly half a century. She still feels his presence, and often thinks she smells shaving lotion when she enters the bedroom. Her nights produce many dreams of which he is the central figure. Some of the dreams are unpleasant and she wishes they were more of the sweet times that they had shared.

Meditating on her life from her birth in the back country to the present, she wonders what her life might have been like had she had a more normal childhood in a more conventional family with her teenage years consisting of parties and dating. She also wonders if she had ever been in love. She knew she had been a good and loyal wife and had fulfilled her commitment "'til death do us part." Being in love was a debatable question. However, she had peace, contentment and the adoration and respect of her offspring and many loyal Christian friends who have sustained and enriched her life by their support.

Whatever the brief or lengthy future holds, there are family to sustain and comfort her. She is happy because she chooses to count her many blessings and is grateful for the father of her children and the many years that they shared and the closeness they felt. The beautiful children they produced who would pass their heritage from generation to generation and, hopefully, keep their family close with love and consideration until the end of time.

CHAPTER 97

The Annual Family Reunion

For the thirtieth year the tables were readied by Georgianna before the first family member arrived. There was extra time for reflecting on the many years gone by while waiting for the first embrace. She looked through the reunion albums and reminisced when she spotted her children and grandchildren in their younger days. She wiped a tear as she saw pictures of family members who have passed on to the other side of Jordan. Frankie is among them, and a feeling of deep sadness for what could have been, and should have been, but now would never be, brought more tears to her eyes.

Frankie's last living first cousin and his sweet petite wife walked through the door, and the tears quickly vanished. "What a treat to see you two looking so fresh and trim."

"You're looking great yourself," they replied. "Where is everybody?"

"The place will come alive any minute," Georgianna said. Georgianna's first cousin, Marshall, and his wife and daughter soon arrived and all were introduced.

Very soon the room began filling up with uncles, aunts, and cousins by the dozen. Lots of hugging, hand shaking, backslapping and laughter filled the room while savory dishes of food were placed on the long table. A special table for desserts and another one for beverages had been arranged. Cora was the last to arrive with her coffee urn. For many years she had made the coffee and, of course, there was Nell's dish of macaroni salad that she always brought to gatherings.

"Where is Ruth with her pot of chicken and dumplings?" Georgianna asked.

Edna, Corbin's widow, reported, "She is sick and it might be cancer."
"Oh, no, I hope not."

Two rowdy great grandsons had to be calmed down. "No running in the building and that's that." One folded his arms and ran to his mother for solace.

The time for announcements had come. Frankie Junior was rounded up to be the emcee. Georgianna sounded the dinner bell with a pot lid and a mixing spoon. Frankie Junior who could be a real comic, welcomed everyone. Happy Birthday was sung, especially for Fubby's oldest daughter's sixtieth birthday. She was Georgianna's right hand when it was time to get the many notices out for the annual reunion.

Georgianna's grandson, Darrel English, announced his engagement to Robin French and the wedding to be held on April 19, 1997.

The oldest family member present was recognized, and who was it? Cora, of course. She had passed her eighty-second birthday the previous March. The youngest was Fubby's great, great granddaughter.

The largest family was of course Fubby's descendants, and the greatest distance traveled was Georgianna's granddaughter and family from Los Angeles. They included a five-year-old and a two-year-old who was the image of her grandmother Katherine and also her great, great grandmother Anna at the same age.

A gracious blessing for those present and the food was prayed. Children were admonished to not look for the number on the bottom of the plate where a few had been marked and offered a small token for one lucky to get a number. Occasionally someone would sneak back for the second plate, hoping for a numbered one. Georgianna's sharp eye usually saw what was going on and intervened, "That's not fair." Then the boy would tuck his head and walk meekly back to his seat. Girls usually did not attempt to cheat.

There was Nettie's delicious fresh apple cake and all the other delicious desserts that finished off the meal. Georgianna was hoping for some participants for a talent show but there were few responses. Malcolm was always willing to give the piano a good workout. Many joined in a great songfest of beautiful hymns. Dela, being a beautiful singer, favored the group with a solo and received a round of applause for an encore, but it was declined.

Shutter bugs roamed around getting some snapshots for the photo album. Georgianna strived to keep the clan together of her and Frankie's family as long as she was alive, and she hoped that her children would continue it when she was gone. Some younger family members dropped by the wayside when parents were no longer there to encourage them.

Departure time approached fast and some had already left when Katherine picked up her flute and began a lively tune. Georgianna grabbed her son by the hand and began to dance, one of her first loves. The crowd began to applaud as Frankie Junior danced his mother around the room while the little folks laughed with glee.

Everyone seemed happy as they retrieved their dishes and bid each other good-bye. "I'll see you next year, if not before," they said.

Soon the room was empty. Georgianna, Ellen, and Lila checked to make sure everything was as it was found. Then they left for a pool party at Frankie Junior's for the grand finale of a perfect day.

THE END

To order additional books, please use coupon below.

Mail or fax to:

Brunswick Publishing Corporation
1386 LAWRENCEVILLE PLANK ROAD
LAWRENCEVILLE, VIRGINIA 23868
Tel: 804-848-3865 • Fax: 804-848-0607
www.brunswickbooks.com

Order Form

❏ *Georgianna* by Fay Logan
   $24.95 ea., hardcover .... $ _____

Total, books... $ _____
VA residents add 4.5%($1.12) sales tax .... $ _____
Shipping – within U.S. and Canada
   $5.00 1st copy .... $ _____
   $.50 ea. additional copy .... $ _____

Total .... $ _____

❏ Check enclosed.

❏ Charge to my credit card:
       ❏ VISA   ❏ MasterCard   ❏ American Express

Card # _____ Exp. Date _____

Signature: _____

Name _____

Address _____

City_____ State_____ Zip _____

Phone # _____